THE NIGHTSHADE'S TOUCH

#3 MESSENGER CHRONICLES

PIPPA DaCOSTA

'The Nightshade's Touch'

3# Messenger Chronicles

Pippa DaCosta

Urban Fantasy & Science Fiction Author

Subscribe to Pippa's mailing list at pippadacosta.com & get free ebooks.

www.pippadacosta.com

CHAPTER 1

For he would be thinking of love
Till the stars had run away,
And the shadows eaten the moon.

~ W. B. Yeats, Old Earthen

As a gladiator, there'd been no need for dance in my life, unless I counted the killing dance I'd performed for years in the arena. And so, when Kellee declared we were visiting a backwater colony called Hapters to "celebrate," I was too curious to decline. But on arrival, it was all I could do to stand on the periphery of the revelry, wide-eyed and uncertain. Saru don't dance.

Drums made of discarded barrels and tins thumped out a beat, instruments stringed from horsehair rang tricky notes, and pipes whittled from wood sent the revelers into a merry frenzy. The human colony, some two hundred lives from a ravaged farming planet, danced and sang and laughed. I wasn't even sure why. There was little cause for celebration in Halow. We had beaten the fae back from

Calicto—driving them out after I'd sent a swarm of wardrones into their shiny new arena—but warcruisers still swarmed Halow's old spacefaring channels, watching for survivor ships. Millions were dead—families, homes, generations snuffed out by the fae who believed it their divine right to cleanse Halow of its human infestation.

I was about to retire outside, when I caught sight of Arran among the dancing throng. Arran, previously known as Aeon. He had eaten starfruit, wiping his mind clean of his entire past. He now danced like he didn't have a care in the world because he didn't. Arran was the first name that had come to me when he had blinked at me and asked who he was. It was fae and unoriginal, but I didn't know his saru name, and Arran sounded a little like Aeon.

I had told him he was saru, that he had been a fighter, but that was all. He didn't know his name for most of his life had been Aeon. He didn't know he was the saru gladiator who had wanted revenge on the Wraithmaker. He didn't know he had spent a lifetime at the mercy of the jailor Dagnu. I had told him his new name, and he had smiled back, shallow and polite, like two strangers bumping into each other on a street.

Aeon was gone.

Arran, on the other hand, was very much here, in the moment, and he had caught the eye of several women. I couldn't blame them. He liked to dance, and he looked good doing it. That was something I hadn't known about him and wondered how it had come about. He'd spent ten years in captivity after I left him for dead, and Sjora—the fae Talen had torn in two—implied he had spent some of that time as more than arena entertainment. He wasn't namu, humans bred for pleasure, so to make him behave as one would have been degrading, even to a saru. But all of

2

that was in the past, no matter how much of it I still witnessed in my dreams. I loved Aeon, but Arran I had to let go.

"Have you seen the buns on that man?"

Hulia appeared at my side, dreadlocks swishing. She took the tankard from my hand, sloshed pink liquid inside it from the cracked drink bowl, and handed it back. Hulia *was* namu, or so Eledan had told me while he'd had her enthralled. On waking, she had stabbed him in the back. For that alone I would have considered her a friend. But even before Eledan, I'd liked Hulia.

"I mean, dayam honey. He has enough thrust to rival my old shuttle."

Her eyes flashed, and I rolled mine. She had managed The Boot, a mishmash of bar and whorehouse on Calicto, and had also acted as something of a pimp, seeing to it that her girls were looked after and paid well. She was also a musicmaker and could lull humans into a sense of safety and admiration. If I thought about it, her being namu was obvious, but I'd missed it because I'd been living as Kesh Lasota, invisible messenger, and I had wrapped myself in so many lies that I couldn't see the truth even when it was right in front of me.

"What did you say his name was?" She leaned a hip against the table and watched Arran clamp his hands on his partner's hips while she threw her arms around his neck. The two of them practically got it on right there on the dancefloor for all to see. Nobody cared. Everyone here was lost to the party, celebrating like this warm night on a nowhere planet might be their last.

"Arran."

She made a face. With his darker skin and sloped eyes, he didn't much look like an Arran, especially when he rocked his hips in harmony with his dance partner. Hulia watched like she would happily take Arran outside to teach him a few moves of her own. "I could put him to work and make a fortune."

"Don't," I snapped with too much force.

Hulia flinched. "Okay, all right, I didn't realize you and he were a thing—"

"We're not."

Hulia frowned with one eyebrow raised. "Touchy much."

I smiled at my friend. I owed her more, a lot more, but Arran's secrets were mine to keep. "It's all right. It's just... complicated."

"What about that one?" Hulia jerked her chin at the only man in the room wearing a coat. The dark fabric matched his dark hair, tied back in a short, unforgiving ponytail. And all that dark worked to brighten his intense green eyes. He cut through the crowd like an apex predator striding through Faerie's jungles and eyed the revelers like he might arrest half of them for wanton behavior in a time of crisis and the other half for breach of the peace. He wasn't wearing his gold star, but he didn't need to. *Lawman* was written in the way he walked, the way he scanned for threats, and the way he pinned me under his challenging glare. I'd also recently seen everything beneath those layers of lawman. He had a body to match his impressive presence and a physique made for stamina *and* strength. A rare combination, but then, he was the last of his vakaru kind.

Hulia caught my too-long stare in the marshal's direction. "Huh, guess not." She snorted something like a laugh. "I hear you have a fae in your harem too. Dayam Kesh,

4

leave some of the sexy for the rest of us." She smirked into her drink.

"It's not like that." I turned my back on the approaching Kellee and feigned interest in the food.

"Being namu means I got a few tricks, *Messenger*, like sniffing out when someone really, really wants to f—*Hullo, Marshal Kellee*." She flicked her hair back and straightened, purring his name and making it sound filthy in a good way. I knew she could flirt, but I figured I'd only seen a fraction of what she could do.

"Hulia," Kellee greeted from behind me. I heard the polite smile in his voice. They knew each other. He had helped her get to safety after Eledan had screwed with her head. She likely also knew him from her profession. The Halow law and Hulia had rarely gotten along. Now there was no law, and we were all on the same side.

"You smell delightful," she gushed. "What *is* that cologne?"

I stomped on Hulia's foot. Her bright, tinkling, seductive laughter turned half the heads in the room, and she sashayed into the crowd, looping a few unsuspecting males in her arms.

I glanced at Kellee side-on and caught his puzzled frown mixed with that superficial smile. Once Hulia was out of sight, he took up her spot beside me and eyed my drink. "What is it?"

"I have no idea. She keeps refilling this." I showed him the tankard. "And when she's not looking, I dump it back into the bowl." The last time I'd gotten too liberal with my emotions after drinking Faerie wine, I'd had sex with a fae ambassador and strangled him with my whip. Granted, I'd thought he was Eledan. But while I wasn't craving Eledan like before, I didn't entirely trust myself not to lose control.

Kellee picked up a discarded cup and sniffed. "Smells like cleaning fluid." He set it back down and turned his attention to the room. "Arran's enjoying himself."

I couldn't read the marshal's flat tone but knew I didn't want to watch Arran anymore. I nodded and made an agreeable sound. Setting down my drink, I grabbed a piece of flatbread and picked at it. Kellee was too astute to miss my mood. His gaze warmed my face. He hadn't said much after Aeon had eaten the starfruit. Hadn't said much about anything since we had survived Sjora and her arena games. He knew something was going on between Talen and me. He didn't like what had happened with Aeon/Arran, and then there was the fact I'd watched him fuck a powerful, immortal fae unconscious. There was a lot going on in everything we didn't say.

A violin, or something like it, started up, but the sound held an electronic note. I instantly recognized Hulia's music and stiffened. She had played like this in The Boot. She had magic. Not a lot, but enough to lightly bespell. There was no harm in it, but it reminded me too much of all the things I'd been hiding from and everything we had lost.

Kellee's hand boldly found my waist, and then he was there, leaning close to my side so that when he spoke, I heard him clearly despite the music. "Do you dance?"

"No, I..." He pulled back, but the electric flutters he'd sparked to life in me felt too good to lose so soon. I dropped my bread and covered his hand on my waist with my own, trapping his fingers against me. "I don't know how," I admitted, expecting him to laugh. I had never danced in my life. It seemed silly here, surrounded by dancing humans, but these weren't my people. I wasn't human, not really.

His fingers closed around mine, and he wordlessly led me to the edge of the crowd. There, he stepped in front of me, took my hand, placed it neatly on his waist, and clasped my other hand in his. He rested his other hand on my hip, where it might as well have scorched a hole through my clothes. I stared at the laces tying his shirt closed. It seemed like the safest place to look.

"Feel the movement and let yourself drift with me," his deep voice rumbled.

My face was hot. I could kill a thousand fae, lie to the Faerie Queen for years, and cut out a prince's heart, but this... this wasn't me. Half of me wanted to run, the other half was too stubborn to let Kellee see me weak. And so I stomped on the spot, with no idea where to put my feet. My heart raced as if I were being stalked in the arena, like I was preparing to fight.

Kellee's hand slipped to the dip at my lower back and his fingers spread there, and to make it worse, he pulled me close so my lower belly grazed his belt and my chest brushed his. I had been close to him before, mostly while trying to kill him. This was different. What was the point in dancing anyway? Was I supposed to enjoy being this close to Kellee without an endgame?

"Just tell me if you want to stop." His words tickled my hair against my forehead.

He swayed to the music. I focused on my feet and the feel of him moving, and soon, everything else fell away.

"I didn't know you could dance." I sounded okay, not like the high-strung mess inside my head.

"There's a lot you don't know."

Of course there was. He was the last of a race the fae

had all but wiped out centuries ago. He looked young, my age, but he wasn't. He looked human, but he wasn't that either. He had a hunger inside him, one that had once looked at me like prey. Marshal Kellee had teeth, literally and figuratively. And beneath all that rugged prettiness lurked something *unseelie*. Something forbidden.

My footing stumbled. Kellee caught me. The music quickened, and so did our pace. His rhythm swept me with him, his body strong in ways that had nothing to do with combat. "We've fought often enough that this should be second nature to you."

"Give me a weapon and I'll know how to dance with you." My hand had moved to his back, inside his coat, so I felt the warmth through his shirt. I didn't remember moving it there, but it felt good to feel the smooth shift of muscle, feel him move beneath my touch. I wanted to feel the heat and softness of his skin under my hands. I had dreamed it over and over and over, and Eledan had ripped those dreams away. I wanted the real Kellee in my memories. Always had, since I'd first seen him walking through the sinks like he, alone, was the law. But in many ways, the marshal, like Talen, was untouchable. I'd seen him fuck a fae general. He hadn't killed her, but he could have. I was sure of it. Their lovemaking was one memory I could have done without. The two of them rocking together, her fae skin glistening magic, his mouth on her shoulder, her breast, his sharp teeth sinking in—

"Then dance like that," he said, bringing me back into the room. "Use your emotion."

If I did that, I'd probably kill him. I laughed at my dark thoughts.

His fingers touched my chin, tilting my head up. Delight sparkled in his eyes. "You don't laugh enough."

Those eyes, flecked with green... sometimes they were black, sometimes rimmed in gold, sometimes red. He had so many facets, all of them dangerous. But I hadn't feared him until I'd seen the truth at his center. The unseelie. Did he know he had the darkest part of Faerie inside him?

The music still played, and bodies moved around us, caught up in Hulia's spell, but Kellee and I stood motionless. He looked down at me, seeing... I wasn't sure. But he seemed puzzled, like I was the mysterious one. He knew more about me than I did about him. I wanted to know more, but getting answers out of him had never been easy. Getting a kiss was even harder. If I rose onto my tiptoes, I could kiss him... and ruin this tentative truce we'd built up over the past few weeks. I wouldn't force him. There were more lies than truths between us. I'd betrayed him. I wouldn't make this decision for him. It had to be his, even if I ached all over for him to lower his mouth, sweep his tongue in and claim me the way the rest of him wanted. I knew what he was, both sides of him. And the only thing that frightened me was never having him know me in return.

The violin sang, its vivid notes weaving a spell through the crowd.

I brought my hands up between Kellee and me, creating space and room to think, but as I did, I noticed the crowd no longer moved. "Something's wrong."

Hulia played, but the rest of her band members gazed slack-jawed like all the others. She swept the bow across the violin, her body locked in its own dance, and the crowd watched her with glassy, unblinking eyes.

Kellee's eyes narrowed, golden edges glowing. "Stop Hulia's song." He cocked his head, listening to something I couldn't hear. "Go."

I shoved through the bodies. "Hulia!" Her eyes had glazed over too.

I heard Kellee's growl and glanced back to see him pitch the bowl of pink water off the table, splashing the entire contents across the floor. Poison.

"We're not alone." Kellee ran from the room, his swirl of coat the only part of him I recognized in the blur.

The floor shook and the strings of lights overhead swung. Thunder followed, but it rolled on and on. A ship. And Kellee was out there alone.

He'd be fine. He was always fine.

"Hulia." I scrambled onto the makeshift stage made of rows of tables. She continued to dip and sway, her body one with the music and the magic. And it was magic she wove. I could taste the sweetness of Faerie sprinkled in the air. This wasn't Hulia's doing. Something mixed with the drink had left an entire people susceptible, including Arran. He stared up at the stage like all the others.

This trance was fae made. It had to be.

I placed a hand on Hulia's shoulder, moving with her. "Hulia, snap out of it."

She didn't respond, just played her hauntingly beautiful music.

I slapped her, putting weight behind it. Her grip on her bow slipped, and the violin jolted in her hands. Silence.

She blinked and touched her face.

"Fae." Kellee was back. He grabbed a table, upended it like it was as light as paper, and wedged it against the door.

"How many?"

Hulia fluttered her lashes and frowned at her audience. "I've never done *that* before."

"Too many," Kellee replied. He turned and scanned the nonresponsive crowd. "Can you play them back to life?"

"I don't even know how I did... this..." She dropped the violin. It clattered to the stage at her feet. "My music doesn't hurt people. I don't hurt people."

Until now, I thought.

We couldn't move them all, not in time.

I watched my friend's face crumble. "It's not you, Hulia. It's Faerie. Something in the wine must have left them susceptible to your song—more than usual." I jumped down, wove through the crowd to Arran, and gently shook him. He didn't wake.

"Why do... this?" She lifted her hands, and I knew what was going through her head. Had they gotten to her too? Made her play at the right time?

"They want them alive," Kellee growled. "Unharmed."

They're harvesting them. My eyes met Kellee's. We couldn't save them. Even if we could reach our shuttle, it only fit a handful of passengers. Talen might be able to save them with his warcruiser. If he had seen the fae approach, there was a chance he was on his way, but we couldn't wait.

"You have to leave," Hulia said. "There's a basement exit. Hurry."

Kellee scooped Arran over his shoulder, and we reached the basement as the door above exploded open. Hulia lifted a hatch in the floor.

I remembered another time, just like this one, when she had saved Kesh Lasota who'd been on the run from Calicto authorities a lifetime ago.

Kellee carried Arran into the tunnel. I dropped down after him and reached up for Hulia.

"I did this," she said, expression remorseful. She glanced behind her.

"No, Hulia, don't go back. They'll take you too."

When she looked down, her mouth hardened with determination. "I can't leave these people alone at their mercy."

I should have been the one saving them. I was their messenger, wasn't I? But I didn't see how we could survive hundreds of fae, and if their ship was a warcruiser, we didn't stand a chance.

"This isn't the time to take a stand," Kellee said from behind me. "We run today and fight tomorrow."

He was right, but it didn't change the fact that I should be taking Hulia's place. Wasn't that what good people did?

"I'll be all right." She smiled for my benefit. "I'm namu. There's nothing they can do to me that they haven't already done," she said, sounding so much like saru. She began lowering the hatch.

"Wait—"

"Go, friend." Shouts sounded behind her. "I'll see you again soon."

The hatch closed, shutting her and the rest of the colony away and plunging me and Kellee into darkness. Kellee's warm hand found mine, and he led me into the dark.

The tunnel twisted and turned, eventually spitting us out high up on a hillside a long way from the huddled colony buildings. A hot wind, spiced with magic, blasted over us the second we stepped outside. We hunkered down behind a mound of rocks, shielded from sight. Above the scattering of colony buildings, a fae warship hung low in the churning sky. Colored light flashed along its undercarriage, washing the entire area in an eerie green hue.

Kellee propped Arran up against a boulder and peered into Arran's unseeing eyes. "It's Benrin's Spite," he said.

I'd heard of it. It was among the fae's many magical poisons, used to steal their victim's will, making them obedient puppets.

"It's not as potent on the skin, but when consumed it can pack a nasty punch. He should come around soon." Kellee shifted position and crouched beside me. The greenish light from the ship reflected in his eyes as he scanned the scene below.

My attention lingered on Arran. When he came around, would he demand to go back down there? Aeon's fight had been taken out of him, but Arran had a reckless wildness. He wouldn't react well to us abandoning the colony. I'd deal with it once he was awake. Or Kellee would. Arran didn't dare cross the lawman.

"There's some activity," Kellee said.

The warship had landed. A flight of soldiers had formed a line leading from the ship's ramp to the building we had been dancing in. How quickly things changed.

A single fae marched toward the colony building where a string of people was filing out one by one like mindless puppets.

Kellee crouched lower. "Sidhe lord."

Sidhe was a collective name the higher families gave to themselves, separating them from the fae riffraff and granting them godlike status among fae-kind. Most made up the court, but others kept out of courtly politics. Some vanished altogether, prefering the wilds of Faerie to the company of their own kind.

I squinted into the wind to get a clear view of the lord. "Can you describe him?" Kellee's eyesight was better than mine in low light.

"Red hair. He's wearing dark earth-colored clothing."

"Autumnlands." Unlike Winterlands, they weren't quick

to anger and didn't make rash decisions. Their strength and determination made them excellent allies and devastating foes. I only knew of a handful who regularly attended Mab's court. Most stayed away from politics.

"I don't see any markings, but he's well covered beneath a hood. He's armed." Kellee's focus sharpened. "With... steel?"

Only four fae were permitted metal weapons at court.

Kellee must have caught the hitch in my breath. He glanced my way, suspicion knotting his brow. "You know him?"

I tried to get a better look, but all I saw was a tall fae dressed in dark clothing. "Not all fae are averse to metal. To tek, yes. But some wield forged steel. I know of only four who do, and all are Oberon's personal guards."

"A guardian?" Kellee asked.

I nodded. In antiquity, the guardians had served the queen, but Oberon had made them his long before my birth. It was one of the reasons Mab had agreed to let me stand beside her when Oberon so kindly suggested I become her guardian. She had argued that a true Faerie queen should not need a personal guard, but she'd taken me on to humor her son.

"What, by-cyn, is he doing out here?" Kellee asked.

"If he is a guardian, he's not here for the people."

"He's here for us."

More specifically, me. It was no mistake that Oberon had sent that particular guardian here. The red hair, the sword —he had to be Sirius. Sirius and I had a history.

I might have looked away if Hulia hadn't walked out of the colony building with enough sass in her stride to have the flight of soldiers uncomfortably shifting their aims.

Kellee mumbled, "They'll kill her," followed by, "Where the fuck is Talen?"

They wouldn't kill Hulia. Namu were sought after. She had worth. They would make her sing, and dance, and love. Some of the best namu were priceless possessions, Hulia included.

She strode up to Sirius, so much smaller than him but carrying enough confidence to look like the one in control. Maybe she didn't know who he was because, had she known, she would have dropped to her knees. Instead, they seemed to be having a conversation, though they could equally have been just staring at each other. I couldn't tell from this distance, but Kellee watched them keenly, either reading their lips or listening. While they faced off, the colonists shuffled up the ramp and out of sight.

"She's insane," Kellee murmured.

I was about to ask why, when Sirius's hand shot out and clamped around Hulia's neck. The guardian lifted the namu clean off her feet. She kicked uselessly at the air.

Kellee's warning growl sparked my internal rage. Not long ago, I wouldn't have cared. I would have blamed her for speaking out, for defying them, but things were different. I was different. Hulia had only ever tried to help people. The Boot had been a sanctuary in a part of Halow the rest of the system had all but forgotten. But more than that, she was my friend, and I'd learned there were few things worth more than friendship in these dark days.

All I had to do was walk down there and trade myself in for her. Maybe, if I did that, they would all be safe. The people too. And I saved people now. I was the Messenger.

"Don't," Kellee warned.

I ignored him and gripped the rock, ready to push to my feet.

"Kesh."

"I have to."

Sirius threw Hulia to the ground.

I shot to my feet but somehow got turned around, and before I could right myself, I had my back against the rock and all of Marshal Kellee in my face. "Use your sense. I know you have some. You can't save her."

He had his hand fisted in my coat, pinning me down. I grabbed his wrist and tried to shove him back, but it was like pushing against a wall. "Get your hands off me, Marshal."

Frustration flashed in Kellee's green eyes. "This is exactly what he wants. He knows Hulia's connected to us. He probably knows we're watching. He wants you to do something stupid, exactly like this. Stop acting their tool and think for yourself."

His words stung. "I'm not their tool."

"Prove it." He shoved off me and went back to watching over the rock.

I twisted and saw the flick of Sirius's cloak as he disappeared inside the warship. Hulia was nowhere in sight. The people had all filed inside, and now the flights were spreading out to investigate the abandoned buildings. My chance to do something, anything, had passed. The fae had captured the colony and Hulia, and I'd watched it happen.

Among it all sat our shuttle, surrounded by fae. We weren't getting off Hapters anytime soon.

"That anger you feel," Kellee said, "shape it into a weapon worthy of the people's Messenger."

My insides squirmed like the time I'd been caught

pickpocketing a fae lord. They'd whipped me for that. But here, now, Hulia had paid the price.

Kellee had to be right. Every. Damn. Time. Part of me hated him for that, but a larger part of me reluctantly thanked the know-it-all marshal for stopping me from rushing in with no real plan—besides throwing myself at their mercy.

"We can't stay here." He scooped up Arran and plunged into the brush.

I lingered a few moments, watching the fae pour through the colony in search of stragglers and us. I was getting Hulia back. I would save those people. And Sirius would feel the bite of my whip. Because Kellee was right. I was the people's Messenger. And this was war.

CHAPTER 2

*A*cres and acres of burned farmland lay like blackened scars across the undulating landscape. We'd crossed the plains during Hapters's cooler, darker hours, but with the planet's two moons watching over us, the night here wasn't dark so much as varying shades of gray.

We could do nothing to hide the trail our passing left in the ash but hope the wind picked up and covered our tracks.

When Arran began to stir, we veered off our path into an abandoned stone cabin. Its squat profile blended in with the landscape. For now, it would serve as a shelter, but we had to keep moving. The fae were looking for us.

Kellee left Arran on a dusty couch and tucked himself against the wall near the window overlooking the track, and there he stayed, eyes glued to the horizon. With his vakaru eyes he had a better chance at spotting movement long before I could.

I drifted about the cabin, checking for weapons, but found none. Whoever had lived here had cleared out anything of use weeks ago, likely right after the fae reappeared and scorched everything human in their path.

Arran startled awake. His attention locked on me first, read me as friendly, and then snagged on Kellee's silhouette by the window. At the sight of the marshal, Arran's expression locked down.

"You're safe," I told him, crouching beside the couch.

"What is this place?" He sat up and swayed, reaching for the back of the cushions to steady himself.

"Farmhouse." I caught his hand and hauled him onto his feet. "You were drugged."

His fingers squeezed mine. Just a thankful squeeze, but a barbed twist of betrayal knotted inside me, because he trusted me, and out of everyone, he was the one who shouldn't. I plucked my hand from his, drawing that line between us. He didn't seem to notice my brush-off as he hunched forward, bracing his hands on his thighs.

"Drugged?" he croaked, running his hands down his face to clear away the grogginess.

"Kellee thinks the fae knew we would be there. They probably had an enthralled human spike the drinkbowl with Benrin's Spite to smooth their arrival."

"Benrin's Spite?"

Aeon would have recognized the poison. I smiled sadly. "It takes away your will. Makes you compliant."

Arran winced and grumbled in disgust. He straightened and sighed but was already shrugging off the weariness. "It didn't affect you?"

"Had I touched it or consumed any of it, it would have." And that had been a close call. Just one touch and I would have been on Sirius's ship, probably halfway back to Faerie by now. Too close a call. We needed to be more careful. Coming here, to the party, had been a mistake.

Arran threw his head back and cast his gaze to the ceiling. His throat moved as he swallowed and the old scar bobbed. "The others got out?" His gaze fell on me.

"The fae have them."

His notrils flared. "*You* left them?"

I spotted Kellee's cursory glance our way. The marshal likely wondered if he needed to get involved. I ignored him and faced Arran's accusations. "We didn't have a choice," I explained, keeping my tone level. "There were too many—"

"You just left them there?"

What did he want from me? "Kellee said—"

Arran swung his accusing glare to the marshal. "And now we're hiding?" He staggered to his feet. "We have a warcruiser, an attack drone, a vakaru and the Messenger, and we're hiding in a shed while the fae do cyn-knows-what with those people?"

Kellee poked his tongue into his cheek and raised an eyebrow. "You wanna go back there with no plan and get yourself killed, kid, go right ahead."

"I never thought you were a coward, *Marshal*." The weight of his lawman title held a whole load of accusations. Marshals helped people. At least, that was how it was supposed to be. A flash of indignant fire sparked in Kellee's eyes, threatening to turn their color.

Holy cyn, Arran did *not* just call a vakaru a coward.

"That's enough!" I snapped. I yanked on Arran away from whatever argument he was determined to start with Kellee.

Kellee's superheated glower tracked us across the room.

Arran yanked his arm from my grip. "Did you put up a

fight?" he asked, voice lowered. He didn't know Kellee could still hear every word.

Faerie save me from impulsive males. I closed my eyes, breathed deeply, counting to five, and pushed my fingers against my closed eyelids. I could see why Kellee had stopped me from rushing in, and now I was trying to talk Arran down. Opening my eyes, I offered my friend a soft smile. His confusion softened and something of Arran's warmth returned. "You were out cold. We were outnumbered. No, we didn't put up a fight. We got out alive, and today, that counts as a victory."

"We ran away?"

"Sometimes running away is surviving. You know this." The words were out of my mouth before I could stop them. He didn't *know* anything.

He spread his hands against the wall and bowed his head. I waited for him to point out my mistake, but instead, he looked up. "They'll be tracking us."

"Yes."

He shrugged. "So, where's Talen?"

That was the ever-present question. Talen had a warcruiser that could swallow a moon and he had Sota, who I'd left charging on his dock, and the three of us were hiding in a shed, as Arran had so accurately summarized.

I cast my gaze across the room to Kellee.

He shrugged. "He's your fae." Implying I should know where Talen was at all times. Talen and I were *bonded*, but right now, all that internal electric sensation told me was that Talen was alive.

He should have been here by now. All it would take was the sight of the warcruiser in orbit to make Sirius back down. The guardian's warship was half the size. So where in Faerie's three systems was my silver fae pilot?

"We can't wait for Talen." I wanted to believe Talen had our backs, but even after all the recent revelations, I felt as though I knew him less than when we first met. "We need to find a ship and get off Hapters. We can signal Talen's ship once we're off the planet. Back on the warcruiser, we can turn this fight around."

Arran pushed away from the wall. "All right. So we need to find an outpost that would have housed transport ships. A place that was abandoned when the population evacuated?"

"Kellee?" I asked. The marshal knew these backwater planets better than either of us.

"There's a town a few klicks north," he drawled, turning his attention back to the landscape outside the window. "It'll take us a day to get there on foot and there's no guarantee there will be anything of worth to find. But, two days' walk east, there's a salvage yard and a landing strip." He hesitated a fraction too long before saying, "There will be vessels there, but anything left behind will need repair work."

When he looked over, his expression carried more than the usual lawman mask. The tightness at the corner of his mouth, the smallest narrowing of his eyes. Arran didn't yet know him well enough to see it, but I did. Kellee was worried.

"Repair work isn't a problem, so long as it's standard tek." I knew tek, and Arran had picked up his old tek habits quickly enough despite losing his Aeon memories. Muscle memory had stuck with him, hence the dancing and his gladiatorial skills and probably a slew of other things yet to be revealed.

"The yard it is," Arran said, striding for the door.

Kellee watched him pass before catching my eye. "The

yard," I agreed. "Hopefully, once Talen shows up, we won't need it."

Kellee's frown silently corrected, *If Talen shows up.*

WE LEFT the cabin far behind and walked along the fence lines sectioning off enormous patchwork fields. Kellee hung back, watching our tail, while Aeon was a whisper in the grass ahead.

They worked better apart.

Kellee hadn't said a single word about the starfruit, but he didn't have to. The vakaru's glances and silences were loud and clear. He preferred Aeon. Aeon, he understood, and Aeon had understood Kellee. They were both battle-hardened warriors. They had bonded on sight. Arran was... different. Arran eyed Kellee like he didn't fully trust the lawman. Possibly because Kellee looked at Arran like he was permanently disappointed. But it was me Kellee was disappointed with. I was supposed to have stopped Aeon from taking the starfruit and losing his memories. I hadn't.

Maybe Arran was picking up on Kellee's innate threat. Arran wouldn't have guessed Kellee was unseelie. The unseelie were little more than a cautionary tale in a land made of myths. But there was no denying Kellee carried the kind of lethal aura that moved most people out of his way.

As I walked through the long grass between them, I wondered if I should have left Arran at a resistance camp. He hadn't asked to leave, but keeping him around was much harder than I'd imagined. Arran was still Aeon, and when he flashed his quick, bright smile, I died a little inside. I still loved him. I always had. But he didn't know me at all.

Since the starfruit, Kellee had gotten colder, and Talen... despite knowing him better than ever, he was still a mystery. He and I hadn't spoken much since I'd asked him to tell me his name and I'd given him mine.

I was trying to make this work. Wasn't that enough? So why did it feel as though everything I was nurturing in Talen, Kellee and Arran was slipping through my fingers? And all the while, chatter in Halow's communication channels spoke of the Messenger who would save Halow from the fae. The mythical messenger who had killed hundreds of thousands of fae during a Game of Lies. I hadn't killed that many, but the legend was growing. I, however, wasn't. Inside, the kernel of truth the myth was built on threatened to break open and reveal who I really was. A saru slave. A nobody. A nothing girl. And Halow was pinning its hopes on me.

Eledan was probably laughing.

Goosebumps chased up my arms as my thoughts darkened around the memory of the Mad Prince. His phantom still stalked me and probably would forever. *Nothing girl.* How could I be a hero when half the time I didn't even know who I was? I was trying, but Kellee's cold shoulder and Talen's distance meant it wasn't enough.

A low whistle pierced the night. Arran's warning signal.

I dropped to my knees in the grass. Kellee would have surely taken cover too.

I waited, listening to the breeze hissing through the grass, until a different whistle pitched into the quiet, dart-like and constant. A slim organic vessel flew overhead and was gone again in a blink. Single-fae ships. Talen's warcruiser carried some, but there was no way of knowing if the vessel was his or Sirius's.

I waited for Arran's all clear, heard the two pips, and emerged from the grass. Grassheads tall enough to conceal fae scouts waved like ocean rollers. We were too exposed here. The fae could be hiding in that grass and attack at any moment.

"We're clear."

My heart leapt into my throat and my hand shot to my whip.

The marshal quirked a single eyebrow and the corner of his smart mouth tugged upward. He leaned in and whispered, "I didn't know it was possible to creep up on the Wraithmaker," as he sauntered past me and plunged into the wall of grass.

I followed, narrowing my glare on the back of his head, watching his ponytail bounce. In the arena, nobody stalked me and lived. "It's not."

"You sure looked startled."

His voice held that irritating note of laughter. The same note I'd first heard in the sinks when I ran right into him. I silently mouthed his words back at him, *"You sure looked startled,"* and said aloud, "Vakaru were made for this shit."

He grumbled agreeably. It was true. The vakaru came before saru. When they hadn't worked out, the fae harvested child saru for their arena bloodsports.

I stepped in his tracks through the grass, watching him sidestep and carve through the field as easily as a shadow. He could probably vanish right in front of me and I'd never see which way he went.

I was slowing him down, and I *knew* how to stalk. He had better eyesight, better hearing, better sense of smell.

Everything about him was made for the hunt, the chase, the kill.

At least a year had passed since we'd met, though for much of that I'd been dreaming, and I still knew so little of his kind. What had his people been like? Did he have a family once? How had he come to be the last vakaru? But I'd recognized the truth of him during the Game of Lies. Unseelie. He'd had his teeth in my wrist, and he'd drawn my blood from my veins and more with it. The dark part of Faerie inside him *would* kill me if it got the chance. There was a monster in Kellee, one he battled every day. Now I was afraid to poke him too much, in case he didn't know what he was. Or worse, he did.

The unseelie's hunger—what I'd heard of it—made Eledan's twisted torture look like child's play. Oberon had defeated them so long ago it might as well have been a fantasy. It was to me. Until I'd seen the real Kellee.

As I followed his path through the grass, I tried to recall what I'd heard about the unseelie, but much of it was nonsense, like the shadowwalkers who snatched oath-breakers from their sleep, or the nightwraiths who roamed with the Hunt, unable to resist death's sweet song. All legends warped by time in the same way the name Wraith-maker had taken on a mythology of its own.

I pulled my coat tighter around me and shrugged off my shivering. I would ask him. Soon. Once we had Hulia back and we'd dealt with Sirius.

Sirius.

More shivers trickled down my back.

The guardian had hated me from the moment Oberon had plucked me from the arena.

In all the years I'd spent as the king's secret shadow,

Sirius had barely wasted words on me when his hate-filled green-eyed glare did all the talking for him.

Had he volunteered to find me? Was this a kill mission, or had Oberon sent him to retrieve me? What of Talen and Kellee? By now, Oberon must have known they were working with me, or I with them. I wasn't yet sure how we all fit together but we *were* together.

The Game of Lies had changed everything. Right up to that point, I could have lied my way out of it all: letting Eledan live, not returning immediately with the Mad Prince, saving human colonies. I could have gone back, dropped to my knees, and kissed the king's hand. All would have been well. Then I'd set an army of drones on every fae in that arena and cut them down like they were nothing more than the grass I walked through. Immortal lives ended. I could still taste their blood in the air, still hear their screams. Kellee wasn't the only monster walking through the grass.

"I'm afraid to ask what's causing that frown."

Kellee's voice pulled me from the depths of my thoughts.

"What?" I blinked and halted behind Kellee's motionless silhouette.

He had stopped at the edge of the fields. Ahead, a small collection of domed dwellings huddled along a river-bank. I shielded my eyes against the slash of crimson breaking over the horizon and glimpsed a strip of white fabric snagged in a communications antenna. It flapped like a surrender flag in the breeze. Maybe it was a coincidence, or maybe someone had risen the white flag when the fae arrived. Whatever had happened here, I saw no signs of life now.

"Shall we take a look?" Arran asked, emerging from the

grass to my left. The morning light lifted the blond streaks in his short hazel hair.

Kellee's eyes narrowed on the domed houses, shadows gathering on his face. "We should avoid settlements. The fae will look at dwellings first."

"We might need supplies," Arran countered and then started down the slope toward the buildings. "It won't take long," he called back.

Kellee watched Arran skid down the bank, a perturbed muscle fluttering in his jaw. I brushed his arm in friendly reassurance and descended the bank after Arran. "You should be accustomed to being ignored by now."

"I thought all saru were obedient."

I grinned over my shoulder. "There's a lot you don't know, Marshal."

He half-smiled as he heard his words echoed back at him.

We crossed a dust-covered road with an eye on the skies and the farmland stretching all around, shadows cast long and lean behind us. Already, Hapters's daylight heat beat down on us.

"We may need to take shelter from the heat," Kellee was saying as we approached the nearest dome, then the wind changed, and the flag fluttered the opposite way.

Kellee stopped dead. His fingers twitched.

"What is it?"

He bolted forward, dashing around the side of the dome. I sprinted after him and saw Arran stagger out from inside and brace himself against the wall, his face flour-pale. He pressed the back of his hand to his mouth, saw me, and shook his head.

Kellee hissed a curse from inside the open doorway.

I smelled it then, the coppery odor of spilled human blood.

Death waited inside.

At first glance my saru mind struggled to piece together what it saw in front of Kellee where he had crouched down to examine the remains. The scattered bodies were unmistakably human, but from their wrinkled and desiccated carcasses, they had been dead for weeks, maybe months. Dark patches marked the walls where blood had splattered. But the ripe smell of fresh death lingered in the air.

"Have you ever seen anything like this?" Kellee asked. He didn't mean the bodies, or the fact two of the six dead were children. He meant the wet scent of the kill, combined with what appeared to be decades-old remains.

"No."

Their clothes were intact, torn and stained in places. One body, I assumed a male from its size, had a pistol holstered against his shriveled thigh. He hadn't reached for it. The children were huddled behind him, and behind them, a smaller female adult reached beneath a dust-covered bed. Opposite her, two others clutched each other, teens perhaps. Now their hollow eye sockets collected dust and their white bones jutted where their skin had peeled away.

The dome was a single-room dwelling. Beds. A table. They hadn't had much. A farmer's family, perhaps?

Kellee maneuvered between the bodies and brushed his fingers to a dark mark on the walls. He rubbed his thumb and fingers together. "Wet," he said. "The heat would have dried it by now. This happened during the night, just hours ago." He cast his gaze at the bodies, his eyes going distant along with his emotions.

"It wasn't theft," I added.

Kellee looked up, remembering I was here, and his gaze shuttered behind his mask of neutral lawman indifference. He looked around us, at the simple dwelling, and then left without saying another word.

Outside, I heard him tell Arran to check the other dwellings and then his boots scraping in the dirt as he walked away. He had seen more death than me, but this had bothered him.

I looked again at the scene, at a father shielding his children, the mother reaching... Someone had come through the door and killed them all before they could fight back. What could have killed so fast?

I stepped between the bodies. Where was the blood? A human body bleeds a startling amount. Six bodies. There should have been more blood, not just a few splatters on the wall. I crouched beside the mother and peeled her collar away from her neck. The skin, darkened and as dry as paper, held two puckered puncture marks, constricted now that the skin had tightened.

I'd seen those marks before, when Kellee had drunk blood from my wrist. Had a vakaru done this? But there were no other vakaru. Kellee was the last.

There were no other obvious wounds on the bodies. No slashes to the throat. No abdominal cuts, no blast patterns. My gaze tracked the woman's reaching hand toward the bed. Light had crept across the floor and crawled over the dead, and as I lifted my eyes, something glinted in the dark.

Crouching, I stretched an arm beneath the bed and touched something cool, hard, and metal. A box. I pulled it from under the bed and flicked open the lid. A hand-sketched portrait of the family lay on top of a collection of

31

trinkets. I pushed the drawing aside and found a brooch. Metal edging plaited around a tarnished green gem. It was likely worthless, just costume jewelry.

I brushed my thumb across the gem, wiping it clean. Tek whirred to life. The silver plaits unraveled, branching outward, turning the brooch into a star-like shape, and at its center, the gem winked green with a swirl of fae magic —life magic.

Tek and magic.

I stared at the impossible thing in my hand.

"Kesh..." Arran's outline appeared in the doorway, blocking the light.

With a start, I closed my hand around the tek. "Yes?"

"Kellee says we need to leave. Now."

I got to my feet, discreetly hiding the brooch in my pocket, and nodded.

Outside, Kellee's outline was a dark blot walking the river's edge, flooded in sunlight. By the time I caught up with him, smoke billowed out of the larger domed house. In seconds, the column had turned black and climbed high into Hapters's greenish skies.

Arran's scowl made it clear he thought Kellee had lost his mind.

If the fae didn't know where we were before, they did now.

But Kellee knew the risk. And he'd set the fire anyway.

We marched along the serene river's waters in silence, and behind us, the lives of a dozen families burned to ash.

CHAPTER 3

We sheltered in a ravine during the hottest part of the day, keeping to the shadows so that any passing ships would miss us. Kellee scouted ahead, leaving Arran and me to our thoughts. He didn't say much, and after the gruesome discovery back at the farming settlement, I didn't feel talkative either. I'd asked Kellee if there was any beast on Hapters that might explain the deaths, but he'd told me predators had been wiped out long ago, when the planet was first settled.

The mysterious brooch sat heavily in my pocket. It had returned to its tarnished state, but now I knew to look for it, the tingling thrum of fae magic tickled my thigh. As to what fae magic was doing on Hapters? I didn't have an answer, but it *felt* wrong. We were deep in Halow territory, far from Faerie. Until the recent discovery of a well of magic on Calicto, the idea that any magic could exist outside of Faerie had been as far-fetched as the fae themselves.

Kellee returned as the day cooled and the light faded, his unshaven chin and dark hair peppered with dust.

"We need to keep moving," he urged, as spritely as when we'd started out. "It's another day's hike."

Arran fell into step behind him and I followed, hoping we could get off Hapters soon so I wouldn't have to keep staring at the long horizon and miles upon miles of flat fields.

We kept words to a minimum but I watched them both. Arran constantly scanned our surroundings, while Kellee strode ahead, relying on his senses to alert him. We hadn't said much since the settlement, and I wished I knew the right words.

Arran fell back into step with me, offering a small smile I'd seen on him countless times before. Memories rushed in. Memories of the times we couldn't talk, but there were other ways a saru could communicate.

He eased my hand into his like it was the most natural thing in the world. I didn't notice until his little finger brushed my wrist, the gentle tip tracing the outlines of saru marks meant to comfort.

I yanked my hand free, startling him. "What are you doing?" I hadn't meant it to sound so harsh, but he wasn't supposed to remember anything about being saru.

He lifted his hands and stepped back. "I er... I'm sorry. I..." His brow furrowed in confusion. "I didn't realize. I was just..."

"Well don't."

And now he looked hurt, and dammit, I didn't want to hurt him. It was just a touch. He probably wasn't aware of what he'd done.

"Right." Arran, usually so open and easy to smile, guarded his expression and withdrew several steps away from me. "I didn't mean to offend."

"It's fine." It wasn't. "It's nothing." It was everything.

34

I turned away from him and saw Kellee up ahead, jogging toward a watchtower erupting out of the skyline. I assumed he was heading toward it to get a better look at our position. An outcropping of boulders jutted from the ground between us and the tower. I veered off and waited beside them. Arran joined me moments later, his hands rammed into his pockets. Around us, heat rippled off the plains, warping the landscape, making Hapters look dreamlike. Huge skies, painted mauve as the daylight faded, pushed down.

On Faerie, something always interrupted the horizon. Huge weeping trees, sprawling jungle, rolling hills, rocks, walls, bars. This endless open space and its emptiness made me want to dig a hole and hide in it. My back itched, senses tricking me into thinking someone was observing us. I never did like vast, open spaces.

Arran leaned against a boulder and watched Kellee's rippling outline cut its way back through the heat haze.

"The yard's not far..." Kellee said, handing a canvas bag to Arran, who peeked inside and beamed. He took out a square loaf and tossed me the bag. I dug around inside and found a wrapped parcel of oatcake. Tasteless, but it chased away the hunger pangs. Now all we needed was water. We had veered away from the river some hours ago, but the dry, ash-scented air had quickly parched my throat and tongue.

Kellee's keen eyes scanned the surrounding land, probably seeing right to the horizon. The light was fading fast. Hapters's twin moons climbed into the sky, signaling another long night ahead. With the constantly waxing and waning light, it was a wonder anything grew on this farming rock.

"You think they've given up?" I asked Kellee.

He looked at me as though silently asking, *"When have the fae ever given up?"* and said, "We'll rest here a while and then make the push to the yard."

He allowed himself a moment to meet my gaze, and this time, a tentative smile touched his lips. Nothing like his usual cocky grins, but it warmed me to see it.

"Why isn't Talen here?" Arran asked from his rock perch. He picked at his loaf and eyed me cautiously.

It was a good question. One I couldn't answer.

I finished my oatcake, brushed my hands together, and looked up at the darkening, greenish sky. Talen should have spotted Sirius's arrival. At the very least, he should have picked us up right after. And now, here we were, a day in, about to find the yard and fix up a ship because my fae pilot hadn't come.

"He'll come if he can." *Maybe he left,* the little voice of doubt mumbled at the back of my thoughts.

Talen had talked about going back to Faerie. He had also mentioned not being ready, but that was then and this was now. There wasn't much, if anything, that could slow a warcruiser. So where was he?

Kellee looked at me, brow tight. He knew something had changed between Talen and me, and the look he gave me had me wondering if he believed I'd pushed Talen away. A few weeks ago, he had walked in on the end of a discussion Talen and I were having—one where things had gotten heated right before I demanded Talen tell me his real name. Something had passed between them in that moment. A warning, a threat, maybe both. They'd been "friends" long before I showed up and upset everything.

I wished I had all the answers, but with every passing hour, the only answer was the one I didn't want to reveal.

"I'm not ready to give up on him yet."

He left us, my internal voice said, mocking my words.

Kellee knew it too. He scanned the plains again, perhaps looking for more than the fae who hunted us. The breeze teased through his hair, playing with errant curls.

Arran jumped down from his rock and dusted his hands free of crumbs. "Then let's get another ship in the air, right?" He beamed at me and started forward. "Sitting around won't save our ass—"

The ground crumbled beneath his boots. Between one step and the next, the earth opened up and swallowed him whole.

Blink. Gone.

I lunged.

"Careful," Kellee threw an arm out to stop me from following Arran into the growing hole in front of us.

"Arran!" I freed my whip and approached the brittle edge, toeing my boot ahead to test my weight.

"...I'm okay," his spluttering voice echoed from deep inside.

I peered into the hole. Hapters's twin moons lit Arran's face and shoulders. Complete darkness coated the rest of him. I tossed my whip over the edge and dangled the tail down. Arran jumped, but the whip wasn't long enough. I lay on the ground, sprawling wide to spread my weight, and leaned farther in. Arran jumped again, grabbing for the whip.

I lurched forward—falling.

I reached at nothing—and then jolted to a halt as Kellee's firm hands locked around my ankles.

"And where do you think you're going?" He hauled me backward. Gravel burned into my hip and stomach where my clothes rode up.

A crack sounded. More earth fell away beneath me. I

twisted back on myself, saw Kellee lift an arm, and snapped the whip at him, looping its tail around his wrist. The tail snagged. The ground fell, and I fell with it.

My arm snapped taut, yanking me to a halt in mid-air.

I hit the wall and coughed dust and grit.

"You okay?" Arran called up.

"Uh-huh." My right shoulder strained, muscles screaming, but my grip on the whip held.

Kellee started reeling me in.

"Wait!" Drop into the darkness with Arran or let Kellee haul me up?

"Kesh," Kellee growled, "you're not getting any lighter."

"Let go."

"What?"

"You heard me." I looked down at Arran's expectant face below. "Is there a tunnel, a way out?" I asked him.

He squinted into the shadows to his left. "Maybe, something... it's too dark—"

"There aren't any tunnels on Hapters, Kesh," Kellee said.

"Let me down," I called.

"No," he grumbled back.

"Let me go, Kellee."

"You don't need—" Arran started.

"Kellee, *let me go*."

Kellee was perfectly equipped to survive on his own. But Arran... Arran who had lost his memories... Arran who I had left once before. I couldn't leave him in the dark again. "Get to the yard and see if there's a chain or rope. Arran and I will be fine."

Kellee grumbled a string of colorful curses and then the whip dropped, and so did I.

I landed in a crouch, minor pain jarring through my thighs.

Kellee's thunderous face appeared in the circle of light above. "Wait there." He pointed a finger at me, and then at Arran. "Do anything foolish and I'll leave the both of you here." And then he was gone.

I coiled my whip, clipped it back to my belt, and turned to face Arran. He blinked as though he couldn't understand why I'd dropped into a hole beside him. I couldn't tell him the truth, but as his throat bobbed, I wondered if he knew anyway.

I plastered a bright smile on my face. "Everything will be fine."

MY EYES soon adjusted to the thick darkness, revealing an oval tunnel mouth. The small amount of light pouring in from above shimmered over curved, smooth walls that beckoned me forward.

I braced a hand against the tunnel's edge and peered deeper inside. "No tunnels, huh, *Marshal Kellee?*" My voice carried far into the dark. For once, Kellee was wrong. This sure looked like a tunnel.

A beam of light plunged into the tunnel.

I frowned at the small tek flashlight in Arran's hand. He shrugged. "The people back in the village didn't need it."

He had stolen it from the settlement. I opened my mouth to complain and then remembered the brooch tucked in my pocket. Aeon and I had stolen from the fae daily. The winner had been the one with the shiniest of trinkets. I usually won.

I entered the tunnel.

"Kellee said to wait." Arran swept the flashlight beam ahead of me, slicing across the back of my legs and sending my shadow dancing against the curved tunnel walls.

"Kellee says a lot of things."

The walls looked a lot like the smooth, iridescent warcruiser tunnels. I didn't see any obvious chisel or machine marks. Had they been grown instead of cut out by human hands?

"We might as well take a look while we're stuck down here," I added. "Where's your sense of adventure?"

A crooked smile brightened his face as he walked alongside me. "I keep it behind my survival instincts."

Arran kept the flashlight beam high, illuminating the tunnels as far as each turn allowed. We hadn't come across any junctions, so there was no chance of getting lost. Once we had explored inside, we'd turn around and head right back to Kellee. He didn't need to know we had ventured into the tunnel without him. No harm done.

"You and Kellee are pretty tight," Arran said, building up to a bigger question.

"Something like that."

"You know him well?"

"I think so. Sometimes. Why?"

"Do you think Kellee's behavior was strange back at that village?" In the moving light, his eyes sparkled and shadows strayed across his face, making him difficult to read.

"Strange how?" The long tunnel pulled our voices into the dark and swallowed them down.

"He burned the whole place, destroying all the evidence, revealing our location."

Evidence? Did Arran think Kellee was guilty of something? "He burned it because we didn't have time to bury them. What would you have him do, leave them there like that?"

"No. I guess not."

We walked on, the silence suddenly heavy.

"Kellee has seen more death than you and me combined but that doesn't make him immune to it." *Sometimes, I think it makes him more vulnerable...*

"It's just..."

I stopped and faced Arran. "Look, Kellee wasn't about to leave those bodies to rot in the heat. That's not his way. It was a risk, but we were already moving on and he knew there weren't any fae nearby."

Arran pointed the flashlight down, drawing long shadows with it.

"There's something not right about him," he admitted, his frown cutting deeper.

If he knew Kellee was unseelie, Arran would either run, or knowing Arran as I was beginning to, he would probably attack the marshal, thinking he had something to prove. Kellee would not react well.

The look on Arran's face, crowded with shadows, held its own kind of threat. It was easy to dismiss Arran as harmless, but he could kill as efficiently as me and had done many times in the past. He'd forgotten it, but the skills were still there, buried but real. The last thing I needed was the two of them clashing.

"Kellee is... complicated, but his heart is in the right place."

"It takes more than heart to make a man and Kellee isn't a man. There's too much you're not telling me."

Aeon had always been observant. Little escaped his keen eyes and quick mind. Arran had been watching

Kellee closely, reading everything between what Kellee said and didn't say. I would have to tell Arran the truth eventually, before he came to his own conclusions.

"There's *a lot* I'm not telling you." I started forward again. "Just stay on Kellee's good side. We'll talk more once we're off Hapters. He's not a bad guy, Arran. That's all you need to know." Kellee would probably disagree with me, but he was wrong about that too.

The flashlight beam swept ahead and plunged into the dark. The tunnel walls suddenly opened, vanishing behind curtains of blackness.

I stepped up to the yawning space. Silence loomed, so thick and loud it hunched over us like something alive, waiting to gulp us down.

Arran took a few careful steps into the gloom. His flashlight halo landed on something upright, flat, and solid. He pulled back, and the beam expanded like a widening eye, highlighting more of the black slab of stone. I approached, noticing how specks of silver shimmered like fish scales beneath the stone's surface. The wall of rock barring our way had been polished smooth and appeared to block the tunnel.

Arran swept the beam higher and higher to where the smooth stone met rough walls. He reached out a hand and wiped off a layer of surface dust, revealing more of the shimmering surface beneath.

I hadn't seen much of Hapters, but this stone didn't look like the indigenous rocks we had passed. I knew exactly where stone like this came from. I'd seen them capping the arches of Faerie's long bridges, seen pebbles made of the same material glitter along Faerie's meandering pathways.

Arran swept his hand farther along the stone and stopped.

Metal letters glittered vertically along a floor-to-ceiling crack.

Fae letters.

He snatched his hand back, looking to me for answers.

I wordlessly held out my hand for the flashlight, and when he handed it over, I ran the beam over the wording. The swirling fae writing had been chiseled into the rock and poured with metal, probably molten iron, before the slab was put in place.

Slowly, word by word, the light revealed its secret.

Time, our prison,

Dark, our sentence,

Light, our freedom.

I handed the flashlight back.

"What is it?" Arran whispered.

A chill trickled down my spine and my breath puffed out in visible clouds. A fae warning, poured with iron and buried on a nowhere planet far away from Faerie. It made no sense.

"Didn't I say not to do anything stupid?"

I jumped and whirled to find Kellee's outline upsetting the dark.

The marshal's eyes glowed golden, like the glow from two distant stars. Arran splashed the flashlight beam across Kellee's face. The marshal flinched away, but not before I saw the dangerous glare he cast Arran's way. He lunged, too quick for Arran to react, and snatched the flashlight from his hand. Then he marched back the way we'd come.

"Do you know what it is?" I asked Kellee, trying to keep in step with him as his long legs ate up the strides.

"Poetic fae nonsense. Leave it alone. We have enough problems with the fae on our tails and you two go hunting for more trouble."

"What's fae language doing this deep in Halow?" Arran asked, trailing close behind me.

"Who knows?" Kellee answered. "Who cares? It's been here at least a thousand years. Let it rest."

Arran caught my eye, his frustration clear. Kellee knew more. A lot more. But by his sharp stride and sharper words, he was in no mood for questions.

A rope dangled into the tunnel from above. By the time Arran clambered out of the hole behind me, Kellee was a few hundred yards away and showed no signs of waiting for us to catch up.

"This is karushit," Arran snarled, brushing dust off his clothes and ruffling grit loose from his hair. "He knows exactly what that is back there. You need to get answers out of him, Kesh."

"I know. I will." I wasn't sure how to go about that. I'd spent most of my time avoiding Kellee's questions, not trying to turn those questions on him. If Kellee didn't want to play Q&A, nothing would change his mind.

"If you don't, *I* will." Arran started forward, following Kellee's tracks in the dust. He was capable of facing off with Kellee. But for all his bravado, Arran was mortal, and Kellee wasn't.

I followed Arran, feeling like I was losing my grip on everything. Sirius had taken Hulia, Talen was AWOL, something had killed the farmers and drained them of life in the hours we had been hiding, and now it turned out the fae had been here before—a long time ago—and Kellee knew a lot more than he was letting on. Add to all that the magic-infused tek in my pocket, and Hapters was turning out to be a whole lot more than a backwater planet.

Time, our prison,
Dark, our sentence,
Light, our freedom.
What exactly was going on here?

CHAPTER 4

*M*etal fencing as high as Calicto's towering container stacks encircled a mile-long stretch of landing area. Rusted spacefaring vessels lined its outer edges like enormous decaying carcasses. Their metal and tek remains stretched far into the distance. Salvage yard was one name for it. Tek necropolis was another. Did all the scrapped ships in Halow come here to die?

Kellee shoved his way through a door in the fence and Arran set about looking for a ship in a good state of repair, while Kellee found discarded panels and drums to barricade the door behind us.

A watchtower loomed over rows of storage and maintenance hangars. Rags had snagged in its scaffolding and flapped in the breeze like the white flag back at the settlement, only these strips looked black like bird wings. Only there weren't any birds on Hapters. No critters at all. Was that normal?

I climbed the exterior steel stairs to the tower and stood at the windows, awed by the vastness of Hapters's

PIPPA DACOSTA

plains stretching for miles in every direction. The landing strip and yard were the largest human-made structures around and easily seen, but at least we were behind steel walls. Anything coming in from the sky we would spot in good time to take shelter.

"Talen, you should be here by now..." Higher, where tiny stars fought their way through Hapters's light, I searched for any sign of the warcruiser, but found none.

Arran caught my eye below, weaving between the smaller ships. The marshal had taken himself off somewhere, telling nobody where, as usual.

Repair a ship, get off Hapters, find Talen, save Hulia, and turn all this around. One thing at a time. That was the easiest way. Just one step built on another and another until I was in control again.

I watched the cloudless sky as unease crawled up my spine. Something was very wrong on this planet. Despite the lack of people—driven off when the fae came—the quiet and the vast openness had my inked marks itching. I hadn't seen a single animal since fleeing the main colony. Not even a fly. Had the fae wiped Hapters clean of all life in preparation for their arrival or had it always been like this?

"Thinking hard again?"

I did my best not to show my alarm and stopped my hand from going for my whip. Damn that marshal and his creepy stalking.

Kellee filled the watchtower doorway, sleeves rolled up, his forearm braced on the frame like he'd been there all along. How had he climbed the metal stairs without me hearing? The vakaru was damn unnerving. His lips twitched around the hint of a wicked smile. He knew he'd startled me. Again.

"I need to put a bell on you," I grumbled, turning my back on him to watch the long view to nowhere. He stayed put in the doorway, and my gaze soon wandered back to him, drawn by his innate magnetism.

He drifted into the watchtower and perused the consoles of equipment—all dead. I'd already tried all the buttons, but I let him take a second shot. He found a flare gun I'd spotted and lifted it from its drawer to examine it. Satisfied, he returned it and continued his appraisal of the tower. A muscle fluttered in his cheek. He admired the panels but his mind was elsewhere. I wasn't the only one wrestling with my thoughts.

"You know Hapters well." It was a statement, not a question.

He jabbed at a few buttons. None responded. "I've picked up a few things over the years."

"Like what?"

His cheek twitched again. He looked out of the windows, scanning the long orange-kissed horizon. "Like how it rarely rains here but there are springs and rivers all over. Like how the crops grow when the smartest minds agree they shouldn't. There are no pests, no vermin, yet life keeps on going here, against all the odds."

Outside, the cooler, darker hours were waning again, giving way to brighter, hotter daylight. Under the approaching glare, Hapters's burned fields still looked ablaze.

"I knew Hapters was Faerie touched but I didn't know —I don't know how deep it goes."

My heart raced, instincts sensing I was close to something—someone dangerous and important, something of Kellee's past. "Did you have a life here?" I asked quietly, wary of getting too close.

Kellee sucked air through his teeth, making a sharp, jagged sound, and swallowed. He didn't want to answer. I couldn't place a time he had lied to me—ever. Even when he'd seduced Sjora, his words had been real. He had asked me if we were friends, if he thought we had a spark, and later, he had told me it was an act, just like my many faces. Only his act was true. Like this one. He didn't want to answer because the answer was yes and if he admitted he was as old as the fae, as immortal as they were, then what was the difference between them? Pointed ears? Harder eyes? Kellee was just as beautiful as them, maybe more so because he had a wild, unfettered nature that the fae effortlessly kept in check. But not him. He *was* fae. Unseelie fae. But still fae. And he hated that about himself.

I had always thought of him like the saru. Human, but made for the fae. I had thought he and I were alike—bred in captivity, chained in service. I'd been wrong. He was no more like the saru than Talen was.

I ached to ask if he had *any* human in him, but I feared the answer.

He had needed me—the face of Kesh Lasota—because he knew if people ever found out the truth of him, they would never follow him. And he so wanted to save people. Perhaps that was the human in him. He wore his golden star and he saved people. That was Marshal Kellee, a hero with an unseelie heart.

He folded his arms and leaned back against the consoles. The lawman mask was back on, locking away my chance of getting any answers out of him. "Tell me about the guardian."

I had been so close to knowing more, and now he was turning the questions back on me. I knew what he was doing. He knew I knew. And yet here we were, playing the same game as always. "Why?"

"I want to know the fae I'm dealing with."

"You're not dealing with him. I am." Sirius would kill Kellee. No leniency. No chances. The guardians weren't just Oberon's pretty trophies. They had teeth, and blades, and magic, and they were known for their ruthless efficiency with those weapons.

His eyes flashed. "Were you lovers?"

It was such an insane, un-Kellee-like question that I blinked at him, and then laughed. *"Lovers?"* I couldn't even wrap my head around the idea of it, or where that thought had come from. "He's a Royal Guardian, Kellee. Do you truly think he would look at me with anything other than disgust and hatred?" And oh how Sirius had *looked* —*watched*—while Oberon had poured poison beneath my skin. My screams, before I learned to silence them, had likely been music to the guardian's ears. My smile writhed on my lips, like a thing in pain, but I kept it there for Kellee to see.

"Devere was a royal emissary," he said. "Oberon's envoy. You didn't disgust him."

I almost laughed again, which, considering the thunder building around Kellee, would have been the wrong thing to do.

He didn't like that I'd fucked Lord Devere, never mind that I'd killed the lord right after. Well, two could play that game. Hadn't he done the same to Sjora? He was being ridiculous. Maybe the last few days had shaken him. They had shaken me. But I expected more from the marshal.

"Jealous?" I purred, remembering all too well how Kellee had sunk his teeth deep into Sjora's breast.

He blinked lazily, unfazed on the surface, but still

waters run deep and Marshal Kellee's were bottomless. "I'm just trying to understand who you are so I can take the guardian out without you getting in my way. If there are feelings between you and him, I want to know now, not when it's too late."

Feelings? I fought my smile, even as it turned bitter on my lips. Sirius had seen more of me than any other fae, besides Oberon, and that wasn't something I was getting into with Kellee now. Maybe never. Sirius likely knew me —the real me—better than Kellee, maybe better than Aeon. Because he had seen me plead with my then-prince, and later, seen me worship Oberon. If I told Kellee any of that, he'd twist it around and make it wrong. "The best thing you can do is stay out of *my* way if you want to live a few more thousand years."

"Is that a threat?" There was no humor in his eyes. Marshal Kellee was dead serious.

I laughed again and turned my back on him so that when my smile cracked and my face crumbled, Kellee wouldn't—couldn't see it.

I had thought we were past all this. I had thought we had found a peace between us. I had thought... we were friends. And now he was treating me like the Wraithmaker all over again. It wasn't just Devere. We were destined to clash and there was no getting around it.

"You haven't answered the question," he said, and for good measure, he asked it again. "Were you lovers, Kesh? It's a simple yes or no answer."

"I don't have to answer."

"You already have."

Haven't I done enough? I'd asked him that after killing thousands of fae. How many dead did it take? How many human lives saved? For Kellee, it would never be enough, because I couldn't change my past. I could answer all his stupid lawman questions and it wouldn't earn me his trust. Maybe it was time to let the dream of Marshal Kellee go?

"You think you know everything. You don't—"

Arran's whistle pierced the sizzling quiet. Outside a hangar, he waved, summoning us down.

"Stay here," I told Kellee. "Keep your eyes on the horizon."

Kellee's gold-rimmed eyes flashed. "Whatever you say, *Messenger*."

Somehow, I didn't swing for him on the way out the door, but if he kept that lawman karushit up, he and I would clash, and soon. I wondered if Talen were here, would he tell me Kellee was angling for a fight. If Talen were here, he'd defuse this tension. He always had before. I missed my silver fae.

ARRAN WAS WAITING for me inside the first hangar, and so was a sleek spacefaring ship the size of our usual shuttle. Some lower panels hung open, wires trailing over the floor, but the rest appeared to be in good condition.

Arran's grin instantly lifted the weight of Kellee's accusations off my back. "Ready to get dirty?" he asked.

"Always." I rolled up my sleeves, eyeing exquisite pieces of tek strewn about the hangar. Kellee's insistent questions fell far to the back of my thoughts where I locked them away.

We got to work.

Arran and I buried ourselves deep inside the ship's

hatches, surrounded by wires and mechanics. Tek glinted. Every piece I touched was a marvel. The air smelled and tasted metallic, just the way I liked it. It reminded me of Calicto, of Kesh Lasota's life before the lies came undone.

Arran knew what tools I needed without my having to ask, and I often handed over a component before he emerged from the hole in the ship's guts to find it. Words were superfluous. I had never gotten a chance to work on something as large as a ship with Aeon, but we had often crafted tek-trinkets together, and then, like now, we'd fallen into a wordless rhythm.

Hours into the repairs, I struggled with an unwieldy exchanger box, shaped in an awkward arch that refused to seat itself back where it belonged. I reeled off a string of curses that would have made Sota blush.

"Want help?" Arran peered inside the cramped hatch I occupied and arched an eyebrow at my colorful swearing.

I puffed my sweaty hair out of my face. "Definitely."

He reached in, forearms and hands coated in grease, and locked his fingers around the grips to haul himself inside. It was a tight fit, the two of us squeezed in close, but we wrestled the tek together until it clunked home.

Arran's victorious grin did something to that blackened thing in my chest I called a heart. And then I became acutely aware that we were both wedged into a space no larger than a delivery chute. I'd been so preoccupied that I hadn't noticed how his thigh was snug against mine, his knee braced against a panel close to my hip, and now that I'd noticed, I couldn't think beyond the feel of him. Something tickled my cheek, hair or perspiration. I brushed at it, realizing too late how filthy my hands were. Arran laughed so suddenly and so freely that all I could do was stare. I didn't recall him ever laughing before. His whole face lit up. On him, a smile looked good enough to eat. Nerves tried to up my heartbeat and breathing. I was supposed to be backing off Arran, not wondering what it might be like to kiss him quickly, just for kicks.

He noticed my lack of laughter and let his fade to chuckles. "You er... you got a little..." He reached out, about to touch my cheek, then stopped when the awkward angle meant he would have to shift closer. Instead, he gestured at his own cheek. "Some... grease there."

"Here?" I brushed at my face.

He winced and twisted his lips. "Kinda all over." He wanted to reach out again, but instead he curled his fingers around a handle and pressed his lips together.

Well, this had gotten awkward real fast.

"You hungry?" he asked.

"Very."

His eyes, once so old, were bright with a mischief I coveted. "We've earned a break, right?"

"Definitely." And especially if it got me out of this hole and away from his delicious temptation.

We dropped out of the hatch into the cooler air. Everything ached from being wedged inside the ship's innards. I stretched out the stiffness, acutely aware of Arran's attention lingering on me. The lack of light and my protesting muscles indicated we had been fixing up the ship for most of the day.

"They're easier to work on than I thought," Arran was saying, making idle talk as we entered sections of the main complex. "It's like the tek wants to be together again."

The lights in the building didn't flicker on like they were supposed to, but enough ambient light spilled in through the many windows lining the corridors. We did a little exploring, Arran in front of me. He had a smear of grease down the back of his neck and in his hair where he'd run his hand through it. His clothes sat askew, twisted from working in confined spaces all day. Metal dust caked the back of his pant legs. Some of it sparkled on his boots. He looked like he'd rolled in dirt and then glitter. I probably looked just as dishevelled. I'd left my coat back in the ship and regarded the stains on my pants and vest. Machine grease was better than blood, any day.

In the sprawling kitchen that must have once catered to the salvage yard's workforce, we found sealed packets of food inside cupboards. Arran and I emptied out anything edible and eagerly tucked in, standing at the counters. He tossed me a flask of water. I took a deep drink, threw it back, and watched him gulp it down.

Memories were everywhere. Sometimes, in Faerie's jungle arenas, Aeon and I would drink from tubular leaves as we passed them, or climb trees and steal the sweet fruit while we could. Dagnu often withheld our rations, knowing the arena was the only time we could fill our bellies. It made us want to go into the fights just so we could eat. Killing was just one part of the show.

"I like this," Arran said. "You and me, I mean." His eyes glittered in the low light.

I slowed my chewing and swallowed hard.

"This, the tek... you." He shrugged. "It feels right."

I set the rest of my packet down, losing my appetite. He was supposed to forget everything. Aeon had wanted to forget it all. Whatever he felt between us, it was dangerous.

He noticed I'd stopped eating and set his packet down. "We were close?"

Dirt smudged his honest face, his eyes true. I wanted so badly for him to know me. "No, we hardly knew each other." The lies burned where they touched my tongue. I reached for the flask. He handed it out, studying my reaction and probably reading some of the lie—maybe all of it.

This was a mistake.

I took the flask, or tried to. My fingers brushed his and I froze, the flask caught between us. I'd tried to hide the weight of my feelings from him, tried to bury it deep inside for his sake. He had earned the right to start over. I could not betray Aeon again by telling him the truth. Some secrets could never be told.

"We were friends. That was all." And that was true. We had been too young for anything else, and when he returned after the Game of Lies, he'd returned broken. Used by the fae in every way. Saving Aeon meant letting him go.

Arran saw the truth in me then. He released the flask.

I drank hard and deep and licked my lips when done. He watched it all, his hands braced on the edges of the counter beside him, keeping still.

"And because we're friends," I murmured, "please don't ask me questions about..." My hands shook, betraying too much. I set the flask down. "...before." I would beg him not to ask if I had to, because if he did, and if he kept asking, I'd break. I so wanted to tell him everything, to bring Aeon back. I had never wanted to let him go and having him here, so close, and the way we had worked on the ship together, his laughter, that playful and mischievous expression of his—I needed that light in my life. I needed him.

"You're a brave woman, Kesh."

I closed my eyes on the pain those words caused, not wanting to see the scar across his throat.

"I feel that. I... I think whatever happened, it was hard for both of us. But our past, it's important. We had *something*. And I'm sorry I let that go. I respect your wishes," he said, sounding too damn understanding. "I won't ask."

My lip trembled. I bit into it and tasted blood, feeling the sting.

"You're one of the good ones," he added. "You think you're not, but—"

"No." The word sounded too harsh, but it needed to be. "I'm really not." I made for the doors, keeping my pace slow though I wanted to run. Once this was over, I would send Arran away, somewhere he could carve himself a normal life, somewhere away from me, because if I kept him around much longer, I'd ruin him all over again.

THE SHIP'S engines growled and grumbled but failed to start. Kellee sat in the pilot's chair, muttering the same kind of growls as he tried to get the small vessel working.

"I thought you fixed it," he said.

"We did." I gripped the back of Kellee's chair, watching his hands dance across the controls. Tek, I could do, but piloting was not in my skill set.

The vessel coughed, shuddered, and then thundered to life. Kellee whooped in joy. Arran fist-bumped the arm of his chair, directly behind Kellee's, and threw an electric grin at me.

I dragged a half-smile up from somewhere and fixed my glare through the screen. "Can we finally get off this rock, Marshal?"

The control panel flashed countless warnings. Kellee worked to clear the worst of them.

"Strap in, Kesh, this could get rough. Half of her is fighting me and the rest feels ready to fall apart, but she should get us orbit-bound."

Once there, we could scan for Talen's warcruiser. If Talen had left... I refused to believe it. Talen would be there, waiting, like always.

I strapped in next to Kellee, instantly regretting the front-row view. The vessel rumbled forward on its little wheels, emerging out of the hangar. The long runway ahead was clear, and beyond, Hapters's moon-bright sky beckoned.

Kellee ramped up the thrust and the vessel screamed off the line, throwing us into our seats.

We'd screeched about halfway down the strip when a deafening alarm rang out. Kellee's mouth twitched, but that was all. It sounded bad, but from his minor reaction, maybe it wasn't. Something clunked off the hull and sparked outside the screen.

"Don't need that!" Kellee yelled over the engine sounds, convincing himself and us.

The vessel's nose lifted, the ground fell away, my gut sank to my knees, and we lifted off toward the wash of Hapters's night sky. That wasn't so bad. We had outrun the fae and Sirius. We would find Talen. And we'd go back down there and get Hulia and the others.

A thunderous explosion barreled forward from somewhere behind the cockpit. Hot air blasted the back of my head, throwing me forward. Straps dug into my shoulders as gravity took hold of my body and yanked me forward. The sky had changed. Gone were the moonlight mauves, and in its place was a world of rock rushing toward us. *We're crashing!*

"Kell—!"

The world screamed, or I did, and then all I saw was light.

CHAPTER 5

*M*y head rang. Blood pooled in my mouth. I spat to the side and reached for something, anything, that made sense among the pain and throbbing noise. White blurs lay strewn about. I blinked grit from my eyes. Deflated crash bags. Thoughts slowly came together: *We crashed.* Those bags were the reason I'd survived. Wires crackled and hissed. Fire snapped and burbled. Instincts tried to get me to stand and run, but my cumbersome body wasn't moving. I was hurt, everywhere and nowhere that I could find. After brushing a blur from my eye, my hand came away black with dark blood. That was bad, but my thoughts were taking too long to catch up with reality. I'd hit my head. That was probably bad too.

A hand looped around my wrist and pulled. I let it happen and may have blacked out again, only to wake as something tugged on my hip. Sota, I guessed. He often nudged me awake when it was time to get up and deliver messages for Merry. Where would my job take me today? Calicto's A sector, perhaps, so I could see all the rich people in their shiny tek-towers.

Someone tall blocked my view of all the glass. Tawny leather-wrapped legs and a heavy cloak. He crouched. I peered up into eyes as green as Faerie's rolling hills.

"We have the vakaru, guardian," a voice said from somewhere behind. The voice didn't matter, because the green eyes held me utterly bespelled.

Guardian. The male taking up my entire view leaned in. Long hair the color of wildfire spilled over his shoulders, and I knew him then. He had watched as I'd screamed, watched as a prince had shaped me into a tek-whisperer, watched as my body had been changed and marked, as my life as a saru had ended and I'd been forged into a weapon for a future king.

I held his gaze as my vision cleared, revealing the guardian in exquisite detail. He was made of smooth, pale Autumnlands skin, stubborn angles, and reddish lips on a mouth quick to deliver the king's orders.

"Kill her companions," Sirius said.

Kellee.

Aeon.

No. Despite the scream in my head, the cry came out garbled and weak.

"You have no say in this, Wraithmaker," Sirius said. His words, like the male they belonged to, were hard and unwavering.

I reached out a limp hand. He batted it away. I tried to push up off the ground, to bring myself closer to his level. Sirius straightened to his towering height. His boot found my ribs, gently rolling me onto my back. He could have kicked me, could have hurt me, but he didn't need to. I was already at his mercy.

I shook my head to hustle my thoughts back into the present. Everything throbbed—my head, my back, all of me—but none of that mattered. Pain was just a symptom. I could overrule it. Saru knew pain every day. I was not its victim.

I saw the yard fence. We had made it outside, but not far. The ship Arran and I had fixed lay in flaming bits. Where were Arran and Kellee?

Something shimmered behind Sirius, its surface smooth like a mirror. It reflected the fire raging inside the mangled wreckage, reflected Sirius standing over me and the fae dragging Kellee's lifeless body away from the flames.

My heart stuttered. Fire blazed or were those my thoughts raging? I reached down for my whip, found it gone, and pressed a hand to my chest instead and called.

Stardust and shadow. Come to me.

Power raced through my veins, power and light and strength and the ravaging wildness of Faerie. It overrode the pain, washing it away and lighting me up. The rich scent of lilies filled the air. Magic.

I climbed to my feet and shook off the tingling.

Sirius had watched me rise and his green-eyed glare burned with indignation. "You are Faerie touched," he whispered.

And then something the size of a shuttle, made of pure darkness and bristling with teeth and claws, slammed into the guardian, throwing him off his feet and into his ship, hard enough to rock it off its struts. I blinked, hardly believing what I witnessed.

Sirius's flight of soldiers let out a chorus of alarms, and the creature turned. Its outline churned. Fire raged in its eyes. Whip-like tentacles thrashed and knotted at the air, as though the air itself infuriated this *thing*.

I'd never seen anything like it, had no idea where it had come from, but I recognized the look in its eyes. Death.

The beast bounded in, clamped its massive jaws around one of Sirius's flight, and crunched down, biting the fae into a gory, mangled mass of flesh and bone. It tossed the body aside and searched for a second.

I sprang toward Kellee's motionless form on the ground, and heard the terrible sounds of flesh tearing and bone cracking behind me.

"Kellee!" I grabbed his shoulders. His face was all scuffed up and his shirt was bloody, but he had shrugged off worse injuries. "C'mon, Kellee." The marshal rattled in my grip, head lolling. I couldn't carry him. I could drag him, but that would be too slow and—

A blast of hot, rancid air blew my hair across my face and warmed the back of my head.

Everything froze but my racing heart.

Fire burned ahead of me, but I didn't hear the shouts, just ticking and bubbling metal, and the huffing, panting snarls of something so close its breaths surrounded me.

It would chew me up the way it had the others. I smelled death on its breath. Death like I'd known as a little girl locked in the saru harvest container. Death like the smell the Hunt left behind. Blood and carnage.

Cold sweat wet my face. Kellee lay at my feet, his eyes closed, and I didn't know where Arran was, and this thing behind me might kill them too. Any second. I couldn't move. Terror had me in its terrible grip. Some ancient human part of me believed that if I froze, I'd live.

Breathing too hard and too fast, I carefully, slowly, turned. I wouldn't run. If I ran, it would chase me, and that was something nobody could survive. I saw the heaving mass of tentacles whipping at the air. Then the slippery, shadow-like skin and its smiling, fang-filled jaws and eyes that saw too much—knew too much. Intelligent eyes. My twin reflections glowed in its pupils. There, I was a splash of light with a thread of silver outline.

The beast growled. Hot, wet breath washed over my face, and a whimper escaped my lips. The beast opened its maw, slowly, like it was tasting the air. Its black barbed tongue writhed in a mouth clogged with torn flesh, so close my eyes watered and my instincts clamored for me to *run, run, run.*

There was no hiding my fear.

Run, fleshling. Let me chase, it crooned inside my thoughts.

It was a monster in the truest sense of the word. Its smell coated my tongue and burned the back of my throat. It had power too, something alien and sickly. Its power clung to me, pulling at my strength. This thing had killed the fae, maybe even killed Sirius, and I was next. Kellee too.

My tears mixed with the sweat and grease on my face.

Run, the saru in me demanded. But Aeon had told me never to run from them. Kellee too. *You don't run from them.* I lifted my chin and stared into its eyes, standing between it and Kellee, and inside, the thrum of Talen's wild power set my soul ablaze. I felt the call of things that didn't belong to me, and I felt Talen answer from somewhere far off. *My silver fae.*

I didn't know what it meant, but this creature did, because under the weight of my stare, it bowed its head and stepped back once, twice, and kept retreating until it turned away and slunk off, folding the night around it.

I waited until I was sure it was gone, until the fire had died down, until I saw that Sirius's vessel had vanished. Only then did I drop to my knees.

"SIRIUS WAS WAITING." Kellee paced, boots striking the floor in even beats. "Shot us out the sky before we'd even made it a few hundred meters. I should have suspected it. They were too damn quiet..." He rumbled on and I watched him stride back and forth. Patches of blood darkened his clothes but he paced with ease. It could have been worse, for all of us.

Arran had been thrown out the opposite side of the vessel. He'd woken to find me numb, kneeling beside Kellee. He'd roused the marshal while I'd mutely looked on, much like I was doing now. Together, we had retreated inside the hangar buildings. Arran now sat in a chair. He'd torn his sleeve open and tied it around a deep gash in his bicep. The bleeding had stopped, but he'd have a new scar.

We each looked as though we had been run through a mangling machine and spat out half dead on the other side.

They hadn't experienced what I had. The smell of the creature, the noise of its burbling growls and the way it had cut through Sirius's flight like they were nothing but toys.

But they had seen the bodies—what was left of them. Neither had commented on the carcasses, but the questions were coming. Kellee would be first to ask; he just hadn't gotten around to the accusations yet.

"We find another ship..." Arran said. He opened and

closed his hand, watching the tendons in his arm move, testing the movement around the cut. "Kesh and I will fix it up and we'll try again."

"That won't be necessary," I said, wondering how I sounded so calm when inside I was coming apart. "Talen's coming."

Kellee jolted to a stop. "Now?"

Talen *was* coming. The tightness in my chest and its accompanying flutters signaled that the bond was getting stronger. Wherever he had been, whatever he'd been doing, he was coming. And he would know exactly what that beast was. He'd glide in and save us, the humans, and Hulia and stop Sirius, just like he should have done two days ago. This nightmare was almost over.

"He'll be here soon," I said, avoiding the sight of Kellee's scowl, catching Arran's instead. Where Kellee glared, Arran just looked... concerned. What did they want from me? I didn't have answers to any of this.

Kellee's eyes narrowed. "Are you going to explain what happened out there?" I heard the real question hidden in his words, *Did you kill those fae?*

"What by-cyn is wrong with you, man?" Arran snapped. "She's in shock. Leave her alone."

Kellee shot Arran a golden-eyed look, heated enough to flash-burn souls. Arran arched his eyebrow and held the marshal's gaze, baiting him into a fight.

I closed my eyes and rubbed my temples.

Was I in shock? Something felt... off. Empty. Numb. Was that normal after what I'd seen? The emptiness started after the creature had left, like it had taken part of me with it. Surrounded by human buildings and tucked safely back inside reality, I wondered if I'd dreamed the whole thing. I hadn't killed those fae, had I? The creature *was* real. Sirius knew. He'd seen it.

I reached down and examined the coils of my whip for blood. Arran had found it among the wreckage. Its edges were smooth and clean. I hadn't killed the fae, but Kellee's glare was right about one thing. I could have.

I needed Talen.

I needed to get off this planet.

I looked at my hands, my palms, and my fingers. Just normal saru hands, meant for serving the fae. Nobody could see the blood on them, but the memory was there. Not from recently, but from far back when I became a killer.

I heard Kellee leave and wondered if he was afraid, because I sure was.

"You okay?" Arran didn't look at me like I was a monster. His soft eyes and gentle smile reminded me of how we would reach through our bars at night and draw saru symbols on each other's palms. They had tried to keep us apart, but we'd always found a way to be together.

I nodded. "I'm all right."

"Okay." He smiled gently, aware that anything sharper might shatter me. "That's good."

"Yeah." Maybe I *was* in shock. I wasn't all killer. Inside, wrapped in all the Wraithmaker myth, I was the same little girl just trying to survive. Aeon had known that.

Arran looked at me. He didn't remember who I was, but he cared. I could see it in the way he tried to smile and failed, in the way his eyes apologized for something he hadn't done.

"Will you sit with me?" I asked.

Without hesitating, he crossed the room and sat beside me. It was unfair to ask him. I knew this was wrong.

When I rested back and leaned into him, feeling his warmth and strength, and when his arm settled around my shoulders and tucked me close, the terrible weight of my past lifted. He understood where Kellee didn't and never had. I needed him close. I needed a friend.

THE WARCRUISER DESCENDED through the burnt orange sky, frothing the atmosphere and casting a shadow the size of an ocean across the plains. I shivered as a cold wind tore across the landing strip, whipping up dust storms. It was an impressive sight. It would have been even more impressive had Talen turned up in time to save Hulia and the remaining colonists. Even as I shivered, heat fizzled in my chest. He had better have a damn good reason for arriving late.

The ship settled on tower-like struts, spreading its massive weight over huge pads, but even with the distributed weight, the earth still cracked, rumbling thunderously across Hapters's empty landscape. Warcruisers, once in the sky, weren't designed to *land*. The fact Talen had brought her down likely meant he had no intention of taking her up again anytime soon. Something about the exertion of low-atmosphere travel. He had explained it once, but I was still grappling with the idea that the enormous ship was alive and sentient.

We entered a strut and took a pod up into the warcruiser's belly. Kellee ground his teeth the whole way while Arran stared at the doors like he wanted to be anywhere else but trapped in a confined space with the marshal and me.

Inside, we split up, each of us silently heading to our

quarters. I must have been special, because Talen was waiting in mine.

He turned as I entered and arched a fine silvery eyebrow at my grease, ash, blood, and dirt smothered coat —the coat he had given me. I tore it off, balled it up like a used rag, and tossed it at his feet.

He blinked quickly and looked as though he was about to say something—explain where he'd been, perhaps—but I strode past, crossed my arms, and yanked my upper garments over my head. I threw those at the bed, acutely aware of his gaze riding my naked back. I couldn't look at him. The angry sizzle I'd felt earlier tightened into a ball of fury. I'd rarely felt anger like it, anger and fear so potent I wanted to spin around and scream, *Where were you!?* Oh, but he felt it—through the bond wide open and beating between us like a thing alive. He felt every nerve simmer, every thought scorch the next. My treacherous body trembled, and no doubt he felt that too. I didn't need to say a damn word.

I freed the whip from its hip loop, dropped it to the floor, and pushed my belt down over my hips. A dart of lust tripped my stride, because that sensation wasn't mine. It shot through the rage like a javelin of fire. I almost turned around and threw everything I felt at him just to see if he could weather the storm. But despite my fury, I was fragile too, and I couldn't lose control. I was too ready to break. Pushing the heady rush down, I stepped behind the drapes, finished undressing,entered the shower and tipped my face up as water hissed from holes in the ceiling, stinging cuts I hadn't realized I'd gotten. I braced my hands against the warm walls as the water pummeled my shoulders. Dirt and blood spiraled around the drain holes.

Talen watched my outline through the drape, perhaps ruminating over his explanation.

I could have died on Hapters. When the ship went down, we *all* could have died. The fae flights could have killed Hapters's people instead of harvesting them. Hulia might be dead. The creature could have eaten us all. And Talen had been missing. He'd gotten away with the mysterious shit before, but I was about done with long fae silences and implied secrets. He was a fae pilot. Rare. Powerful. Enigmatic to a fault. And while he had never explicitly said he was on our side, he sure behaved like he was one of us.

The warm water soothed my quivering, but it did nothing to ease the ache in my head from clenching my jaw too tightly or the roll of my stomach every time I thought of how close that creature had come to sinking its teeth into my face. I'd seen people killed, killed people myself, and I'd seen some of Faerie's worst butcher each other for entertainment, but I had never seen anything dispatch the living the way that thing had.

I half expected Talen to be gone when I tied my robe and stepped out, but he hadn't moved from the spot dead center of the room, like a museum centerpiece. His long silver hair was tied in a loose ponytail down his back and threaded with a thin strip of leather. He wore loose-fitting leathers, not the snug scout kind, but something similar to what human males wore on Calicto. He would never pass for human. Or casual. Without trying he still looked mythical. Eyes the brightest shade of violet and a body sculpted and shaped by an artisan. I had to fight every saru instinct not to drop to my knees. I had served Queen Mab for years. I'd learned to kneel before learning to walk. I'd lived among his kind—survived them—and he was like them in every way, and yet... not.

He looked me in the eye, his face a blank mask.

I cinched the belt on my gown tight, using about the same lethal force I'd used to kill a lordly envoy. Then I planted a hand on a hip and waited.

Virtually motionless, he waited right back. His silences had always been heavy, but this one was suffocating.

Would he say he was sorry? Would he explain where he had been? Would he ask if I was okay or would he just stare at me until I wilted like a human flower he'd plucked from Earth a thousand years ago?

"Did you enjoy the party?"

That was what he'd decided to open with? *Did I enjoy the fucking party?* He must have seen the rage flash in my eyes because he flinched. "Try again," I coolly advised.

His penetrating gaze narrowed. "I—"

"If anything comes out of your mouth that isn't an explanation of exactly where you've been then I can't be held responsible for what happens next."

He paused and frowned, wrinkling his perfect brow. "A fae warship arrived."

"Yes it did," I agreed. Having seen Sirius stride from inside it and hidden from its flight with Kellee and Arran, I knew all about the warship.

"With a guardian aboard," Talen added.

"I noticed."

"An Earthen vessel in orbit was observing from afar. I chose to observe it in return."

"You didn't think we might need help with the guardian and his ship full of fae?"

His fine, elegant eyes narrowed further. Apparently, he didn't like my tone. "The three of you are capable. The human vessel was the first one seen in Halow since the fae's arrival. An alliance with Earthens from Sol could prove invaluable."

My rage fractured a little. That was a good point. "Go on..."

"The ship appeared to be observing Hapters, and then it vanished before I could secure a communications link. When it was clear they were gone and not just stealthed, I turned my attention to Hapters and attempted to track the guardian's personal vessel, but he is using a shuttle with stealth capabilities. I could have tracked its path from the colony, but I would have needed to descend into the planet's atmosphere, limiting my firing capabilities. I waited to see where the ship emerged and planned to arrive once it did. Unfortunately, I lost its signal, only for it to reappear near the landing strip you were sheltering in." His eyes were cold, just like the facts. "I felt your call."

The sound I made might have started as laughter in my head, but it sounded more like a growl when it left my lips.

He *felt my call.* While I'd stared down a monstrous creature three times my size and capable of chewing up immortal fae like kibble, he had *felt my call.* I grinned and knew it wasn't a pleasant smile. "I know that too." I approached him and stopped far enough away so I didn't have to tilt my head to look him in the eye, but I was close enough to feel the magnetic pull thrumming between us. "And?"

As a Calicto messenger, I'd intimidated my way into many dwellings. Some folks didn't want a messenger on their doorstep, but payment was contingent on the delivery of the message. I could be very persuasive when I had to be. With the right words, the right attitude, and a flash of the whip and pistol, most people buckled. Farther back, in the arenas, some saru hadn't so much as raised a hand against me before I took their lives.

But right now, Talen looked back at me as though his explanation was perfectly fine. Then something cracked in that perfect fae stoicism.

"You had Marshal Kellee," he said.

The two of them weren't mutually exclusive. "I needed *you*." I jabbed him in the chest with a finger. "And you weren't there."

He didn't give an inch. He lifted a hand like he might touch my face, but if he did I'd either lash out or fall into his touch and wrap myself around him. Maybe both.

I turned away from him and folded all the rage and fear neatly away like I had all the times I'd witnessed the worst of what the fae could do. "Talk with Kellee," I said, collecting the clothes I'd tossed away earlier. "He'll tell you everything that happened. I need to find Sota..."

"I don't understand your anger," he said, sounding hurt.

A pang of guilt almost had me apologizing.

"It's simple." I sighed. "I needed you. *We* needed you, and you weren't there." His frown said he still didn't get it. Maybe that was the point. He was fae. He'd made a choice, one that could have killed us, but it was already in the past.

"Go talk with Kellee." I picked up my discarded coat and felt the brooch thump against my leg. I'd hoped to ask him about it, to ask him about the creature too, but he was already heading out the door, long ponytail swishing.

"Talen?"

He paused in the doorway without looking back.

"I gave you the only thing I owned. There is nothing left. You know everything about me. You know me now, just like you said you did when we met. I gave you more than I've given anyone else alive." Arran didn't count. He didn't remember. "And in return, all I've gotten from you is a wall of ice."

He hesitated at the threshold, weighing his words. But instead of apologizing or offering some part of him in return, he said, "I wasn't aware there was a price on your affections."

CHAPTER 6

The table was Sjora's—the fae general who originally owned our ship and the same general Talen had torn in two. I approached the edge and realized it looked a lot like Devere's table, the one he had fucked me against and I'd left him dead beneath. I hadn't been back in that room since and had no plans to ever go back there. Ever. Maybe I could have Talen ask the ship to swallow that room up and turn it into something else.

This room was brighter. Talen and Arran were seated at the table on opposite sides. Arran's knee bounced and his eyes darted. Talen sat so still he appeared to be carved from stone. Both looked up as I approached.

Sota buzzed in low and took up his usual position behind my shoulder. "Tension. Knife. Just saying," my drone mumbled so only I could hear.

If Sota could pick up on the tension, it had to be thick. I had to do something about that, which was one reason I'd called everyone here. One key player was missing from my meeting and I shouldn't have been surprised.

"Where's Kellee?"

Arran looked at Talen. If anyone knew where Kellee was, it was the fae.

"I passed on your message," Talen said, as though that absolved him of any responsibility for Kellee's absence.

"And?" I asked.

"He's chosen not to come."

I didn't own the marshal. But his behavior undermined my already precarious position. Arran had come because he thought he had something to prove and Talen was here because I *did* technically own him. Kind of. Kellee could do whatever the cyn he wanted and regularly did.

I stood at the end of the table. The silver threads of my coat shimmered. I wasn't even sure why I'd chosen to wear it here. It was part of the Messenger myth. The coat and the whip. Wearing both helped me believe my own legend. Helped me *become* that legend.

"Did you question Kellee about what happened?" I asked Talen.

He dipped his chin in an almost indiscernible nod. Faerie forbid he waste too much energy on actual words.

"Do you know Sirius?" I asked him.

"No."

A nice, clean answer. If only Talen answered every question like that.

"He's one of Oberon's personal guardians. He has Hulia and the rest of Hapters's people. First, we need to get her and them to safety. We can do that now, right? Using this ship?"

Doubt darkened Talen's expression. "Not from the surface. I would have preferred not to land at all, but now I have, it will take some preparation to get her spacebound again. It will be days, not hours, before we're ready for orbit."

"Can't you threaten Sirius from here?"

"Not without risking punching a hole in the planet and killing everyone here. Warcruisers aren't known for their finesse."

Dammit. We had enough firepower to send Sirius running and couldn't use it. "He knows we won't risk killing civilians."

"I can talk with him," Talen suggested.

I almost laughed. He said it as though he could walk right up to Sirius, pat the guardian on the back, and catch up on old times like fae buddies. "You said you didn't know him."

"I don't. But he'll talk with me."

I *did* know Sirius. The first chance he got, he would use Talen to draw me out. "He knows you and I are working together. If he agrees to meet, it'll be to capture you and use you as bait. We tried that plan once. It didn't go so well."

Talen's lips danced around a smile that never quite appeared. "I'm not so easy to capture."

"Sjora captured you—" I started, and wished I hadn't when a sudden fierceness turned his expression from mildly helpful to scathing disgust.

"I *gave* myself to her," he replied, tone dead flat.

He had. He had given up his freedom for what would have been forever to keep Sjora from killing me, Kellee, and Arran. I hadn't thanked him, not with everything else happening. And now he looked at me the same way I'd probably looked at him.

I wet my lips, guilt squirming inside. Maybe I shouldn't have been so hard on him. He had put himself in harm's way for me several times. Relationships weren't something I knew how to foster. With Talen and Kellee, all my emotions got tangled up into knots. I had no idea where to start unraveling them.

And this was why Mab had kept me away from the Faerie courts. Playing well with others was an art I had no hope of mastering.

"Kellee captured you for..." Arran spoke up. "What was it... a few hundred years?"

Talen eye rolled so hard it was almost human. "Marshal Kellee didn't capture me. He and the Halow law provided me with adequate accommodations away from Faerie."

Arran arched an eyebrow and shot me a look as if to say, *Can you believe this guy?* "'Accommodations' implies you could have left whenever you wanted." Arran smirked. "That's not how prisons work."

Talen smiled back. "Isn't it? I could have left at any time and often did."

Arran brought his fist to his mouth and coughed, "*Karushit.*"

I wondered if all these secrets between us would destroy us before we could begin our so-called Messenger mission. Too many egos and too many unknowns. Sota was the only one I trusted to behave, and that was saying something, considering the drone had a habit of doing his own thing when he felt like it. A glitch I could never fix and didn't feel inclined to. Sometimes, Sota's instincts proved right.

"Pass the popcorn," Sota uttered, lifting my mood. He had skill for knowing when to distract me.

"So we can't threaten Sirius with the cruiser?" I asked, bringing everyone back on track.

"Not while grounded," Talen confirmed. "Spacebound, I could overpower his flight, but he'll use Hapters's people as a shield."

So far all Talen had provided me with were more problems. I needed solutions. "How do I get them back? How do I fix this?"

The pair blinked at me.

I wished Kellee were here, he would have had an answer.

I dropped into Sjora's chair—now mine. "There's something else, something you don't know."

Talen tapped his finger against the tabletop and I wondered if this was what he'd been waiting for —the truth.

"There's something else out there. I..." Its heavy breaths sounded in my memories, moist panting touching my neck. I shook off the sensation. "After the crash, Sirius found me and dragged me from the wreckage. He was going to kill Kellee and Arran, but he didn't get a chance."

"You didn't kill those fae?" Arran asked.

I rolled my lips together and swallowed to clear the scratch in my throat. "Sirius and I... He had me." A muscle ticked in Talen's jaw and my heart flickered in return. His rising emotion now mine too. "Something killed his entire flight. It wasn't me. It was a creature ... I saw it tear them apart..." I ground my teeth, remembering the sound of bones splintering. "When it got to me, it... stopped. I stood between it and Kellee, and it backed down."

Talen leaned forward, his gaze intense. "Describe it."

I wasn't even sure I could. When I reached into my memories, the image of the creature slipped away like it was made of smoke and mirrors. I shook my head, struggling to grasp it. "There's more. Arran and I found tunnels—"

"With fae writing." Talen leaned back. "Yes, Kellee

said." He looked away, thinking. "I'd like to see the tunnels."

"Why?"

He side-eyed me. "I'm curious."

"Have you been here before?"

Talen pinned me under his gaze. "Me? No."

Something about that answer felt off, like he was wriggling around the truth. "*Time, our prison, Dark, our sentence, Light, our freedom.* Do you know what it means?"

"No." He continued to hold my gaze, as though he could pin me down, force-feed me the words, and make me believe.

"Why are you lying?"

"I'm not lying." He reached for his chest and rubbed absently near his heart, the same place I felt my anger burn. "Some truths could put you in danger."

I smiled my toothy Wraithmaker smile. "I survived for over twenty years on Faerie without you there, not answering anything. I've maneuvered my way around wild and courtly fae alike. I think I can make that call myself."

"We weren't bonded then."

"And that makes a difference why?"

He looked away. Again.

"Shall I just..." Arran started to rise. "I'll just go see—"

"Sit down," I ordered.

Arran sat.

The non-answers from my friends, my team, were driving me insane. I couldn't continue like this. "I'm just about done with karushit answers and fae vagueness. Give me a straight answer, Talen. The thing I saw outside, what was it?"

"I do not think it is wise—"

"What was it?"

"Without seeing it—"

"Kellee told you about the deaths?"

"He did."

"Are they connected?"

"I'm unsure—"

I slammed a hand against the table. "What is it, Talen?"

He swallowed and shifted restlessly in the chair. "The beast you stared down was unseelie fae."

Unseelie fae, here, on Hapters, deep in Halow. Unseelie who no longer existed and hadn't since Oberon wiped them out. Unseelie, like Kellee.

The life-well on Calicto. The unseelie here. The tek and magic brooch in my pocket. *Time, our prison.* It all meant something. Something Talen knew. He was watching me—not just watching, but scrutinizing my expression, trying to read my thoughts as well as my feelings. And I felt it then, the slippery ice-water touch of fear running down my back. His.

"I thought the unseelie were a myth," Arran said, "like the Hunt."

"The Hunt isn't a myth," I said, straightening, but my thoughts were back on Hapters, back in the dome where we'd found the dead family. Kellee was unseelie, and he wasn't here. Kellee who could move like a wraith through worlds and who fed off the life of others. The puncture marks on the desiccated bodies. He had burned the evidence, just like Arran had said.

"Kesh?" Talen stood, because I was backing away from the table, from them.

"I er..." I waved him off and hurried for the door.

Outside the room, I told Sota, "Find Kellee."

"My sensors are limited while we're inside organic matter. But I cannot locate him on the ship."

"Find him, Sota."

My drone buzzed off down the corridors and disappeared from sight, no other words required.

I marched on, listening to the thud of my boots and the beat of my heart. Talen would feel the heady concoction of emotions and anxiety I radiated through our bond, but his faeness was the last thing I needed. Talen and Kellee, when it came to them, I couldn't think straight.

Kellee couldn't have killed those people. He was good. Sure, he had his demons, but we all did.

I veered through corridors and down slopes, following a path I had memorized over the past few weeks. The chamber I entered glistened. On one side of the walkway lay a perfectly still pool. I'd discovered it while exploring the massive cruiser and kept it a secret from the others. I had no idea what the pool was for—part of the ship's environmental systems maybe—but I'd fallen into the habit of visiting the pool's mirror-like surface when I needed space to think. Space *alone*.

I'd barely gotten comfortable at the water's edge when Arran entered. He casually sat beside me, one leg drawn up, his forearm resting on his knee. He didn't speak, and I didn't feel the need to fill the silence. Anyone else and I would have asked them to leave, but Arran's presence soothed my rattling thoughts.

"I can go if you want," he said after a few moments. "But I figured you don't really want to be alone."

How did he know? "No." Softer, with a smile, I added, "Stay. Please."

He nodded once, looking ever serious, and then a light, easy lift of his lips banished any remaining tension. "Everything you've done, everything you're trying to do... it's not easy. If it were, we'd all be heroes."

Is that what he thought I was? A hero. No, that had been Aeon's destiny, not mine. Aeon who had dreamed of freedom for saru. Looking at him now, it was easy to believe he might have achieved great things. Where I was all hard edges and cruel efficiency, he had a relaxed confidence that put others at ease. Even now, in the ship's strange alien environment, he looked as though he belonged. But he had never been a pushover. He had his limits, like the rest of us. Lines he wouldn't cross. Did Arran have those same morals?

"What happened to the unseelie?" he asked, cocking his head at the pool. Side by side, our reflections gazed back at us.

I leaned closer to the water's edge and dipped my fingers in, upsetting the reflections. "Oberon destroyed them, or so most legends agree. All the Light Fae—the sidhe, the fae ruling Faerie today—combined their magics with Oberon's and buried all the Dark Fae—the unseelie—below ground. Other legends say Oberon tricked them into riding into the night sky in search of a powerful weapon, but the weapon was long ago shattered into a thousand pieces, and that's where the unseelie stay—all the monsters of Faerie trapped between the stars, where the light can't reach them, forever searching for something that doesn't exist."

"Do you think there's any truth in that?" He watched me wiggle my fingers in the water, sending ripples outward. Our reflections blurred, color mixing with the dark beneath the surface.

"Yes. I'm certain Oberon trapped or killed the unseelie, but as for how..." I knew Faerie's king well. Like all fae, he couldn't lie, but he could embellish, and oh they loved to paint the dark with light. "Truths get twisted over time, especially when the winners tell the stories."

"Talen thinks it was the unseelie you encountered... Have the unseelie ever been seen outside of Faerie?"

"Not that I know of, but... all of my knowledge stems from saru myths and those myths are sometimes romanticized. Kellee and Talen know more." Between them, they likely knew exactly what was happening here and why, but they didn't trust me enough to tell me.

I pulled my hand back from the water and watched our reflections reshape.

Arran's reflection looked over at mine. "You care for them?"

"Sometimes, I wish I didn't." Arran tilted his head, likely wondering how caring could be such a bad thing. I twisted to look him cleanly in the eyes. "I was someone who cared for nothing and no one. I walked through life, detached from it all. I was a ghost, to tek and to others, never allowing myself to stray from my path. One simple thing drove me forward: Oberon's orders. I lied, I cheated, and I've killed following those orders. I only cared about not disappointing him."

If my words unsettled him, he showed no sign of it. "Must have been lonely."

It had been, but I hadn't realized how much until I'd looked at Eledan and seen my loneliness in him too. "I was a hollow thing," I admitted. *Nothing girl.* "And then Kellee and Talen woke me up from that dream and... everything changed. I cared what happened to them. I care now, even as they shut me out. I care more than I understand and it hurts to care. I care for Hulia and those people Sirius captured even though I don't know them. I care because what the fae are doing throughout Halow is wrong. I care about the billions of lives already lost and the people left behind and I want to do something to stop all the hurt, but I don't know how."

"I think you're missing the point."

"I am?"

"The hurt is a good thing. It means you're free to care. You're not that hollow thing anymore."

I laughed softly. "Tell that to Kellee."

Arran shifted, stretching a leg out, getting more comfortable, if that was even possible. "Kellee keeps his distance because he's afraid of what you do to him, and Talen... Talen thinks you'll break if he pushes you too far." Arran's little smiled bloomed into something mischievous. "They don't know you very well."

And he did? I smiled along with him, my mood lifting. "Not even the Dreamweaver could break me. Although, he tried..." Eledan's laughter tickled my thoughts, but I let it slip away, still smiling when my thoughts were my own again.

"You're amazing, Kesh Lasota." He blinked innocent eyes at me—eyes that held too much understanding. The woman in front of him had killed an arena full of fae and apparently had the confidence of two of Faerie's immortal creatures, and she rode a fae warcruiser through Halow and freed innocent civilians: the Messenger myth—the good to the Wraithmaker's bad—but just like the Wraith-maker, she wasn't real. He didn't know all the lies she'd been built on. He looked at me like Sjora had looked while talking of Eledan, the mad prince, and his sacrifices. Like I was that hero.

I wanted to believe him, but I wasn't sure I could. Not yet.

"You really think Talen's afraid to break me?"

"I know he is. When you broke him free of his bond with the ship, you almost died. Kellee told me he stole you away afterward and how he nearly lost his shit searching the ship for you, then Talen reappeared with you in his arms, sleeping like a babe. If you believe they don't care for you, you're mistaken."

"You've been watching us closely."

He shrugged. "What else can I do from the outside?"

Those words held a longing that hurt to hear. "You're not on the outside, Arran," I offered carefully.

"I am." He looked down into the pool. "You all know me, but I don't know you. I might have fit before I lost my memories, but I don't anymore."

"There wasn't any time before. Kellee and Talen have spent more time with you as Arran than..." I almost said *Aeon*. Almost. "...who you were before."

"Kellee doesn't like me and Talen... I can't even begin to guess at what he's thinking."

He had it all wrong. "Kellee likes you. If he didn't, you'd be dead, and Talen..." I didn't even know where to start with Talen. "They can be... intense."

He snorted. "That's one word. But not you."

"Not me what?"

"You're not *intense*. You're just you."

I was pretty simple once you peeled off all the layers of lies. "I'm saru." I smiled. I pulled my gaze from the pool and found my friend looking back at me, his eyes honest and true, his smile loose and playful. Arran had a simple, saru-like honesty in every word, every gesture. On Faerie, everything was out to seduce and manipulate, with layers upon layers of deception, but saru weren't like that. The fae saw it as a weakness, but it was our strength.

Arran looked at me and he wasn't hiding secrets. He didn't have any to hide. He was just Arran, just a guy who liked to play with tek and dance with strangers. Just a guy sitting with me beside a pool. Someone who listened without a price.

"How do I save Hulia and the others?"

He drew in a deep breath and looked out over the pool. "Misdirection."

"Like... a distraction?"

"Lure Sirius out. Keep him occupied. Strike from behind when his attention is elsewhere."

Spoken like the gladiator saru I knew. "He'll expect a trap."

He shrugged. "So give him one. And then add another."

I turned Arran's words over in my mind—an idea forming. "And the unseelie creature?"

Arran clicked his tongue. "Talen's eyes lit up when you mentioned it. He knows what it is. Let him deal with it."

I had stared into the creature's eyes and seen only darkness looking back, a darkness so thick I wasn't sure Talen's brightness could overcome it. But he had an affinity for Faerie's creatures, and the unseelie were still part of Faerie. I needed time to think on Arran's advice—advice freely given with no ulterior motive. I was more grateful than he could ever know.

"Thank you," I told him.

His smile turned crooked. He looked down, almost shyly. "Any time." His gaze skipped to the pool. "How deep do you think it goes?"

"I've no idea."

He got to his feet, and in one swift motion, he pulled his shirt over his head. "There's one way to find out."

I caught a tantalizing glimpse of his gladiator physique before he dove into the water.

"Aeon!" I yelled, jumping to my feet. I'd used his real name and didn't care. Idiot! He had no idea what was in there. What if it was a drainage system that this ship periodically purged?

The surface ripples faded.

The blackness settled. Seconds passed too slowly. He wasn't surfacing. My heart thumped in my throat, in my head. I started tugging off my coat and stepped to the edge. I couldn't swim. Nobody had ever taught me. What if he didn't come up? I had to go in there. I clenched my hands into fists. "Aeon?"

He broke the surface with a gasp and grinned. "The look on your face..." When he dragged a hand through his wet hair, sweeping it back, delight flashed in his eyes. With his hair back, his dark skin and darker features took on a rugged masculinity I'd forgotten he had—or hadn't wanted to acknowledge. He wasn't Aeon the boy anymore, that much was obvious.

I glowered. "I hope ship parasites eat you."

He laughed and kicked onto his back, splashing me. "Water's warm, Kesh." His smile beckoned. Water lapped at his chest and tugged at his dark pants. He looked right at home swimming in an alien pool.

My glower sharpened. Where had he learned to swim? Like me, Aeon hadn't known how to swim. There wasn't much call for it in the arenas and Dagnu didn't waste time teaching saru what they didn't need to know.

I folded my arms. "I can't swim."

"You can't?" He bobbed upright and swam forward to clutch the pool's edge near my boots. "Huh... I found one of the Wraithmaker's weaknesses? Are there more?" he asked, intrigued.

"No." Hundreds. He was one.

I started for the door before he got any ideas about climbing out and presenting me with an image of Arran I could do without. "While you're splashing about, the grownups have a mission to plan."

"I could teach you..."

Swimming was a useful skill to have, but the time spent next to him—not touching—would be torture. "Thanks, but I like to keep my feet on dry land."

"You're missing out."

I looked over my shoulder. He still clung to the side. Water streamed down his face, beading and licking down his jaw and neck, right where I'd like to run my tongue and mouth and maybe nip at those golden shoulders the water lapped at. Hope widened his eyes. He made no attempt to hide his feelings—it was all there on his face, wide-eyed hope and the spark of playful desire. He wanted me in there with him, and cyn help me, I wanted it too.

I laughed and left the room, somehow keeping my feet moving away from the delectable sight of a friend who was all grown up and alluring in all the right ways. "Faerie help me survive these males."

CHAPTER 7

"*Y*ou did what?"

Kellee ignored my question and tossed a compact personal interface onto the meeting table. He had finally reappeared after Sota had found him back at the salvage yard.

"Can you make it work?" he asked.

I glared at him. He'd gone back down on Hapters's surface without telling anyone, doing whatever the cyn he pleased, like always. What if the unseelie creature had picked him off? Nobody would have known. What if he was down there doing *other* unseelie things?

I shoved that last thought aside.

"Next time you get ideas about going off on your own, will you at least let me know first?" I asked, testing out diplomacy instead of clashing.

"Why?" he asked.

"Why?" I echoed. *Because we're a team, Kellee. Because I care about you. Because you're all I've got and I don't think I can do this without you.* "Just let me know, okay? It's hard enough to keep track of everyone on the ship without you disappearing whenever you please." *Because I need you.*

He made a disgruntled, dismissive sound. "I thought I didn't need your permission. I'll be sure to run every decision by you in the future." The dangerous gleam was back in his eyes. He dropped into the chair to my left, leaned back, and kicked his boots onto the table, appearing at ease.

I snatched the device he'd brought back and turned it over in my hand. A personal data bank. Most of the working personnel on Hapters probably had one to track their working hours, documents, taxes. Sota could easily crack it open and spill its secrets. "Are you looking for something specific?"

"Any mention of strange events or the tunnels."

"I thought there were no tunnels on Hapters, Marshal?" I smiled, finally getting that dig in low and sharp.

He wasn't amused. "There didn't use to be."

"When you were here before. When was that, a few hundred years ago?"

"Give or take a few centuries." He knew exactly how long it had been. He didn't become a marshal by giving vague answers. Once again, he was shutting me out.

"I think you and Talen know exactly why there are tunnels down there and what the fae writing is for. But you won't tell me, probably because you think I'll run right back to Oberon and tell my beloved king all your dark, dirty secrets."

"Pretty much exactly that, yeah."

The data bank groaned in my tightening grip. "You're an asshole, you know that?"

"Have you looked in the mirror lately?"

I worked my jaw around what would have been a dry laugh. "Oh, okay, we're doing this now, huh?"

"I'm not doing anything. I brought you that. A thank you would have been nice, but instead you demand I have to tell you every fucking thing I'm doing because you're the Messenger and I'm just the vakaru, here to follow *your* orders like a good pet soldier."

Was that what he thought? "That's not—"

"I don't wanna hear it, Kesh." He dropped his head back and ran a hand down his face. "I just... Let's get this ship spacebound, scare the glitter out of Sirius, and save some people. Can we do that?"

"That's what I'm trying to do. Had you been at my meeting—"

"Oh, the meeting, right. The one where Talen artfully avoided your questions and Arran spent the whole time making eyes at you."

He had asked Sota about the meeting. That was the only way he could know. I slammed the databank down and shoved it across the table at him. He caught it before it could fall off the edge.

"Crack it open yourself. Ask Sota, seeing as you're both getting along so well."

His glare intensified and a touch of gold rimmed his eyes. Gold was the first stage, black the next, and red when it was too late to turn back.

"Back off from the kid," he warned.

Now I wished I hadn't given him back the databank so I could throw it at him. "Excuse me?"

"Aeon. Leave him alone. Let him have a life, a good one, without you in it."

If I hadn't already been angry, his words might have

hurt more, but a dart of pain still hit home—and there it burned. "You, Marshal Kellee, need to stop talking."

"No, *you* need to hear a few painful truths."

"I don't know what's gotten into you."

"You don't?" He stamped around the table, putting himself inside my personal space. If he thought he could muscle me down, he was mistaken.

"People are dying on Hapters," he said, "and all over Halow, but they have hope, because they've made up this fantasy hero who'll save them all, only I know their hero, and she's more likely to turn on them than save them. She might even hand them over to Oberon for a new matching set of fancy warfae marks—" I lifted my hand to slap him. He caught my wrist an inch from his face, his eyes ablaze and his teeth sharp behind his snarl. "Don't like the truth?"

Damn him! I grabbed him by the collar and shoved him back, so close I felt his trembling rage that matched my own. "You don't even know what the truth is. You're so caught up in the horrors of my past you can't see what we could do together, what we could *be* together. You, me, and Talen. And Arran too. We have something special. I get why you're angry, I understand you're afraid—"

"I'm not afraid." He looked down at his fingers gripped around my wrist. It was the first lie he had ever told me.

"We're all afraid, Kellee."

I thought he might break. The wildness in his eyes burned hotter, golden edges sizzling. I knew what was coming. He would tell me I was a paper lynchpin holding up the hopes of millions and how he would expose me for the nothing girl I truly was, but instead of speaking, his mouth crashed into mine, and before it occurred to me to fight him off, I was kissing him back—with my tongue, my lips, with my entire body. Lust stoked my anger, because damn him, he wasn't winning this. His kiss bruised my mouth, his teeth scraped my lip, close to cutting. I nipped back, pinching the corner of his mouth between my teeth. His sharp intake of breath was all the cue I needed. I broke the kiss and clutched his jaw in my free hand, holding him still while I pinned him under my stare. His grip on my wrist tightened, teetering on the edge of pain, and the fire in his eyes burned hotter still. We had each other captured, controlled. I wanted to hurt him, knowing he could take it, and likely *wanted* it too. All the times we had fought in the arenas, those games had been foreplay. He would not win this one.

I pushed him back against the table's edge, feeling him tense and resist, but he let it happen, let me pull him down to my level so I could lift my face and taste him again, this time slowly. I tasted his lips first. Ironically soft, considering how sharp his words could be. He opened a little, letting me take more, and I relaxed my grip on his jaw. His responding kiss was a careful question, more of a teasing ask than the earlier demand. This gentleness wouldn't last. Tension quivered through him. He held himself in check, like a nocked arrow on its string. I spread my hand on his chest, felt his heart thud, his raw power reined in. The darkness in him paced its cage. Part of me wanted to set it free, knowing it would be reckless and wanting it even more. I'd wanted the marshal since I'd first laid eyes on him, but back then, I'd been a different person. Now, I didn't have to pretend. His kiss wandered from my mouth, skimming my chin. As his hand found the back of my neck, claiming me, his other freed my wrist and cupped my ass. Sinking his fingers in, he pulled me tight against him. What would it feel like to be this close to him with nothing between us?

Hot skin on skin, his body beneath me as I rocked... I wanted him that close. Wanted it so badly I was forgetting my anger.

I turned my head away and let Kellee's warm, fluttering breaths land on the curve of my neck.

Talen stood in the doorway. Watching. His bright fae eyes dared me to call him out.

"He still there?" Kellee whispered, vakaru senses always alert.

Without answering, I ran the tip of my tongue up Kellee's neck to the back of his jaw. Talen watched. I didn't need to see him to know. Our bond was alight, sharing my lust and his. The fae shared most things, including love-making. The thought of Talen joining us freed a rush of pleasurable shivers. I lowered my hand and rubbed my touch up Kellee's inner thigh, seeking proof of how much he wanted this. And oh, how he did. Skimming my palm up the hardness straining against his pants summoned a twitch and growl from the marshal. Need pulsed hot between my legs, aching to be filled.

Kellee breathed, his voice wrecked. "Do you care he's watching?"

His rough whiskers grazed my cheek. In answer, I kissed his mouth, thrusting my tongue in. He growled again, low and deadly. The threat heightened my senses so that his touch strummed a part of me I never knew existed. He cupped the back of my head and crushed me with a kiss so rough, so demanding, that his teeth cut. I tasted coppery blood and groaned into the feverish attack.

Blood.

A shudder racked Kellee, and he whined pitifully, the sound new from him. He yanked my head to the side, exposing my neck, and bared his fangs. Their curved, pearly smoothness looked almost beautiful with the red madness of his eyes.

A blur of silver shot between us.

Talen tore Kellee from my arms and slammed him into the wall so hard it was a miracle he didn't drive him right through it. Talen's right hook landed next and drove the marshal to the floor, where he swam close to unconsciousness.

I felt a whole lot of things. Some of them mine, some of them not. Lust, disappointment, anger, and... fear. None of those emotions belonged to me.

It happened so fast, and was so unexpected, I had to recall the string of moments and piece them together. The madness had started with blood.

I dabbed at a thin, precise cut on my lip. My fingers came away glistening red.

Kellee had been about to sink his teeth into my neck, maybe tear my throat out.

Talen, convinced Kellee wouldn't fight back, turned. He didn't need to say a word and neither did I. He had saved Kellee from making a terrible mistake, and perhaps even saved my life.

And there we stood. Kellee swimming close to unconsciousness, Talen a granite block between us, and me, out of my mind with lust and anger.

"Well, *karushit*," Sota drawled, swooping into the room. His single lens, trained on the semiconscious Kellee, swiveled up to Talen. "That answers who'd win in a brawl and I just won a bet."

"I WANT you two to trade me for the people," I said and

was met with less than impressed expressions from my *team*—if team was the right word for them.

We had gathered in the pilot's chamber, where traditionally a pilot was fused with the ship. Silver veins scarred the ceiling, like lightning frozen in time, where Talen had torn himself from the ship's grasp.

Despite the memories here, the walls thrummed with a warm, comforting glow. There was no table, no furniture, just a raised area where Talen's bond had almost torn me apart. That was where we sat now in a messy circle. Sota silently hovered behind me. Kellee lay casually on his side, head propped on a hand. He seemed... normal, considering what had happened between us only a few hours before. Talen sat beside him, one long leg crooked, the other stretched out so his leather boot almost brushed my knee. Side by side, their differences were stark in contrast: dark and light.

Arran sat crossed-legged to my left, arms braced behind him. We were together, and that mattered.

Here's the Messenger myth, I thought. All of us. I would do everything in my power to keep that myth alive. Sometimes fantasy could be stronger than reality, if the people *believed*.

Sirius had already made it clear he wanted me alive. The others were expendable, but not to me.

"Hand me over," I continued, "the people will go free, we'll buy time to get this ship into orbit, and then we'll muscle in and threaten the fuck out of him with a warcruiser."

"I don't like it," Kellee argued predictably, although much of his dry conviction had fizzled away. His gaze was crisp and honest. A dusting of shadow marred his cheek where Talen had struck him, only visible because I knew to look for it. Maybe the punch had knocked some sense into him. "What's stopping him from killing you?"

"He won't. Oberon's orders supersede all."

Kellee clenched his jaw.

"It will work," Talen replied, calm, smooth, controlled, like he hadn't knocked Kellee flat on his ass with one of the sharpest, deadliest punches I'd seen thrown. And I'd seen and taken many hits in my years. "He only wants Kesh. He'll forget the rest of us. With the deal done, he'll drop his guard. I can track him once he withdraws from Hapters and overpower his ship."

I glanced at Talen's knuckles, expecting to find them grazed, but his hand, dangling over his knee, was healed. And Kellee had once believed Talen had no fight in him. The marshal had gotten that so very wrong. Lately, he'd been making mistakes.

A ghost of a smile tugged at the corner of Talen's mouth, and we shared a fraction of understanding in a single moment. He had probably been looking for an opportunity to hit Kellee for centuries. Most people who knew Kellee wanted to punch him.

"But, before we do the trade," I said, steering my thoughts back to the task at hand, "we need to find and contain the creature I saw, otherwise Hapters's people are as likely to get killed at home as they are by Sirius. Talen?"

"It will submit to me," the fae said matter-of-factly.

Submit to me. His words made me want to chip deeper and mine for more answers. "How do you know it won't try to kill you?" I asked.

"From what you've said, it's a lower creature. I have a talent with some of Faerie's base creatures. That's assuming we can find it. The dark fae excel at hiding."

"I'll track it," Kellee said. "It reeks of the dead. I

thought the scent all over Kesh was dead fae... but I didn't have all the facts." He paused, letting the fact that nobody had told him about the fae-eating monster until a few moments ago sit heavily in the silence between us. "I'm tracking it alone. I can't have you all stumbling about in the dark behind me. At best, you're distracting, and worst, it's dangerous."

"I don't think you should—" I started, but Kellee's razor-like glance cut me off. "Okay. Sure. Fine. Go do your thing, just don't die while you're brooding out there alone."

"Brooding?" Kellee pulled himself into a sitting position, muscles flexing beneath his shirt. "Did you just accuse the last vakaru of brooding?"

Talen huffed a small laugh. I got the impression I had stepped into a Faerie trap. One with teeth.

I shooed Kellee's glare away and turned to Arran. "You and Sota keep an eye on Sirius's main ship, the one near the town. Strictly scouting. Do not engage the fae. Send Sota back and forth. I want frequent reports on any activity. If I don't get those reports, I'm calling everything off and we all return to this ship. No questions asked. I don't like that we have to spread out for this, so let's stick to the plan."

Nods all around. Good. We were making progress. Perhaps we could make something of this Messenger and her men myth.

"And what will you do?" Kellee asked.

I waved Kellee's PI reader in the air. "I'm gonna find out what was going on around here before the fae came." The magic/tek brooch sat heavy as a stone in my pocket, and the more I thought on it, the more impossible it became. Magic and tek—two opposing forces that were rarely combined. I was one example of how tek could work with magic—Oberon had made me that way—and Eledan's tek-heart was another. The brooch was important. A mother had reached for it in her last moments, and I needed to know why. Seeing as Talen and Kellee weren't talking, I'd get my answers without them.

Kellee looked at me curiously, trying to read my thoughts on my face. I barred everything from my expression, like I had for years. He saw nothing I didn't want to show him.

"Let's get to work."

CHAPTER 8

hile the others went their separate ways, Kellee told me to follow him.

We walked the corridors, Kellee content to stay quiet until we reached his chamber. Not long after claiming this room as his, he had torn down the bright fae fabrics and bundled them into a corner, leaving the chamber stark and exposed with no dividing walls between the bathing and sleeping areas.

I entered behind him and noticed the bed hadn't been slept in. So he slept elsewhere on the ship? He had never liked the idea of living inside a living entity. Wherever he got to rest, it would be secure and defendable.

"Tell me about the creature," he said, striding across the room, shrugging off his long coat, and tossing it on the bed. The shirt went next, up and over his head, revealing the exquisite musculature of his tanned back. A few nicks and dimples marred his otherwise flawless skin. Old scars. He'd had a long time to collect them and those were just the visible ones. He likely had hundreds more that weren't visible.

The chamber door closed with a heavy clunk, jolting me from my thoughts. "It's the size of a single person shuttle..." I continued to explain everything I remembered while Kellee efficiently stripped, but I found my description of the creature lacking. When I'd thought back the first time, I'd remembered black eyes, but then I remembered peering into those black eyes and seeing other colors. Or its shadowy outline was sometimes solid, sometimes smoke. Claws and teeth. Talons and tentacles. The more I tried to remember, the more my recall failed me.

"It's not you. Some of Faerie's creatures are known to cast glamour, a way to obscure their appearance so your mind can't piece the memory together."

Great, illusions. I shouldn't have been surprised. My coat had much the same ability to cloak my appearance.

Kellee had replaced his shirt with soft, gray and black, breathable leathers over a figure-hugging undergarment that looked as though he'd painted it on. The pants went next. I crossed my arms, wondering whether to look away or pretend seeing him virtually naked didn't arouse me. We'd had our hands on each other not long ago, and I recalled exactly how the hardest part of him had fit against my palm.

He tugged on pants that matched the jacket—completing the scout leathers. But these were fitted to his vakaru physique, not the svelte form of normal fae. Fae leathers couldn't be bought; they were all made by hand. So where had his come from? Sonia—Devere's saru—was the only person who could have made them. A ridiculous stab of jealousy at the thought of her measuring Kellee's assets had me looking away.

"There's something else you should know," I said, still puzzling over the riddle of Marshal Kellee, who now looked disturbingly fae in his fitted leathers. He had once warned me never to compare him to fae. I figured he didn't look in the mirror much.

He combed his fingers through his messy hair and used a thin strip of leather to tie it into a ponytail. He hadn't met my eyes since leaving the pilot's chamber, and his darting gaze and hard press of his lips indicated his thoughts were far away.

"It's unseelie," I said.

He dropped his hands from his hair and frowned. "Unseelie? Impossible." But he wasn't surprised, just confused. The unseelie were myths, but not to him. He hardly reacted at all.

"I know what I saw."

His frown deepened. "Your description is unreliable."

"Because the thing used glamour."

He hesitated and looked across the chamber, his thoughts turning his gaze heavy. "This far from Faerie... how would it survive?"

"You said this planet has a weird history. Crops growing where they shouldn't... And the unseelie... they're different from the seelie. They don't follow rules, right?" *You know this,* I thought. *You are unseelie.* But I hadn't yet confronted him about what I knew, and while our relationship was so fragile, I wasn't sure I could.

His eyebrows lifted. "True."

"There was a magical reservoir on Calicto, right under Arcon. Maybe there's one here too."

"Unlikely," he scoffed.

"Why, because you'd know?"

"Something like that." He tightened the belts and straps and tugged on a pair of boots. When he straightened, he looked utterly fae. Broader, built for warfare, but still fae in the striking maleness. I preferred him in the coat, wearing his gold star, snarling at criminals. Like this, I almost didn't recognize him. He kept so much of the real Kellee locked away. I doubted I'd ever see the truth of him.

He approached, his eyes on the door behind me, and would have walked right by had I not touched his arm. The touch was light, but it brought him to a halt.

He looked at my hand and then up into my eyes. "I'm..." The break in his voice betrayed emotion he otherwise kept expertly hidden. "...relieved he was there, earlier."

He meant Talen, because neither of us was under any illusions. Kellee would have sunk his teeth into my neck, and he wouldn't have stopped there.

"I'm sorry for my behavior." He drew in a breath and added, "You drive me crazy, Kesh. All of me. All the time."

My own apology tried to fall from my lips, but I swallowed it and dropped my hand from his arm. I dug into my pocket and handed over a comms unit. "Stay within range. If you have to go farther, let me know."

He plucked the comms from my hand and pressed it behind his ear. "I'll find it."

"I know you will." When Kellee had his target in sight, nothing could stop him, not even Faerie's own monsters.

He eyed the door like he wanted to be outside, running through the night. He could, but something held him back. His hard eyes softened, and when he looked at me again, more of the smart-mouthed marshal from Calicto shone through. "I am sorry," he said again. "For many things. I've been hard on you, and I... This place... this war. For so long I deliberately forgot who I was. That's no longer an option."

I knew that feeling. "I understand and it's fine."

"No, it isn't." He lifted his head and looked away, but I caught the flash of pain across his features. "I want this to work. We have something remarkable. I want *us* to work." Us. Kellee, Talen, and the Messenger myth.

"So do I."

His eyes searched my face for the truth. He didn't trust me, but he wanted to.

He had told me time and time again how he wasn't a good man, when all I'd seen was evidence to the contrary, but if he knew the truth inside him, he likely believed he had a lot to make up for. In his heart, Kellee knew he was unseelie. How could he not?

"It can work." His glare intensified.

I smiled. "A messenger, the last vakaru, a champion, a wardrone, and a fae pilot. There's never been a crew like it. We'll make it work."

He nodded and strode from the chamber like a fae soldier from a sidhe's flight.

I was halfway back to my chamber when the comms crackled and Kellee's smooth voice poured into my ear. *"You said you wanted an apology. You got one."*

"I seem to remember, way-back when you made that promise, you said I'd get an apology *any way I liked*, Marshal."

Laughter lifted his voice. *"So how would you like it, Kesh?"* Hidden among that laughter, implications simmered, hints of long, pleasurable moments, of Kellee's mouth roaming where his hands had already ventured. Nervous flutters shortened my breaths. I'd wanted all of him, and he'd shown me what I was teasing. I still wanted it, perhaps more so.

"I've got ideas." Most of them involved Kellee naked,

spread before me like an all-you-can-eat vakaru buffet. Now I knew blood flipped him over the edge, I relished the thought of walking the edge between pleasure and having my throat torn out.

"Will I like these ideas?"

"Bring me a monster and you'll find out."

He growled low and the comms cut off. My chuckling laughter echoed through the ship's corridors.

Silver veins glittered through the pilot's chamber ceiling and the background *thud-thud* of the ship's two hearts accompanied my thoughts while I sat on the floor, an ocular link filling my vision with the PI's information. Daily entries, the airstrip's comings and goings—most of the information had me glazing over. But there were snippets of interest. Reports of sinkholes opening close enough to the strip to alert Hapters's maintenance crews. Missing crewmembers. Tremors. Isolated, each report didn't mean much. But in hindsight, I noticed a pattern and the pattern drew a picture. The fae had been here to Hapters past, and they had left something unseelie behind. Maybe all the fae activity in Halow of late had stirred it awake, or perhaps it had always been awake but in hiding. The message on the buried slab was part of that.

Time, our prison,

Dark, our sentence,

Light, our freedom.

Time. Dark. Light. Faerie's driving forces. Its foundations were built on those three elements. Take one away and Faerie's foundations weakened. But why leave the stone here, on Hapters? And why was the unseelie creature awake now?

What if there's more than one?

I tapped my comms. "Kellee, where are you?"

Kellee took a few moments before drawling, *"Soaking up the rays."*

I arched an eyebrow and chuckled silently to myself. "Your sass is showing."

"It's hard to stay stealthy while talking to the devil on my shoulder."

I was the devil now, was I? "I thought you said I was a male-eating arachnid?"

"That too. Do you want something or may I return to stalking the unseelie?"

I hesitated. There was little point in throwing guesses his way. Better to have him focused. "Just checking in."

His light chuckle sounded down the comms. *"Trust issues, Kesh?"*

I was not getting into a comms conversation about trust. "Let me know when you find something."

"You said that already." I heard his smirk. *"I'm starting to think you like the sound of my voice."*

I tapped my comms, cutting off the signal and his ego. I cut the ocular feed too, and looked up at the silver-veined ceiling. Talen was in the ship, doing whatever he did when he vanished. I knew he was close; the constant flicker from our bond made sure of that.

A floral-scented breeze tickled my hair against my cheek. I turned my head toward the shift in the air, narrowing my eyes at the empty chamber. The walls throbbed their soft orangey hues, but something had stirred the air.

I put my hand down, spreading my fingers to stand,

when the cool, hard kiss of metal touched the side of my neck. The blade nicked my skin, stinging.

"Do not move, Messenger."

Sirius.

Panic reared up, dumping ice water through my veins. How had he gotten in?! I couldn't see him, but I could smell his fae combination of warm leather and Faerie's intoxicating blooms. Blood trickled down my neck.

"Where is the pilot?" the guardian asked, his accent sharp and refined.

I clenched my teeth. His words had landed warm against the back of my ear, putting him so close he could probably feel my heart racing. "I don't know."

He shifted, and I felt his weight against my left shoulder, but I couldn't see him. If I could reach around and twist, I could maybe pull him over me. He wouldn't cut my throat. He needed me.

I shifted the placement of my knee, pressed against the floor, and my hand, moving my weight to one side.

Sirius's fingers brushed behind my ear. He tore the comms unit free and threw it out of sight. "Now throw the whip away."

I swallowed. The blade cut deeper, spilling more blood into my coat collar. He pushed the sword deeper, angling it so it lodged under my chin.

"The whip."

His tone revealed no emotion. And why would it? He was a sidhe lord and the king's guardian. And I was the girl Oberon had plucked from the arena for some inexplicable reason only the king knew. Sirius had always looked at me like he was waiting for the perfect opportunity to cause an *unfortunate accident*. Well, here was that opportunity. But he wouldn't dare return to Oberon with my carcass.

I dug my fingers under the whip's loop and unhitched it from my belt, using the movement to dip my shoulder further, but the more I twisted, the more I realized I couldn't *see* him. The air shimmered like the heat haze off a shuttle's cladding. He wore glamoured clothing, like my coat. I couldn't see anything of Sirius to know where to grab him. I needed another plan.

His body crowded against my back. The ghost of his hand brushed mine and tore the whip free, tossing it across the chamber.

I had other tek-tricks sewn into my coat, but I needed space to reach them.

"Stand. Slowly."

Keeping my hands loose at my sides, I rose to my feet.

"Your other guardians all left, but the pilot is still here."

He had been watching the ship, likely alone. We would have seen a flight of fae lurking nearby, but not one stealthed guardian. This subtle thinking was exactly what made the guardians so lethal.

Sirius's sword dug deeper, forcing my chin up. "Where is Talen?"

I began to deny Talen was anywhere nearby, when an icy voice declared, "Right here."

CHAPTER 9

*S*irius threw me aside. I skidded on a knee and twisted, about to spring back toward the blur, but Talen moved in, like a snap of lightning. Sirius's ghostly outline shimmered. They clashed, two forces of Faerie slamming together. Blast of snarling magic erupted, coiling around the macabre dance.

Talen dropped low, tackling Sirius. Both flickered, blurring in and out of my limited sight, Sirius's foggy blur engulfing Talen. Light poured along the guardian's sword, and flashes of silver lit up a storm of Autumnlands reds.

Pain snapped through my thigh. Talen grunted, and then pain flared across my knuckles. Blood splatters dappled the floor.

Sirius's stealth fell apart, revealing the guardian on his knee, his sword thrust upward through Talen's thigh. Blood—so much blood. Talen's.

Before I could lunge in, Sirius yanked the blade free and slammed the pommel into Talen's jaw. An echo of his pain smacked across my chin. "Stop!"

Talen grabbed Sirius's extended arm and slammed it

over his knee. Bone cracked. Sirius howled. And Talen's violet eyes flared with victory. He was whip-fast and just as sharp. He cracked a fist across Sirius's cheek. More bone shattered, and Sirius fell to his hand, spitting blood.

Talen could do worse. Much worse. He wasn't even using his considerable magic. He was... playing. But I knew the guardians. They never went down easily. If Talen didn't end it—

A knife flashed in Sirius's left hand, hidden from Talen's sight.

"Talen!"

The guardian thrust the blade upward, punching it deep into Talen's chest. My silver fae jolted. Sirius ripped the dagger free, opening a sucking gash across Talen's midsection. Dark blood poured from the wound.

Talen's fury stuttered. His eyes met mine. *Fight*! I screamed inside. He could do more than this. He had done more than this in the past. Why wasn't he calling his magic? Why wasn't he fighting like I knew he could? He could call the ship's tendrils down and pull Sirius apart just like he had Sjora.

The delay was all Sirius needed.

The sword's tip swept across Talen's chest, from his left hip to his right shoulder, almost cleaving him in two.

I bolted forward. Sirius swung the sword toward me. "Hold!" he yelled, forcing me back by the point of his blood-soaked blade.

Talen dropped to his knees, his hands spread across his chest, trying to hold himself together.

"Fight him!" I screamed.

His eyes rolled. The bond pulled breathlessly tight. It snapped, yanking out his magic. I wobbled, my body shocked by the void of power. Talen fell forward, collapsing facedown in a pool of his own blood.

No, no, no... This wasn't supposed to happen. Not like this. Never him.

The ship shuddered and groaned around us. All the chamber doors slammed shut.

The guardian staggered to his feet, his sword still poised to open my throat. "What have you done?!"

The guardian licked his lips and spat blood and bone to the side. His broken face was already popping and cracking back into place. He'd be fully healed in moments... but Talen. Talen wasn't getting up.

"WHAT HAVE YOU DONE?!"

Sirius's green-eyed glare shuttered in the face of my screams. "What I must. Your king needs you, Wraithmaker."

I blinked at him, hardly hearing the ludicrous words. Talen was bleeding out, his silver hair, fanned around him, soaking up all that blood. Too much blood.

He would be okay, he *would*. I'd seen him almost bled dry and he had recovered. He had healed before, and he would heal again. And he would tear Sirius limb from limb, if I didn't get to him first.

"We must leave here," Sirius said.

The doors were closed and I couldn't control the ship... *The ship* had locked us inside. I smiled at Sirius. We weren't going anywhere.

Sirius's expression ticked. The guardian didn't like the sight of my smirk.

"He was connected to the ship." I kept my breathing measured and tone level, kept the sight of Talen out of my mind. My comms were gone, so I couldn't reach Kellee.

Arran and Sota wouldn't be checking in for at least six hours. I was on my own.

"No, he was not," Sirius denied.

"The doors are closed because he's dying."

"No."

"No?! You know nothing about us, Sirius!"

He lowered his sword from my chin and wiped both sides of the blade across his thigh, cleaning Talen's blood from the blade. "Pilots fuse with their ships. They do not walk freely. My reports were incorrect. He cannot be the pilot of this vessel."

Anger burned so brightly I had to swallow hard and stop myself from lunging at him. "Try the doors."

Sirius looked up, studying the silver infecting the ceiling.

Maybe I could get the sword out of his grasp and turn it on him. But I'd barely lifted a boot before he flicked his sharp-eyed glare to me. "Try anything and I'll drag you out of here unconscious. Oberon was vague on the condition in which I should return you to him." He studied me, sizing me up from head to toe. I'd changed since he had last seen me at Mab's court. I'd been a queen's killer, a tek-whisperer, and a messenger. I'd found the mad prince, torn out his heart, and handed the heart and him over. I'd also killed thousands of fae at the Game of Lies. Sirius knew only one thing for certain. He could not trust me.

"Our king sent me here for you," he said, sheathing his sword inside its leather scabbard. "Have you forgotten your allegiance?"

My fingers twitched. I had tek-flashers and nasty little razer-bots, but none of those things would free us from this chamber, and they'd do little more than distract Sirius. I had to think smarter.

"I hadn't, until you killed Talen."

Sirius backed up so he could keep me and Talen in his sights. "Your Talen is not dead, just severely weakened. If you care for him, you should have surrendered, preventing this unnecessary violence." He brushed his fingers along his cheekbone, now healed. His precise words, his posture, everything about him declared courtly fae. I never believed I hated them and their world, not until this moment.

"What were Oberon's orders for him?" I asked, matching his tone.

"Your companions are to be killed."

Oh, Oberon. My companions are worth so much more alive. "So why haven't you?"

He glided to one of the doors, his steps almost silent. The door stayed closed. "As you rightly pointed out, we are trapped. If he is connected to this ship by some inexplicable union, I need him to open those doors."

"You believe me?"

Sirius cruised closer, his eyes on Talen. "Your male was more than I'd anticipated."

He had no idea just how dangerous we were. Apart, we might not appear to be much. But together? Together this guardian would not stand in our way. In *my* way.

"Why did you not return to Faerie with Prince Eledan?" Sirius asked.

I might have killed him for real had I spent any more time with him. "I was captured." I moved to Talen's side, listened for Sirius's protest, and when he gave none, I knelt and swept Talen's blood-matted hair back from his face. His eyes were mercifully closed. I touched his neck and felt the light flutter of his heart—too light, but he was alive.

Sirius peered down at me. "You do not appear to be incarcerated now."

"I bargained my services for freedom." I had helped Kellee save people, and in exchange, the marshal had given me some freedom. It had been true enough, in the beginning. Now, everything was much more complicated.

"And the thousands dead at the arena?" the guardian asked. "*Was* that your doing? Are you the Messenger?"

If Sirius survived this and returned to Oberon, he would tell the king my every word. I had killed other fae to keep my secrets close, including Devere and a nameless scout.

My only weapons against the fae were lies. Was I the Messenger? If I answered yes, Oberon would kill me. No, and I might have one last hand to play against the Faerie King. That seemed like too important an opportunity to pass up for the sake of truth. "Marshal Kellee made it so I had no choice," I lied. "I wanted to live. It's all I've ever wanted."

"Marshal Kellee?"

"The vakaru."

Sirius's eyes narrowed. "Then you are Oberon's?"

I bowed my head, conceding. "I always was. I still am."

He strode back to the next door and tested its seals. I couldn't see his face, but words held weight and he couldn't deny them, even knowing how I had lied in the past. He loved the king. So did I. We had that in common, if nothing else. That love was another weapon I could wield.

I watched the guardian check all the doors one by one while listening to Talen's soft breathing. I would lie to keep them safe. I'd stack lie upon lie and cheat again and again if it meant Oberon left them alone.

After checking all the doors, Sirius stopped beside me. He looked down at Talen, likely puzzling out why he mattered to me. "Your attachment to this one is strong?"

"Yes," I murmured.

"Does he know you are Oberon's?"

"He does."

"Is he social or war-making? I don't recognize him."

"Talen has been away from Faerie for a long time. I think he was... reluctant to return." Was I revealing too much? I didn't think so. But when I looked back and up at Sirius, his arched eyebrow and the curious gleam in his eyes made me wish I'd kept that kernel of truth to myself.

"Was he residing in Halow before Prince Eledan's sacrifice?"

"Yes."

"Then he is resistant to tek." Sirius's gaze sharpened. "A valuable skill in this new war."

What Talen was, and wasn't, was a mystery I didn't want to get into with Sirius, but the flicker in his gaze implied he was intrigued. I could use that.

"Let him live."

Sirius slid his gaze to me, his brow tightening. "You have forgotten your place, saru."

I wasn't kneeling, if that was what he expected. Not anymore. "No, I just made a new one." Sirius balked and rolled his shoulders like a bird ruffling its feathers into place. He looked again at Talen's face. "Oberon's orders were specific."

Damn the king for his sweeping words that changed lives a hundred million light-years away from his glass palace. "He hasn't met him. Talen can be useful."

Sirius's left eyebrow twitched. "I saw."

"Sirius." I straightened and faced the guardian. At my

height, I was eye level with his chest, and while the position would normally have my insides knotting, he and I were in Oberon's service. He *knew* me. "This fae is worth more alive. Oberon will be grateful you spared him."

"You do not speak for the king."

"But Oberon will be displeased to learn you killed a fae as unique as Talen."

"How is he so unique, *calla*?"

Calla—it meant *little one*. I stalled at the term. To him, I was a little thing. Mortal, short-lived, fleeting, naïve, Oberon's plaything. But in some cases, it was used as a term of endearment. That couldn't be his intention here.

I pointed up. "He did that."

Sirius admired the silver above us. "Beautiful, but I do not know what *that* is or why I should care. Is there anything else about him I should know?"

Stardust and shadow. Convincing Sirius of Talen's worth was the only way to save his life. It had to be worth a few secrets, didn't it?

"Do not say..." Talen rasped, stirring awake. "...another word."

CHAPTER 10

The bond was back, flickering like a fragile wisp. Talen heaved himself up onto a hand. I'd have been angry with him for hardly fighting Sirius if he hadn't looked as though the Hunt had marked him for death.

Sirius stood over him, the Autumnlands fae aglow with golds, browns, and the russet reds of his long, tightly braided hair. His pale, slightly freckled face would have been handsome if not for his cold, stubborn detachment. He had all the confidence of Faerie's prowess behind him and used it to look down on Talen.

Talen struggled to keep his head up. His eyes flicked to me and away again. This weakness had to be an act. A stalling tactic, perhaps? But why? Couldn't he use the ship to pluck Sirius off his feet like he had Sjora?

"The Wraithmaker says you are valuable," Sirius declared in his oh-so-courtly manner.

"Did she?" Talen drawled, fatigue drawing out the words.

Sirius watched Talen struggle. "She thought to convince me to spare you."

He winced, and something inside my chest twinged in sympathy. I rubbed at it to massage the ache away. Talen's leathers glistened wet in places, the cuts across his chest and gut likely worse behind the torn leathers.

"Would you like to continue the argument?" Sirius asked.

"You mean, would I like to beg for my life?" He looked up, lashes fluttering, eyes heavy. "Oberon once cherished all life. Has he forsaken that now, as Faerie has forsaken him?"

Talen *knew* Oberon? No, he couldn't. He would have said before now... like he'd told me all the other truths he hid inside?

Sirius's green eyes widened with the same surprise. "The girl says you've been away from Faerie a long time. What would an outcast know of Oberon's rule?"

"I know Faerie will never accept him as Her king. He is weak, made weaker by the mistakes he makes."

I blinked at this revelation.

Sirius backhanded Talen. The *whack* sounded like the retort from my whip and drove me into action. I reached inside my coat, clutched the razor-bots, and froze. The guardian's steel was at my throat again. I hadn't even seen him move. For all my tek, all my training, I wasn't fae. Aeon had often reminded me to never fight them head-on. I wouldn't win.

With my head back and the blade biting into my neck, I eyed Sirius down my nose. He regarded me coolly in return, knowing it was only Oberon's words from a million light years away that kept him from separating my head from my shoulders. My cheek tingled with the echo of Sirius's blow, but Talen shielded me from the worst of the pain. I didn't care who Sirius worked for or about all the lies I could tell. Nobody hurt the Messenger's men. "Touch him again and I'll shove that sword so far down your throat it'll ring your Faerie balls like bells."

Sirius recoiled as though my words could deliver on the threat. His mouth fell open, thoughts racing to catch up with my threat, and then, impossibly, his rich, deep, masculine laughter poured over me like honey and silk, all things smooth and tempting. The laughter staggered him backward and disarmed the aggression building between us. Humor banished the mean scowl he'd worn since I'd seen him again, and animated his face into something charming.

The shock of seeing him laugh vanished when I remembered Oberon had ordered this laughing guardian to kill Talen. I pulled a few buttons from my coat and launched them at Sirius. The little bubbles of tek sprang to life, popping out tiny razor feet, and as a swarm, they sank into his hair. His laughter cut off. He whirled, reaching into his hair to tear the bots free. They buzzed and hissed, burrowing deeper, searching for skin.

The doors whooshed open—under Talen's mental command. I scooped an arm around Talen and pulled him to his feet. We staggered from the pilot's chamber, chased by a hail of furious roars.

"You need to get out of here..." Talen said. He wasn't light, and with every step, he leaned more heavily into me. "Find Kellee."

Struggling to hold him, I staggered on, but Sirius would be coming after us. "I'm not leaving you with him."

"You are Sirius's priority," he hissed. "Not me." His balance wavered. I tried to keep him upright, but we fell against the wall. Blood bubbled through his hand pressed against his chest. I couldn't move him. He needed time to rest, to heal.

"I'll be fine." He tried a small smile. A smudge of blood marred the corner of his mouth and cheek. "You know I will be. Go. I can keep him running circles inside the ship for hours, but I'm too weak to move."

I eased my arm from under his and gently supported him as he slid to the floor. "Just kill him. You can..."

His lips twitched, part grimace, part smile. "I don't want to."

"But he'll kill you. He has orders."

"I don't think he will."

Think didn't fill me with confidence. I scrubbed at the smudge on Talen's cheek. Seeing it there was wrong. I'd seen him hurt too many times, felt his pain too often. He didn't deserve this. "He almost killed you—"

Talen lifted his hand and rested soft fingers on my cheek. He was so ridiculously gentle, even now while trying to keep me safe. "The Hunt will claim me, but not today."

I pressed my hand over his, cupping it closer to my cheek.

"Find Kellee and Arran. Take Sota—" Talen dropped his hand and touched my coat. His gift, enhanced, changed. Part of the myth. "This will hide you. Do as he did. Take the guardian's warship. His ship... you will find it most... accommodating." His smile sharpened. "I'll keep him here."

"You can stop this."

"The guardian is following orders. Had I killed you, Kesh, for following Oberon's orders, we would not be here today."

"That's different." He was looking at me as though I'd

let him down, like he expected more, like I was supposed to be the Messenger, not the Wraithmaker. "Just maim him a little?" I suggested.

Talen chuckled and dropped his head back against the wall. "Go. Be the Messenger and save the people. When you return, I'll have the guardian on his knees."

"Give me your word you won't die." It was an impossible ask. He could not guarantee such a thing.

His bright violet eyes locked on mine, suddenly intense. "You have it, Mylana."

I backed off, hating that I had to abandon him. But Talen would never go back on a promise. He would never lie.

Behind me, a door whooshed open, and behind that, another and another, opening a clear path to the exit pods. Forcing myself to turn away, I stepped through, and left my silver fae alone.

No, not alone.

Safely inside the pod as it descended to the surface, I touched the wall, spreading my fingers wide, and whispered, "Keep him safe."

NIGHT BLANKETED HAPTERS'S PLAINS, soaking the burned fields in milky moonlight. My coat took that light and whipped it around me, turning me into a blur, but I still felt exposed as I emerged from the warcruiser's shadow and jogged across open ground. I had to get in contact with Kellee and let him know Sirius was on the ship, but I'd lost the comms. I needed another way. Something he would see from miles away.

I slipped back through the salvage yard's fence and

climbed the watchtower. From the top, I could make out the scarring of our crash site and the twin watchtower in the distance, close to where a sinkhole had swallowed Arran. There was no telling which way Kellee had started tracking or if he was within sight. He moved fast when he wanted to. He could be hours away.

With the flare gun Kellee and I had discovered in hand, I stepped outside the watchtower onto the metal deck. Hapters's wind tugged at my coat and whipped my hair around my face. Far below, dead tek vessels took on strange, irregular shapes as though they were all enormous creatures rotting away.

I raised the gun, aiming it into Hapters's near-dark sky. Kellee had better see it. I only had the one shot.

I fired. The gun kicked and the flare shot skyward, trailing purple light like a shooting star. Up and up and up it went until it arched over and dove back toward the ground, fizzling to nothing.

I clutched the rail and waited for my night vision to return. All four corners of the watchtower revealed the same endless plains stretching toward the horizon. The only interruption was the mass of Talen's warcruiser that, unlit, looked like a mountain that hadn't been there a few days before.

"C'mon, Kellee."

He wouldn't ignore the flare. And he couldn't have missed it. He would come. And together, we'd take Sirius's ship and save the people right out from under the guardian's nose. The hunt for the unseelie creature would have to wait.

HAPTERS'S MOONS drifted across the sky, moving the shadows around inside the tower. The link between Talen and me flickered and thrummed, a sign he was alive, just like he had promised. Once Hapters's people were safe and Sirius was dealt with, I needed to sit that silver fae down and prize answers out of him. It had never occurred to me to ask him if he *knew* Oberon, but after the way he had talked to Sirius, he had more than a passing knowledge of Oberon's rule. So many secrets lay between us. His secrets, not mine. I had no more to give. Maybe he and Kellee would trust me if they saw me save Hapters's people. It might go some way to balancing the scales, tipped a long way down on one side after the slaughter at the Game of Lies.

The tower shuddered.

I might not have noticed it had I not been sitting on the floor, tucked in front of the dead control banks. I dropped my hands to the metal flooring and waited, wondering if I'd felt anything at all. Another shudder, this one strong enough to rattle the windows. Distant earthquake? Perhaps the warcruiser was firing up—

Twisting metal screamed a long, drawn-out sound.

I shot to my feet and peered through the windows. Shadows layered the hangars far below but nothing moved.

Something tinny clanged near the entrance to the yard. I homed in on the sound and tried to make sense of the sight below. The fence was gone. No, not gone. Ripped open and shoved aside like someone might yank up weeds and toss them away.

It had been fine when I'd walked through the doorway a few hours before.

I left the watchtower and stood against the rail,

searching the ground for any sign of what could have warped the fence.

Nothing.

Something that big couldn't hide. Unless...

I touched the soft fabric of my coat. Fae magic. It could glamour itself.

It could be right in front of me and I wouldn't know. Or behind...

I backed away from the edge. The smell of warm, wet meat drifted on the wind. Reaching for my whip, my heart sank. I'd left it in the pilot's chamber in my rush to get Talen away from Sirius.

The tower groaned again, complaining about the weight... The creature was here, climbing higher to get to me.

I darted inside and scanned the control banks for anything I could use as a weapon. Nothing.

A window to my left cracked and popped apart, spilling broken glass.

I couldn't climb down. I'd fall.

Trapped.

A growl bubbled all around me, the sound thick and wet, boiling from the insides of something not meant for this world. Hisses came next, mixed with snarls and huffs and the horrible leathery sound of tentacles lashing and grinding.

I'd seen this thing bite fae in half.

I was not fae. Not as fast, not as strong. But I had my coat and some tek-flashers. It would have to do.

Standing in the center of the watchtower, I spread my stance, dropped my hands, and pulled the coat's magic around me, hiding in plain sight. My heart thudded too damn loudly, hammering through my ribs. That creature would surely hear it, and if it was anything like Kellee, it could probably smell my fear. I couldn't hide forever.

The walls stilled. Rattling glass fell silent. Moonlight poured in through broken windows, washing across the floor and catching tiny glass shards. And I waited.

I'm not done yet.

Talen's magic tingled on my fingertips and traced down my spine, both sharp and smooth. The creature probably sensed that too.

Snarls simmered right outside the door. Air quivered in the doorway. Saw-like panting moved closer. It was here, so close, but virtually invisible.

Cold sweat broke out across my skin. The thing snuffled closer, cracking and warping the doorframe around its bulk.

Sickening moist breath blasted my face and the hissing snarls rolled over and over... forming *words*?

"Niiiight... sssshhhhade." The words dripped like poison from its invisible lips.

The air rippled and the unseelie's glamour peeled apart, falling off wrinkled, furred skin. A beast-like head emerged. Red eyes blazed—intelligence sparkling. Teeth glinted inches from my face. It could kill me in one clean bite. But these things, these creatures, they were not dumb animals. Unseelie. The intelligence in its eyes was real. It saw me, but did it know me?

I opened myself to Talen's touch and let his golden light wash over me. The power, like the fae it belonged to, was alien, but so right. Light blasted outward from my body, and the creature reared back, smashing its head through the ceiling. Debris rained down. It roared and clawed the air blindly. I sprang back, but its claws snagged my thigh, catching and digging in before tearing out again.

The wound burned. I clamped a hand around it and hobbled backward. "You want me?"

Power danced up my back, snaking like a whip, and sank its own claws into my flesh. It didn't hurt, but it was too much, too soon, too *different*, and briefly, I struggled to see past the light.

The creature landed on all fours with a thunderous boom, yanking my focus back to it. It hunched low, half-moon teeth bared. Its eyes glowed, fiery and eternal.

"Come and get me," I beckoned, backing onto the deck.

It sprang. I saw the rippling muscles bunch and release, saw the claws spread, its maw open, and lips peel back. The doorway I'd backed through exploded around it, and in that fraction of a delay, I lunged sideways. The creature howled as its weight carried it forward, through the rail, and over the side. Its howl rang out as it fell. More than sound, it touched my blood, my soul. And then it came to an abrupt, silent end.

Its hulking shape lay on the ground far below.

I stared down at it, Talen's magic withdrawing until I was sure the creature wouldn't spring back to life, and then I pulled myself back into the tower to wait for Kellee.

CHAPTER 11

*K*ellee whistled low at the stinking carcass of something that looked, in daylight, as though Faerie had chewed up a bunch of its freakish creatures and vomited them back up.

"Well, we know one thing," he said, smirking up at the tower and back at me. "They sure can't fly."

He had arrived shortly after daybreak to find me sitting on a drum of spare tek parts far enough away from the carcass that its stench didn't have my eyes streaming.

Kellee used a boot to prod its back. Muscle and skin wobbled. He screwed up his nose, then shielded his eyes to look at the tower again. The claw marks scaling the sides and smashed windows told the story better than I could. "You all right?"

"Uh-huh." I got to my feet and brushed off bits of dirt and glass. "We need to get moving."

Kellee's gaze snagged on the gash across my thigh, where the creature's claws had caught me. Dried blood darkened the frayed edges. "You sure?"

"It's fine. C'mon..." I started for the mangled gap in the

fence. "Talen is keeping Sirius busy on the warcruiser. We need to get to the community and Sirius's ship, while we have an opening." I was outside the perimeter fence by the time I realized Kellee wasn't behind me.

He stood beside the dead creature, his gaze skipping from its claws to its pearly fangs. All things that looked eerily familiar, only bigger.

"Marshal!" I barked, jolting him out of his thoughts.

He jogged to my side and we strode across the dusty plains in silence, the morning light beating down hard. Kellee queried me about Sirius's arrival on the warcruiser and I told him everything. We had been walking for what felt like an hour, much of it spent in silence, until the plains turned into scorched fields. Ash stirred and settled as we passed. "I think the fae buried that creature here. *Time, our prison.* It's a warning and it's plural. There might be more than one."

Kellee's eyes darted along the horizon, always scanning for threats. He'd gained a dark shadow of whiskers over the past few days. The ponytail had lost most of its hold and hung loose, while the rest of his mop of dark hair brushed his jawline. The heat had curled his hair in places and the breeze teased messy bangs across his eyes, forcing him to run his fingers through it and sweep it back. "You're right."

"You know for certain?"

"No. But what other explanation is there?"

"You tell me. You've been here before."

He pinched his lips together and hid his grimace by rubbing perspiration and dust from his face. "Not for that..."

"Then why?"

His eyes were on the horizon again. Maybe he wasn't

looking for threats, but something else. "Hapters was my home a long time ago. I had a family. We farmed. It was... They were good times."

I stopped dead in my tracks and in a few strides, Kellee stopped too. He hesitated, knowing the questions were coming, and reluctantly turned to face me, his expression tired.

"You're a farmer?"

Old sorrow clouded his eyes. "Was."

I started walking again and let him fall into step beside me. Kellee was *old*. Old in the same way the fae were old. When you live that long, things change, people die, loved ones too. "I'm sorry."

"I'm not. The years I spent here were some of the better ones."

Kellee. With a family. Absurdly, I readily imagined it. He would make a good provider. A good father. Stern, but true. Honest. Proud. But he had survived and they hadn't. What a terrible curse to carry, to watch those around you eventually die. Friends, lovers, family—all of them gone, and any new friends would eventually pass too, leaving you forever alone in the world.

I had always envied the fae their immortality, and perhaps on Faerie it was a blessing, but not in Halow. Kellee once told me how everything around him had changed and he no longer belonged. I had thought I understood, but I hadn't, not until now.

After a few hours of walking at a solid pace, we came to a rocky outcrop. Kellee handed me a flask of water. His pace had been relentless, and he didn't show any signs of fatigue other than wilting a little under the heat. I'd kept up—barely. Sitting on a rock, I took a few swigs of water, grateful for the respite, but Talen was with Sirius and each minute was another chance for the guardian to get a message back to his flight.

Kellee stood watch, ramrod straight and virtually motionless. He looked into the sun, and the light lent his face a bronze glow, accentuating the sweep of dark eyebrows and darker lashes. He was remarkable to look at.

"It said something to me," I said.

He looked down at me on the rock, frowning. "The creature spoke?"

I shielded my eyes from the harsh light. "It made a lot of noises, but it definitely said *night shade*. Does that mean anything to you?"

His brow pinched. "Nightshade?"

He knew something. But would he tell me? I handed out the flask, making him come closer. He grabbed it, but when I didn't let go, his dark eyes flicked up.

"Tell me," I pushed.

"We're assuming it wasn't referring to the plant?" He tried on his cocky smirk like he could distract me with all that pretty. It was a cheap trick that had never worked on me.

"Don't vague-answer me, Marshal. You and Talen think you can feed me just enough karushit to string me along, like I'm a naive saru who'll believe anything. I killed that thing back there. It said Nightshade. You owe me an answer."

"I owe you now?"

If he brought up the whole *I work for Oberon and lied about it* issue again, he might find his flask shoved somewhere painful.

He breathed in and held it long enough to give him time to think of a suitably vague answer. "*The* nightshade is an unseelie myth."

I released the flask. He hooked it onto his belt, against his back, and squinted into the sun. The light caught the greens in his eyes, sparking them alight. "They used the name to identify an unseelie ruler, something all-powerful. It was supposed to save them all in a war to end all wars. Clearly, it never did, because the unseelie are gone, and as far as the myth says, nobody could organize them when Oberon and the queen wiped out the unseelie for good. I don't know whether the nightshade was real or a fairytale. Maybe *Oberon* knows. You should ask him."

I smiled up at my last vakaru and his attempt to distract me, yet again, from the facts by dragging my past into the conversation. He was angling to get a rise out of me, and he wouldn't get it.

He was right though. The unseelie were all gone from Faerie. Like the vakaru were gone. All but one. "I've never heard of it."

"A saru wouldn't have. Unseelie myths are forbidden tales. Somewhere in history it became bad luck to say the word *unseelie*. Younglings believed the Hunt would snatch you away for uttering it. Oberon would have his people believe the unseelie didn't exist." The fire in Kellee's eyes dulled. "He likes his Faerie pretty."

"Then how do you know about them, Marshal?"

The corner of his mouth twitched. "I've had a long time to collect fairytales."

Because you are one...? "Do you think that thing I killed was the nightshade?"

"No." He swallowed. "That *thing* was a pest."

If that was just a pest, what were the more powerful unseelie like? "If it's a myth, why did it say nightshade and why to me?"

Kellee's expression stiffened, becoming guarded. Question time was over. "C'mon. A lot of folks are waiting on the Messenger."

I admired the deadly elegance in the way he walked away and considered how he could summon claws and fangs and how his blood was poison. I remembered how he had fucked a fae general unconscious. Marshal Kellee was undoubtedly unseelie. A monster wearing pretty camouflage. But he didn't think like one, did he? Nerves churned my gut into knots. I had never feared him. Through everything, I had trusted his sense of honor, but the beast could override that. It almost had when he'd tasted my blood. He would have hurt me had Talen not stepped in.

I was playing with fire by inviting a monster into my heart. But Kellee's good outweighed any bad. I had witnessed that myself, time and time again.

I brushed dust from my hands, accidentally snagging my finger on the tear in my thigh. The fabric tore. I cursed the loss of yet another set of clothes and got to my feet, feeling remarkably rested considering my showdown with the creature. Kellee marched on, a gray and black smudge in the heat haze. While he wasn't looking, I poked my fingers into the slits across my thigh and brushed the smooth skin beneath, looking for the cut. I jabbed around some more, searching for scabs.

There weren't any. But it had cut me. I'd felt the claws slice me open, felt the burn. The blood around the tear was mine. Hours later, the wound was gone.

"Keep up, Kesh," Kellee hollered.

I hurried after the marshal, my thoughts slipping away as fast as my grasp on what I knew for sure.

138

ARRAN'S broad grin at the sight of Kellee and I was almost enough to settle my rattling nerves. Sota whooshed in, scanned me with his all-seeing eye, and grumbled a string of Calicto sink words that had Kellee lifting an eyebrow. I waved Sota off, knowing the questions would come later.

"I didn't think I'd see either of you for a few days. What happened?" Arran asked, keeping his voice low.

We sheltered behind the mound of spoils dug out from the escape tunnel—the same place Kellee and I had first seen Sirius emerge from the warship. The ship in question still sat outside the colony, its miniature-cruiser appearance shimmering under Hapters's ever-changing light. Hulia was in there. Was she *entertaining* the fae as all namu were supposed to?

"Plans have changed," Kellee whispered back. He peered over the top of the rocks.

Arran noted the cut across my thigh but knew better than to ask. I'd walked in on it so nothing needed to be done. He took up a spot against the rocks beside Kellee.

"Talen has Sirius distracted." I crouched behind them. "Now's our chance to get in there."

"What do we have?" Kellee asked.

"A few guards posted near the ramp." Arran nodded toward them. "No comings or goings. Very little activity."

"They're waiting," I added.

"Yeah," Arran agreed. "But for what?"

"Word from Sirius that they can let the prisoners go," Kellee said.

"Or kill them," Arran suggested.

Kellee studied the scene, shoved off the rock, and headed into the undergrowth. "Stay right here." The bushes swallowed him, and he was gone.

Arran continued to observe the fae below. I moved to

his side, trying not to recall how, when we were younger, we had spent hours hiding and stalking through Faerie's arena undergrowth.

"We're supposed to trust Kellee's coming back?" he asked.

"He's scouting the other side, checking all angles before we commit to going in," I explained. "You can trust him, Arran."

It would take more than words before Arran believed me, but ironically, he trusted me, and his nod said that was enough, for now.

"Talen's keeping Sirius busy, huh?"

I explained the events back at the warcruiser, but instead of easing Arran's worry, it increased his concern.

He watched the buildings below, scanning for any sign of Kellee. He wouldn't see him.

"You okay?" I asked.

He nodded again, but his look lingered. Whatever he was thinking, it was enough to make him rest his hand on mine on the rock. Had I been a good, decent person, I would have pulled away and shut him down, but the brush of his hand on mine said all the things we couldn't. Sometimes, all it took was a touch for one person to understand the other, and it had always been that way with Aeon. Now, as Arran, nothing had changed between us.

"When this is over, we should go somewhere," Arran suggested.

My battered heart leapt at the idea. "Where?"

"Somewhere away. It doesn't matter where. Just away from all this. When was the last time you relaxed, had fun?"

Fun? "Probably in The Boot when I was just a secure

messenger, before the fae came, before Eledan changed everything." So much had happened since then. That woman with her cocky attack drone and simple life? She was long gone, buried with the rest of old Calicto. She'd been a dream anyway. Pretend. But in her moments, she'd had fun. More than I'd ever had during a lifetime on Faerie.

But how could we have fun when Halow was crumbling around us? How could we rest, knowing so many were losing their homes, their lives?

I took my hand from beneath Arran's. Fun wasn't for the Messenger. "I don't think that's a good idea."

He touched my arm, drawing my eye back to him. "Don't shut me out."

I knew what it felt like to be shut out. Kellee and Talen routinely kept me at arm's length for reasons they believed a saru couldn't possibly understand. In the beginning, it had been justified. But now? If I shut Arran out, he'd have nothing else. No one else. "I won't."

Kellee stepped out of the bushes like he'd never left. He saw Arran's hand on my arm and a flash of annoyance darkened his eyes. "A simple distraction drawing the guards away from the ramp should suffice. We know there's at least a flight of fifty inside, from what we saw when they took the people. Kesh, slip in using your coat's glamour and see what you can discover. They won't expect it, and with Sirius away, their response to an attack will be slow and disorganized."

"We don't know how long we'll have. Let's do this now." I straightened.

Arran handed me his pistol. "Take this."

I nodded my thanks, tucked the weapon out of sight, acutely aware of Kellee's judgmental glare on us both, and turned to meet that glare head-on. "Try not to kill anyone," I told him.

"*Me* not kill anyone?"

I shrugged. "Talen has a hang-up about killing fae. Mostly me killing fae. But if I can't kill any, neither can you."

"Since when?"

"Since the Game of Lies, apparently."

Kellee's eyebrow lifted. He hadn't been on board with my premeditated murder spree at the arena either. "Are you shitting me?" He flicked his hand open, releasing five razor-edged claws. "What am I supposed to do with these? Wave them menacingly?"

Passing him, I patted him on the shoulder. "Maim them."

Kellee murmured, "Maybe I'll aim for Talen's legs when we get back."

It was banter, I hoped.

"Be careful, Kesh." Arran's warning washed over me as the coat hid my next step into the dark.

Sota dove in low, tucking in close enough that my coat's glamour absorbed his outline too. "You're hurt." He finally said what he'd been thinking.

"If you scan closer, you'll see I'm not."

"But—"

"Later, Sota. Let's get this done."

THE FAE HAD LEFT the township undamaged, a departure from their usual burn-it-all-for-Faerie routine. It could be a sign they intended to release the prisoners, or that they hadn't gotten around to cleansing Hapters yet. I figured it all depended on Sirius's orders, which were ultimately Oberon's. The king had killed billions of Halow people, so why save these?

Your king needs you, Sirius had said. Strange words. The only time Oberon had *needed* me was to woo Mab, then hunt and kill his brother on tek-infested Calicto. Now that the king had Faerie, he no longer needed me. *Your king needs you.* The saru in me quivered with anticipation at the thought of being needed, or perhaps it was fear dancing at the edge of my thoughts. I pushed those thoughts and feelings away. They were of no use to me a million light years from Faerie.

Hapters's waning light folded around me as I slipped between abandoned single-story storage buildings and crouched at a corner, eyeing the ship's open ramp. The guards would sense something was amiss if I tried to sneak by them too close.

A moment later, an explosion rocked the air. I didn't bother looking for the source. Kellee knew how to cause a decent distraction. It worked. The guards bolted from their posts and headed deeper into the township.

I was sauntering toward the ramp when three more fae marched out of the ship to replace them. Being in glamour didn't make me entirely invisible. Had they been looking directly at me, they would have seen the light wobble. Luckily, they were all looking toward Kellee's pillar of smoke. I slunk inside.

The ship was a smaller version of the cruiser, right down to the grown, smooth glowing walls. Somewhere, there would be a pilot, likely permanently fixed in place. A fate Talen had avoided. I shuddered at the memory of seeing him strung up, puppet-like, and hurried on.

As a ship grown for war, it didn't have a cargo hold, but

if it was anything like our cruiser, it likely had prison cells in its belly. That's where the people would be, but I couldn't break them out. The prison bars would be bone and needed to be coaxed open. I had to go straight to the source.

"You have a plan?" Sota whispered near my ear, still tucked close and hidden inside my glamour. The corridors were curiously empty. There should have been more fae aboard...

"Kind of."

My stride tripped as we entered the womb-like pilot's chamber. The pilot, what was left of him, was halfway swallowed by a wall. Only his torso and head were free to move. Vampiric vines looped around his arms and latched into his veins on his inner arms and behind his shoulders. The ship had *absorbed* him. Would it one day swallow all of him down?

He had been handsome, once. But now dull, dark hair trailed in long strands down either side of his lean face. His eyes were black and unseeing. His skin, from his torso, to his face, to his lips, was a single shade of gray so pale it almost glowed from within—like the ship's walls.

I approached, still cloaked, nothing but a whisper of movement giving me away.

"You step lightly." His voice held a jagged edge, as though it faintly echoed, one voice over another. Once, it would have been smooth and made for the telling of pretty untruths at court. *"Not fae."* His head tilted. *"Saru."* And then, with a small gasp, *"Wraithmaker."*

My glamour fell away, no longer required.

Sota drifted up from my shoulder. "Guard the door," I told my drone. He sailed into a position giving him a direct line of sight to observe anyone about to interrupt us.

The pilot blinked dark fathomless eyes. He could feel exactly where I stood and hear Sota's motors. He didn't need sight to see. "You know who I am?"

"Faerie's touch surrounds a human shell. You are unmistakable." A pink tongue swept across his lips. The only color on him. *"Do you mean to kill me, Wraithmaker?"* His teeth flashed as he spoke, as though he would like to see me try.

My reputation was growing. "No." I studied where the ship grasped at his chest. Small tendrils suckled at his skin, countless tiny mouths slowly devouring him. This would have been Talen's fate. It was cruel, but why was I surprised? "Am I speaking with the fae or the ship?"

"We are one."

I waved my hand in front of his eyes. He didn't react. He looked vulnerable, but my body would broadcast any ill intent and I'd seen how quickly these ships could defend themselves. Attacking him would likely get the doors locked and the prisoners killed. My death and Sota's would follow soon after.

"How much do you know of me?"

"I know you. You are saru, birthed by Faerie and risen from the earth. You are the Wraithmaker, marked by a king and pulled by his strings. You are the Messenger, sent to hold back the dark. A message to all."

His mind had been tainted, but I'd be a fool to dismiss his words as insanity. The human myth, the fae myth, they didn't matter. Only one truth had any worth here. "I am saru. I live to serve. You understand?"

"We do."

I braved stepping closer even as every cell in my body wanted to cringe away from the sight. He didn't have the sweet floral scent of the fae. He smelled like the warcruiser, like a rich Summerlands breeze loaded with pollen or a bracing Winterlands wind that bit and nipped, like something changing and untamable.

I lifted my hand, holding it close to his cheek, but didn't touch him. "What if there's another way?" I asked.

"Another way?"

"Change is coming." I pressed a hand to his cheek, expecting it to be as cold as he looked, but his skin was soft and warm. He didn't feel sickly. "What if we did not have to serve them?"

He chuckled darkly, and the ship shuddered. *"My choices ended long ago."*

"Kesh?" Sota rumbled.

"It's okay." I brushed my thumb down the pilot's cheek, felt him lean into me, and touched his lips. He had been beautiful and proud and strong once, like Kellee. I looked again at the surrounding chamber. Perhaps, this pilot was still all those things, but changed in his form. I was standing in front of a fraction of what he was.

Magic tingled through my fingers, summoning a glittery glow to his parting lips. "I have a ship and a pilot," I told him. "And both are free. They are not slaves—"

"We know," he whispered and his mouth turned down. *"We hear her. She speaks of a silver fae like no other and the saru with fire in her heart, a vakaru relic, and a champion. She says you and yours have just begun. Her name is Shinj. She wants you to know her name. And she asks that we help you, Wraithmaker."*

Talen's ship had a name and knew us. More than that, she was sentient enough to understand everything going on around her? Shinj. I'd known she could think for herself and I'd sensed there was more to her, but to have her name, to know her intention, it was a rare gift. "Will you help me?"

"*We refused to, until this moment.*" His lashes fluttered over blank, unseeing eyes. "*We see you. We see all of you, who you were, who you are yet to become, the thread of light running through you. Some shine brighter than others, and you... you are blinding. We will help you, Messenger, but you must do something for me in return. A bargain, a trade. You must agree.*"

I might have been saru, but I'd spent enough time at court to know better than to agree to any bargain with the fae without knowing the terms. "What are the stakes?"

"*I ask only a small thing. Worth nothing to you but everything to me.*"

I tried to guess at his meaning. Few things were worthless to me. I had nothing, so everything was worth something. But if this thing truly was worth nothing, I could give nothing away to save the people. It was a trick. It had to be. "Truly worth nothing to me?"

"*Truly.*"

"Free the people now and I'll agree."

His eyes closed. "*It is done.*"

"And your price?"

"*Kiss us.*"

What? I schooled my face, though he didn't see me and could likely read the fear surrounding me. I had already touched him and he hadn't pulled me into the ship, so why did I hesitate? A kiss *was* nothing. A kiss for the lives of Hapters's people.

I swallowed and tilted my head, leaning in. *Just a kiss...*

Sota's motors whirred. He watched closely, always ready for the unexpected.

My lips touched the pilot's. Magic fizzled sharply on my tongue. He opened, just a little, and returned the kiss so gently I wondered who this fae had been before for him to kiss with such reverence. His sweet sigh brushed my lips as we parted. The kiss *was* nothing, just a brush, a tease, but it left the taint of sorrow sinking through me, heading for my heart.

"The nightshade, Messenger. Beware."

"You know of the Nightshade?"

"You are right. There is another way." He bowed his head but kept his haunting eyes on me. *"Now kill us."*

I stepped back. Once. Twice.

"Kill us." His voice had lost its echo, making each word solid, real.

"That was not our bargain."

"It was. Kill us, Messenger. It costs you nothing."

I lifted Arran's pistol, aiming between the pilot's sorrowful eyes. I understood now why he had wanted the kiss. To feel again, one last time. It was wrong, what they had done to him. I wished I had known him in another life.

"Free us, Messenger." A single diamond-like tear rolled down his cheek.

My heart hardened against all the injustice of Faerie, against the abuse of its own beautiful creatures. This was no life at all. His freedom cost me nothing.

I pulled the trigger.

CHAPTER 12

*T*he fae flights scattered throughout the township discovered that Hapters's people weren't as manageable when not drugged. Once the people dispersed, digging up their buried weapons, the fae fled the township, probably hoping to regroup under Sirius once the guardian returned—not anytime soon if Talen had his way.

I wasn't needed, and as the people drifted back to their homes and lives, I sat down on the ship's ramp. Behind me, the ship had fallen silent and cold, its lights extinguished. Sota drifted above, motors humming.

I'd seen countless saru take their own lives. I'd thought them fools, thought them weak. But I realized they had looked into the future and known, without any doubt, that the future was not a place they wanted to be. Arran had taken the starfruit to avoid his future and his past.

He was right. I had mastered my saru existence by making myself cruel.

The nameless pilot who had wanted something as simple as a kiss had known me better than I knew myself.

And I'd thought to go in there and champion saru companionship, as though the pilot and I were the same. I was a fool. A weak, unworthy fool.

Kellee climbed the ramp and looked down at me. After a few moments of silence, he regarded the dead ship and said, "I thought we weren't killing any fae?"

I stood, shoved the pistol at his chest, knocking him back a step, and walked away.

I wandered aimlessly, watching people pick up the pieces of their lives. Faerie's march on Halow could not be allowed to continue. Faerie wasn't beautiful; it was a lie. Halow, in all its natural human messiness, was the true beauty. Faerie would devour it whole the same way that ship was devouring itself. I couldn't let it happen.

And there was one way to stop it.

Your king needs you.

Oberon.

"MESSENGER?"

I'd been wandering so long the sky had turned dark and I'd lost track of time. A woman leaned out the doorway of a domed dwelling. Her eyes crinkled with kindness. She stepped back and wordlessly invited me into her home.

Talen needed me. Hapters was a long way from safe. Kellee was somewhere nearby, doing his marshaling, helping people return to their homes. "Thank you, but I can't."

Hulia, in a halo of dreadlocks, appeared behind the older woman. "Kesh, you look dead on your feet. Come eat, drink. You've earned it." She saw me wavering and added, "Get your ass inside."

Sota buzzed in over my shoulder, not about to hang around and wait to be told twice. The home was compact, with all the rooms built around a central living area. The older woman who had invited me in joined a stocky man in a kitchen, where food bubbled and simmered. My stomach grumbled and my mouth watered. I hadn't eaten much of anything in days and the gentle thrumming of the bond inside me implied Talen was fine. Maybe I could afford a break.

The middle-aged pair had stripped out of the ragged clothes the fae had clothed them in and wore the simple cotton over-garments of folks used to working the land in hot weather. The man said something to the woman, and her responding laughter was true, honest. It was a delight to hear.

Hulia cleared a table, wiping it clean of dust that must have blown in when the fae had raided the house. She grabbed a bowl of fruit and set it down in the center and then added smaller bowls, clearly familiar with the house.

"Sit," Hulia ordered.

I knew better than to argue. "I can't stay. There are—"

"Yeah, yeah, yeah, there's more shit to save. I get it." Her glare twinkled. She came around to my side of the table and pulled out a chair. She quietly added, "Let Janet and Miquel thank you the only way they can. You can get back to hero-ing when your belly is full and you don't look ready to collapse."

"That bad?"

"It's a good thing you don't have mirrors on the warcruiser, huh?"

I winced. "It's been a long few days."

We drank and ate, making polite conversation. Janet was an engineer, Miquel a farmer who spent much of the

151

year isolated on the vast expanses of wheat fields. I gleaned from the conversation that Hulia had known them a long time. Longer than she had known me. They served bite-sized parcels of spicy meats and apologized for it not being *enough*. Nobody had invited me into their home before. Nobody had offered me a seat at their table and spoken to me as though I were... like them. Not saru. Not the Wraithmaker. Just another friend. The fae had taken me too young from the saru for me to have known. Aeon was the closest thing to family I had. This light and laughter around a feasting table was such a simple thing, but oh so precious. What would it be like to laugh and love with my friends, Kellee, Talen, and Arran. Would we ever have a moment like this, not fraught with tension? I wanted this for us. It was a dream, but I hadn't given up on all my dreams, not yet.

"Your drone is powered by *lumines*?" Janet asked as she cleared the table.

I'd almost forgotten Sota was with us. He had settled on a shelf, doing a fine job of blending in like a large, beaten-up, red-eyed metal soccer ball. He'd been watching the scene like I had.

"Lumines?" I asked, unfamiliar with the word.

"It's what they call magic," Hulia explained, her smile cracking around its edges.

"Oh, er... yes. He has some." They could tell Sota had life magic in him? "I'm surprised you noticed. Tek and magic aren't supposed to mix."

Janet laughed softly. "When you've lived on Hapters a while, lumines get into your bones."

They were talking about Faerie magic and were more right than they realized. It infected most everything it touched over a long period. If these people knew about magic, what else did they know? "Hapters does have some unusual characteristics," I said, steering the conversation toward the tunnels.

Janet beamed. "It's the secret to our yields. Hapters keeps on giving year after year."

Did they know it was fae magic boosting their crops? A glance at Hulia's straight face indicated not.

"We learned a long time ago how to combine lumines and tek."

"Combine them?" I tried not to appear too interested, but Hulia's narrowed eyes flicked my way in warning, or was that fear in her gaze? Why would she fear this conversation?

Janet continued to clear the dishes away, smiling like her world was perfect and she hadn't spent the last few days trapped inside a fae vessel. Maybe she hadn't been too concerned, but the people here were already familiar with the magic that powered the ship, the magic the fae wielded.

"The Giver came and showed us the way," Janet said. "We are forever grateful for his generosity."

"I'm sorry, I haven't heard of them... Who is the Giver?"

Janet's crinkled eyes shone with pride and something akin to love. "He died and was resurrected to show us the light."

A religious leader?

Miguel filled my glass with water. I thanked him and took a sip, noticing how Hulia stared into hers. I was missing something here... "The Giver taught you how to combine tek and magic?"

"Oh no, he showed us the lumines and we saved *him*." She reached inside her shirt and plucked out a brooch, just like the one in my pocket. "He made our future real," Janet explained, "and made us see a world of possibilities. We built that world for him here. He has promised to return one day and see all we have done, see that his dreams are real."

The water lodged in my suddenly dry throat. I coughed. "Dreams?"

Miguel rushed to refill my glass. I waved him off and threw a look at Hulia. She continued to stare into her cup, studiously avoiding me.

They didn't mean *Dreams*. They couldn't. I looked at the brooch in Janet's hand. The tek encircled a red gem—a dormant, cold, hard thing wrapped in metal vines. But if I tilted my head, if I turned those vines loose and twisted them into a cage-like shape. Oh no.

The brooch was a symbol to these people. A talisman in times of need, used for protection. That's why the mother had reached for it. She had been praying to her god in her final moments. But I'd seen it before in another form.

A tek and magic heart.

My thoughts raced to everything I knew of Eledan. For a thousand years, it was believed he had been slain in the first war. An angry mob had torn out his heart. But he had survived, his fae heart replaced with tek. Here, on Hapters?

I still had the brooch in my pocket. A talisman to the Dreamweaver. Hapters's messiah. I wanted to rip the piece of jewelry from my pocket and smash it under my boot.

"Thank you." I stood. "For the meal. But I really must be leaving."

"Kesh...?" Hulia began.

The Dreamweaver had been here. He had beguiled

these people and made them worship him. They loved him. But he wasn't a benevolent god. He was fae. A Prince of Faerie. Oberon's brother. And as capable of darkness as he was of light. He had used these people. Why or what for, I didn't know. But the fact he had been here was enough. It was all a lie. It always was with Eledan. *Illusion.* I needed to see inside Hapters's tunnels. I needed to go back to that slab of stone and its iron-poured writing.

"You're too kind," I mumbled. "And I wish you all the best for the future..." Sota hummed into the air and buzzed out the door after me. "Find Kellee," I told the drone. He shot off, zipping between homes, leaving me standing outside in the dark alone.

"Kesh, wait," Hulia called.

"He was here."

"I know." Hulia stopped beside me. Patches of light from nearby houses and their tiny windows peppered the pathways and Hulia. "I was going to tell you but then it seemed like it didn't matter. He's not here now. And so what if these people think he's their god? It's harmless."

"*Harmless?*" I could hear his laughter, hear it so far away but it might as well have been in my ear. "You don't know him..."

She lifted her hands to placate me. "I understand. He had me in his thrall for a few hours. With you... I know it was a long time. I know it was hard."

He'd had me for nine months. And forever. Turning my mind over and over and over. "He's not kind," I snapped. "He's not a hero. He's certainly not a god. Eledan is fae. He's fae, Hulia. He's not even here and these people are his puppets. That should tell you enough."

"Don't lecture me about the fae!" Her eyes flashed. "We all have wounds to bear. I'm sorry I didn't tell you.

You were only staying for the party, but then the fae came and... It's over now, and these people can—"

"It's not over. There's something left over here, something *unseelie.*" *Beware the nightshade.* And now Eledan's past was all mixed up here too.

Her eyes widened.

"There are tunnels. Do you know anything about that?"

"Tunnels, what? No. What do you mean, *unseelie?*"

"I mean, dark fae supposedly gone but not so much." I pulled in a breath, tasting hot dust and night. "You need to ask these people what they know about the unseelie. Try to find out if there's anything dark in Hapters's past. I don't believe for one second that Eledan was here and he's not in some way connected. Find out what you can and make sure they stay inside. I killed an unseelie creature, but there could be more."

Her double eyelids flickered. "You killed an unseelie? For real?"

"On the plains, we found a family, all killed. The mother was reaching for this." I plucked the heart talisman from my pocket, fighting the urge to toss it away. "Eledan has one just like it that's keeping him alive."

She looked at the talisman seeing its true meaning. "They think he's coming back."

"Of course he is, because he knows there's power on Hapters, just like there's power on Calicto. I will find out what's going on. I will stop this, and then I'm going to do more." I heard the Kellee from my past offering me a chance to make it right, heard Talen say I was *everything*, heard a boy once tell me a hero would come and save us, and I heard my king's voice whispering that I was his secret to keep. All of it had brought me here to a township on a faraway planet where its people worshipped the Dreamweaver as a god and the unseelie lurked beneath our feet. None of this was an accident.

I squeezed the talisman in my hand. "I can make a difference. I can stop Faerie from conquering Halow. I will stop this war." As I said the words, it felt as though something larger than me clicked into place. Something cosmic, something more than my deep-seated fear of the Dreamweaver, more than Hapters and its rogue unseelie. With all the magic here and the tek-heart in my hand, I wondered if my pledge had carried far between the stars to Faerie and Her king.

CHAPTER 13

We trudged back to the warcruiser in near silence. Arran attempted to make conversation with me, but I was lost in thought. Kellee was a silent brooding storm. Sota happily chatted with Arran, his man-crush on the gladiator gleefully on display.

When we rode the pod into the warcruiser, Talen stood in front of the doors, looking every part the perfectly in control fae. Nothing of his wounds remained. He was back in his fae leathers, his hair elaborately twined in braid upon braid. Nothing had changed besides the storm in his eyes. That was new, and he looked ready to take one of us to the wall—probably me, probably because of the pilot I'd killed. I held his gaze, waiting for the words.

Instead of speaking his mind, he said, "Sirius is in the meeting room." He kept the storm from his voice.

"Alone?" Kellee asked.

Talen slid his glare to the marshal. An eyebrow quirked at Kellee's fae leathers and no doubt the fact the marshal—with his errant curls, scuffs, and general disheveled prettiness—

looked as though he'd stolen those leathers from someone worthier. My smile ticked at one corner. I liked how Kellee fucked up all the fae prettiness whenever he encountered it. "The ship will not permit him to be incarcerated."

"You are the ship," Kellee grumbled, shoving by his sometimes friend, sometimes enemy.

Arran looked between me and Talen, uncomfortably. I gave him a nod that sent him on his way. "Go with him, Sota."

The drone bobbed in the air behind Arran, asking about the rules for a game of rock-paper-scissors. On the walk back, they had been figuring out a way for Sota to play.

Talen waited until the voices had faded before lifting his gaze to me. The emotional storm churned in his violet eyes, crackling with lightning. "You're safer with me than either of those males."

He was probably right. Kellee either wanted to fuck or fight me, probably both at the same time, and Arran had a habit of rushing into things before thinking. But for Talen to voice the possessive thought was unlike him. Something had him wound so tightly he was about to break. Sirius, probably.

I pulled the talisman from my pocket and held it out on my palm. "What does this look like to you?"

He didn't look down, didn't reach for it, didn't even blink. His gaze drilled deeper into mine, accompanied by careful, measured breaths that rhythmically lifted his chest. I'd seen him enraged, seen him sorrowful, but this was something else. Maybe I shouldn't have sent Arran away with Sota.

"Talen?"

"What you did—"

This *was* about the pilot. I lifted my chin and stared back at the fae. "What I did was necessary. I freed the people. The flight escaped, and while they're scattered, they're not a threat, but we'll need to deal with them. The pilot..." His eyes flared and the storm surrounded me—his magic, so real, so present, that it pushed in from all around like invisible, intangible water. I'd drown in it if he let it all go. "He asked to die," I whispered. "I'm not apologizing for that."

"I know." He started forward, the storm breaking its barriers, and before I could think to protect myself, he was in front of me, his hands wrapped around my upper arms, his head bowed, forehead touching mine. Old saru instincts tried to drop me to my knees, but he wasn't hurting me. "You saved the pilot." Talen breathed the words. "I saw it all. I know it cost you. Kesh... I... I would take you away from all this. Take you far away to the corner of Halow where Faerie cannot reach you."

I looked up into his eyes and fell into Talen all over again. He never wasted a single word, so when he spoke, everything held weight and reverence. And he had offered to save me in such a foolish, unrealistic, almost romantic way that I would have laughed if he hadn't looked ready to snap. Nobody did intense like him. "I don't need saving," I said. "But there are hundreds of thousands of people who do."

"I know. I know that too." He spoke as though the words pained him. "I know more than you can imagine."

"So how about you tell me some of it?"

His eyes flicked between mine, his gaze so damn intense it might burn me to dust in the next second. "I want to. I want to tell you *everything*, Kesh. All of it. I wish I could."

But he wouldn't, and we were right back at the beginning, a wall of secrets and lies between us. I closed my eyes. "Let go, Talen."

He did and stepped back, shutting down. The storm had passed and he was just Talen again—ice and fire, stardust and shadow in one perfect faerie specimen, but back under control.

"Any time you feel like revealing all these secrets, you know where I am..." I left him standing in the corridor and didn't look back.

SIRIUS WAITED in the meeting room. Lucky for him, Kellee had stayed by the door, though he shot the guardian his stoic, unshakable lawman stare.

"There isn't time for this," the guardian hissed, looking even more pissed off because he had chopped off chunks of his long red hair, leaving it in a haphazard mop around his angular, stubborn face. My tek-razors had taken some removing. I felt a pang of loss over his missing locks. He had looked lordly before, and now he looked like those wild sidhe lords who shunned the royal courts in favor of Faerie's hills.

"Said by an immortal who has all the time in the worlds." I had my whip back, its weight clipped reassuringly to my belt. Sirius's gaze dropped to it as I approached the table. Apparently, he and Talen must have come to an agreement, because he wasn't broken or kneeling—as Talen had promised—but he did look forlorn, as though someone had taken his favorite toys away.

"Send the vakaru away," Sirius snapped.

Kellee snorted. "This vakaru does what he wants."

Sirius's smile wasn't pleasant. "A vicious, mindless race. Oberon should have killed you with the rest instead of sparing you."

Oberon had spared Kellee?

A whisper in the air was all the warning I had. Kellee was suddenly standing over the guardian, his right arm raised, claws poised to tear the guardian's throat out. "Kellee! Don't!"

Kellee's lips rippled, curved fangs bared. "If it were up to me, your immortal life would have just been severed at the root."

Sirius's mouth twisted. If he laughed, Kellee would cut out his throat and gut him.

I barely had control of Kellee at the best of times. If he killed Sirius here, we could lose a valuable contact. "Kellee, leave us."

The marshal snarled, making sure he had the last word, and flung Sirius away. Sirius's gaze tracked the marshal all the way out the door. It wasn't until he had left that I realized Sirius had gotten exactly what he wanted: me, alone. I dropped my hand to my whip and kept the table between us.

The guardian's face was the picture of fae arrogance. He was in my ship, surrounded by his enemies, and he still looked at me as though I were just another one of his household's saru playthings. That glare might have held more weight, but his messy hair diluted the effect.

"Your retinue is impressive," he said tartly. "For a saru."

"What did you mean when you said Oberon should have killed Kellee?"

"Didn't he tell you?" Sirius's green eyes flashed with malice. "Did you not wonder how a single vakaru survived? It is only by our king's leniency that your vakaru lives." Sirius sat himself at the table, draping all his guardian self into a chair like a feline sprawling in the sun. "Kellee stood by and watched the fae snuff out his people. One by one."

The glee Sirius took in retelling the tale made me want to spring across the table and choke the life out of him. Kellee would never have stood by and let his people be killed. Never. Sirius was twisting the truth and I couldn't afford for him to drive a wedge between us. We did enough of that without help from outsiders.

"You came here for me?" I asked.

"Yes."

"Oberon ordered you to retrieve me?" I reworded the question, remembering I was speaking with a fae.

"He did."

"And to kill my friends?"

Sirius bowed his head. "Indeed."

"But Talen is alive and the two of you appear to be fine. He bargained with you?"

Sirius wet his lips, his mind crafting the right answer. He reached up and ruffled his hair, and then frowned when his fingers combed through it too quickly. "There are few of Faerie's creations I fear. I do not fear the king, though many do. I do not fear the Hunt, though perhaps I should. Your Talen, I fear. We bargained. We forged a truce. I will speak no more of it."

Interesting. "You won't kill my friends?"

"No."

"Any of them?"

He sighed. "I cannot give you my word if I do not know who your friends are. And what is your definition of friend?"

"You don't need to kill anyone. You're here to take me back to Faerie. Can we agree on that?"

"Yes. And we should be leaving. Time is not our ally. Our king needs you."

Old longing reared its ugly head. The need to be seen, the need to be loved. A king's promises whispered into my ear. I shook my head. "He's been doing just fine without me for a few thousand years. He has Faerie. He doesn't need me."

"Times are changing." Sirius got to his feet, doing so slowly when he saw me tense. "As much as I disagreed with your tutorage, I rarely saw Oberon happier than when he was with you."

I glanced at the door. If Kellee so much as heard a single word of that...

"With you, he did not have the weight of the court on him. With you, he was different."

No, no, no, sweet lies. They meant nothing. "He just trained me to fight, Sirius. You know this. I'm one in a long line of pet saru. Something for him to occupy his days with. A distraction, at best."

"No," the guardian whispered. "I wish it were so, but Oberon... He has an unseemly fascination with you. I have tried to explain it, to understand it, and failed. You have somehow beguiled him and now you must return. The king has never had more enemies and fewer resources. He never leaves the palace. Every day his light darkens further. I would see him returned to his former glory for the sake of the court, for the sake of Faerie, and if you can assist with that, I will not stop until you are returned to his side. The king needs his Wraithmaker."

I swallowed and hoped Kellee wasn't listening, because what I said next would destroy everything I had built between us. But it had to happen. For Halow. For the namu and saru. For all the lives holding out hope that somebody would save them. I had never wanted to be the Wraithmaker, and I hadn't asked to be the Messenger. But nobody else would be.

"I will go back with you to Faerie, and I will go willingly, but first, I need your help. Yours and your flight's."

"With what exactly?"

"An unseelie problem."

"WE'RE WORKING *WITH* THE GUARDIAN?" Kellee rolled his eyes and slumped in his seat at the meeting table. He pinched the bridge of his nose as though this meeting were too painful. I'd sent Sirius from the room and called everyone in to discuss how to proceed from here.

"The guardian is working with us," I corrected. "Big difference."

"How, in cyn, did you get him to agree to that? Wait. Don't tell me. I don't want to know. It's taking all the control I have not to walk right out of here. Maybe I can find an abandoned farm somewhere and grow barley for the rest of my long and hopefully uneventful days. There's no way you, Kesh, can fuck barley up." The marshal huffed and added, "You do realize venturing into unmapped tunnels with a royal guardian by our side is the definition of stupid?"

As reactions went, Kellee's could have been worse.

Usually, his brutal honesty was refreshing, but not now. I needed him with me on this. I was trying to do right and move forward. I needed his support, not his side-eyed scowl.

I flicked my gaze to Talen. The fae stood at the back of the meeting room, leaning against the wall like a lethal statue. He appeared to be engaged and acknowledged my glance with a lift of an eyebrow, but the fact he had isolated himself spoke volumes. That and the distant focus, like he was only going through the motions.

Arran's fingers tapped lightly on the tabletop. He saw me looking his way and smiled reassuringly. At least I could count on him to stand beside me.

"I suggest we vote," Sota said. The drone hovered in the air between Arran and Kellee. He had been mostly quiet since the incident with the anonymous pilot, which meant he had a lot to say. Time for our usual debriefs wasn't on our side.

"That's actually a good idea," Kellee agreed. He lifted a hand. "I vote 'fuck no' to having a sidhe guardian tagging along while we hunt deadly unseelie monsters. The only one he wants alive is Kesh, and the rest of us he'll accidentally kill because Oberon ordered it to happen. He'll wriggle around his word. They always do."

"I vote yes," Arran said.

Kellee groaned, nipping the sound off when it turned into a growl. "Of course you'd agree with Kesh."

Arran bristled. "What do you mean?"

"I mean, you'd fling yourself over the edge of a cliff if she told you to."

Arran folded his arms and glared back at the marshal. "I trust Kesh."

Kellee chuckled. "And that right there is your problem."

I was ready to snap at them, when Sota added, "I vote no."

Why had I programmed my drone to have an opinion on everything? I couldn't even rely on him to back me up. What was I doing here? I needed them with me, not divided. I needed everything they could be if we were to make a difference where it counted, and I couldn't even organize them enough to go rooting around tunnels on a faraway planet. But they could be united. All of them had one thing in common: their dislike of the fae. All but one.

All eyes turned to Talen, aware his was the deciding vote. His brow knotted, messing up his perfect lines and hardening his expression. I couldn't tell if he was annoyed with them, with this entire situation, or just frustrated at being here when he had already admitted he'd prefer to take me away from all this.

The silver fae blinked emotionless eyes back at us. "Having the guardian's flight search Hapters for signs of unseelie habitation is a far better use of resources. Hapters's people are at risk. If there are more rogue unseelie here, they will kill again. We need to deal with this threat and move on."

"And that's a yes." Kellee was on his feet and heading for the door before the last word had left Talen's lips. "When you're all dead, be sure to remember this conversation and which one of us is always right."

"We leave in fifteen minutes," I told the others and jogged to catch up with the marshal. He would have vanished the second he'd left the room if he hadn't wanted me following, but instead, he strode down the winding corridors, the soft lighting warming his gray and black leathers.

"Hey." He ignored me. Stubborn, arrogant son-of-a-sluagh. "Hey!" I caught his arm and tugged him around. A warning flared in his eyes. "You and I need to talk about a lot of things—"

"Now is not the time." He started to turn away.

"No, it's not, so shut up and listen." I waited for him to keep on walking. He thought about it but must have decided I wasn't a complete loss. When he faced me, a muscle twitched in his cheek. "We rarely see eye to eye, but I respect you, Marshal Kellee." More than he could imagine. "I'm just asking you to respect me in return."

"I will." He nodded. "When you've earned it."

I blinked, his words striking so deep, so fast, they cut off any reply. Hadn't I done enough? The arena, saving the colonies alongside him, freeing Hapters's people. I looked into his dark eyes and only saw disappointment, like he already knew how this would play out and I'd fail him. Again. When would it be enough? When would he forgive me? I then remembered that my heart believed I knew Marshal Kellee, but I never had, not really. Eledan had seeded an idea of the marshal in my head when he'd had me running circles in the illusory prison. The marshal I'd spoken to during those long nights of loneliness wasn't real. The one in front of me was. Despite everything, we were strangers. And my heart ached to think we might always be.

"Kellee." I swallowed, refusing to wilt under his glare. "You must believe I can make a difference, otherwise you wouldn't be here."

He looked away, and the muscle in his cheek fluttered

again as he bit down on whatever he wanted to say in reply.

"You promised you would help me be the Messenger. I need your help now."

"*You* aren't the Messenger." His top lip twitched. He flicked a hand back down the corridor. "We are. Talen, Me, Sota, even Arran, and you. We're the Messenger. I'm here for that. We can make a difference, all of us, so long as you don't tear us apart, Kesh."

For once, we agreed. I wasn't the people's hero. We all knew it. I was just the face of the myth: the coat, the whip, the saru slave risen out of the dirt. It was a great tale. But Arran, Talen, Sota, and Kellee—they were the Messenger. They could be the people's hero. They were more than I could ever be. They gave hope to a star system barely clinging to life. And that was precious. I understood now. When Kellee looked at me, he saw a threat to that hope, because I'd betrayed him once, and in his mind, I could betray him again. He trusted Talen—his enemy— more than me. He trusted Arran and Sota more than me. And now I'd brought Sirius into our midst. Oberon's guardian. My king's most trusted advisor. A king who had made Kellee watch as he slaughtered the vakaru.

"I was wrong," I admitted. "But I didn't understand how wrong I was until now. I was the Wraithmaker. It was all I ever knew. I lived to serve my king. Nobody and nothing else mattered to me."

The quiet pain showed in his eyes. A trust betrayed. He had seen me at my worst. He had helped pull me back from the nowhere place the Dreamweaver had trapped me in. He had pinned his hopes on me. This proud man who had lived a hundred lives alone, this last vakaru.

I pressed a hand to his chest, feeling the soft, warm

leathers beneath my palm. If he pulled away, we might never know each other, but he didn't. He looked down, his expression raw and open, his heart strong where it beat beneath my hand. "We were both wrong."

He pressed a hand over mine and closed his fingers. His hands weren't the soft, smooth hands of courtly fae. His were the hands of a male who had worked the fields and gripped weapons, who had fought for more lives than I could know. Inside, I ached to know the real Kellee.

"I've been someone's slave my entire life. Now that I'm free, because of you, I'm still trying to understand who I really am, but I know one thing. I won't ever let you down, Marshal Kellee."

He lifted my hand from his chest and brought it to his lips. His lips brushed the back of my fingers while his eyes never left mine. The touch of his lips in a kiss so light it was barely there at all was so unlike Kellee that all I could do was watch and feel as that small brush of a touch held me utterly bespelled.

He lowered my hand and released it. "I have never known anyone like you, Kesh Lasota. I want to believe you, to believe *in* you. But you are Oberon's, and for all your pretty words and promises, you will always be Oberon's."

My heart stuttered, because he was wrong, so very wrong. If he would just give me a chance to prove it.

"Do not deny it." He backed off. "It would be a lie, to both of us."

I watched him turn and walk away, wanting so badly to call out, to deny it, but I feared beneath all the need and want between us that Marshal Kellee was right.

CHAPTER 14

*H*apters's night was warm and velvety, reminding me of Faerie's long, sultry hours, clad in wisp-punctured darkness. Day and night weren't linear on Faerie. Night came only when many desired it and was banished again when Faerie's people sought the light of day. The wax and wane of desire and indifference made Faerie and its people unpredictable, but it also made no two days the same.

Was Hapters more than it appeared too?

Kellee strolled far ahead, his outline little more than a flickering candle inside the moonlit heat haze. Sota and Arran were closer, Arran tossing his daggers in the air while Sota dipped and bobbed behind him. Next came the guardian, his every step delivered with purpose. His dark, earth-colored leathers and cloak almost had him blending in with Hapters's fields. If he wanted, he could slip away, but the guardian was used to people seeing him and obeying him. He was not subtle.

Behind me, Talen slipped through the night, Hapters's

twin moons painting his silvery hair a milky white. In my silence, I was struck by how impossible we all were.

Don't tear us apart, Kesh.

Kellee's words haunted me like the Dreamweaver's. I wouldn't tear us apart. I had every intention of making the Messenger a legend worthy of Faerie, but keeping everyone together and on the right track wouldn't be easy, especially when I thought of the things we must do.

"The stars are beautiful here." Talen had drawn up beside me and fallen into my pace. He lifted his face, lips quirking gently at their corners.

I followed his gaze, through the pale greens of Hapters's high atmosphere, and spotted a few stars desperately competing with the moonlight. The stars were unfamiliar here. They had been unfamiliar on Calicto too, on the rare occasion they were visible through Calicto's domes. The nightscape on Faerie looked as though someone had spilled a line of glitter across the sky. I'd often watched their path through the bars of the window in my cell (when permitted), and later from the tower Oberon had kept me in. Hapters's stars were lifeless and dull in comparison, and yet Talen looked at them as though they were brighter than anything else in the sky. What did he see that I didn't?

My gaze fell from the sky to the fae admiring them. He was like those stars, I realized. Not Faerie's brilliant fireworks, but something distant, something so far away that if I blinked, it might vanish. I had bound him to me, captured him, to control him, but it seemed he had captured me. I couldn't hope to hold something like him for long.

"Why are you here?" I asked, checking the others

ahead to make sure we were heading in the right direction. Sota said something that Arran laughed at.

"Why am I here on this mission, on this planet, with you?" Talen asked. He turned his head, resting the weight of his precision gaze on me. A flicker of humor softened it. Softened *him*. Outside, wrapped in Hapters's warm night, he seemed happier and lighter.

"With me." I likely wouldn't get an answer, but it wouldn't stop me from chipping away at his barriers. "You called me a thief when we first met."

"I saw too much in the young saru standing outside my glass cage. I didn't understand how you were there, how you had a queen's magic wrapped around you and living tek attached to your hip." He flicked a glance to where my whip sat now, peeking out from beneath my coat.

"A human can't steal magic. It must be gifted," I reminded him. Then I recalled the wound in my thigh and how it had miraculously healed in hours. I remembered other things too, such as how I had recovered from the Dreamweaver's affections with Talen and Kellee's help. I hadn't been bonded to Talen then. Perhaps Eledan hadn't taken all his mother's magic like he'd thought.

"And yet you are the only human I've ever known who has wielded fae magic without it ravaging their mind."

I let his words sink in, let all their hidden secrets and things he didn't say permeate the air and my thoughts.

Nothing girl.

No, she is everything.

I would be a fool to ignore how there was more happening here, more I didn't understand, but Talen did. The fae with all the secrets. "You knelt to me." It had been the first time I'd seen a fae shed tears. "Why?"

"I begged you to free me." His smile grew. "Perhaps I wasn't speaking of Kellee's cage."

"You weren't?"

"Free me from this prison. Do this one thing and I will be yours," he repeated wistfully. The memory of those words was so vivid that I saw him on his knees again, his hand pressed to the glass. And just like back then, my saru heart fluttered, an eager, fragile thing.

"Sure sounds like you meant the glass cage." I kept my tone light in the hope he would keep talking and not shut me out like all the other times I'd tried to get answers out of him.

His smile stayed. "There are many prisons, Kesh. Some are visible, and some are not as obvious."

"In that case, which prison was I freeing you from, if not Kellee's glass one?"

He looked over, met my inquiring gaze, and his smile faded. "The same one you are trapped in."

I opened my mouth to deny I was inside any kind of prison, but Kellee's sharp whistle shattered the moment.

We had reached the hole into the tunnels. It had widened since we'd left it, turning into a crater, with multiple tunnel mouths branching off to cyn-knew-where.

"Sota, can you do an infrared sweep and see how many tunnels there are and where they lead to?"

Sota buzzed upward. The rest of us lingered near the edge of the sinkhole, equal parts intrigued and wary. Even Sirius eyed the hole in the ground with trepidation. But it was Kellee's reaction I sought, and by the hard stare he sent my way, he knew the evidence was grim.

"There are, within range, fifteen tunnels," Sota reported. "Half intersect at various locations beyond this plain. One appears to head toward the settlements. One terminates precisely four hundred meters from here."

"Where that tunnel terminates, is there anything beyond it?" I asked, thinking of the foreign stone Arran and I had discovered.

"There is a substantially cooler pocket nearby."

"Cooler by how much?" Kellee asked.

"Hapters surface temperature is on average twenty-five degrees. The pocket is approximately twelve degrees."

It could be a cavern or water. In fact, water could have formed the entire tunnel network. "Irrigation?" I asked the others.

"Perhaps," Kellee replied, not convinced.

I caught Arran's gaze, his eyes glittering with anticipation. In the arenas, we had always stuck together, and when we weren't together, we'd always had a plan. The others looked to me for answers. All but Sirius. The guardian peered into the hole in the ground, his ruthless mind turning over clues and possibilities. All of this, every second, every word, he would report to Oberon.

"Sirius, stay topside," I said.

He grunted and jerked his chin at Arran. "Have the saru guard the hole."

I freed my whip and arched an eyebrow at the guardian. "*The saru* isn't likely to sabotage this mission. You, however, are less of a threat up here than you are down there."

"I am the king's guardian. I follow my king's command. Not yours, Wraithmaker."

I held the guardian's stony glare, silently reminding him of our deal. *He helps me, I help him.* "Are we having a problem?"

He lifted his chin enough to declare his defiance, and

then stepped back from the edge. "I've decided I will stand watch."

I ignored Kellee's narrowing eyes, saying, "Sota, stay close," and stepped off the edge into the hole.

Talen landed effortlessly beside me. "If we split up, we'll cover more ground," he said. Splitting the team to explore the tunnels made the most sense. We could cover more ground and everyone here was more than capable in combat. But splitting up would make us vulnerable.

Kellee dropped in next, followed by Arran. I scanned the three males, each wearing their own fierce intensity. Whatever our problems, and we had many, these males were here, standing with me. That meant more than they'd ever know. Pride thrummed warmly through my chest, lending me a new kind of strength.

Sota drifted down. "Splitting up is how people get dead."

"No splitting up," I told them. "Not yet." The tunnel Arran and I had already explored beckoned. I ventured in. The sweetness of freshly dug earth hung in the air, and it was noticeably cooler than before. "Talen, I want you up front with me. Kellee and Arran, watch the rear."

Talen moved up, but so did Kellee. "What deal did you strike with the guardian to have him obey you like that?" In the dark, with only Arran's and Sota's flashlight to guide us, the gold surrounding Kellee's dark pupils flashed. Nothing got past him. I held his gaze, answering the challenge with my own. I would tell him. Later.

"C'mon," I spoke up. "It's time we found some of Hapters's answers."

Kellee's attention cut deeper now I hadn't answered him. He didn't like being kept out of the loop. Well, now he knew what it felt like.

The tunnel swallowed us just like before. This time, Sota's high-intensity beam flooded the path ahead with brittle white light, washing every shadow away. But when we approached the wall of black rock, it absorbed even Sota's artificial light, peeling it away from the tunnel edges and guiding it in. I'd never seen anything bend light that way. The others saw it too but said nothing. Acknowledging Faerie's magic was another way of giving it power.

The old fae words glittered like spider webs lit by morning dew.

Time, our prison,
Dark, our sentence,
Light, our freedom.

Nobody spoke. Talen stepped forward. The iron inlaid words began at his eye level and climbed higher. He looked at them with the same awe as when he had admired the stars in the sky, as though they held a wonderment I couldn't possibly understand. When he touched the swirling trace of the first word, he hissed and yanked his hand back. Iron. *Pure* iron from his reaction. I expected him to move away, but he tilted his head, frowned, and then slammed his hand against the words.

And everything caught fire.

The blast of heat and light shoved me back. I leaned into it to keep from falling, and then as quickly as it had blasted outward, it blinked away, leaving the entire wall of black stone sparkling as though sunlight lit it from behind. Every internal shard, every sparkle blazed, scattering a kaleidoscope of color across Talen's face and clothes, lighting him up and searing the image of him aglow into my mind.

He cradled his fist against his chest. The light still blazed, but Talen's pain-riddled face had nothing to do with his hand and everything to do with the rippling brightness in front of him.

I stepped farther away, squinting into the light. At first, the sparkles appeared to be random, but slowly, an image took shape, one I hadn't seen since I'd left Faerie almost six years ago. Inside the wall, hidden by the dark and only visible with the light cast behind it, was a map of Faerie's night sky.

"What is that?" Arran whispered.

"Something that should not be here." I moved back another step, reading the entire view. I only recognized a small section of the map, the part visible from the crystal palace, but I could trace the imaginary lines between the stars as easily as the lines across my palms.

I tapped a finger against my palm, discreetly alerting Sota and using our ocular link to have him store several still images for later study.

Talen looked over his shoulder, past me, straight to Kellee. "Eledan was here?"

Why did a map of Faerie's sky have anything to do with Eledan and how by-cyn did he even suspect Eledan of being here?

"A long time ago," Kellee replied, his voice pitched low. "We don't know if he saw this."

"He did," Talen replied solemnly like he was delivering a death sentence.

"Oberon has Eledan locked down tight," Kellee said.

Arran pulled my gaze to his. He had the same questions in his eyes that I did. They were keeping us in the dark. Anger and frustration fizzled hot and sharp where pride had glowed before.

"I wouldn't be so quick to dismiss Eledan." I heard the coldness in my voice and liked it. I liked it even more when Kellee and Talen looked at me, both needing my answers.

Eledan might have been buried in a hole somewhere, but if I believed the illusion of him I'd witnessed in Arcon, the mad prince had means of escaping. At least part of him did. He could dreamwalk. Neither Kellee nor Talen knew that and I couldn't think of a way of telling them without them twisting the words into an accusation against me.

The heavy weight of the talisman in my pocket reminded me of how Eledan could weave his way into human lives and linger there like a malignant tumor. Did he still linger in mine?

"What do you know?" Kellee asked.

If I told the marshal how I'd potentially spoken with Eledan before the Game of Lies and had kept it a secret all this time, he would never trust me. "Just that a fae with his abilities probably has other means of getting what he wants. Why don't you tell me why his seeing this is so important? He has seen Faerie's night sky his entire life."

I looked between them, at the silent conversation they were having with their eyes, excluding the rest of us. Damn them, their secrets, and their distrust. We couldn't go on like this. They would have to trust me or the Messenger would never be anything more than a myth. "One of you had better start explaining this or this ends right here, right now."

Talen's gaze slid to me, lingered for a few pensive seconds, and then he faced the wall and its glowing star map. "Three star systems in total," he began. "All viewed from Faerie." He pointed at a cluster of bright lights. "Sol with Earth at its center." At another. "Valand." Lower and lit by a tight cluster of stars. "Halow." At the heart of each system, marking them like laser points, an intense red light pulsed.

So, it was a map. Why did they both look as though this map was a whole lot more than that. "And?"

"Three systems, each with a fragment of Faerie hidden within them," Talen said grimly. The red stars throbbed hotter. Beacons. Targets. "The unseelie are not myths, and they are not gone, but they are forgotten. This map shows exactly where to find them and potentially the means to free them." Talen turned his back to the map. Backlit, his expression was difficult to make out. But more than that, his outline blurred, losing its solid edges, crafting shadow where no shadow should be—inside the light.

Once more, Talen's gaze fell to Kellee. "If Eledan saw this... he may have already found the pieces."

Kellee held Talen's gaze, the two of them sharing the weight of something bigger than a map to the unseelie hordes.

Kellee's jaw twitched.

"It must be destroyed," Talen said.

"Wait." I stepped forward, but Talen was already turning toward the light, his hand reaching outward. "Don't!"

Kellee's grip encircled my arm, holding me back. I tugged, but his grip held. I would have swung for him if Talen's touch hadn't connected with the map at the exact same time as Kellee's arm wrapped around my waist. Light poured in from all sides, so bright and so hot that my fury at Kellee for holding me back dissolved under the scorching onslaught. There was a noise too, like rock breaking, earth moving, worlds breaking apart. And then a silence so thick it smothered me.

"Kesh!" Sota flew to my side. "I can't see!"

I shoved Kellee back, clasped Sota in my hands, and peered into his red lens. "Are all your sensors out?"

"All of them. Only infrared is functioning."

"Use that. I'll fix you..." I trailed off as I noticed the rock the map had been etched inside was warped and twisted. There was little left but veins of silver.

Talen had destroyed it. He lifted his gaze to me, his eyes downcast because he felt the thin thread of rage flowing through me. The map could have been valuable. We could have kept it safe, could have used it, but more than that, he and Kellee had taken the decision away from me. Because I was saru. Because there was more happening behind all this that I didn't understand. And they continued to keep me in the dark. I was just a face to them. Just the Messenger myth.

An animal screech erupted from the black space behind Talen, sounding like claws on glass.

Talen whirled.

Sota shot from my grip. "Incoming!"

A wet, earth-rich wind blasted from deep within the darkness, and a wall of air, broiling with wings, claws, and fangs, poured over us.

CHAPTER 15

*A*t the Game of Lies when the kelpie had tried to drown and trample me, I'd been at the mercy of Faerie's whim. When the tunnel beneath Hapters's plains filled with the same kind of wild vortex of chaos, I felt the same helplessness, as though Faerie had me in her enormous grasp and could crush me at any second.

Creatures howled as one, pouring into the tunnel like a monstrous storm funneled into a narrow space. Their claws tore up my back and slashed my face. I fought to bring my hands up as a shield, but leathery wings beat the air and sharp teeth snapped, snickered, and flashed.

Someone called my name, but the noise and pain swallowed that too. Dropping to my belly, I crawled forward. The screaming winged beasts sailed overhead, occasionally clipping my clothes and hair. I'd lost Sota somewhere in the melee and the ocular link was filled with so much chaos that I'd had to shut it down. One reach at a time, I moved forward, blocking out their screams.

Something collided with the side of my head hard

enough to dull the noise, and stopping seemed like a grand idea.

A figure carved through the storm, broadsword slicing in an arc through the winged monsters ahead of him. His magic licked around him like flames. His reds took on a life of their own, lighting his clothes, his hair, all of him ablaze like a torch battling the dark.

He cut the winged beasts down and stepped over their flailing bodies. Eventually, the stream learned to swerve around the male, and as he reached down for me, the beasts swerved around us both. I took his hand and scrambled to my feet. Sirius turned and led me back. A scream came at us. He cut the thing down with one deadly swipe. It slammed into the tunnel floor. The body was the size of a male fae, with the same humanoid figure but wrapped in leathery wings. It had claws and teeth that crowded its too-wide grinning mouth.

Sirius continued onward.

I tore my bloody hand from his. "Wait! The others!"

"Their survival is not my concern!"

"You said..." A winged fae dove above our heads. Sirius cut it out of the air, practically severing it in half. It flopped to the ground, bucking and flipping, and then stopped moving altogether.

The guardian's emerald eyes scored into mine. "I said I wouldn't kill your friends, not that I'd save them." He held out his hand again while the walls moved and the dark fae screamed their hideous song.

"I can't leave them."

"If they cannot save themselves, what good are they to you?"

Arran's sharp whistle penetrated their howls, coming

from ahead, behind Sirius, and what must be the way out. Arran was okay. That meant Kellee and Talen were probably okay too.

I took Sirius's hand. Cool flame danced up my arm. I almost yanked my hand back, but the touch wasn't hot. It flickered and licked over my torn coat, summoning something of Talen's golden magic from within me and lighting me up in the same way Sirius glowed. The guardian cut a path to the crater hole.

I grabbed the dangling rope and climbed out to the sight of Hapters's sky simmering with dark fae. They fanned outward, blocking the light from Hapters's twin moons and cawing into the night. I might have thought it beautiful if I hadn't felt the sting of a thousand cuts.

Kellee was running... toward me. I frowned, wondering where the others were and why Kellee was clutching his side, his face fierce with determination. "Run!"

Run?

The air shimmered between us, bending around something larger than us, exactly as it had bent around the unseelie in the tower.

There were more of the unseelie monsters, just like I'd feared.

I freed my whip, aglow with magic that wasn't mine, and saw the new unseelie's eyes burn red through the rippling illusion.

Air rippled to my right. Another one.

More than two.

How many?

Too many. And all cloaked.

I had never fought in a battle before. Never seen anything more than organized arena combat. This wasn't a one-on-one game to entertain an audience. The sky writhed with wings and talons. Screams drowned out my cry for Kellee. And the smell of wet meat, of blood and bone and dead things left to rot clogged my throat. And inside it all, I felt small, like I was in the eye of a storm I had no chance of controlling.

"Nightshade," a deep, wrangled voice gurgled to my right. The word was wet, the stench of its breath like poison.

I had always believed I could fight and kill anything and anyone. That I was the Wraithmaker and invincible. But that belief slipped away.

The beast in front of me charged, its illusion sloughing off. I saw Kellee leap, saw his claws flash and sink in, saw the beast rear up.

Something wet and thick and warm pushed against my neck and rode up my cheek. I swallowed and heard the *thing* make a deep, rumbling sound. A laugh.

"A fleshling with power. Mmm..."

It huffed, blasting me with its breath, and then reared. I saw it towering over me, saw its claws spread just like Kellee's, saw its mouth yawn wide, opening to devour me in a single bite.

Sirius slammed into my shoulder, knocking me off my feet. I hit the ground, rolled, and the terror that had clamped me still snapped loose. But it was too late for Sirius.

The beast's mouth came down. The guardian plunged his sword inside its throat, up to his own elbow, but whether he missed the mark or if he'd acted too late, the strike did nothing to slow the beast down. The beast's massive mouth slammed shut around Sirius's arm, sword and all. It jerked its head, lifting the guardian into the air, lashing him left to right like a rag doll.

I was running, whip cracking, but too late. We were too small and too few to fight so many monsters.

The beast shook the guardian and then tossed Sirius aside, done with him. I cracked the whip, zipping open the beast's left eye. It reared and howled in agony, turning toward me and away from where Sirius had fallen. I skidded in, slipping between its forelegs, and there I planted a string of tek-razors. Jaws snapped in. I rolled aside. The razors exploded behind me and peppered the beast's underbelly with holes. It screamed, whirled on me, and froze.

In my left hand, I held up the brooch as high as I could stretch my arm. The talisman throbbed its magical beat, and to my surprise as much as the beast's, the tek flung silver vines outward, unraveling, twisting, becoming something bright and alive and hungry in my hand. The people of this planet knew it could protect them. That was why the mother had been reaching for it. She'd been too late. But I wasn't.

The talisman glowed a deep undulating glow, light like Talen's inside me. The light of Faerie.

The beast dipped its head, and its one good eye darted, as though the thing were ashamed to be seen.

Snarls rippled across its lips. And then slowly, begrudgingly, it pulled its glamour over itself and slunk away.

It wasn't over.

The sky was so thick with dark fae that barely any light leaked through their swirling vortex of bodies. The plains below them rippled with moving shadows, the ground alive with the unseen.

Hapters was theirs.

TALEN HAD GUIDED SHINJ, the warcruiser, over the town-ship, enabling us to collect our shuttle, Hapters's remaining colonists, and Sirius's scattered flight of fae scouts. The warcruiser groaned her displeasure, but she loosened up as we climbed through thinner air and eventu-ally entered the planet's orbit. Below us, the once peaceful farming planet bled black like rotten fruit.

I'd wanted to help these people, but somehow, I'd condemned their homes to the unseelie. This wasn't my fault. If Kellee and Talen had told me even half of the truth, I could have planned. I could have prevented this.

"Sensors back online," Sota announced from his favorite shelf inside my chamber. He had been rebooting while I had walked the ship, helping people get settled. I knew how unnerving it could be inside a sentient ship, especially as their last visit to a fae ship had been as pris-oners. I assured them my ship was different. Some believed me. But some looked at me like Kellee sometimes did—with a heavy dose of skepticism.

"Good." Earlier, I had spread Talen's coat out across my bed. The dark fae had torn it to strips, but it was resealing itself. I too had healed the thousands of cuts in a way that wasn't possible for saru. More questions circled my thoughts as I watched the coat shimmer.

The collective injuries of the crew were minor. Nobody had died and the people were safe. All but Sirius.

"How is the guardian?" I asked Sota.

"Unconscious but stable."

We would struggle to control the fae scattered among

the survivors without Sirius, but we had time before they organized themselves. The fae flight had also regarded me with skepticism, suspicion, and outright hostility. I couldn't blame them for that. As the face of the Wraith-maker and the Messenger, I was hated and loved on all sides. Around Talen, who had walked the ship beside me, Sirius's flight had regarded us curiously.

Sota hovered off his shelf and drifted across the room to where I stared at the coat.

"I want to ask you a question," the drone said.

I looked up. He wasn't usually careful with his words. Perhaps Talen was rubbing off on him. "Then ask it, Sota." I smiled reassuringly.

"The others haven't noticed, but they don't see you like I do."

He didn't need to say any more, because he was Sota and he saw all the things the rest of us missed.

"I noticed immediately after you rebooted me on Arcon. You exhibited fae characteristics then. They've been increasing, changing you. I've heard the others speak of a bond. Are you bonded with Talen?" Was there a hint of sadness in his voice?

"Yes."

"It's changing you."

"Yes, it is."

"Did you know it would?"

I looked my friend in his single lens. "No. It's... I don't think he meant for it to get this far. The initial bond wasn't as strong as it is now. But after I helped him break free of this ship, the connection between us widened. Something changed. I don't know how to explain it. It feels more solid. And it's changing me."

"He knew it would." Sota's lens didn't waver. He had an

unnerving ability to stare through people, like he was doing with me now. He knew when my heart rate increased and when my temperature fluctuated. He knew every nuance of my face, every flicker, every twitch. Sota was a walking lie detector. Perhaps that was why I had never lied to him. Never needed to.

"What makes you say that?"

Sota's lens narrowed. "He wants something from you."

"What do you think he wants?"

"I don't know, but I think it will hurt you."

"Talen won't hurt me. He can't. The bond ties us together. If he hurts me, he'll hurt himself."

"Not hurt like that, Kesh. A different hurt. A heart hurt."

I blinked at my drone, at the artificial components glued together by plant extracts, tek tiles, and Faerie magic. He still wore his battle scars from the time Kellee had torn him open. A few dents here and there, imperfections that made him perfect. What could he know of heart pain? Of the sting of rejection or the ache of losing someone you loved? I hadn't made him to *feel*.

"Do you know what that feels like?" I asked him quietly.

"Like an error inside I can't correct. Like when I hard-reboot and feel myself falling, even though my sensors indicate I'm not moving. Like an answer that should be simple but eludes me."

Holy cyn, the things he was describing sounded exactly like grief, perhaps even human despair, but where had it come from? I hadn't programmed anything like that into his system. Eledan had reprogrammed him, but the mad prince wouldn't bother adding emotional feedback when all he'd wanted from Sota was a means to control me.

"If he hurts you, I will hurt him," Sota said clearly, precisely.

I should have told him it wouldn't be necessary, should have ordered him not to hurt my friends like I had ordered Sirius. But somewhere inside, I had always believed Talen would hurt me too. It was why I'd asked him to seal the bond. Because he was fae, and they did not know any other way.

"C'mon," I told the drone as I headed for the door, leaving my self-healing coat on the bed. "Let's get some answers."

I HAD ASKED the ship to *remodel* the pilot's chamber, not knowing Shinj could hear or understand me, or if she would even listen. Much to my surprise, she had. Talen seemed surprised too as he drifted between the clearly defined seating areas, all grown from the walls and floor. Kellee eyed it all like it might swallow him if he sat down.

"I like it," I said as I entered the room, alerting them to my presence. "Sit. We have a lot to talk about."

Neither of them obeyed.

Kellee had ditched the fae leathers in favor of his well-worn duster. He had showered the dust and blood off and bore a striking resemblance to the cocky lawman I'd first met in the sinks. Even his smile played on his lips. All he was missing was his star. Getting off Hapters agreed with him.

Talen also looked more like his usual self, carved from unyielding rock, smoothed off, and polished to the height of fae elegance. Not a strand of hair was out of place. He sent long looks my way beneath long lashes. My saru heart did its usual flicker at the sight of him. He felt it, and the corner of his mouth ticked.

They were both in for a rude awakening.

"Close the doors."

Talen tilted his head. A knot gathered between his sweeping eyebrows. Even now he didn't trust me. But eventually, the doors whispered closed, sealing me, the two males, and Sota inside the pilot's chamber. Arran was with Sirius. He knew what was about to happen and had told me he was happy to sit this one out.

I eyed each male in turn. They waited. Kellee sat and kicked his boots up on the low table, crossing his legs at the ankle, pretending to be completely at ease with the growing tension.

"We can't do this if we're all lying to each other," I began.

Kellee snorted.

Talen blinked innocently, as sweet and harmless as candy.

"The two of you have known each other a lot longer than you've known me. You're both *old* in ways I can't begin to imagine. You've both seen and done things, been part of things, I'll never fully understand. But I'd like to. I want to know you, and I want to understand you—not like you understand each other, I know I'll never share that connection, but enough to know who I am dealing with. Because right now, we're strangers, and with each day that passes, I know you less and less."

Talen looked at me as though he was afraid to look away, and Kellee looked everywhere but at me. They were so very different but equally stubborn in their stoic silences.

All I heard was Sota's gentle humming behind my

shoulder. I sighed and approached the bench opposite the table from Kellee. I sat, gave them a few more moments of silence, ready to be filled, and said, "I'll tell you a secret. Then you tell me a secret. A trade of secrets, if you will. Can we do that?"

Kellee arched a dark eyebrow. "That's a dangerous game."

"It would be worthless if it wasn't."

He flicked his eyes to Talen, saw the fae fold his arms, still unblinking, and nodded. "All right, let's do this. It's been coming for a long time."

"I'll tell you one of my fears. I have many, but this one... it's been on my mind a lot."

Talen finally moved. He shook his head, his braids rippling. "You don't have to do this."

"I want to."

"No, this is not the way it should be." He started for the door.

Kellee's gaze dropped from the fae to me. I held the marshal's oddly challenging glare, a flutter of excitement stirring way down low as his gaze dared me to say something, do something, to stop Talen.

"Sota."

The drone buzzed to the door. I didn't look, knowing the drone now blocked Talen's path.

"We can play this game the easy way or the hard way," I said.

"You would use your drone against me?" Talen inquired, a dangerous note in his voice.

I turned in my seat and saw Talen cast his narrowed gaze over his shoulder. We were just getting to the truth, but he felt it enough to know this was a dangerous game indeed.

"You destroyed that map in an instant. If we are to continue this charade that the Messenger means something, then you'll sit with me, Talen, and you'll help me understand who you really are and what you want."

He lifted his chin. "There are myths far darker than the Messenger out there. It is those we should be addressing."

"Why did you destroy the map?"

"You know why."

"No, I don't. It showed the sites of the unseelie. So? It had been there for a thousand years and you put your hand on it and turned it to molten rock in seconds. What was really on that map?"

My stubborn, cold, distant fae looked through me. Hair of silver and eyes like Faerie's sunfalls, his touch rooted around my heart, a stranger. But he didn't have to be.

"Tell her," Kellee grumbled, indicating he knew something, probably most things.

Talen sent his gaze across the room, far from me, from us. "I cannot," he whispered.

"You can't or you won't?" Kellee asked.

I fought the urge to look at the marshal. It almost sounded as though he was on my side.

"Can't."

I heard Kellee move, sensed he had leaned forward. "But there's nothing to stop me from telling her?"

Talen's expression ticked. "Are you so sure you know?"

The marshal glared right back. "I'm not just a pretty face." His smooth words were barbed.

Stardust and shadow.

He has another name, one he guards as closely as I guarded my heart.

An affinity with Faerie's creatures.

Eledan had been on Hapters a long time ago, and there the people had fixed him, made him a tek-heart, made him their messiah. That map had been there just as long. The unseelie too. Talen feared Eledan's knowledge of the map and the whereabouts of the unseelie. He feared it so much that he'd destroyed the map before anyone could fully understand what it showed.

Talen, who I had seen walk among the fae and have them hanging on his every word. Talen, who could control a warcruiser by asking nicely.

I looked up at the silver veins marking the pilot's chamber ceiling and remembered how he had torn himself from the ship—right here. I remembered how I had seen something of him take the light and twist it. And I remembered falling through the Dreamweaver's darkness to find my silver fae. Only, what if it hadn't been the Dreamweaver's darkness at all?

"You're the Nightshade." It felt right. Every time the beasts had attacked me and spoken that name, I'd been aglow with Talen's magic. He was so different from anything I'd seen or heard of on Faerie. But he was light and the Nightshade was dark. Wasn't it?

I looked up. "You are, aren't you?"

His lips twitched as though he might smile at my foolishness. "No."

"Then what?!" I snapped.

"I'm stardust—"

"Sweet cyn, fuckin' fairies and their drama," Kellee growled.

"Oberon—" Talen began.

"Doesn't need to know, right Kesh?" Marshal Kellee held my gaze. "Because if there was ever a secret you needed to keep from the king, it's this one. You told Talen

197

your saru name—no, he didn't tell me it, because he has integrity. I figured it out because I can't miss the way he looks at you. Do you have integrity, Kesh? He's about to put his life and the lives of billions of people in the hands of an infamous liar and killer. Because he trusts you. Because he knows you." Kellee tapped his fingers to his chest. "He *knows* you inside. I think he's a fool, but what do I know? I'm just the last vakaru. So, Kesh, can Talen trust you?"

A knot twisted in my throat, so I almost choked on the word. "No."

Kellee blinked. "What?"

"Don't tell me." Panic contracted my heart in my chest. "You can't trust me."

"Kesh?" Kellee growled the warning inside my name.

"Because you were right. As much as I want to believe I'm my own person, I can't be sure. Talen is obviously important. I thought I needed to know who he was, but..." I thought of Sirius and my agreement to return to Faerie with him, to return to Oberon and somehow end this war from the inside. I had killed a queen I loved. I could do the same again. I had that power. Nobody else did. I couldn't give that up. But going back made me vulnerable. And the Dreamweaver... Without a collar, he could get inside my head. He had at Arcon. The illusion of him had plucked secrets right out of my thoughts. I couldn't know the truth of Talen and go back to Faerie with that knowledge. I didn't trust myself enough.

"Don't," I said again. "I'm sorry... I want to be your hero, but I can't."

"Kesh?" Kellee pleaded.

"Open the doors." I got to my feet. So much for

getting answers. All I'd done was expose myself as the fraud they had always believed me to be.

The doors stayed closed, and Talen looked at me with apologetic eyes, breaking bits off my heart. Kellee's gaze was worse, as though he understood. *I can't be the person you want me to be.*

"This won't work." I divided my attention between them. Kellee's dismayed face and Talen's regret. I wanted so badly to be like them, to be the hero Aeon had ached to have come and save them all. But I wasn't there yet, and no matter how I tried, I might never be. "Do you want to know my secret?"

"Kesh—" Talen stepped forward, reaching as though he could stop me.

I lifted a hand, holding him back. They needed to hear this. "Eledan... He got to me. He got to me in a way I can't brush off or pretend didn't happen. He pulled out my fears and made them real. He... he has a name for me. He's not gone. He's still up here"—I pointed at my head—"in a way I think might be real." I paused, waiting for their argument, waiting for them to stop me, and I saw the same two hopeful faces who had brought me back from the Dreamweaver's grasp all those months ago. But while I'd physically recovered, mentally, I was a mess and was only now realizing how much I still had to heal.

"He calls me the *nothing girl*. Because he knows, underneath all this pretend Messenger costume, I'm just another saru. He knows the truth. You are right not to trust me. What I want doesn't matter; it's what I do that matters, and I *am* Oberon's. I always was, from the moment I slit Aeon's throat. I can't stop being his by saying the words. It'll take more and I'm not ready. I'm sorry. I'm sorry to the both of you. I never meant for it to go this far. The

Messenger is just a dream, just like the life you'd have with me."

I turned my back on them and strode to the farthest door. "Open it, please." I couldn't hide the depth of my pain from Talen, but at least he knew my words were true.

The door opened, and it was all I could do not to run.

CHAPTER 16

Asleep, Sirius looked like a chiseled god from Talen's Old Earthen history books. The tipped ears gave his fae genetics away; those and the ruby shades of red in his hacked-up hair meant he couldn't possibly be human. Of the four royal guardians, he was the one who had both fascinated and frightened me when Oberon had first taken me aside.

I'd willingly fallen into admiring him as I'd sat beside his bed, waiting for him to wake. It was difficult not to look and easier to dream than to live the life rapidly unraveling around me. I'd rarely gotten so close to the guardian. He had made sure to always keep his distance.

The guardian's golden lashes fluttered, but he stayed asleep, his chest rising and falling steadily.

He was my key to returning to Faerie without being shot through the heart on arrival. *Your king needs you.* Oberon was Sirius's weakness—and one I would gleefully exploit.

His eyes snapped open. Green blazed and then locked on me. He gasped and jolted upright.

"Easy there." Arran swooped in, but Sirius wasn't looking at him or me.

He lifted his right arm. Four tek-fingers and a tek-thumb curled inward.

"It was the best we could—" I started.

Sirius lunged for the nearest figure—Arran—snatching with his intact left hand. The grab was sloppy, giving me time to fling myself between them. Sirius grappled pathetically with me, his tek-hand and wrist limp at his side. We tussled, and the sheets slipped and tangled between us. A frenzied wildness had fallen over him.

"Easy!" I tried pinning him down, only for him to buck me off, and then with a jarring *thwump*, the guardian and I fell in a heap on the floor. I had him pinned, one leg straddling both of his, while I had his good hand wedged against the bed, bringing me so close to him I felt his trembling as though it were my own. He blinked, unsure where he was. Recognition softened his glare, and I became aware that I was propped on the guardian's lap. Then he lifted his tek-hand. Light slid across the bare metal fingers. Shock widened his eyes. Fear too. He shook his head and scrambled backward, shoving me off him.

"It's okay..." I hadn't expected this, though perhaps I should have.

"No, no, no...." he murmured over and over and over, holding his arm out as far as possible.

I glanced behind me at Arran.

"I could put him out again?" he suggested.

I shook my head. "He just needs time... to adjust."

"Get it off," the guardian growled, more animal than fae. He yanked on the metal limb.

"It's fused." He'd need to hack at his flesh with his sword to get it off.

He pulled again, baring his teeth and putting considerable strength into it. His abs quivered and glistened with perspiration.

Arran and I had built the arm and borrowed the ship's abundant life magic to bind the tek to the sidhe lord. Now, I wondered if that had been the wrong thing to do. But a guardian with a missing arm was no guardian at all.

"My sword. Saru!" he barked at Arran. "Get me my sword."

"It's gone," Arran replied flatly.

Sirius swung his glare on me. "You did this."

"I... we fixed it."

"You did all of this!" He sprang.

I swung an open-handed slap he could have avoided had he been thinking clearly. My palm struck the side of his face, sending a fiery bloom up my arm and shocking him to a halt. "Your arm is gone. You can't grow limbs back. If you ever want to wield a sword for the king again, you'll need this tek. Without it, you're useless to Oberon."

His fury was so thick I could taste it, but after a few nostril-flaring moments, he retreated against the bed. "This cannot be. Don't you see? I cannot go back to him like this, calla." He lifted the arm and gawked at it like it was a hideous disfigurement. I found its sleek metal beautiful, but I understood why Sirius might not.

"He will shun me," Sirius whispered. "Or worse." A shudder ran through him. "I have failed him." He sagged and stared at the arm, now resting on the sheet covering his lap.

"You're alive. The rest we'll deal with when the time comes."

I left the guardian muttering to himself and posted Sota by the door, just in case he got any ideas about rousing his flight and taking the ship for himself. He wasn't mentally sound enough, but he would recover quickly, and then I'd have an angry, clear-thinking guardian on my hands.

Arran stayed with me as I walked deeper into the ship, passing people busying themselves in the corridors and children sprinting from one end of the decks to the other. I found my secret pool, rolled up my pants to above the knee, and sat on the edge, dangling my feet in the water. If there were any ship parasites, I was beyond caring.

The map, my confession, the unseelie, and the knowledge of what we had to do weighed me down. I needed space, and time to collect my thoughts.

"Mind if I join you?" Arran thumbed at the pool.

"Go right ahead." I braced my arms behind me and watched him pull the shirt over his head, revealing rippling abs that Hulia would have been measuring for profit. He kept his pants on and dove in, quick as an arrow. I quelled the nerves at the sight of the water swallowing him whole and waited for him to resurface. When he did, he was almost on the other side. He swam on, focused as though he had a goal in mind. He moved effortlessly through the water, barely making a ripple. Again, I wondered who had taught Aeon to swim and who had taught him to dance. There was much about his past Arran and I didn't know. There had been no time to get to know Aeon again before he ate the starfruit, and now there never would be. For him to swim like he did, for him to dance like he didn't have a care in the world, there must have been some good in his past somewhere.

"Where do you think you learned to swim?" I asked, unable to contain the question any longer.

He started swimming back toward me, a gleam in his

eye. "Maybe a sweetheart taught me on a world far from here?"

Well, that sweetheart certainly wasn't me. "Maybe."

He swam up to my legs and folded his arms beside me, propping himself on the edge. "The meeting with Kellee didn't go well?"

"That's an understatement."

"They're fools."

I managed a smile. "I'm the fool."

"Never."

His faith in me was sweet, if misplaced. "I have all these grand ideas about making a difference, ideas a friend had once given me, but surrounded by Faerie's creatures, like Talen and Kellee, I sometimes forget I'm saru, and when I remember, I realize I can't do these wonderful things because saru serve, and no matter how we try to change, we can't, not really." The tragic pilot's last plea for freedom haunted me. We were all trapped in servitude under the fae, even the fae themselves.

Arran considered my words. He propped his chin on his folded forearms and lifted his dark eyes. "You've already done so much. How can you doubt yourself?"

I leaned closer and spoke softly. "Do *you* think we can change?"

Aeon had believed it. He had believed it so fiercely that I carried that belief with me to this very day. A belief that we were more than what Faerie made us. My friend— the one who looked back at me now with no knowledge of his dreams or beliefs—had believed in heroes. But I wasn't asking Aeon. I was asking Arran.

He considered it. "Yeah, we can change. Everything changes, given enough time."

"Not the fae."

"Yeah, well, that's their loss. Change is a good thing."

Change is coming. Sonia—a saru who had lost everything she had worked for, a woman braver than I—had told me that.

"What's next for us?" Arran asked.

"I'm... I don't know. I can't see us shoving the unseelie back into the hole they crawled out of, so I guess we'd better find somewhere safe for Hapters's people until we can figure out how to get rid of the unseelie. After that..." *I go back to Faerie with Sirius.* "I don't know."

Arran's eyes sparkled. "Do you have time for a swim?"

"Here?"

"Why not?"

The water looked bottomless, as though things could get lost in its depths, never to be seen again. And then there was Arran, half-smiling up at me, his face hopeful. There were a million reasons why getting in the water with him was a terrible idea.

"I'll keep you safe," he said, sincerely.

I had never doubted that. "Arran, we can—"

He laughed, cutting off my friend-zone talk, and grumbled, "Get in the water, Wraithmaker." The sideways look he threw me was pure Aeon mischief, the same look he'd toss my way when he was about to stoke Dagnu's rage, just because he knew how to get a rise out of our fae jailor, the same look he'd toss me when he had stolen something precious from a fae lord. "This is one of those opportunities you don't say no to. Unless you have lives to save somewhere?" He kicked off the side and swam backward, splashing me. "Is the Wraithmaker scared of a little water?"

I rolled my eyes. *Yes.*

He kicked water at my face. "Make me stop."

"You're annoying."

"Oh, I'm annoying? Like this?" Another flick.

Fat drops landed on my clothes. I wiped them off with a scowl.

He changed course, and with a few broad strokes he was by my legs, peering up through his wet lashes. He rested his hands on my thighs, and when I didn't protest, he dropped them between my thighs and eased my knees apart, placing himself between them. "Still annoying?"

The right thing to do would be to tell him to stop, to walk away like all the times Talen had walked away from me, but I didn't want to and he didn't want me to, so what was so wrong about any of this?

"Tell me to stop." He ran his hands down the outside of my thighs where the wrinkled fabric bunched, bringing him so close he had to crane his neck to see my face. His eyes were kind and proud. They always had been. His face was open and unguarded. With me, he was Arran, no lies, no games.

Placing his hands on either side of my legs, he heaved himself out of the pool, soaking me in water and bringing his wet, smiling face an inch from mine. His eyes were bright and dancing the way they did before the arena. My heart raced, catching his excitement.

His arms quivered where he braced himself.

I hadn't moved, hadn't said a word. If he kissed me, I'd kiss him right back, because with Arran, everything was as it seemed. He had no secrets, none that he remembered. He was just uncomplicated, fun-loving Arran. But he deserved more, didn't he? I'd take him and twist him, break his heart. It was what I did. I'd already killed him once.

He must have seen my thoughts cross my face because

his excitement waned. "Guess not." He dropped back into the water and disappeared below the surface.

At times like these, I almost wished Oberon were here so I'd have orders to follow. How did free-loving humans make unguided decisions every day of their lives? How did they not make mistakes over and over and over? Or maybe they did. Maybe mistakes were the point?

I unlaced my waistcoat, dumped it to one side, and pushed myself over the edge, sinking legs first into the pool. Warm water tugged at my fitted undervest, lapping at my waist, and licked higher as I lowered myself all the way in until the surface rippled around my shoulders and chin. The fact I couldn't feel the bottom of the pool had my heart stuttering with fear.

Arran broke the surface in the middle of the pool, shook his head, flicking wet hair out of his face, and spotted me. His smile broadened. "There she is." He swam up to my side. "Not so bad, right?"

Fucking terrifying. I clung to the edge. "Is it deep?"

His lips twisted. "Very."

"Lie and tell me it's safe." I narrowed my eyes.

"Where's the fun in safe?" His deep voice rumbled.

"So, how do we do this?"

He blinked, and I noticed how water had beaded at the ends of his dark lashes. We had once cried in each other's arms, and his lashes had glistened wetly then too.

"Do what?" he asked, forgetting himself.

"Swim."

"Swimming, right. So, you *do* want me to teach you?"

I was in the damn water, wasn't I? "What else would I want?"

A dirty smirk tucked a corner of his mouth into his cheek. "We start by letting go."

My heart skipped. "Of the edge?" I wasn't sure I could do that.

He reached around and braced his arms on either side of mine, pinning me in. My heart raced for different reasons now. Thoughts too. Some of them nonsense. Most of them fearful.

He dropped his right hand below the surface and I felt his soft touch on my hip. Just light enough to steady me. "Hold on to me."

I didn't want to let go of the edge. Panic teetered at the edges of my thoughts.

"I've got you," he said, his voice deeper, darker, closer. "I'll always keep you safe."

I let go of the edge and grabbed his braced arm. It felt like corded steel beneath my grip. I settled my other hand on his shoulder and let him hold me in the water, away from the edge. This wasn't so bad. More floating than swimming, but it was a start. I smiled, and so close to Arran, the smile felt strange and new on my lips, like I was letting him see it for the first time. I didn't remember ever trusting anyone so completely, except maybe when I had opened myself to Talen to save him. But that was different. I hadn't had a choice. Here, now, nobody was trying to kill us, and nobody would die if I got this wrong. This mistake wasn't life or death; it was just Arran and me.

"In another world, there's a guy just like me and a girl just like you."

"Oh?"

"They're in a pool together."

"He's teaching her to swim?"

His eyebrow flickered. "She thinks he is."

"He's not?"

"He faked the whole thing to get her in the water."

"Oh." My soft smile grew. "That's... sly of him."

"Yeah, well, he tried to ignore it, but that didn't go so well."

"Ignore... what?"

He winced like he wanted to back away, but that couldn't happen now that we were here, pressed together in the water, him holding me up. Arran's smile turned serious, and I thought he was about to say something terrible, something that would ruin everything. "How strange it is to love someone he's never met."

But how could that be? He had forgotten everything, hadn't he? I smiled, maybe even laughed dismissively. "You can't—"

"I can."

He had forgotten his memories, but not his feelings. Aeon was still alive inside him, inside the emotion.

I brushed my fingertips against his cheek. Did his feelings for me make this worse or better? Was this wrong?

"You...?" *Love me?* I couldn't say it, because if I did, it would make it real, and frightening. No one had *loved* me before. Was it even possible to love someone like me?

"I tried not to," he said sadly and shrugged. "You don't feel the same, an—"

Fate and Faerie be damned. I kissed him. As I pulled myself close, I thought the widening of his eyes might be fear, so the kiss was quick and sharp. I hesitated and almost let go. But he cupped my face and kissed me like I was something to be savored, something to cherish, somehow gentle and possessive all at once. And I kissed him back, carefully, slowly, feeling the softness and warmth of a mouth I'd seen smile and laugh and joke too many times to count. I'd seen him scream, and rage, and cry. I'd seen him break and rise again. I'd loved him for years.

Loved him since he had been locked in the cell next to mine and he'd fought back. He wasn't Aeon but he was, and I was done trying to figure out what was right and wrong in this world. I was done playing the martyr.

He broke the kiss, bumped his forehead against mine, and peered into my eyes. "I've wanted to do that since I woke up in a new world with you looking at me like I'd lost my mind. It was the first thought I had, and I didn't even know who you were—or who I was."

I bit my lip to stop it from quivering. He was killing me. Each word cut deep, turning out all my fears.

"Nothing has felt as right as this..." He stroked my cheek, his thoughts lost in my eyes. "As real as this."

I leaned into his hand. His strong, calloused fingers spread and sank into my hair. In the past, his hands had been torn and bloody, clenched around bars. When he kissed me a second time, the intent behind it deepened, becoming stronger, hungrier. Doubts fell away. I threw my arms over his shoulders and pulled him closer, needing to feel him, to banish any space between us. He pressed me back against the side of the pool, but I wasn't trapped like I would have been with Kellee, and somewhere inside, the parts of me beyond thought recognized I wasn't afraid of Arran. There was no bond toying with my emotions, no teeth about to sink into my neck and tear me open. Arran didn't want anything from me. He was just Arran, and with him, I was Mylana again. Not the Wraithmaker, not the Messenger, not a distant, unobtainable hero with the hopes of a billion people pinned to her sleeve. Just a girl with a dream that someone might love her just for her, even after all the horrible things she had done.

With Arran, I was free.

The kiss ended softly and he brushed his cheek over

mine, bringing his mouth close to my ear. "I should probably teach you to swim, right? If I don't, it'll look like I got you in here for other reasons."

With my body buzzing to be touched and my head awhirl, learning to swim was the last thing on my mind, but I wouldn't rush this. It felt too good, right now, right here, with Arran looking at me like I was a long, cool drink on a hot Summerlands day. He was a gift. He was my hope.

"Okay, teach me to swim," I agreed. "But you've got your work cut out. I mostly just sink."

a few hours after my impromptu swimming lesson, I found a disused room not much larger than my old Calicto container. Benches had been grown from the walls, and a table had sprouted from the floor in the middle of the room, making it the perfect meeting chamber.

Sota sailed in. I pointed him toward the flattest wall. "There."

His lens extended, widened, and splashed a twinkling image across the smooth surface.

"I wonder if I can dim the lights in—"

The lights behind the walls dimmed. Apparently, the ship was listening.

"Hey, sugar, you called?" Hulia sauntered in to gape at the glittering image painted on the wall. "What is *that*?"

"A map of the star systems as viewed from Faerie."

"Holy sweet cyn on a tek-stick, that's... *beautiful*." She touched the image, upsetting the projection, which now coated her hand and arm. She let the captured star map paint her hand, and then frowned and withdrew. "Some of these stars aren't there anymore. The fae took them."

Took them meant destroyed. Tiny stars snuffed out, like the billions of lives they'd cradled before the fae returned.

I folded my arms and chewed on my lip, trying to make sense of the billions, perhaps trillions, of pinpricks of light. Each system had a red point at its center, just as Talen had said before destroying the real map.

"Your drone has the best resolution I've ever seen. What is that, like fifteen terrapixels? It looks real."

Sota hummed appreciatively. "Twenty. Size does matter."

Hulia chuckled. "Oh, Sota. I missed your sweet tek-ass."

"Not as much as I missed yours."

Hulia laughed harder. I rolled my eyes at the two world-class flirts. "Can we focus here?"

"Already am," Sota purred.

I fought my own laugh. "Sota, take the snark down a notch."

Hulia took up a spot on Sota's other side. "How come I'm here and not your entourage of Buns, Dark, and Icy?"

"Buns, Dark, and Icy?" I shook my head at her wicked grin. "Never mind, I don't want to know."

"Have you bedded all three yet?"

I wouldn't even acknowledge that question.

"She hasn't," Sota replied.

"Sota!"

"Are you insane?" Hulia exclaimed. "What the hell is keeping you? Give them to me. I'll dirty them up for you."

Oh, by-cyn, why had I thought bringing Sota *and* Hulia into this discussion was a good idea? "Hulia, just—"

"She did get hot and heated with Buns a few hours ago," Sota said.

Wait, what? "Sota, how do you know I was with Arran?" More to the point, how did he know Buns was Arran, unless he and Hulia had been talking? Of course they had. Sota was a terrible gossip, only matched by Hulia.

"I keep track of all the important individuals on the ship, and you spent exactly fifty-three minutes inside Arran's very personal space."

Hulia was giggling again. "That is *not* enough time to do the dirty in all the right ways."

I opened my mouth, stumbled over my words, and said, "He was teaching me to swim."

"Uh-huh." She made a point of staring at the map with her tongue firmly stuck in her cheek.

"I'd bang him," Sota said, "if I had all the right equipment."

I covered my face with my hands.

"You and me both. At the same time," Hulia agreed.

This was serious, and I could hardly keep a straight face. Damn them. "If neither of you have anything constructive to say, you can leave."

Hulia planted a hand on her hip and eyed me around Sota hovering between us. "Just say the word if you want any pointers. I bet I can coax out the namu in your uptight saru ass." She continued to stare, waiting for me to say something. "Did you kiss?" I didn't get a chance to reply as she read the admission on my face. "You did! Was it fast and hard or slow and soft?"

"I'm starting to regret our friendship."

"You can tell a lot by the first kiss. Fast and hard

usually means he'll be a royal pain in the ass, but slow and soft, those are keepers. So, which was he?"

I smiled at my friend, hiding my true thoughts behind the too-bright grin. "Duly noted. Now can we focus on the Faerie map and not Arran's buns?"

"Is this a hypothetical question?" Sota asked.

"No!" I laughed. They were both impossible.

"So, why am I here instead of your entourage?" Hulia asked again, once we had all settled down. "Icy alone looks like he could stare his way out of an iron box."

"*Talen* destroyed this map on Hapters and I... I don't want him knowing I have a copy. Kellee and Talen are tight, so it's just us."

"Ah." Hulia turned serious. "All right." She silently studied the map. "Well, I haven't been out of Halow much, but I know for sure that red dot in Sol is on Earth, so maybe the others are all locations in the systems' major centers?"

"Close."

"What *are* the red dots?"

"Unseelie, apparently. Or the location of something that can free the unseelie in those systems. It sounds like Oberon scattered and buried the unseelie throughout the three systems, Sol, Valand, and Halow, but right now, it's all guesswork. Talen wasn't specific before he melted the original map and the dark fae escaped."

"Talen released the dark fae?" Hulia asked, her singsong voice dropping to its darker tones that could sing a person into a coma.

I'd assumed the dark fae's escape had been an accident, but what if he'd known the dark fae were behind the map? He wouldn't do something so foolish as deliberately free them, would he? He had made mistakes before... This had to be a mistake—one that had cost a community its home, but a mistake all the same.

"What are you thinking?" Hulia asked.

"How little I understand all of this." *How little I understand Talen.*

I turned all the things I knew over in my mind. Too many times over the past few days the dark fae had uttered the name nightshade—the prophesized unseelie ruler who was supposed to rise up and lead the dark fae. The dead pilot had used his last words to warn me that the nightshade *watches*. Talen wasn't unseelie, but I suspected he wasn't seelie either, despite the light fae looks. But I'd asked Talen if he was the Nightshade and he'd denied it. He couldn't lie. Clearly someone or something was or had been the Nightshade, and the unseelie thought it important enough to mention it a few times before attacking me.

"Hulia, have you ever heard of the Nightshade?" I asked.

"Unseelie badass. A fairytale told to baby fae to frighten them. You think this map has something to do with the Nightshade?"

"Yeah, I do."

"Well *shiiit*."

"And I think Eledan knew it too. He was here. He spent time on Hapters. He saw the map. He knew the unseelie were here along with whatever magic source is feeding Hapters's crops, the same source the Hapters people call lumines."

"You're right." Kellee leaned against the doorframe, arms folded, looking every inch the smart-mouthed marshal who'd been standing there the whole time. Stealthy bastard. He wore all black under the lawman duster and had dug out his gold star. It glinted the same shade of gold as the rings around his dark pupils.

"Marshal Kellee is here," Sota announced, five seconds too late.

"Annnndd that's my cue to leave." Hulia headed for Kellee, still blocking the door.

He shifted out of the doorway. "You don't have to go."

She paused and raised an eyebrow at me. "A namu's gifts are better spent in the pursuit of pleasure, not war play."

Kellee gave her a dry look. "We've all evolved well beyond our intended design." He approached the map and looked it over, giving nothing away as though he were admiring a dinner menu. "No namu has ever stabbed the Dreamweaver in the back," he commented. "Yet, for a plea-sure-giver, you managed that pretty well. I also watched you try to slap down a royal guardian. I think I'd rather have you on my side, Hulia, than the snakelike namu of old."

Hulia's shoulders straightened with pride. She loved to be complimented and Kellee had found her weakness. "All right, Marshal. I'll stay."

He nodded once and the matter was settled. When he turned, projected stars speckled on his face. He thumbed over his shoulder at the map. "Knowledge of this map stays in this room. Should this get out, half of Faerie will come after Sota. Your drone's life depends on it."

"What?" Sota balked.

"The map is safe," I assured him. "Sota is secure. He can't be hacked."

"Didn't Eledan do exactly that when he turned Sota against you?" Kellee asked.

"Eledan is a fae who knows tek. He's one of a kind.

Plus, I deliberately left a programming door open for him so he could find out who I really was. Sota's databanks are encrypted. Nothing inside him gets out without my permission."

"Doesn't matter," Kellee said. "If anyone learns the map is on him, he'll be the most wanted piece of tek outside of Faerie, and they won't be kind in cutting him open."

Sota shuddered, rippling the map across Kellee.

"Understood," I agreed. "Sota's got this."

"I do?" Sota asked.

Kellee stepped out of the way of the projection. A silence settled over us as we waited for his opinion. "It's not a map to the unseelie," he said.

"But Talen said—"

Kellee's look cut me off. "You need to stop listening to his words and instead listen to his intent. There are things he can't say, exactly like lies. Listen to what he *isn't* telling you."

How was I supposed to do that? Talen's silences were everywhere.

Kellee sighed and looked through me, gauging my worth. "It's a map to the fragments of polestar."

I frowned. So did Hulia. Sota's motors whirred in a way that told me if he'd had a face, he'd have frowned too. What by-cyn was a polestar?

Kellee half-smiled at our collective ignorance. "I forget how young you all are. The polestar is a Faerie artifact, plucked from Faerie's sky by Queen Mab. Oberon and Mab used its light to overpower the dark fae—the unseelie —and drive them out of Faerie forever. Then, against Mab's wishes, Oberon broke the polestar into four pieces and scattered them so the unseelie could never be summoned back to Faerie."

"Four pieces? Why didn't he destroy the polestar completely?" Hulia asked. She had moved to a bench and sat down, looking wide-eyed and overwhelmed.

"It can't be destroyed, but it can be broken up or altered to resemble other things."

"Where was Eledan when this was happening?" I asked, the missing pieces of my puzzle slotting into place.

Kellee's eyes darkened at the mention of the mad prince. "History neglects much of Prince Eledan, besides his prowess as his brother's general. As second in line to the throne, Faerie's history cares little for the mad prince's past."

"Exactly how old *are* you?" Sota asked.

Kellee's smile twitched. "It was before even my time, but I make it my business to ask questions and always have, long before I became a lawman."

Questions he was now answering. What had changed to make him trust me? "And this map shows where the pieces are?" I asked.

"Considering the targeted locations, I'm guessing so. Halow"—he pointed near Hapters—"Sol, Valand, and there was one on Faerie."

"Why have a map?" I asked. "Doesn't that defeat the purpose of hiding the polestar to begin with?"

"We don't know the map was Oberon's. In fact, it probably wasn't. Someone else left it on Hapters eons ago, knowing time would swallow it. They probably always intended to return, but we got to it first."

"Someone who controlled the unseelie enough to station them here to guard the map and its fragment?"

Kellee nodded.

"The Nightshade?"

He scratched absently at his neck. "The unseelie had a ruler. Not born royal—the unseelie don't care for how rich a bloodline is. Their leader is tested and proven." He swallowed with a click. "The legend is Oberon killed the Nightshade in his crusade to banish the dark fae. Something or someone left the map there, hiding it long enough for these things to fall into myth. It could have been the Nightshade, if you believe the legends, but it could also have been Mab. She was known to leave Faerie on occasions. She left to forge the peace treaty with the humans during the first war. She could have buried the map on Hapters then."

"Would Mab go against her son's wishes?" I asked.

"She knew her son's ambitions. It was a matter of time before Oberon came to reign. This map could have been her backup plan, only she didn't get to use it..."

Because I'd killed her. An awkward moment stretched on.

Kellee cleared his throat and continued. "A thousand years ago, the fae fought with their human experiment." He turned his gaze back to the map. "Mab formed the peace treaty, giving up Faerie's sister systems to the humans. The fae withdrew from Halow, leaving their secrets behind. Hapters was settled and farmed, its inhabitants unaware of what lay buried beneath them. I was here for years and had no idea this went so deep. Bits of Faerie are all over Halow. People forget the fae were here first. They were, and still are, the protofae. They were the beginning of everything, the beginning of life."

It was a lot to take in, but one thing was clear: Oberon had wielded the polestar. It was a weapon fit for a Faerie king. A weapon fit for revenge. If the mad prince got hold of it, there was no knowing what he'd do, and he'd already been all over Hapters, twisting the planet around his fingers. "If Eledan saw the map, do you think he used it to find the pieces of the polestar?"

"When Faerie thought him dead, he had a long time to scour the systems for lost treasures. He was here. Yes, I think he saw it and used it. It's a good thing he's back on Faerie and far away from all this."

I thought of the magic and tek talisman. A trinket fashioned in the vein of Eledan's new heart.

I eased down onto a bench. *But Eledan isn't far away... He could be right in the room with us.* It was time Kellee heard the truth. "Something happened to me back on Calicto, right before the arena." I dared not look at Kellee. "I found Sota and tried to fix him, but I couldn't make him right."

The image of the map flickered as Sota cut the projection. He swiveled to face me. "Then how am I here if you did not fix me?"

And here it was, the moment I admitted just how compromised I could be. "*Eledan* was there."

"Like Devere?" Kellee asked, assuming I'd imagined Eledan.

I squeezed my eyes closed to block out the memories of Devere and his death. "No, not like that. It was... different. He wasn't imaginary. He wasn't physically with me either, but he was there and he knew things. He helped me fix Sota. He was *real*."

"He *helped* you?"

I winced at the accusation in Kellee's tone and met the marshal's guarded expression. "It's why I can't let you tell me about Talen. There's a risk the Dreamweaver can get inside my head whenever he wants, and I can't stop him, unless I wear a collar."

Kellee held himself still, motionless but for the twitch of his cheek. "How is it possible the Dreamweaver can mentally transcend millions of light years?"

I stared back, refusing to shrink from his tone. "Where there's a strong enough font of life magic—his magic—he can find me." Unfortunately, life magic was abundant in Faerie and apparently outside of it too. Arcon was built on it. It flowed through this ship like blood through its veins.

"Does he still walk your dreams?" Kellee asked, his tone slipping into the neutral lawman mode like it did every time he wanted to hide his feelings.

"No."

"Have you seen him since Arcon?"

"No."

"I did not detect Eledan after you brought me back, Kesh," Sota said to reassure me.

"I know, Sota, but I can't shake the feeling it was real. I don't have a good enough imagination to concoct the things he said or the way he looked." Scruffy, tired... a startling contrast to how I'd known him.

"Did he say anything we can use?" Kellee asked.

I'd spent the weeks since Arcon and Calicto trying to forget everything about Eledan.

I brushed a hand down my face and sighed hard, then looked up at Kellee's guarded expression. "Just that he was incapacitated, but he could still be anywhere his magic was at its strongest." And he'd tried to reel me in, tried to make me want to fall into the dreams with him again, fall and dream and dance with the Dreamweaver in the nowhere spaces. I'd been tempted. I didn't need to say it.

From the wariness in Kellee's eyes, he knew. He always had.

"We have to assume it was real," Kellee said. "You should have told me this before now."

"Yes, I should have, but you aren't the easiest person to talk to."

His lips twitched. "You could be a spy for Eledan, but you didn't tell me because it might annoy me?"

"Back off, Marshal," Hulia warned in the voice she used to scare angry and intoxicated revelers. "Or do you always blame the victim of a crime?"

"I'm not blaming her." He laughed darkly. "But this is about more than Kesh. Knowing Eledan can get to her is damn important. It makes her a liability."

Hulia's laugh came out laced with disbelief. She got to her feet and squared up to Kellee, rising onto her tiptoes to do so. "Doesn't that star on your chest mean you protect people?" Her third translucent eyelid flicked across her eyes, a sign she was one wrong word away from losing her namu composure.

Kellee peered down from his vakaru height into Hulia's narrowed eyes. "No offense, Hulia, but you don't know all the facts."

"I don't need to. Kesh is my friend and that means I help her, no questions asked. How many friends do you have, Marshal?"

I loved my friend in that moment.

She looked at me. "Any time you need me, I'll be here for you."

I nodded, afraid if I spoke it would come out all wrong. She left, leaving Kellee staring at the wall, his cheek flickering. Sota buzzed quietly in what would have been a thick silence.

"You were right not to ask any more questions of Talen," Kellee said. "Knowing Eledan can get to you, even here, changes things. I'm not the bad guy here, Kesh. You are and you know it."

I leaned forward and rested my elbows on my knees, clasping my hands together. "I wish I wasn't. I wish I was different."

He swallowed hard. "I don't." When he faced me, the golden glow in his eyes had died down, leaving him more like his normal self. "I'm hard on you because I want this to work, but every time we get close to something good, something else pulls it apart again. You're a brave woman, Kesh. You're not... a nothing girl. Eledan is poison." Kellee approached the table. "I don't wish you were different. I wish *things* were different. This war, and us, all of us... We can make a difference, and that's worth more than you or me."

Oh, I understood that. He had always been good. It was why I was going back to Oberon with Sirius. Would Kellee understand that I was walking away, not for him, not for us, and not for Oberon, but for Halow's right to be free?

"If Eledan has the polestar, or knows where it is... there's no knowing what he'll do with it. He'll kill Oberon, but I doubt he'll stop there." A thought occurred to me. "Can the polestar be used for good?"

He blinked, surprised by the question. "It's a Faerie artifact. Good, bad, they aren't Faerie notions; they're human ones. It can be used for anything its wielder desires."

"Could we use it to drive the dark fae back into their hole on Hapters or out of Halow altogether?"

His eyes darted, ideas forming. "Talen could... maybe. But we're not fae. It won't respond to us."

Weren't we? Talen's magic was changing me, and Kellee was two rounded ears away from being fae.

"On the map, where's the nearest piece?" I asked, my insides fluttering as a plan formed.

He closed his eyes. When he opened them, they were the truest shade of green they'd ever been. "Valand," he said with a growl that failed to hide the fracture in his voice.

The vakaru home. *Kellee's* home. "We should go there."

He swallowed and this time didn't succeed in hiding all the emotion on his face.

We were going back to where Kellee had been made in search of a piece of the star that could either save us or condemn us all.

"Thank you," he said, "for being honest with me. I know it cost you."

I tried to smile but didn't have it in me. "The truth is often painful, right?"

His expression was haunted. "More than you know."

CHAPTER 18

The warcruiser didn't ordinarily have windows, but after Talen had asked Shinj nicely, she grew one so we could view our approach to Valand. Talen hadn't asked why we had left Hapters or where we were going, but he watched carefully, his secrets and silence deafening.

Two days after agreeing we needed to go to Valand—days in which I'd spent much of my time checking on Sirius and learning how to swim with Arran while stealing long, lazy kisses in the pool—Kellee grunted at me to follow him to the viewing deck. He stood there now, on a raised platform, facing the window, lit by starlight.

I drew up next to him, trying not to feel too exposed in front of the great curved window holding back the vacuum of space.

When I had escaped from Faerie to find Eledan, I'd been so focused on finding the prince that I hadn't had much time for sightseeing or stargazing. But now, I watched as Halow's pinpricked black slowly gave way to hypnotic swirls of purples, greens, and golds. It was so beautiful I didn't have words for it, just feelings. Lots and lots of feelings swelled inside, threatening to bubble over. I wanted to step closer to the screen so I could see how the multicolored stars grew from specks of dust, to marbles, to planets. Some with rings, some peppered in storm eyes, some all purple or green. Each one was a part of Valand.

Halow wasn't like this.

I'd seen snippets of Halow's starscape. It was mostly black with scattered systems. But Valand... My saru heart swelled at the stunning sight. Tears were brewing in my eyes, and I had no idea why. I felt like a child seeing a galaxy of stars for the first time and didn't know how to voice my wonder.

I had my hand on the screen before I realized I'd moved. The ship thrummed beneath my touch. And beyond, Valand's galaxy of color sparkled. My dark, brooding vakaru had come from *here*?

"Kellee, it's..." My glee turned cold at his expression. He stood there, wrapped in dark colors, like a thundercloud on a Summerlands day.

"It's dead," he said.

I pulled my hand back. How could something so beautiful be *dead*? Not all of it, surely. An entire star system couldn't die, could it?

He joined me at the screen. His ghostly reflection shimmered on its surface beside mine.

"It looks exactly the same now as the day I left it all behind."

This was difficult for him. I wasn't certain, but I suspected he hadn't been back in a long time. Maybe not since Oberon had wiped out his people.

"Which one is your home?" I murmured.

Color danced in his dark eyes as he scanned the canvas of stars. "There. Named Valand, like the system it's cradled in." He tapped the screen and the ship helpfully ringed the planet in question, making it stand out from its neighbors. It had its own rings too, one made of golden dust and another of red, around a surface of greens.

For a people made for war, their star system was the most beautiful thing I'd ever seen. But there was no pride in Kellee's face, no wonderment, just cold, flat acceptance.

The fae warcruiser sailed closer to Valand, probably the first fae ship to enter Valand's space in centuries. I knew the fae had wiped out the vakaru, but why hadn't the humans colonized Valand? Sjora had said Valand was slumbering, but what did that mean?

"Where's the fragment of polestar?"

Kellee's eyes clouded over. He turned away from the screen, leaving me alone on the viewing platform. "I'm not sure," he said, leaving. "We'll start at the capital city."

I considered going after him, but I knew better than to crowd Kellee when he didn't want to talk. Instead, I faced the Valand system and wondered why Oberon would be so foolish as to destroy something so beautiful. It didn't seem like something the king I knew would do. He adored beauty in all its forms. But I hadn't seen what was left behind. Beauty sometimes hid an ugly core. Faerie was proof of that.

THE WARCRUISER SETTLED into Valand's orbit, and Kellee piloted our shuttle down into Valand's atmosphere. Below, the land shone in a multitude of greens. No oceans that I could see. As we drew closer, the patches of green adopted solid rectangular shapes, reminding me of Sjora's patchwork clothes, all stitched together with green thread.

Closer and the patches became miles upon miles of interlinked walls surrounding enormous step pyramids that climbed skyward. Everywhere I looked, the ground had been shaped and molded into a vast metropolis built of green rock, like a jewel glittering green from every angle. Closer still and Kellee piloted the shuttle through valleys between towering pyramid peaks, making them look like manufactured mountains. I'd seen similar structures in Talen's Old Earthen books, built as temples to the stars long before human tek had carried humankind to them.

I peered out from the window, expecting to see other ships in the sky or movement in the crosshatched streets below, but nothing moved in the sky or on the ground.

My companions' faces all looked grim. Kellee, at the flight controls, was a simmering pot of silent emotion about to boil over. Talen sat at the back, eyes closed as though resting. Arran flicked his daggers through his fingers, his eyes darting over the abandoned city outside.

Sirius was here, soaking up the shadows at the back. I'd insisted on him coming, much to everyone's disagreement. Nobody wanted the guardian with us. By the guardian's stoic look, he didn't want to be here either, but leaving him on the ship with his loyal fae flight would have invited an insurrection. Better to get him off Shinj and distract him from his mission and his new arm. He'd twisted his cloak to his right so it hung over his arm, concealing it. He watched Valand's green land scroll by just like the rest of us.

Kellee set the shuttle down in the middle of an open plaza boxed in by high walls. A proud step pyramid loomed over one end.

The shuttle doors hissed, equalizing the pressure, and the ramp descended.

The quiet hit me first. A silence so big and so complete I could almost touch it. The city air hung motionless and dry. Grit crunched under my boots and group's boots behind me, the sound of our passing too loud in this abandoned place. The emerald pyramid climbed ever higher, turning us into small, inconsequential things.

"It hasn't changed in all these years," Sirius remarked. His voice sailed on and on and on into the silence until the emptiness swallowed it down.

Quiet washed in again. The paths underfoot would have flowed with people once. Houses and temples, streets and parks. Hundreds of thousands of vakaru. Mothers, fathers, children. Now gone.

The creeping sensation of something watching us intensified, and the fine hairs at the back of my neck lifted. Despite the warmth, shivers rippled through me. I looked back at Sirius and saw a haunted look in his unguarded expression. Something terrible had happened here.

Kellee marched far ahead, toward the terrace of steps leading up to the pyramid. Whatever he was going through, I had promised him he wasn't alone.

Talen drew up alongside me and bowed his head to whisper, "I cannot go with you."

"Can't or won't?" I asked, remembering Kellee's method for pinning Talen down.

"Won't." He lifted his gaze and fixed it on the distant Kellee. "Don't lose him in the past."

I nodded and hurried to catch up with Kellee. Arran followed, but I waved him back and shook my head. His eyes narrowed, but he reluctantly nodded and hung back with Talen and Sirius.

Sota came in next, humming too close to my shoulder.

"I don't like it here," the drone rumbled. "My sensors itch. The silence is alive."

I knew how he felt. As beautiful as everything was, the silence was cloying. Nowhere was this quiet. This place wasn't just empty, it was a vacuum. "Stay outside the temple. Keep an eye on the others."

He whirred. "I should come in with you. The marshal's heart rate is elevated. He is angry."

"Yes, but not with me. Stay outside. I'll be fine. He won't hurt me."

I climbed the steps before Sota could argue that Kellee already had hurt me, multiple times. A huge stone doorway, three times my height, marked the entrance. I stepped through, feeling small compared to the grand columned entrance chamber. A path stretched dead-straight through various halls and chambers to the center of the pyramid, where light plunged in from above, highlighting a platform and an empty dais. Kellee stood in the spotlight, his face lifted to the light that couldn't penetrate his shroud of darkness.

I approached carefully, respectfully.

He yanked the band from his ponytail and ran a hand through his hair, mussing it around his face only to rake it back and hold it there. The firm set of his jaw revealed how he kept his emotions locked down. I'd rarely seen him so still.

Something had once rested on the dais. The entire central chamber had been built to house whatever had sat upon the stone plinth. A statue to a god, perhaps? Did the vakaru worship a god or gods? They were known as a violent race, but I'd seen no evidence of warfare so far, just astonishing engineering and architecture.

Drifting out of the light, I wandered the chamber,

eyeing jagged marks on the walls. The scratches weren't part of the original design and looked chiseled into the stone. There was no rhyme or reason to them, and the more I looked for them, the more I found, until I realized they were everywhere. Always scratched in fives. I'd seen them before on the inside of Kellee's cage on the warcruiser when Sjora had kept us both caged. I saw them in every one of the fae Kellee had killed. I pressed my hand to a patch of marks, fingers spread to match their pattern. Vakaru claw marks.

What happened here? I ached to ask, the question right on the tip of my tongue, but Kellee still looked up into the beam of light, as though looking for answers too.

A fight, a battle, or had they been trapped inside and tried to claw their way out?

There was nothing here to answer why Oberon had killed them all. The vakaru had unseelie in them, but that couldn't be the only reason the king had wanted them gone. There had to be more to it. I knew Oberon's wrath was legendary, but had he feared the vakaru so much that he'd wiped them out? What was it about the vakaru— Oberon's own creation—that had offended him so?

"I still hear them." Kellee's voice filled the quiet, chasing it out of every corner and crevice. "Like it's happening again."

He bowed his head and stepped back from the plinth. When he looked up, molten gold ringed the edges of his dark pupils, making his eyes shine. "We built these pyramids higher and higher, thinking we could reach the stars. We built them for the fae. We built this entire world for the fae. Because we loved them." He snickered a dry, ugly laugh. "I know *you* understand that."

"I do," I whispered.

"The fae we served were like the stars. We thought they were gods. We thought..." He laughed. "Oberon was a god. We worshiped him and bled for him and would have brought all the worlds in all the systems to their knees for him."

I knew exactly how that felt. I may not have lived for as long as he had, but I had loved the fae just as fiercely, loved Oberon as though it were a madness. I would have done anything for him to see me, for him to love me in return. I had done anything.

"Then the humans fought back and we went to war," Kellee continued. "We killed them in the hundreds of thousands. We tore through the humans, tore them open and drank from their veins until we were mad with blood-lust." His grimace twitched and the golden ring in his eyes darkened, bleeding red. I could imagine the sight, the ferocious loyalty of the vakaru and how powerful a weapon they must have been.

Kellee dropped his hand from his hair so the locks fell, obscuring his face. "Humans who looked like us, talked like us. They had built machines, and we tore those down. They'd built spacefaring tek that carried them through the stars, just like the fae, and we... I..." he corrected, again, and wet his lips. "*I* started seeing them differently. These humans... they weren't gods, but they were clever, and powerful, and they didn't want to fight us. We knew it." He circled the empty plinth and the column of light. "In the beginning, it didn't matter. Our love for the fae blinded us to everything else, and then the humans came here and brought their tek with them, not to make war, but to make peace. The fools." His smile almost returned. "There was one human..."

He pressed his lips together, but not before I saw them

quiver. My marshal was slowly, carefully coming undone, and all I could do was watch as his layers peeled away. "... one brave woman." Kellee's dangerous glare speared me, issuing a challenge: Stay. Listen. Do not run. "She walked through our number, through a city full of monsters, unarmed, her chin held high like none of us could touch her. She wore a gown of green silk laced with glittering tek. I had never seen anything so foolish or so beautiful. Any one of us could have torn her down, but something about her... The vakaru watched her approach. She walked right up to me, her eyes full of fierce determination, but no fear. Despite all the things we had done, all the humans we had slaughtered, she did not fear us."

Kellee closed his eyes, either to hold back the memories or to see them clearly. The pain on his face was too raw, too real. I hated to see him hurting, but a large part of me wanted more. He was talking, telling me who he was like never before. He never showed his feelings, not really. He was always guarded, always in control. But here, now, he was revealing *everything*.

"She looked me in the eyes." He opened his. They glittered with unshed tears. The next words he pushed out in a hiss. "I *had a choice*, she said." His breath hitched, lodging in his throat. "My people need not kill for the fae. We need not bow to them or live by their rules. We did not have to be their slaves. We could be free to choose our own path, a vakaru path."

Kellee threw his head up, freeing the tears. They slid quietly from the corners of his eyes, wetting his face. He wiped them away. "I... made the wrong choice," he whispered, losing his voice.

A knot formed in my throat. Mistakes, I knew those all too well.

"I killed her, right here." He looked down, his eyes alive with the past. When he looked up, right at me, his upper lip pulled back, revealing growing fangs. "I killed her for *your king*." He pointed, his fingers tipped with growing black claws. "I killed her because Oberon would reward me. Because I adored my god. I loved him, like you still love him." Kellee swayed on his feet and I stepped forward, but his glare held me back, and when he next spoke, the sadness and pain and sorrow made him seem so small, made him seem like just a man with the weight of a billion lives on his soul. "And he murdered my entire people because I'd invited a human here. Because I'd let her in. Because I'd listened to her. I begged him. I got down on my knees right outside, with tens of thousands of proud eyes on me, and I begged him to hear my pleas. I begged him to kill me for my mistake—*not my people, not my vakaru.*" He smiled but it was an anguished grin. "I knew then, before he decided, I'd made the wrong choice. I knew it was all a lie. The fae and their magic and their pretty words. They were lies, all of it. And he knew they were lies too. So he killed them, Kesh. Every. Single. One."

Kellee lifted his head, and the vakaru peered into my soul. Sharp intelligence glittered in its glare. It was a terrible, powerful creature. A born killer. But proud and strong and honorable.

My unseelie monster, my Kellee. It hadn't been his fault. Oberon hadn't killed them because of Kellee's choice. Oberon had created the vakaru. He knew they were unseelie—he had made them that way. Oberon had destroyed them because he *feared* them.

"It's not your fault." I held my hands out, showing the vakaru I was unarmed and no threat. "The unseelie—"

The wildness snuffed out of Kellee's eyes and he

barked a bitter laugh, because the words were pathetic and could do nothing to change the ancient past. *His* ancient past.

"And here you are..." He smiled, and it broke my heart wide open to see the sorrow in his smile. "Centuries later. The Messenger with a choice. I see that brave woman I killed in you. I see her every time I look at you. I see myself in you too, a stubborn war chief who believes he can save his people. I see my past in your eyes and my mistakes. You have the same choice I did, and damn you, Kesh, if I don't see you making the same mistakes... knowing you'll do exactly the same as I did. He'll ruin you. He'll destroy everything you know, everything you love, because it's what he does—what *they* do. You *have* to see past everything they made you. You have to be better than them. You have to choose for you, nobody else, not even your king."

I hadn't known Kellee at all. But now?

"I know you think you understand, but you don't. You want to, and I believe that, but until you stand in front of Oberon and deny his power over you, you're still his. Until that moment, you'll always be his."

I understood why Kellee looked at me the way he did, why he fought me, why he lifted me up and then pushed me down again. I saw it all in his eyes. Saw the hope, the fear, the terrible knowledge that his world could come crashing down again, and I wanted so badly to make the right choice. For him. For me. For a race long dead and those still fighting today.

He and I were the same. The fae had made us, we loved them, we'd die for them, we'd kill for them. Until there was nothing left. Until we had climbed a mountain of bones to reach the stars, only to realize their light had died long ago.

"Thank you," I said. No other words were necessary. And in that moment—as I looked at the last vakaru, his eyes ablaze with fire, his claws sharp, and tears streaming down his face—I knew I'd made my choice and it would be the right one.

He nodded sharply and wiped a hand across his face, sweeping away those tears. "Faerie be damned." He dropped his head, but the empty plinth caught his eye once more. With a sudden roar, all his emotion broke over him. He slashed at the plinth. Rock split and crumbled, tumbling to the floor, where it shattered into rubble.

Sota whooshed in, gun ports open and trained on Kellee's back. I shot out a hand, warning the drone off, but Kellee dropped to his knees, spent and empty. A gentle rumbling upset the quiet, and miraculously, the fallen stone shook and trembled, debris bouncing and shooting off the floor, back into its original positions, remaking itself before my eyes.

Magic.

He had told me Valand was immortal. But it was more than that. The silent city was trapped in a single moment. Never permitted to change. And it would stay that way, forever. Oberon had done more than wipe out Kellee's people. He'd stopped the passage of time on Valand entirely.

Kellee rose to his feet, and I saw a man who'd been staring down the barrel of a gun for centuries. Because he was trapped in the same moment, cursed to live with the belief that his choice had killed the vakaru, cursed to be alone with that knowledge for all eternity. This planet, this system, was a tombstone.

I locked my jaw, swallowed the painful knot in my throat, and blinked back the unshed tears, because my pain, my sympathy, solved nothing. But I could make changes. Just like a single kiss gifted to a fae pilot who had wanted to feel one last time, just like a starfruit given to take away the agony, or just like a boy's hand in mine as we reached through our bars, change happened one small step at a time. Kellee and I could make a difference.

"We'll make it right, Kellee."

I wasn't sure he'd heard me. He breathed hard, staring at the remade plinth, seeing and hearing the past all around him. Then, with a growl, he cleared his throat and turned to me, pinning on his lopsided lawman smile that touched his gold-rimmed green eyes. "Let's go find this polestar."

CHAPTER 19

I emerged from the pyramid with a new perspective on the silent city and Marshal Kellee.

"You have the talisman?" he asked, squinting into Valand's greenish light.

I dug the talisman out of my pocket and held it out. It sat on my palm, as innocuous as the brooch I'd thought it was. But the magical throb warming my hand and beating in waves up my arm made it clear it was no ordinary piece of jewelry. The fact it was a replica of Eledan's heart had me itching to throw it as far away as possible and leave it behind for Valand to claim.

I dropped it into Kellee's hand. The marshal's eyes narrowed as he lifted it and turned it over in the light, watching its facets catch fire. "After the original Hapters people fixed Eledan's heart with magic and tek, I figure he had them make more, watched where they got the magic and how they threaded it through tek, and used that knowledge to root out Hapters's secrets, including the map."

"But how does that help us find fragments of the polestar here?"

"Us? It doesn't." He tossed the talisman into the air, caught it, and started down the steps, his gait lighter than before. "But it came from Hapters, a planet saturated in early fae magic right alongside the trapped unseelie and likely a piece of the polestar too. Faerie magic knows its own. Talen can make this trinket dance for him."

I joined Kellee on the straight path back to the shuttle, catching his smile and sending one of my own back. He had shown me his painful truth, and finally, I was beginning to know my marshal. Seeing that lopsided smile anew and knowing what it cost him spread a strange, comforting warmth through my chest. Maybe he and I would be okay. Now all I needed was for Talen to open up. He didn't have to tell me all his secrets, we all knew I wasn't ready for that, but the silver fae's silences felt as heavy and laden with dread as Valand's.

"Talen's been quiet lately."

Kellee nodded. "In the prison, he once spent a whole year in silence. He has the patience of the ancients roaming Faerie, watching time pass them by."

I'd heard the tales of ancient fae who had lain still for so long that Faerie had reclaimed them. Saru said Faerie ate them, made them part of her sprawling meadows, or her warm Summerlands breezes, or her secret murmuring brooks. I wasn't sure how true such things were, but I had no wish to lose Talen to that kind of silence.

Back at the shuttle, Arran was sitting on the ramp, twirling his daggers, eyeing Sirius as he strode along the inside of the long, high walls.

"Where's Talen?" Kellee asked Arran.

"Went that way." Arran jerked his head at the path

branching off the main thoroughfare, through the wall and out into the city. "I opted to babysit the fae most likely to kill us all while Kesh wasn't looking."

Kellee's eyebrow arched. "Good move," he praised, prompting a grin from Arran.

Kellee started down Talen's path. "Kesh?" he called back. "C'mon. We shouldn't stay here longer than necessary."

Arran smiled up at me. "Go with him. I'm fine here, and Sirius isn't showing any signs of staging a coup." He stood and sheathed both daggers inside his thigh straps. He lifted his chin and lost his smile. Some of the cold gladiator in him hardened his eyes and closed off his expression. "What happened in there?"

"I saw something of the real Marshal Kellee."

Arran glanced after Kellee. "Do you trust him?"

"Implicitly."

"Then so do I."

What? No argument? No fighting? I shouldn't have been surprised. Of everyone, Arran had never questioned me. "Thank you."

He looked up and back at Sirius. "Kellee's right, though. This place feels wrong. We should get this done and move on. I can't shake the feeling there's something else here."

I felt it too, a crawling itch between my shoulder blades. "If Sirius gives you attitude, remind him this will be easier for him if he works with me, not against me."

"Sirius is *armless*," Sota quipped, dipping in to hover close.

Arran frowned.

My drone did not just go there. "Sota, really?"

"Too soon?"

Arran chuckled and nodded at Kellee's shrinking outline. "Go, or he'll leave you behind."

I kissed him on the lips, meaning for it to be a passing touch, but I failed to resist him the moment he looped his arm around my waist and pulled me against him. A flicker of heat sparked to life and pulsed low. Arran's kiss deepened. The feel of him, hard and soft, right and wrong, made that real, fragile part of me flutter to life. Need and want and fear mixed together, because the closer I got to him, the more I wanted to explore the man he had become, but he had resisted going farther, and I was in no rush.

When he broke away, I was breathing too fast, my heart racing to match all the crazy thoughts in my head.

"When we get back ..." He tucked my hair behind my ear and searched my eyes, looking for answers I shouldn't give him. "We need to talk, just you and me."

"We do?"

He closed his eyes and backed up. "They need you."

The fresh intensity in his eyes made me wonder if there was part of the kiss I hadn't understood, if there was something happening between us that I didn't understand either. "Arran—"

"Go," he said. "I'll be right here when you get back."

I searched his face. Had I said or done something wrong? Whatever it was, it had to wait. Kellee had almost disappeared inside the heat haze. "Sota—"

"I'm staying," the drone said before I could issue an order.

I hesitated on the path and looked back at them. Arran and Sota. Maybe Sota had sensed something too. He and Arran had grown close these past few weeks. "Don't stray too far," I told them and jogged after Kellee.

The marshal passed through a stone archway into a formal garden made up of a jade brick pathway and several planted terraces. Despite row upon row of trees and bushes, all shaped and pruned to within an inch of their lives, the garden was as silent and motionless as the rest of the city. It didn't feel real. But it wasn't dreamlike either. It just felt *frozen*.

"You were a..." The word stumbled off my tongue. "...king?"

Kellee's soft laugh echoed through the motionless garden. "Ask Oberon and he'll tell you I was a savage. The sidhe lords called me *Droch-fhoula*, my people called me *Kell-eigh*—war-lord. But a king?" Laughter danced in his eyes. "Never that. I didn't rule the vakaru. Nobody rules the wild things of Faerie, manufactured elsewhere or nurtured by Faerie herself. I was chosen."

"Droc-oo-la?" I echoed, trying to pronounce his fae name.

He screwed up his nose. "Stick with Kellee."

"What does it mean?"

"Bad blood." He strode on, long legs eating up the path. "The sidhe were not wrong." He had locked his gaze ahead and didn't notice or care about the gardens we walked through, but I found their frozen elegance unnerving. The crawl of a gaze on me was stronger here, riding my back. I even turned to check no one was following.

"Whatever you're doing with the kid, don't fuck him up."

There was no point in denying it, but I'd be damned if I would let Kellee make me feel bad for something that felt as good as my feelings for Arran.

He took my non-answer as his cue to continue. "I

245

don't own you. I can't stop you. But I can ask you not to hurt him." He looked over. "He didn't survive you before."

I kept my thoughts to myself and off my face. Talen had once told me I didn't know what love was. He'd meant real love, not the manufactured kind all saru felt for the fae. Arran loved me. He didn't understand why, and neither did I, but it was real. And I loved him back.

But I also loved Aeon and wasn't sure if what I felt was an old love or a new one.

"I don't want to hurt him," I admitted.

"You already are."

I stopped on the path. We had climbed several sets of steps, passing deeper into organized rows of trees until the city's walls had vanished behind motionless leaves and static branches. Kellee took a few sides before stopping and looking back. He looked at me with too much understanding.

"Talen is Talen..." he said, that sentence oddly making sense. "And you and I, we're like fireworks, the dangerous, out of control kind." There was a Kellee and me? "I don't have a problem with your divided affections, and we both know Talen prefers to share but Arran—" Kellee rubbed his eyes and looked around him as though seeing the pruned forest for the first time. "Shit, this is not the place for this..."

He'd seen the kiss and more. He had seen whatever it was that had spooked Arran.

Kellee sighed and approached me so his next words were softer and just between us. "He's just a kid, Kesh."

"He's not just a kid. He's been through as much as I have, if not more. Saru live a lifetime behind bars before we even reach adulthood."

"Yes, as Aeon. But he chose to let all that go. Now it's your turn to do the same."

But I'd just found him again.

Kellee was suddenly close, all his understanding, his past, his knowledge written on a face that didn't carry the scars on the outside, but they were all there, below his handsome surface. "I'd give almost anything to have the people I loved back, to have my mistakes wiped clean, but not if it meant hurting them all over again. Leave the past far behind you, Kesh. Let the ghosts rest. You know I'm right."

I sighed out any denials. "One of these days, you'll be wrong."

"When I'm wrong, people die." He turned, coat fanning as he paced through the trees.

I watched the marshal stride into the green and knew he was right. I had to stop this thing with Arran before it went any deeper—if it wasn't already too late. But just the thought of letting him go hurt in ways I'd rarely experienced before. It was a deep pain, with no source, nothing I could fix with a med-gauze or pain suppressors. I'd felt the same hollow pain when I'd revealed my truth to Talen and Kellee.

When I caught up, Kellee mumbled, "I've spent too much of my life trying to track Talen down and here I am again, stalking his wayward self, playing cat and mouse."

"He's close." I could feel the bond tugging me ahead, letting me know we were going the right way. "You know who he is, for real, right?"

Kellee didn't answer, but his "don't-ask" glare did.

"Good, don't tell me. I just... Just tell me this. Is he good?"

The marshal looked down the straight path, deeper

into the organized forest and far into the distance. "It's all about choices, Messenger."

"That's not an answer."

"Yeah, well, it's all I can give you."

"He's bonded with me, Kellee. I feel him inside, getting stronger." *And he's changing me.* I couldn't admit that, not yet. Not here, where words carried far and wide. "This is important. You even suggested I take up the bond, remember? You wouldn't have done that if he wasn't good."

He winced, as though he'd forgotten that conversation. "All right, yes. I think he's good."

"You *think* he's good?"

"He's fae, and there's a lot I don't know. He's never told me his name, but Talen doesn't tell you the important things. It's all in the silences... the unsaid. I didn't sit on my hands for the three hundred years he was incarcerated. I dug around and got answers. He's powerful, he's a Faerie outcast, a pilot, he's on the run, and he has his own agenda, which is why we're traipsing through this damn forest after him."

I stopped. "Kellee, wait."

The marshal frowned back at me. "What?"

I took his hand in mine, delighting briefly at its roughness. "Can you show me a claw?"

"What?"

"Please."

"Why?"

"I need to... explain something and it's easier if I show you."

He eyed me suspiciously, but let a nail grow into a sharp, slender, curved blade. I turned my hand over and flicked my finger along the under edge of the claw, running its razor edge over my fingertip. My skin painlessly peeled open and a pearl of blood welled. "There, I need to—"

His eyes shot open. He snatched my wrist and yanked me into a run after him. *"Go, go, go..."* He stumbled and shoved me ahead of him and then spun. I saw claws glint, saw his fangs lengthen, his eyes blaze. And all around, arching above him, behind him, the perfect trees began to rustle and *move*.

One branch struck fast, lashing in like a whip. Kellee swung and sliced through it, severing its gnarly fingers. Another struck, plunging in from behind, but it didn't wrap around him like I'd expected it too. It punched *into* his shoulder, wrenching a cry from Kellee. He spun, cutting himself free. His glare found me. *"Get out of here!"*

I freed my whip, but in the next second, it was snatched out of my hand so fast my palm burned.

The trees thrashed and hissed, turning their branches on me and thrusting them in. One tore across my shin. Another struck my face, slicing my cheek open. Something hooked around my ankle and yanked, and before I could tug free, it pulled my leg out from under me. My back hit the path, then my head, and I was hoisted up and held aloft like a dangling saru on a fish hook.

The frenzy ended as abruptly as it had started.

I swung upside down over the path and caught sight of Kellee dangling the same way, his coat hanging halfway to the ground.

"What the cyn, Kellee?" I snapped, twisting keep him in my sights.

"Blood," he said, like that answered everything.

"Blood?! I was trying to show you something."

"I know what happens when you *bleed*."

"Not like this." Speaking of blood, much of it was

rushing to my skull, flushing my cheeks and making my head throb. "Your forest likes blood?"

"You're surprised?"

We dangled quietly, branches groaning under our weight, but none would break. We weren't that lucky.

"Are you hurt?" he asked.

I had swung back around and saw the sheepish look on his face. "I'm fine," I huffed. My itching skin meant the cuts were already healing. My coat kept falling over my face and had ridden up to my elbows. I didn't even know where my whip was. The trees had taken it. "Why are they keeping us here."

"Snacks."

I closed my eyes. Snacks. Right. We were tree food. How very... Faerie.

"Your face? I saw the cut..."

I opened my eyes and felt Kellee's glare drilling into me.

He cocked his head, staring harder. "You're healing."

"That's what I was trying to show you before your trees tried to eat me."

He gaped, or I thought he did. He'd swung around, facing the opposite way again. I was about to ask him what he thought it meant and how we were getting down, when I realized his upside-down coat was jiggling. Was he... laughing? This was hardly funny. His carnivorous trees were about to eat us and he was... I saw the laughter in his eyes, saw his lips twitching... He was snickering? At the sight of my glower, Marshal Kellee laughed loudly and freely, shattering the deathly quiet. I was turning away from him again, and although nothing on Valand was remotely amusing, my own laughter threatened to bubble free.

"The all-mighty Messenger is..." He laughed harder. "... hanging by her ankle from a tree."

The laugh escaped me, and by the time I'd swung back around to see Kellee, my sides ached. It felt good to laugh *with* him.

Talen cleared his throat. He stood on the path below, looking up at us. "I followed the sounds of hilarity."

"Hey." I waved, gulping down the laughter. "This is all your fault."

"I don't see how," Talen replied, violet eyes glittering at the absurdity of finding me and the marshal hanging from trees. "These aren't my trees."

"We were looking for you."

One eyebrow sprang upward. "You knew exactly where I was."

"Yes. No. I mean..." I growled and rolled my eyes, ending the roll on Kellee. "So, what happens now? Do either of you speak tree?"

Kellee got himself back under control. "I always hated these fucking shrubs." He rocked his arms, swinging into motion. I didn't have enough upper body strength to haul myself upright and fluttered my lashes at Talen instead. Talen stopped watching the marshal with mild interest and clicked his fingers. The grip on my ankles vanished. I plummeted, twisted, and somehow landed on my feet. My knee clipped the path, but I was upright and hadn't slammed onto my ass or broken anything.

"A little warning next time?"

Talen's secret grin was on his lips and gone again before anyone but me could see it.

Kellee had enough swing to grab onto a branch. He heaved himself into the canopy and then sliced off the branch fingers clamped around him. He dropped to the floor in a balanced crouch and straightened to his full height, wearing the kind of marshal stare that wilted flowers.

"I'd have freed you too," Talen offered.

Kellee's glare thinned. He tugged his coat back into place. "Do I look like I need a fairy to save me?" Kellee tossed him the talisman. "Don't answer that." The fae snatched it out of the air. "The polestar," Kellee declared. "It's what we're here for. Will you make yourself useful and help us find it?"

Talen eyed the talisman and tossed it back. Kellee caught it.

"I know where it is without that trinket," the fae said.

Of course he did. He was Talen, lord of secrets and silences. He turned back the way he'd appeared and headed down the path, his long hooded coat a silvery river running down his back.

Kellee veered into the trees and emerged a few seconds later with my whip. "I guess we're following the fae." He handed the weapon over. "I'd apologize for the trees, but they haven't had company in a while, and if you're going to bleed all over a vakaru garden, you should expect to get eaten."

"Noted."

We walked together, following Talen's slash of silver ahead, until the motionless, sentinel trees ended at a step pyramid as high as Arcon's back on Calicto.

"It can't be in there," Kellee said, resting a boot on the first step. "We built these pyramids. If there was anything of Faerie here, we would have noticed."

Talen gave him a look that said he really wouldn't have. "Some things cannot be found without intention."

Meaning the polestar needed to be deliberately sought out. We headed inside.

The pyramid was hollow, its insides cavernous. Shafts of light streamed in through holes punched far above.

"What is this place?" I asked.

"A temple." Kellee watched Talen drift up the straight path, heading for the raised platform at its center. "To our gods, the *sidhe*." His sharp teeth flashed.

Light shivered down Talen's back, and when he dropped his hood, it sparked in his hair as though to emphasize how easily the fae could make themselves appear divine. Talen wasn't even trying—the plain cloak, the simple leathers—yet he looked magical. It was easy to understand how ancient races had worshipped them.

Talen stepped up onto the platform and knelt at its center with his head bowed.

I waited, expecting something to happen. The silence stretched on. "What's he doing?" I whispered.

Kellee snorted. "Who knows." He circled the platform, dropping down a step into a lowered area. "I'd have sensed Faerie's touch long ago if it were hiding here. I know every inch of this temple and the others. There's no mystical weapon on Valand."

A flicker of power sparked inside my chest. It wasn't mine. But when Talen didn't react, I ignored it and followed Kellee's trail around the outside. "You didn't know there was magic on Hapters."

"I did, but I was using it to farm and I had no intention of digging up the past so it could screw me over again."

"Are your hungry trees not Faerie touched?"

He threw me a half smile. "You're full of questions, huh?"

"That's what happens when you start answering them. Why *did* you start answering?"

Kellee ascended a few steps onto a raised pathway. I joined him, putting us both in front of Talen, who still knelt on the platform. The only entrance or exit was behind the fae. "Because you walked away from answers before, on the ship, when Talen offered you the truth," Kellee replied. "If you were still under Oberon's thrall, you would have gotten your answers, no matter the cost. That honesty... that's the first real thing I've seen of you since you revealed exactly who you are. Be honest with me, Kesh, and we'll get along just fine."

He smiled in that crooked way of his, inviting me to challenge his words. He didn't know how I planned to go back to Faerie. I could tell him, but he would try to stop me. He might even succeed, and I couldn't allow that. I had to go back, for him, for Talen, for Hulia, for the people everywhere still running from Faerie.

Kellee lifted his head and frowned at the crux of the pyramid, where the four sides combined to the inverted point high above us. "The trees are unseelie," he explained, answering my earlier question.

"Unseelie is Faerie too."

"Not anymore."

"There was something here," Talen said. "But it was taken."

Darkness pooled at the point above the platform—above Talen. I hadn't noticed it before because it seemed as though it should be the darkest section of the pyramid, but now the darkness was... growing. I watched, fascinated as the dark's edges dripped down the undersides of the pyramid's sloped ceilings liked spilled ink.

"*Talen*," Kellee growled. "We've got company."

Talen snapped his head up at the same time as a stone slab slammed down over the exit, sealing us inside.

The shadowy droplets coalesced, forming humanoid shapes. *Sluagh*—restless souls discarded by the Hunt—but then I saw the claws flicker from reaching shadowy hands. Not sluagh... similar, but something else. I unclipped my whip and let its tails fall free.

One or two we could handle, but the dark was growing, flooding the ceiling, dribbling the things in a steady stream across the floor. And then I heard the laughter. Laughter like I'd heard for months while trapped in dreams, laughter that licked over my skin, strumming my flesh to life with hate and lust and all the feelings the Mad Prince summoned.

"No..." I gasped.

The Dreamweaver was here.

CHAPTER 20

*I*t was impossible. The Dreamweaver couldn't be here. If he had been real in Arcon, it was because he'd had enough life magic there to open a doorway to step through. There was no life magic here.

"You are too late," Eledan's liquid voice purred as the blackness stalked down the walls.

Not possible. Not real.

I clamped my hands over my ears but still heard his words rolling over and over. *Too late, too late, too late.* Turning, seeking the shadows, I was sure I'd see him there, his blue eyes arresting.

"I hear him too, Kesh." Kellee's claws sprang out, glinting with the last of the light. "Stay with us!"

All around, the temple's light was being snuffed out, shaft by shaft, going dark. Soon, there would be only darkness, and *he* would be inside it. He always came in the darkness. He was the darkness. The sweet darkness my dreams were wrapped in.

I'm not his. I'm not.

I lashed the whip's tails in the air. It cracked viciously.

The liquid-like creatures covering the walls flinched away, and my thoughts cleared, but then Eledan's laughter whirled like a storm inside the pyramid, filling up the space as real and thick as the silence before it.

He's not here.

"*Wraithmaker...*" he whispered, in my head or aloud, I didn't know. I couldn't tell what was real and what was illusion. And the worst of it was, a small part of me wanted this, wanted him to be here.

"Kesh!"

Not Kesh.

Wraithmaker.

The Faerie King's hired killer.

Liar, loser, nothing girl.

"It's an illusion! Fight it!"

Kellee. His voice found me among the chaos like it always had. *Illusion. Just illusion.* I raised the whip, whirled it above my head so it hissed like a living thing and struck at the creature slithering closer. Its outline glitched, there and gone again, jolting through time. Both here and nowhere.

Not sluagh, but something else... Something stronger. Something rooted in this world. They were... *people.* Once.

"Kellee!"

He wasn't moving. The flickering sluagh-like creatures rushed him in a wave as one.

Kellee lowered his claws. His shoulders dropped, and he stood defeated, his face lifted to the cresting wave as it slammed over him, devouring him in its broiling dark. When the dark parted, lapping at the jade floor, Kellee was gone.

"No!"

I ran to where he had been standing and scooped my

258

hands through the dissipating blackness. He had to be here. They couldn't just take him away. He had been right here. There was no way out. He had to still be here.

The black crawled back up the walls, limbs and claws just broken pieces inside the hungry darkness, taking Kellee somewhere inside it.

He'd given up.

He hadn't fought them at all.

The darkness above swirled at the pyramid's inverted tip, like water down a drain, and then it was gone. Light spilled into the temple, flooding every corner, every platform, and bathed Talen where he stood. Where he had stood the entire time, doing *nothing*.

"Where is he?" I demanded.

He didn't move, didn't reply, didn't blink.

Kellee was gone, and Talen had done nothing. Just watched. Like always.

I ran onto the platform and glared up at the perfect, expressionless fae. "Where is he?" Anger throbbed inside, aching to break free. I knew my hands shook, knew I breathed too fast. "Damn you, answer me!"

"They took him."

"Who took him? Took him where?"

Talen lifted his gaze over my head as though I wasn't even there. His gaze darted, thoughts far away. But it wasn't good enough. He wasn't good enough. He could have done something. Anything. *They* had taken Kellee!

I slammed my hands against his stone-like chest, shoving him back a single step, and glared up as he peered down. "Where is he, Talen?"

"I was right... I always saw the light. I knew... But Eledan was here. He could have more pieces. He saw the map. He knows—" He cut off his mutterings, believing

259

he'd said too much despite none of it making any sense. His gaze wandered again, and he turned away.

No, he doesn't get to walk away from me, not anymore.

I grabbed his wrist and pulled. Power crackled up my arm, darting straight to my heart where it burned. When his gaze swung back around, his violet eyes flared with indignation. I'd seen that look a thousand times before, but never on him. *How dare a saru touch a fae.*

Instincts demanded I let go, but I clamped his arm harder. "If this bond means something to you—if I mean something to you—then answer me. Where is Kellee?!"

He looked at me, his lips a thin line, his eyes cold. Did I even know him at all?

When he tried to walk away the second time, I let his wrist slip from my grip and threatened, "If you walk away from me now, it's over. I'll find a way to carve out this bond the same way I carved out Eledan's heart. Don't think I won't do it. I may not have earned the right to ask you your name, but I've earned the right to understand what's happening here. You owe me, Talen. And you owe Kellee."

With his back to me, I saw his shoulders stiffen. "The vakaru took him home."

Those things were vakaru? "But they're all dead."

"Yes."

I circled around to stand in front of my fae, blocking his route to the exit. "Can we get him back?"

"Yes."

Listen to what he's not saying. His frozen gaze, his shuttered face. He didn't want me to know what was going on here. We could get Kellee back, but it would cost us. Cost him. Would Talen save a marshal who had kept him prisoner for over three centuries?

Talen bowed his head and stepped around me, giving me time to reach for him. I didn't. Instead, I watched him walk to the stone slab covering the door and turn it to dust beneath his hand.

"Why didn't you stop them?" I asked.

He waited for me to catch up, and when I did, I realized the sadness tugging at the corners of his mouth was real. "Kellee was right. The fragment of polestar isn't here. The Dreamweaver stole it long ago and left the illusion behind as a warning to any who followed."

The fact Eledan had part of an ancient Faerie weapon was something I filed away for later. "Why didn't you stop them, Talen?" He could have. He *was* light. I'd seen it in the tunnels, seen him wield it when breaking free of Sjora's hold.

"Because," he sighed, "I am not who I once was."

He had told me that before, in moments when he wanted me to understand something I hadn't yet grasped. Something he couldn't speak. *My name is stardust and shadow, and it cannot be spoken aloud.*

"Do not ask again, Kesh. It is my fault you already stray too close to the truth. The secrets I harbor are my burden. To speak them would..." He trailed off.

"What happens if you speak your secrets?"

His focus softened. "In the past, people died. People I cared for."

"Could Kellee die like them?" This was not over. "Talen?" He didn't answer. I had a marshal to save, and damn his vagueness, I was getting him back no matter what. "How do we get him back? At least tell me that."

Talen walked out into Valand's green light. "With blood."

I braced an arm against the shuttle's door rams and squinted at Valand's pyramids. Nothing had changed, but in my mind, the sharp edges and glittering greens now had cutting edges.

Blood would bring Kellee back.

Great.

"This entire system is made of violence," Sirius said. He appeared beside me. The last I'd seen of him, he had been checking the perimeter walls around the plaza for anything unusual. "Valand is a culmination of violence and warfare," he continued. "Can't you hear it?"

I couldn't hear a damn thing besides the rapid thumping of my heart.

Talen approached from Kellee's pyramid, his silvery outline shimmering like a mirage. *With blood.* I was to bleed on the plinth inside the pyramid at the right time, or so I'd finally managed to wring out of him as we'd returned from the hungry forest.

Sirius's gaze followed mine. "You were right. Oberon should meet him."

"Oberon can't have him." The words were out before I realized I was supposed to be Oberon's faithful servant. Sirius's gaze settled on me. I guarded the panic from my face. If I didn't highlight my mistake, then it wasn't a mistake at all. Sirius had heard it. Not a word was uttered on Faerie without it having weight and meaning. And my words had a whole lot of both tethered to them.

"You are a puzzle inside a puzzle, calla," he admitted.

"It'll be dark soon." The warcruiser was moving in, guided by Talen, to cast her shadow across the city and herald a forced night. We needed the shadows to smooth the way, or so Talen had said.

We had failed to find anything related to the polestar, and we'd lost Kellee. And Talen, like always, was right in the middle of it all. I wasn't sure I could take much more of his cryptic answers and layers of secrets. I'd pushed him away, despite aching to have him close, but it only made me want him more, and with every non-answer, every stubborn silence, every cold shoulder, I was reminded of how he and I were worlds apart.

"How is your arm?" I asked the guardian.

Sirius tensed. "Functional."

As answers went, that was probably the best one I would get. "Show me." I faced the tall wall of reds that made up Oberon's guardian and held out my hand.

"I'd rather not." A muscle in his square jaw twitched, and he glared at the approaching Talen.

"Would you have preferred not to have an arm?" I asked coldly.

"Yes."

Well, that was ridiculous. "I thought—"

"You mutilated me."

"No," I said carefully. "I gave you your sword arm back."

I heard metal *slink* across metal from beneath his coat and wondered if he'd clenched his tek-fingers into a fist.

He continued to glare across the plaza. "I wouldn't have been wounded if not for you."

"You might have saved my life back on Hapters, and I am grateful for that, but you didn't do it because you chose to. You were following Oberon's orders. This isn't my fault."

"Isn't it?"

"What do you want from me? I'm not apologizing for fixing you."

"I want us to leave. Now." Finally, he looked down at me. "We go back to the warcruiser and return to Faerie where you will take up your place as Oberon's shadow. All of this"—he gestured with his left hand at the silent city —"whatever is going on here, is irrelevant. Only Faerie matters. Only Oberon matters."

"No." I watched Talen's silvery outline take shape. "I think it's entirely relevant."

"Your vakaru was an animal. Leave him."

Sirius didn't see my smile. I liked my animal. "And Talen?"

He considered the question. "He would make a valuable ally."

"What did he say to you, Sirius? Why do you no longer want him dead? What did you and Talen agree on?"

"In exchange for my word that I would not harm you or the people on Hapters, he told me something the king needs to know."

And what could Talen possibly know that was worth all that? "What did he tell you?"

Sirius's eyes glittered with knowledge and relief. "He told me how Faerie will be saved."

"Talen told you that?"

"Yes."

"Talen told you how to save Faerie from withering away?" Talen, who was supposed to be on our side, supposed to be part of the Messenger myth, had told the king's guardian knowledge so valuable that many would kill for it and many had died for it. We were meant to be saving the systems from Faerie, not making the fae stronger. "You believe him?" I asked, sealing my shock deep down where Sirius couldn't see it.

"He cannot lie."

That was right. He couldn't. Just whose side was Talen on?

"How can Faerie be saved, Sirius?" I asked.

"That is knowledge Oberon will hear from my lips and not yours."

Powerful knowledge indeed. "I'll remove that tek-arm if you tell me."

He scowled, shattering all those handsome male angles, making him seem cutting and hard. "Not even the promise of being made whole again and being rid of this tek could make me reveal this knowledge and certainly not to you, someone known to betray those closest to her."

I glared back at him. "I haven't betrayed Oberon. I've done everything he's asked of me."

"And yet the Dreamweaver still lives."

My mouth twitched. "I'll rectify that the next time I see him."

He smirked in a way that had me wanting to free my whip and square up to him. "Your weak saru mind cannot withstand the Dreamweaver."

Ugh. Fae. "Maybe your new arm will whittle down some of that fae ego you lord over every other race."

"We are protofae. Everything you see, hear, touch, taste, and breathe belongs to us."

I shook my head and descended the ramp. How different my view of Faerie and its children was now. At one time, I would have agreed with him. A fae like Sirius could never see the truth outside of Faerie. He was blind to it, just like I had been. "You." I pointed a finger at Talen. "With me."

He watched me stride past him, heading back the way he had come and then looked up at the approaching warcr-suier and her shadow. "It is not dark yet."

"We need to talk before I *bleed*."

When we entered the pyramid, the light had changed, softening the edges, but the crisscross claw marks on the walls were still visible. I stopped at the plinth, exactly where Kellee had stood... where, long ago, he had made the wrong choice and killed the human woman. I wasn't losing him to the past. I wasn't losing any of them.

I plucked a dagger from my belt—borrowed from Arran—held my wrist over the stone plinth, and pushed the tip in.

"Not yet!" Talen lunged in, but abruptly stopped when he saw the look on my face.

"I survived Faerie for over two decades," I told him. "I survived the saru harvest, survived Dagnu and a thousand battles in Faerie's arenas. I survived the queen, survived Oberon pouring acid under my skin to make me a tek-whisperer, survived the warfae markings never meant to touch mortal flesh. I survived the so-called affections of every fae who thought they could play with a saru and throw her away." He flinched. Good. "I survived the worst of them. The Dreamweaver got inside my head and under my skin until I didn't even know my own name anymore. I survived what he did to me."

My words settled in the following silence.

"Don't make me add you to that list, Talen. Because whatever or whomever you are, if you hurt me, I will survive you, and I'll stop you. Don't make me your enemy."

"I'm not your enemy," he replied firmly.

"You told Sirius how to save Faerie."

"Yes."

Yes?! "By-cyn, Talen, tell me I can trust you. Promise me that."

He closed his cool fingers around my hand and drew the knife away from my wrist. "You *can* trust me."

"I wish... I wish I knew you. The real you, beneath all the secrets."

"Do you really?" He still had my hand in his. He pressed it to his chest, and his heart galloped beneath my palm. "I wish the same. But you do not know what you ask of me, Mylana."

Because he wouldn't tell me!

He was too close again, too Talen, and just like before, his presence filled this room and drowned me in the feel of him, the overwhelming sense that he was more than this fae standing in front of me. More than I could understand.

"I cannot speak the things you wish to know, but some answers you have already seen." He pressed his other hand to my chest. "The bond was a mistake. It was meant to temper something in me. I saw power in you, and I thought I could calm these things inside if I was bonded to a mortal, but I didn't know... I didn't understand who you are, but I do now. I know you. I see you."

Why was there sadness in his eyes?

"I can't tell you who I am." He swallowed and said carefully, "But I can tell you who you are."

"There is no mystery in me."

He smiled his sorrowful smile and lifted his hand to press a finger to my lips. When he pulled away, I sensed the weight of his words and the truth barricaded behind them.

"Talen, this isn't about me."

"You're wrong. It has always been about you."

You're wrong. She is everything.

"The magic you feel," he breathed, "the power you believe is mine, it was always in you, Mylana. Just a spark so small it could be hidden among the saru, where you grew, where you survived."

I pressed my hand over my heart because an ache was spreading, a terrible, hollowing emptiness that threatened to change my past, my future. Everything.

"My lana," Talen said. "It has meaning. You know this. It's why you guarded your name so fiercely, and it's why you told me, because you had to breathe life into it, and I knew for certain from that moment."

Mylana. My slave name. The only truth of me I truly owned. "Talen, Kellee needs us—"

"It means *my star*." The words were free, and the truth with them. "You don't see it. You can't see it. No one can but me. I saw it in you from the moment we met. There is a light in you, Mylana. Put there by Oberon. You are a caged thing. You always were."

His words clicked into place, like a key slotting home in its lock, but I dared not open the door those words had revealed. "You can't do this, Talen. You can't say these things."

"I can. Because they are true."

I flung my gaze at the chamber door behind me. The light was fading. "You can't do this now. It isn't fair. I am saru. I am... I am the Wraithmaker. My past... is mine. Not theirs, and not yours to twist like Eledan tried to. I will always be saru." I placed the back of my hand on the plinth, watched my veins throb in my wrist. Saru. My blood ran red. "I was born of the earth, grown for the fae, and harvested into their service. I fought with everything I ever had to survive, to be saru. Faerie can't take that away from me." My voice shook, parts of me cracking open. "Your words can't take that away from me."

"I'm not taking anything of yours, just revealing more." Talen appeared in front of me. His eyes were bright in the gloom. "You are saru, but you're more. Eledan knew it. He took Mab's gift of power and knew then. It's why he didn't kill you when your usefulness was over. Why he kept you. Why he calls you the nothing girl, seeking to wear you down, and why he haunts you still. It's why you're changing. You feel the truth, Mylana. You always have. You seek the polestar in distant places when a fragment is within you, and always has been. My lana, a name, the gift of truth, given to you by someone who hid you in plain sight. Who gave you that name?"

"I don't know." I'd always had it. It was the center of me. My first memory. My single truth. The one thing I truly owned. And now? What was he saying? That something of Faerie had named me, that *Oberon* had named me? That my king had hidden a secret in me?

I lifted the dagger. What little light shone through the door licked down the blade and sparked at its tip. And behind it, gathering in the shadows, Talen's bright power rippled outward.

The blade plunged down, sinking deep into my forearm. The pain meant nothing against the screaming inside my head. I tore the blade free, spilling blood where a vakaru war chief had once killed a human woman, sacrificing her to the sidhe gods. Talen's outline glowed now. I blinked, catching sight of something impossible. I'd seen it before, just for a second when he had torn free of the warcruiser. Hidden inside the light, hidden so deeply behind Talen's blazing star-like glory, twin shadows beat as one.

Not shadows...

Wings. Wings made of Faerie's darkest night, pricked by a thousand distant stars.

He couldn't speak his name, but he could show me.

Talen wasn't made of light. He was hiding inside it.

The truth made liars of us both.

All around, smoky wraiths twitched in and out of time, blurring Valand's past and present into one. Wraiths bubbled from the floor, the walls, from between the blocks, and seeped from the score marks. They turned to Talen, and on their unseelie lips, they whispered, *"Nightshade..."*

CHAPTER 21

*a*saru and a fae, both and neither. A lie and the truth. We were coming undone.

I pushed it all away, but I couldn't push away the sight of the shadows crowding Talen's back or the knowledge burning in his infinite silver eyes.

Stardust and shadow. Death and darkness.

I saw it in him now, the terrible yawning power, as though he could reach out and snuff out the stars of Faerie's sky one by one.

He knew how to fix Faerie.

He knew my name.

He knew too much.

He *was* too much.

The walls and floors bubbled and boiled with vakaru wraiths. But Talen speared his gaze into me, pinning me still as my blood flowed down the plinth's sides.

Fear clutched my heart. The Talen I'd known wasn't real. He never had been. The truth had always been there, lurking in his silences, in the things he didn't say, in the power he kept controlled.

I had asked to know him, the real him, and now I looked upon the truth. But I hadn't been prepared for this. Fear's jagged edges hacked at our bond, and Talen's infinite eyes widened with an echo of terror.

"*Nightshade...*" the wraiths hissed, filling the air. Vakaru who were unseelie at heart. The Nightshade's unseelie.

The enormous wings made of shadow flexed wide, like they might consume entire worlds, consume me.

I stole a step backward, thoughts spiraling out of control. I'd brought him here. I'd freed him. I'd freed the unseelie ruler. And now he had a warcruiser. He had the unseelie on Hapters and the vakaru wraiths. He had me... Had he somehow steered us all here to this very moment?

And now Kellee was gone, and the vakaru were... rising *all around.*

I couldn't think past him, couldn't breathe around the weight of his power. I turned, sensing the enormous pressure of Talen's storm pushing down, and ran from the pyramid.

"Kesh?!" Arran was running toward me, Sota hot behind him, but so too were the wraiths. They flowed in, thickening inside lengthening shadows, until they rose as one and crashed over Arran and Sota, washing all signs of them away.

No, not Arran. Not Sota!

"No!" I screamed. "You can't have them!"

Talen was doing this. Back at the temple, he hadn't been looking for the polestar. He'd likely already known its pieces weren't here. He had been waking the vakaru. On Hapters, he had freed the dark fae. Wrapped in light, I'd missed the darkness in him. He'd calculated every move, and I'd fallen into his trap the moment he had knelt to me, with tears in his eyes, asking me to free him. He hadn't meant the prison, just like he'd said. He'd meant for me to free him and the unseelie.

I ran, seeing Sirius on the shuttle's ramp, his tek-arm outstretched and glistening. Just a few more strides. My boots thumped against the stone path. Blackness flooded across the plaza, rushing in from all sides to swallow Valand's green stones. It looked like water, deep and hungry. And in seconds, it would slam into me. I'd drown and disappear like the rest.

Arran was gone. Kellee had been taken.

But I wasn't giving up. The darkness couldn't have them. I was getting them back.

I hammered up the ramp, feeling it tilt upward beneath me as Sirius hit the button to close the door. A second later, the ramp slammed shut, followed by the combined outraged roar of a thousand lost souls.

Talen.

Oh by-cyn...

What had he done?

Wraiths crawled over the shuttle's screen, their twitching outlines a mass of heaving shadows.

Sirius recoiled from the screen. "Where are the others?"

I gripped the back of the pilot's chair and fixed my attention on the pyramid entrance far across the churning black waters. Talen hadn't come out. "Gone."

"Gone?"

"The wraiths took them, the same way they took Kellee."

"Then we should fly out of here and be rid of this forsaken place."

I couldn't leave Kellee, or Arran, or Sota. I wasn't leaving at all. The wraiths hadn't killed Kellee. He'd vanished, so they'd taken him somewhere. With any luck, Sota and Arran would be in the same place. I had to go to them. I had to find them. If Talen was right, if I truly had the light of the polestar within me, then he wouldn't let me die. He needed me and the fragment Oberon had hidden inside me.

"I have to go back out there."

"Where's Talen?" Sirius demanded.

The Nightshade is Talen.

Was it true? My silver fae, my gentle, quiet, powerful, proud fae. Could he truly be the vanquished unseelie ruler?

I knew only what I'd seen. He could control the unseelie. He had woken them on Hapters, woken the ghosts of vakaru here, and now, he could stop them. I pressed my hand to my heart and felt the bond lashing like bait caught on a hook, trying to free itself before it was swallowed whole. We *were* bonded. He wouldn't hurt me. He *couldn't* hurt me.

"Sirius." I breathed in and held that breath, Talen's touch fluttering around my heart. "Things just got a whole lot more complicated."

The guardian's expression shut down. "What happened?"

"Talen is not who I believed him to be."

I am not who I once was... I winced at the echo of Talen's words. Maybe he wasn't the monster from the myths, but he certainly wasn't someone I knew.

"But he won't hurt me," I said aloud, mostly for my benefit. The second I opened the shuttle door, the wraiths would rush in. Sirius would be gone too, and they would surely swallow me moments later.

"You're opening the door?" Sirius asked, already seeing the answer in my determined expression. "Why? We can leave right now and return to Faerie. Why would you risk your life for them?"

For Arran, for Kellee, for Sota, I'd risk it all. Perhaps even for Talen too. It was too early to tell. "They are each a part of me, a part of who I want to be." I didn't expect Sirius to understand, but perhaps one day he might, if we survived the next few minutes.

Sirius blocked the door. "I cannot allow this. I lost my arm to keep you safe, and now you insist on walking out there? The king tasked me with bringing you to him, and I intend to uphold that order." He looked as though he might tackle me. He'd probably win too.

"Can you fly this tek-shuttle?" I asked.

He swallowed, the answer obvious.

"Then you don't have a choice." I dropped my hand to my side, hovering it close to the whip. "Get out of my way, Sirius."

"Your life is worth more to the king than your love is worth to them."

That was probably true. But I couldn't live with myself if I walked away, whether my friends loved me or not. I stepped around Sirius. "Don't worry. I have a knack for surviving."

The guardian sighed behind me. "Until you don't."

I hit the button and the door seal cracked open. Time held its breath, and then the wraiths plunged inside.

VALAND. But so very different. Movement and life and laughter. I blinked into the glare to clear my vision. Color swirled, mixing like the color in Valand's sky, but it wasn't my eyes that were blotted with too much color. The world was... blurred.

I looked back, expecting to find the shuttle and Sirius, but the space behind me was filled not with spacefaring tek, but with people. Stalls lined the walls, bright awnings cast over them like flags, and the people drifted between them. Not fae, not even close. Broader, heavier, stronger, but beautiful nonetheless. Children wove between the groups, dragging sticks behind them so they clicked over the stones, punctuating the rise and fall of the crowd's swell of collective voices.

This was... *before*.

I wandered forward, letting my feet carry me in no particular direction. They spoke a language I didn't recognize, but I didn't need to understand them to know they were happy. *Life* bubbled everywhere, in their smiles, their voices, the way they touched one another, and in their eyes, rimmed in gold. Vakaru. All of them. But this wasn't a warring race. These weren't soldiers. They were just... people.

A shadow washed over the plaza and the chatter of a thousand people died. I followed their gazes and looked up into the sky. A ship blocked out the light—a world-eater. Enormous, even by warcruiser standards.

The vakaru fell to their knees, and the scene swirled. Colors bled away like paints washed in the rain, swirling into a storm of gray. When it settled, I set my eyes on the only spot of color left: a fae I hadn't seen in five years.

Oberon.

The prince stood in the center of the plaza, his blue robes threaded with cold silver. No crown, he wasn't yet king, but he regarded the kneeling vakaru like one. *No, not like a king... like a god.* His glittering eyes skimmed my way. I dropped to one knee and bowed my head, facing the stone. I had knelt to him a thousand times, I had wept at his touch, but never had it felt so wrong as it did now.

"Droch-fhoula has failed you." He spoke in fae, a language I knew well. His words rippled through the vakaru.

A man to my right sobbed into his clenched hand. I blinked at him, at the sight of this strong male vakaru crying so freely, at the child clinging to his father's leg, eyes locked on their god.

"You have failed me," Oberon said.

No. I lifted my head and looked at my king. *No, it is you who has failed them.*

"You harbored a human among you, invited her onto your soil. Faerie's soil. You listened to her poisonous words seeded with rebellion."

Oberon's voice carried far into the silence. More sobs followed in its wake.

I stared at my king, stared into the past. *Don't do this.*

"Your chief believed her blood sacrifice would suffice, but the betrayal is rooted far deeper and must be torn from this land. Faerie will not suffer betrayers."

"Mercy!"

Oberon's unblinking gaze settled on the speaker. *"Mercy?"* he asked.

More cries for mercy darted about the vakaru, and with each voice, Oberon's gaze thinned, turning brittle. He was not merciful.

I rose to my feet in a sea of Oberon's kneeling subjects and opened my mouth to beg for them.

"Please," Kellee said.

He stood among them, a splash of color in the gray, his head lifted to the king while someone beside him clutched his hand. A young woman or a child, I couldn't see. But others also reached for him. He wore the same simple clothes as his people, patched with colors. Long dark hair fell in waves down his back, tied with feathers and beads, making the firm cut of his jaw and the pride in his eyes more prominent.

He walked forward, through his people. The woman's hand slipped from his, and others brushed their hands over him, their reverence clear. They loved him.

Oberon watched Kellee approach, his face unreadable.

Kellee knelt before his god. He looked up, eyes pleading. "My lord, the mistake was mine."

"A mistake indeed." Oberon lifted a hand. His sleeve spilled down his arm, revealing thorned ink spiraling from elbow to wrist. He clicked his fingers.

Light blazed. There and gone again in a blink. And for a moment, nothing had changed. Then the wailing started. The wrenching sound of loss chilled my blood.

"My child!?"

The male vakaru to my right watched his child's little hand, nestled in his, dissolve into smoke and shadow. He grabbed for his son, perhaps to stop what had already been done, but his arms sailed through the nothing space left behind, turning his child to dust.

My thoughts stuttered.

"No!" Kellee roared. From where I stood, I saw how his claws sprang free, how rage and fear and grief raced across his face, and how Oberon looked down on him as though nothing had changed.

Oberon had come here to kill this world, to end his unseelie experiment the same way he wanted to end the human one. It wasn't Kellee's fault, but history remembered it this way.

Oberon's left hand shot out. He caught Kellee by the

chin and jerked him to his feet. *"You continue to defy me even as your people die."*

"Don't take them, don't take my people. Not my vakaru!"

Another flick of Oberon's right hand. More light. More screams. But the vakaru ran. They burst apart, fleeing. There was nowhere to hide. Oberon's ship likely had them all pinned in its sights. The blasts of light came from the world-eater in orbit. A click of his fingers and people died. It was so... easy.

Kellee knew then that all was lost. "You are no god." He swung for Oberon, but the prince brought his arm around, his fae marks blazing, and Kellee's claws clashed against them as though striking a shield.

Oberon's thin lips curved into a sharp smile. *"The vakaru die here today, but not you. You will forever be apart from them, forever alone, forever wishing you had saved your people."* The prince pulled Kellee close. *"I admire you, Droch-fhoula. Without you, the vakaru would be beasts. You brought order to chaos, but they have served their purpose, and now all this must end. Everything but you."*

Oberon flung Kellee down, lifted his hand again, and scanned the crowd of scattering vakaru. They gathered their children and clutched one another, sobbing, begging, pleading to their god, and Oberon watched and heard it all. The click of his fingers echoed in the silence that followed.

Screams gone.

Begging cut short.

I blinked, and it was over. The shadow of Oberon's enormous ship had vanished, as had the king.

And Valand was empty but for a single vakaru abandoned in the plaza. He looked tiny, suddenly, in this big, empty world.

"Kellee?"

The name rippled far and wide, turning over and over and over, and the colors at the edges of my sight blurred, reminding me this was all happening somewhere else. Some*time* else.

He lay half-sprawled on the ground, his head down, claws out, bathed in Valand's unforgiving light.

He didn't look like my Kellee. He looked like a wild, colorful, messy version of the dark, somber marshal I knew. Would this Kellee even know me?

"Kellee..." I said, softer this time. He didn't move, didn't look up, but his shoulders heaved with the effort of keeping himself under control. I kneeled and reached out a hand toward his, acutely aware that a twitch was all it would take to slice me open. "Kellee, pl—"

He snapped his head up, and for a second, the beast looked through his eyes. Then his focus softened, and the haunted look fell away. His appearance stuttered, flickering like the wraiths, so that my Kellee was back—long coat, pulled-back ponytail, and a few hundred years' worth of anguish gathering in his eyes. "Kesh, you... you saw that?"

I gripped his shoulder, sinking my fingers in. "Listen. Oberon was always going to kill your people that day. He came in a ship grown to kill worlds. It didn't matter what you said or did. You couldn't have saved any of them."

Kellee searched my eyes, his face a mixture of confusion and grief. I didn't know what it was like to lose everything, but I knew Oberon. The king had come here to kill a world and cleanse Faerie of anything unseelie.

Kellee gripped my arm, locking us together, his gaze fused with mine. "You're here."

Had he thought I'd leave him? I mustered a small smile.

He pulled me into his arms, clamping me so close I could feel his heart thumping and hear his breaths fluttering, but above it all, it was his trembling that had me gripping him so damn tightly. Kellee was never afraid, he never showed weakness, he didn't falter, but now, in my arms, his tremors told me he was more real than I'd ever known him.

"You can't stay here... in the past." Talen's words came back to me. *Don't lose him to the past.* And with it came the terrible knowledge that the Nightshade was waiting on the other side of all this. "Kellee, I need you with me. We need you with us."

"Why didn't Oberon kill me?"

I clutched Kellee's face in both hands and held him still. "Marshal, we need you. You can make a difference. You told me if Oberon kills you, he wins. You're wrong. He wins when you let him win. Don't let him win. Come back with me. There are things happening outside of the past. I need you, Kellee. Halow needs you. This Messenger needs you."

The look in his eyes had my heart beating too fast, like he was seeing me anew, and it frightened me more than Oberon ever could. I knew who he wanted me to be, and I knew I'd let him down in the past. The unguarded hope in his eyes was real and raw, and he was laying all that hope on me.

He touched my face and tilted his head, as though figuring something out. Frown lines creased his brow. "I don't deserve you."

"No, you stupid, stubborn fool, you don't. But I don't deserve you either. So we're even. Let's find Arran and Sota and get out of here."

Kellee pulled away and looked around him. He scrambled to his feet, his frown deepening. "This isn't now."

"No, you said Valand was timeless, and now we're stuck in its past." I shielded my eyes and saw a flying blur streaking toward me. The blur quickly became a ball of lethal tek. Sota whirred to a halt a few feet in front of me, guns armed.

"Kesh, everything is an echo," he said. "We're here, but not here, and they are there and here. It's confusing."

"It's confusing for all of us."

Arran jogged up to us, daggers in his hands. "Anyone wanna tell me what's going on? There was a ship... a fae. Was it Oberon? I saw people."

He had seen it all too.

"Where are they?" Kellee whispered.

"Who?" Arran asked.

"The dead. They were right here..."

I closed my eyes and felt the lashing barbs of the bond tugging me back. When I opened my eyes again, they looked to me for answers. "Talen has them."

CHAPTER 22

Outside the pyramid, shimmering colors flickered whenever I tried to focus on them, but inside, all was still.

"He was right here." I stood at the plinth, saw my bright red blood staining its sides, blinked, then watched that blood fade away. The wound on my wrist had healed, leaving no trace behind. My human mind struggled to place the real and the unreal together. The present, the past, the future. The vakaru wraiths had pulled us into the past. But Talen... He was still in the present.

"Talen's here?" Arran asked.

Was he Talen, or was he something else? "The Nightshade."

"He's not the Nightshade," Kellee dismissed, circling the plinth.

"Then he's something, Kellee. Something dark and powerful. Something the unseelie call the Nightshade."

"I thought he was light fae." Arran reached to touch the claw marks that scored the walls and pulled his hand back when they appeared to move.

"So did I."

"You asked him and he said no. He can't lie." Kellee stopped in the same place I'd last seen Talen—back in the present—and peered across the chamber at me.

"Whatever his name is, it doesn't matter right now. He's out there and we're here. He freed the fae on Hapters, and I think he's here for the vakaru wraiths." He was collecting unseelie, resurrecting them or waking them, or something I couldn't afford to think on while we were trapped in time.

"You still feel him?" Kellee asked. He braced his hands on the plinth between us.

I nodded. I felt him as though he were standing next to me. Listening. Watching. Like always.

"Then he hasn't left us."

"Yet," Arran added.

Kellee shot Arran a look. "He's Talen. Whatever you both think, I've known him longer than your combined lifespans. Maybe if Kesh had stayed with him instead of running, we'd know what that reason was."

I swallowed. Maybe I should have stayed, but that hadn't seemed like an option at the time. You don't linger in a room with that kind of darkness and wait for it to swallow you. "How do we get back?"

"Blood," he growled. "With vakaru, it always comes back to blood."

I lifted my arm and regarded my smooth wrist.

"Not yours."

Arran tossed Kellee a dagger. He caught it, clamped it between his teeth, and rolled up his sleeve. Freeing the dagger, Kellee flexed his fingers, stretching the tendons in his forearm, increasing the blood flow. "It must be my sacrifice." He pressed the blade into his forearm and pushed toward his palm, opening the vein in his wrist. Blood flowed freely over his hand and dripped from his fingers onto the plinth.

"He showed you the truth, like you've been asking all along. Don't run from him." Kellee lifted his gaze and locked it on me, holding me in the moment as the air rippled, the walls bowed, and Kellee's past shimmered out of sequence, peeling back to reveal the now.

The sensation of the ground and walls tipping leveled out, and with it came the storm of snarling growls. I'd expected to find Talen in the pyramid with us, but we stood alone, and outside, the mass of noise swelled, crashing through the silence.

Kellee dashed from the room. Sota shot over my head, and Arran and I followed.

I didn't know what we would find, but the sounds of tearing, of wet snarls and vicious yowls, sounded like animals in pain.

Outside, the warcruiser hung in the sky, casting a shadow over the silent city, only now it was no longer silent. The walls, the plaza, they *moved*, painted in living shadow.

Sota shot forward, high above the plaza, and zeroed in on the bright eye of the maelstrom: the shuttle and Talen. But this wasn't my calm, composed Talen. He was something else. He blazed with a light almost too bright to look at for long. Silver eyes scored the dark waves churning around him, and twin shadows danced in the air behind him—his wings, made of smoke and glittering dust.

Between him and us, the countless dark shapes of the vakaru swelled again and again, but each time, Talen's light held them back.

It wouldn't last.

There were too many, and as bright as he was, his light wouldn't be enough.

"We have to help him," Kellee yelled over the thunderous noise. Claws glinting, he eyed the sea of vakaru, but there was no way through.

If Talen was the Nightshade, shouldn't he have been able to stop them? He wasn't attacking at all. They slammed into his light over and over, wearing him down, and he did *nothing*.

Kellee was right. We had to help him.

I flicked my palm, activating the ocular link with Sota. Instantly, my vision flickered, seeing through the drone's eye from above. Sota had a grid spread across the ocean of wraiths, each one marked with a red-dot target.

"Help him," I told my drone.

Sota's gun ports jolted open, and the drone opened fire, peppering the vakaru with searing precision blasts, tearing their shadowy form to pieces. The flanks surrounding Talen crumbled, and Talen straightened, widening his phantom wings. His gaze speared straight to me—through me—sinking a hook into my chest, around my heart, and yanked. I'd staggered and fallen to a knee before I had a chance to draw breath.

"Kesh?" Arran was beside me, his hand on my shoulder, but I couldn't look at him or anyone. I cut the link with Sota so only Talen occupied my thoughts. The vakaru boiled around him, slamming into his light and recoiling—a light now throbbing brighter. Its heat beat in time with my heart, and Talen's power sang, bursting to life between us.

If his words were true, if there was something hiding in me, some fragment of the polestar, then was this light... mine?

I am yours, he had told me. *Free me.*

He knew me. He always had. But I was only beginning to know him.

"They're retreating..." Arran said, his voice far away and getting more distant as I fell into my thoughts of Talen.

Sota ceased firing.

"Vakaru never retreat." Kellee drifted forward, toward the ocean of ghosts. "They're *kneeling.*"

More light beat over Talen, sweeping up the enormous arched wings, igniting their smoky outlines on fire, and I felt it inside me, a power so great, so consuming, it might swallow me, this city, this entire world whole.

I am not who I once was.

Whatever he was or wasn't, he *was* mine.

His eyes pleaded with me to know him, to understand, pleaded with me not to be afraid. But I was afraid, and he was right. Nothing would ever be the same again. I pushed against the weight of power and stood to look Talen in the eye from across a sea of long dead vakaru.

The rippling darkness stilled.

Silence flooded back into the city.

And just like that, Talen had an army of wraiths kneeling before him. And they weren't alone.

Kellee knelt too, his head bowed.

Only Arran and I stood facing the dark-winged Nightshade, because despite his denials, he could be nothing else. And here, he was the god the vakaru had been waiting for, the unseelie myth and legend brought back with my help.

Talen lifted his hand and closed his fingers into a fist. He hadn't blinked, hadn't taken his eyes off me, but his gaze wasn't a challenge. He was afraid. Not of the vakaru, but of... me.

Above, the warcruiser filling the sky yawned backward, shrinking, until Valand's light once more washed over the plaza, boiling the dark-loving vakaru away. But something told me they weren't entirely gone. Just... somewhere else, ready for the one who controlled them to summon them.

When the light hit Talen's wings, they also simmered away to nothing. He blinked, the light sloughed off him, and he was just violet-eyed Talen again, the hair cascading around his shoulders the only testament to the wildness we had all witnessed.

"Who is he?" Arran whispered.

Kellee rose from his kneeling position. "Wrong question." He started forward.

My attention skipped from Talen to the marshal and the bond loosened, allowing me to breathe freely again. "*What* is he?" I whispered.

CHAPTER 23

*F*ear.

I had always mastered it before. Mastered it like I'd mastered my time behind bars as the fae's renowned gladiator. Fear had stalked me my entire life, but it had never won.

On the warcruiser, I tucked myself into a corner of a makeshift "bar" Hulia had set up inside the ship's belly, selling or trading the likes of water and some other concoction she had cooked up. Hulia had always been an opportunist with an eye on filling a need. Chairs and tables had grown in random places across the floor of what had once been a storage chamber. Hapters's refugees kept to their half of the room, while the fae—the handful who deigned to make an appearance—adopted a table in the opposite corner. They didn't so much as sit and enjoy themselves as glower. They were here for one purpose only: to watch their enemies closely.

I was alone, lost in my thoughts while feeling the part inside me that belonged to someone I feared. Fear had me wanting to cut the bond out. Fear drove me inside my own thoughts, wanting to flee back to Oberon and pretend none of this had ever happened. But I hadn't let fear rule me before and wasn't about to let it now. I would confront Talen. Soon.

I expected Arran, or Sota, to find me. Talen wouldn't come where Sirius's flight might observe him, and Kellee was probably with him. So when Sirius stalked through the bar, sending some of Hapters's people scurrying, it was enough to stall my thoughts.

"When do we leave?" The guardian loomed, tall, broad, and overbearing, even with the hacked-up hair and tek-arm hidden beneath his cloak. Or maybe it was because of his new look that he garnered terrified glances from not only Hapters's people, but his flight as well.

"Sit," I told him.

His auburn eyebrow arched.

"Please."

The guardian arranged all his considerable presence into the chair, filling it with dark reds and earthy browns. I noticed how his cloak and leathers had frayed in places. The magic holding it together was weakening this far from Faerie. Or perhaps the tek grafted to his arm was eating at his prowess.

"We're going back to Hapters," I told him.

"Why?"

"Because Talen can deal with the unseelie problem and get those people their homes back." I hadn't yet asked Talen. But I would, and if he refused, well, then I would know whose side he was on.

Sirius's smile was razor thin. He leaned forward. "I was in the shuttle on Valand. I saw your fae control, contain, and then banish the vakaru wraiths. On Hapters, he *freed* the winged dark fae. What makes you think he'll put them all back in their box for you? You are delusional if you think a sidhe lord of his caliber will answer to you, a saru."

I didn't reply.

"Come with me now, calla." Sirius reached out with his metal hand and settled it on mine in an oddly intimate gesture. The touch was cool and hard, utterly devoid of magic. "We must return to Faerie, to Oberon."

And leave Talen free to unleash all the unseelie for reasons I didn't yet understand? How could I? "Where is Eledan?" I asked, prying my hand from beneath his.

Sirius frowned at the change in subject. "The mad prince is contained."

"Oberon had me kill his brother to clear the path to the throne. I tricked Eledan and tore his heart out, but he still lives." *And he knows too much.* He had sought the polestar for centuries when Faerie thought him dead. He had its pieces, but not me. Was I the last piece? There was so much I didn't know, but I would know. From now on, my questions would be answered. But first, I needed to know Eledan was far, far away.

The guardian stared back at me. He had known or suspected Oberon's plans for me for a long time. How could he not? He had witnessed the king train me and subject me to Faerie's poisons in another of his experiments. Sirius and I had always had an understanding. I was Oberon's secret obsession, and he observed without comment.

"Wherever Eledan's body is contained, it may not be enough. His mind is free." I swallowed around the knot in my throat, hearing that distinct laughter all over again. "He wants revenge on Oberon."

"You know this for certain?"

"Eledan is within his rights to kill Oberon for what

the king has done, and much of Faerie will stand with Eledan. Sjora thought him a hero, and I doubt she's alone in that admiration. I also know Eledan was searching for an ancient Faerie weapon, its pieces cast throughout the stars, and he found some pieces. If he has them all, we need to know where he took them and maybe we can... destroy it." *Use it.* I could use it against Faerie. Use it to stop the war, to stop the fae, to free the saru, the namu, and the humans—when the time came, which it would. "I am trying to save Oberon by tracking down all the pieces. He'll need the polestar." Lies. All of it. If Oberon had hidden something of the polestar inside me, that had been his mistake. I wouldn't give it up. Now more than ever, I had a chance to make things right.

"You're searching for the polestar *for* the king?"

"Yes." I held his gaze like the professional liar I was.

He regarded me as though the harder he stared, the more he could unravel my lies, but few could see past them. Frowning, he leaned back and glanced around us. His flight and Hapters's people were watching us, the king's guardian and the Wraithmaker having a little heart to heart alone.

I was surprised Sota wasn't here recording the entire conversation to share with Arran.

"You are his guardian not because you follow orders," I added. "He has a thousand fae who answer to his every word. You're Oberon's guardian because you love the king. When we return, and we will, you'll have the knowledge of how to stop Faerie's decline and I'll have the polestar. With those two things, nothing will be able to stop Oberon, not even his brother. That is how we must return to Oberon. Triumphant."

How easy the fae were to seduce with their own karushit.

Sirius nodded. "I will not wait forever, Wraithmaker."

I placed my hand over Sirius's metal hand. "We will return to him with gifts he cannot refuse." And Sirius knew, without something to smooth his path, Oberon would frown upon the guardian's new arm. Many would see it as a failure, a defect, and it could ruin his standing among the court. Sirius needed all the help he could get.

"After we return to Hapters, we must depart for Faerie, willingly or not. Refuse and our deal is void, including our agreement to keep your companions safe. Nothing will stop me from fulfilling Oberon's decree." He stood and was about to leave when a stray thought stalled him. "The guardians were not always Oberon's. We are Faerie's protectors first. You would do well to remember that, calla."

He left, and the room released a collective sigh. Sirius had enough fae on the ship to overpower Hapters's refugees. He couldn't overpower Talen, but they already had an *agreement* in place. The guardian would soon stop playing nice. I didn't have much time.

The chatter lifted again, and I lost my thoughts beneath the murmuring.

After everything that had happened on Valand, I had to face Talen, preferably before we arrived on Hapters.

I tapped my palm. "Sota?"

"Yes, Kesh?"

"Where's Kellee?"

"Third level, aft chambers, with Arran."

"And Talen?"

"In his chamber, where he's been since returning to the ship."

I thanked my drone, acknowledged Hulia and her observing presence behind the grown bar, and headed deeper into the ship.

I WATCHED Kellee and Arran spar for strictly professional reasons. Kellee was fast and brutal, whereas Arran had a grace that came from honing his skills for entertainment. I'd fought Kellee and knew he preferred his opponent to see the threat coming. Arran used all the tricks to distract and disarm.

It was over too soon, both breathing hard. I made a concerted effort to keep my eyes from roaming the exquisite display of bare chests. Neither were fae, so I could admire as much as my sexually repressed saru mind could handle. And that was a great deal.

"Kesh!" Arran beamed, spotting me.

Kellee made a sound, like a grunt of acknowledgment, before scooping up his shirt and heading for the opposite exit.

"Kellee?"

He stopped. His grip on his shirt tightened.

"We're good, right?" I asked. It seemed too small a thing to say after everything I'd seen on Valand, but Kellee wasn't the sort to *talk*. His actions did the talking for him.

He smiled over his shoulder. "We're good."

"Have you spoken with Talen yet?" Arran asked after Kellee had left, eyes turning serious.

"No, not yet. I..." *I'm terrified.* "Can we go somewhere?"

Arran's grin faded. "It's not me you need to be with." He ducked his head and passed by, leaving through the doorway behind me. Of course, he was right. I knew exactly where Talen was. These days, I always did. And I should have been with him. He was too important to let slip through my fingers, but how could I speak with him after everything I'd seen?

The walk to Talen's chamber had never felt so long, and with every step, the echo of our bond beat inside my chest. None of what I had seen was okay. Nothing about any of this was *fine,* and it wouldn't go away unless I faced him. Doubts tried to undermine my every step. He controlled the ship, controlled the unseelie, and by-cyn, he even controlled Kellee. What if he was like all the others on Faerie, and this was just the real him shining through?

He was powerful. Too powerful. We had the bond, but he didn't control me like he could control Faerie's monsters. I was the only one who could face him.

I had to do this.

The door to his chamber opened, and there he sat on the end of the bed, his back straight, and his expression indifferent as he settled his gaze on me. And it was all I could do not to turn around and run. But I'd run from him on Valand, and I couldn't afford to give in to those instincts. I wore my coat, my whip was secure at my hip, and Sota was just a mental summons away. I could face the Nightshade as the Messenger. For the sake of Halow, I had no other choice. Kellee would be proud.

"You ran." He said it as though he had only now just realized. His perfect brow crinkled, and those fiercely intense eyes softened.

I took a single step inside, and the door whispered closed behind me, shutting me in with a creature of unseelie legend.

"You ran from me, Kesh." He lifted his chin.

"Talen—"

"You asked to see the truth of me. I showed you." His gaze flicked away. "And you fled."

Another step closer. He could lunge from that bed, turn into something dark, something unreal, and swallow me down in seconds, and there was nothing I could do to stop him. Throughout all this, he had always been fae, and I was saru. I was changing, yes. I could heal quicker, but I could still die like any other mortal saru.

The bond was the only thing keeping me in the room, because it meant he couldn't—wouldn't hurt me.

He stood, and I jolted back, losing the ground I had gained. The downward tilt of his lips sliced straight to my heart.

Why did it have to be like this? Why couldn't he just be Talen again, the quiet, reserved fae who liked to cook and read, the fae who had run with me through our prison? But there had always been more to him. I'd only seen what I'd wanted to see.

Lies, just like the lies I'd once been made of.

"I couldn't tell you," he said. "I can't tell anyone. The words... After I was expelled from Faerie, it was made so I couldn't speak them. It is dangerous to speak them. They have a power of their own and Faerie hears all." Even that admission pained him. He stepped closer again, and this time I fought off all my instincts to back down, to run, to kneel, though my saru heart beat against its bars.

He took another step, bringing him within arm's reach. He looked like Talen—poised and restrained and proud. But that was his armor. The thing I had seen on Valand was powerful and deadly and made of all the worst bits of Faerie.

"I will never hurt you." He couldn't lie, but someone

like him talked so easily around the truth that every breath could be a lie and I wouldn't know it.

He slowly reached out, wary, as though any sudden motion might startle me. His fingertips brushed my face so lightly I wondered if I was imagining the touch. Part of me—the saru part—wanted to brush against his hand, to lean into him, to let him embrace me, because it would be so much easier that way.

"Are you the Nightshade?" I asked. I'd asked before, and I knew the answer, but it was the wrong answer.

"No." He closed that last step between us. His hair, unbraided and free, fell forward, framing his face.

"Are you unseelie?" I asked, words tripping as fear ate away at my barriers.

"Yes." He brushed the backs of his fingers against my cheek, the touch more insistent. "And seelie."

"Both?"

His fingers threaded into my hair, drawing it back from my face, and pleasurable tremors spilled through me.

"How is that possible?"

"All things are possible on Faerie. Time stands still, dreams are breathed to life, stars can be plucked from Night's embrace and given a heart to beat." He pressed his hand over my heart and our bond flared, washing wave after wave of warmth across my skin.

I had heard those words before. Kellee had spoken them... *Plucked from Faerie's sky...* He had been talking about the polestar. Oberon had broken the polestar apart and scattered the pieces to prevent anyone from using the polestar to bring the unseelie back. But the king had kept a piece for himself, and here I was, facing the unseelie's mythical leader. It seemed so... fantastical, like a myth a saru would concoct to whittle away the long hours behind bars.

Thoughts tumbled. *It can't be destroyed, but it can be broken up or altered to resemble other items.*

Talen had known all along. He had asked me to help him, to free him, to share this bond with him. He had steered and guided my path with his small touches and subtle hints. He was not of Winterlands, or Summerlands, not of the ruling courts, but of something else entirely. He was the wildness of Faerie, the parts the courtly lords never could control. He was part of the dark, part of the night, part of the monsters, the wild and hungry, part of chaotic Faerie. All the parts Oberon had sought to destroy.

I looked into Talen's eyes and saw the truth of him looking back at me.

I had been asking the wrong question all along. *I am not who I once was.* The real answer was right in front of me, peering back at me, caged and hidden for so long.

"*Were* you the Nightshade?" I asked.

"Yes," he whispered.

I was expecting to feel more fear, to have to fight to stand so close to him, to have him touch me, but the great weight of fear lifted, and all I felt was relief.

There was the truth. He wasn't the Nightshade, but he had been and could be again. That was why Sjora had used her last breath to say she knew him, why he had dared not speak the name, why he had stayed away from Faerie. As Talen, he was not the unseelie's chosen ruler. He was hiding in plain sight.

"You see now why I cannot speak the words?" he whispered. "Why I could not tell you my name."

Stardust and shadow.

"Talen..." I touched his cheek and danced my fingertips down the side of his face and along his jaw. So perfect. So measured and controlled. All of it camouflage. He hid *inside* the light.

"Did you free the dark fae on Hapters?" I asked.

He was so close I saw every flinch, every tiny line gather around his lips, every miniscule narrowing of his eyes. And now that I knew what he was, I saw the poetry in it all.

"They had been locked away for a long time. The magic used to hold them there had faded. They were already breaking free. My presence spurred them on. I didn't realize how fragile their cage was until it was too late."

"And the vakaru? The truth, Talen. I need to believe you, otherwise it's over. The Messenger, the myth, the good we can do—if I can't trust you, it's all over."

He cupped my face and my heart beat furiously. He could crush me in his hands, turn my feelings inside out, but through all this, he had never once hurt me. Right from the moment we'd met and he had dropped to a knee, he had helped me. When Kellee had first freed him, Talen had asked after me. Time and time again he'd tried to keep me safe. *Only because he knew what you are.*

"The vakaru were lost long ago," he said. "Oberon trapped them in time and shadow, forever reliving their demise. I freed them and bought the Messenger an army."

"Or yourself an army?" I pressed my hands over his and lowered them.

"I am not who I was once." He sounded like Sota, hung up on old code, and I wondered if every time he said those words, he believed them a little more. "Oberon painted me as a monster." He took my hands, still on his, and folded both over his heart. "You know I'm not. You feel the truth in me as I do in you. I know you, as you know me. It was the only way. The bond means we cannot lie to each other. I know you're afraid, and you sense the same in me. And more..."

Oberon had killed the vakaru, I'd seen the past and knew how the king worked. He would not stop until he wiped out everything he despised. The Nightshade, weakened and separated from the unseelie, had done the only thing he could do and withdrawn. The victors had spun tales of unseelie monsters. What was the Nightshade, really? A monster to some, but a hero to others.

I felt the thud of his heart beneath my hand, saw the truth in his wide eyes, and felt the broil of emotions that weren't mine. Strong, mixed feelings of anger and fear, but more too, of anticipation and hope. I did not have it in me to understand something like him, but I knew he was *good* and perhaps that was enough.

I knew too much.

"Kesh..."

I stepped back, out of his hands. If I went back to Faerie, how could I keep all this from Oberon? The polestar, the Nightshade. Oberon would know the moment he saw me. He always knew my secrets, as small as they had been all those years ago. But now my secrets were big.

"Kesh, please..." He stepped forward, reaching. "I couldn't tell you. I wanted to. For so long, I wanted to."

We had the fate of Faerie tied between us and I was the weak link.

"Mylana..." The plea in my name broke me open.

"I... We need to go back to Hapters," I said and backed away toward the door, "to control the unseelie there and give the people their homes back... Then we should separate. We can't... we can't be together. We can't do this." The Messenger and her crusade ended with us. I had to let them go. Talen. Kellee. Arran. It was too dangerous to keep us all together. Eledan knew what I was, and he'd been searching for the other pieces. To what end, I wasn't sure, but it couldn't be good. He would come for me. If Oberon didn't use me first, Eledan would. But if I found the pieces, I could control the polestar, couldn't I?

"You can't do this alone," Talen said, guessing my thoughts.

I needing space to think. I needed to speak with Kellee and Sota and Arran. This involved all of us. "If what you said about me is true, if I am—"

"A star made flesh."

I smiled at the pretty words. The Wraithmaker was not a creature of light, neither was the Messenger, but she could be a harbinger of change. "I am vulnerable to Eledan and to Oberon..." *And to you.* "I must master all these elements conspiring against me. I can, I've done it before. I've always survived, thrived, and I will do the same, but... not with you."

"We are stronger together. Not just you and me, but Kellee and Arran, Sota too. It will take more than the fragment of a star to stop Oberon."

"Is that what you want? To stop Oberon? Or is there more?" Of course there was more. Had he just been Talen, I could have believed stopping Oberon was his only concern, but as the Nightshade, he had his own motives.

"I..." He turned his face away. "When Oberon drove the Dark Legion out of Faerie, he did not understand the consequences. Faerie is hurting. She needs to be made whole."

He had no intention of stopping Faerie at all. He wanted to heal Her.

Left alone with the guardian, Talen had conspired behind my back. His intentions were good, if you were fae. But what would become of saru, namu, and humans?

"Kesh?"

I lifted my hand. I could not play these games with him, with *them*. I didn't have it in me to outthink the fae. I never had. "You told me once I did not know real love."

He didn't reply, but his hands clenched at his sides.

"Maybe I still don't, but I think love is accepting and understanding someone so completely they can tell you they're a monster and the feeling doesn't go away. If anything, it gets stronger. I am afraid of you, the real you, but I understand, Talen. I understand what you must do for your people." He listened in that silent way of his. "And you understand that I cannot stand with you."

"I had hoped we might stand together."

I was beginning to see why Kellee had knelt to him. It was a shame we would likely one day be enemies. But that day was not today. Today, all I saw was Talen, the hopeful, honorable silver fae whose streak of dark humor often had me secretly smiling.

He offered me his hand. "Run with me." The door opened by his silent command.

I looked at that hand, at the open door behind him and the faintest smile flickering on his lips.

"Run where?"

"To the stars... if you can keep up."

Now there was a challenge. He had told me he would never hurt me and the bond ensured he couldn't. So what awaited me if I took his hand? His smile, knowing it as I did now, sent a lick of illicit pleasure way down low.

I closed my fingers around his, locking our hands together. Power tingled under my palm and sparked through my fingers. The power of Faerie, mine and his.

Delight sparked in his eyes.

"Run, *my lana*." And with that, he turned and ran.

Still wrapped in leathers and wearing boots not meant for marathons, I sprang forward, freeing my grip so I could fall into a racing stride. Light rippled through the walls, driving us on, beating with the same pace as my boots, my heart, and his. Talen let me gain on him, and then, ahead, the corridors appeared to swing around, and Talen sped away. I grinned. Of course the walls moved. He was the ship. He could shape our path however he liked.

We ran, and just like during the Game of Lies, magic sparked to life, its electric fizz spreading through my simple saru flesh and bone, setting me ablaze. I ran, chasing the streak of silver ahead, and my muddled thoughts and fears fell away, clearing to a precise point. Chase. Catch. It was freeing, and exhilarating, and a gift.

All too soon, Talen slowed. He barely seemed out of breath, whereas I had to work to fill my lungs with enough air to stop me from passing out.

"She likes you," he said, placing his hand on the shimmering wall. "Always has, since you defied Sjora." There was a looseness to his smile, as though some of his ice had thawed.

"It's an... honor," I panted.

We strode on, entering sections of the enormous ship I'd never ventured down, and since we hadn't passed anyone, I assumed few, if anyone, had explored this deep. There were probably whole areas closed off to passengers.

Deeper and deeper we walked, until the air cooled and took on a flowery bite, reminding me of Faerie's fresh nights before they lingered too long and grew stale. And then a room appeared ahead, its expanse a chamber of blackness.

I jolted to a halt in the doorway as Talen slipped into the shadows. Glitter hung in the air like motionless snow. Where Talen walked, the sparkles shifted around him and settled back into place in his wake. *Like a million wisps*, I thought, but none moved unless Talen was near.

"What is this place?" I entered and the bright speckles parted in front of me.

"Navigation."

The specks of light were... stars? Whichever way I turned, the stars shifted, inviting me inward.

"Each one of these specks represents a star," Talen explained. "Each cluster a galaxy."

I tried to snag one, but it darted away, only to return to its spot once I'd stopped harassing it. "The ship is doing this?"

Talen nodded. "It's how a pilot navigates. Usually we don't have to be here physically to pilot, but I wanted to show you. *She* wanted to show you."

I wandered, watching the stars shift and dance, delighting in their random shimmer. The more I drifted, the more I heard a distant sighing, so soft and quiet I could have imagined it. "The stars sing?"

"You hear it?" His light chuckle was playful and a delight to hear. "Of course you do. Yes, they sing their forever song."

He was behind me and all at once so close. When I looked up, the mischief of the run was long gone, replaced by a deep sincerity. This time, when his fingers eased into my hair and his palm brushed my cheek, I leaned into the touch. How could I not?

"You know me." He drew me close and rested his forehead against mine, filling my world with him. "Like I know you. Like I've always known you."

He tilted his head and closed his eyes as though the touch was all he sought. His mouth brushed mine, his lips cool and soft and oh so tempting. I parted my lips and closed my eyes too, feeling the kiss travel deep, the touch spilling darts of magic across my tongue. And I kissed him back, tasting sweetness and light and power and how it all hung on the edge of fear. He was afraid, just like I was.

He called to the part of me born of the earth, to the practical saru in me devoid of all magic and all things mystical. I had dreamed of being among them, of being loved by them, of pleasing them, of serving them. But I had never dreamed something as bright and untouchable as Talen would look at me as he did now, as though I was the beautiful one, the divine one, the one worth all the stars in the sky.

The kiss ended, and it felt like we'd been standing there forever, surrounded by galaxies, and yet like no time at all.

"I see you battling every day." His thumb brushed my bottom lip. His next words settled where his thumb had tracked. "I see you fighting a war inside, one of loyalty and of a love you have no control over, and I admire how you dare to change your design. Kesh, Wraithmaker, Messenger, Mylana. You have a light in you, one you rarely let shine. Most don't, won't, or can't see it, but as the darkest creature in all of Faerie, I do. Whatever name you choose, you are my star."

He had shown me all of him, and I wasn't running, not anymore.

I kissed him again, with no barriers and no regrets. He

came alive beneath my touch, taking everything I gave. We stood among a million stars and came together like stars might. Sliding his hand down my back, he walked me backward, his touch hastening, mouth seeking more and more of me. His kisses roamed down my neck, each one freeing shivers and ramping up my need to touch him, feel him, taste him. His mouth, somehow hot and cold, scorched where once a collar had held me under control.

I became dimly aware of my back against a wall. My fingers dug at all the laces and buckles holding his jacket closed, locking him behind his armor. When those ties refused to unravel, I pushed my fingers down the front of his pants and yanked him close. An unadulterated growl rumbled through him. He caught my wandering hands, lifted them, and pinned them to the wall. There, he held me, the smile on his lips broad and tantalizing like something forbidden. Trapped, I wanted to nip at that smile, to take it and own it. I pushed my shoulders off the wall to reach him. He teased away, his smile growing. He liked to tease. Wasn't he just full of surprises.

"I've wanted you since I saw you." His eyes flicked up, shrewd beneath their fine lashes. "Wanted it more since you first had your hands on me."

I'd stolen many forbidden touches, but the one that stuck with me the most was when Devere had brought him to me, out cold and covered in blood. I had lain next to Talen after cleaning his wounds, my hand in his. "You were aware of me?"

"Always."

It was my turn to smile. "And while you were bathing after Sjora tried to bond you with the ship, nothing but a wisp of a curtain between us, do you remember? Were you aware of me then?"

"Always," he whispered against my mouth.

I laughed, turning my face away. "You have a mischievous streak."

He pressed in, all of him, so I had no doubts about how much he wanted this. "No more secrets."

"No more secrets," I echoed, feeling somehow exposed but strengthened in this new freedom. He ran a hand down his jacket, pulling open all the frustrating little buckles I would likely have torn free. He shrugged the garment off and tossed it away. Then, as I watched keenly, he crossed his arms over his shirt and pulled it over his head, whipping his hair with it, until the shirt was also gone and I saw those entrancing circular patterns on his chest and how they interlocked and wove over the curve and flow of fine, sculpted muscles. Some swept up, over his pecs toward his shoulders, while others dipped low, riding the abs, funneling toward the defined v and vanishing beneath the waistband of his pants. And I took it all in like a typical saru, by staring and losing my thoughts in a merry chase around the gift he presented.

Those marks weren't pilot markings. They were unique to him, to the Nightshade, and I couldn't think of anything I wanted more than to trace each and every one with my tongue, as low as they could go.

But I wasn't moving, and he was there, within reach, waiting, and I still had my back against the wall and my hands off the goods.

Talen cocked his head, accentuating that wicked gleam in his eyes. "You don't need my permission. Have your way with me, Kesh."

His words had power, and they quickened my breaths and heart and tightened my core. "Be careful what freedoms you allow, fae. I might take them all."

"I might just beg you to."

That was all the permission I needed. A single long step brought me close against him. Warmth radiated off his naked skin, urging me to touch. I placed a finger on the largest mark over his right pec and trailed its path to where it looped beneath his nipple, and there I leaned in and ran my tongue along the rest of its curve, hearing Talen hiss inward.

I roamed my tongue lower, tasting his sweetness. Almost sinking to my knees, when he caught my hand and pulled me upright. "You don't go down on your knees for me."

He swept an arm under my legs, and before I could squeal a protest, he scooped me up into his arms. No one had carried me this way since I was a little girl, and I laughed at the insanity of a fae carrying a saru.

"Amusing, am I?" That voice licked at my desire like his tongue might.

He unceremoniously dropped me on a bed. We were in his chamber. How...? The wall behind him sealed around a hole he had carried me through. "That's how you get around so fast?"

"Is that really what you want to focus on?"

There was a shirtless fae lord at the end of the bed, his long hair gathered to one side and twisted into a loose ponytail seemingly of its own accord. He looked every inch the prime male specimen with eyes of violet and a body that wouldn't quit. But the most alarming part was that he was all mine. And he was waiting —for me.

I propped myself up on my elbows and wondered how far he would go on my word alone. "Strip."

He wet his lips with the tip of his pink tongue and

untied his pants laces. The leather fabric strained around his arousal, leaving little to the imagination.

A *saru* aroused him. I aroused him. How was that even possible?

It shouldn't be.

It was wrong.

This was wrong. But by-cyn, I had never let *wrong* stop me.

Talen left the laces loose and approached the bed. He moved like molten silver, and my saru heart beat so fast at the sight of him approaching I couldn't decide whether I was afraid of the punishment for observing all this, or if it raced in anticipation.

He braced an arm either side of my legs, then a knee, and prowled up my body until we were eye to eye.

I struggled not to drop my gaze, not to spread myself before him and beg his forgiveness for daring to look and admire and want what was forbidden.

"You aren't saru with me," he said. "Stop thinking like one."

I hooked my right leg around his and pulled, shifting his weight to one side. I shoved him over and pinned him down beneath me. Now I had his wrists locked under my hands and his firm body pinned between my thighs. "You're not nearly naked enough."

"And you're still fully dressed," he observed, his eyebrow permanently arched.

That was fair. I sat up and tore my waistcoat off, leaving a loose cotton vest. Not at all flattering, but easily dealt with if he wanted it gone. I planted my hands on either side of his shoulders, fixed over him as though he were my prey. "I have something in mind."

"You do...?"

After a quick glance to my left at the shower behind the drape, I faced him again, catching the approval on his face.

"Naked *and* wet?" he asked.

"I want you in every way, but mostly wet."

He brought his hands up, touched my hips, and then rode his hands beneath my vest, brushing their warm solidity over my stomach. It might have been the first time I'd felt his hands on parts I normally covered up and I couldn't help the small groan that fell from my lips. Then he kissed me, flipped me on my back, and scooped me up again, all in one swift, blurring motion, delivering me to the shower before my head had a chance to stop spinning. Warm water cascaded from above. Its pitter-patter soaked my shirt through and plastered his hair to his face and shoulders. Talen set me down on my feet and skimmed his hands up my back, sending tingles through my dark warfae markings. He couldn't possibly see them, but he knew exactly where they curled and swirled because his fingers traced their lines. Need throbbed low. A need to be close, to be *filled*.

I threw my arms around his shoulders and yanked him down to my level, kissing him like this was the only moment we'd get. His hands dove and cupped my ass, roughly jerking me against his hard bulge. There were still too many layers between us.

Everything we had done, every kiss, every touch, had been asking permission, testing boundaries, but I wanted more. I wanted the real him, raw and in my hands. "I'm not sure I can do this gently." I already sounded wrecked.

"I know I can't," he growled low in my ear.

He pulled at my pants fastenings, tearing some. I lost track of where I had my hands, my mouth. I just needed to feel him closer than this. My vest was gone, and then his warm hand found its way inside my undergarments, stroking and teasing. I only had to think how I wanted his tongue there, and in the next gasp, he was on his knees, water pounding us both. He yanked my pants down over my hips, clasped my thighs in his hands, and swept his tongue deep, but slowly, oh so slowly, over the most sensitive part of me. A few more sweeps and his tongue quickened, swirling lightly, teasing in the same way the rest of him did.

You don't deserve this.

Nothing girl.

I turned my head away but couldn't banish the voice. I had been here before, with Talen on his knees in my dreams, and Eledan had taken him from me. Or Talen was Eledan and I'd let him have all of me, because I'd wanted so badly to be loved and touched like I was worth something to them.

Talen's mouth on mine pulled me back from the memories. His body, wet and hard, smooth and trembling, anchored me to the moment, and the Dreamweaver's wicked laugh faded beneath the sensation of Talen's touch. I dropped my hand, cupping the smoothest, hardest part of Talen. He bucked and braced an arm against the wall over my shoulder. His racing breaths fluttered against my ear.

This impossible myth of Faerie legend was mine. And I planned to never let him go.

I pulled on the loose fastenings of his pants, freeing all of him, and slowly rode my thumb over the sensitive tip. He twitched in my grip. Raw, naked desire flashed in his eyes, sending a heated throb between my legs. Sweet cyn, if I could make him look at me like that, what else could I do? He knocked my hand aside and lifted me against the wall. My pants fell free. He hooked my thighs around his hips and paused—his arousal nudged almost home. I clung to his shoulders and bit my lip to keep from demanding he thrust in deep. He had more control than I did. I sank my nails in and tilted my hips. His hardness pushed in and he was in my arms, his body moving with mine. Power and magic sang, coming to life beneath my skin and his. The black warfae marks spiraling around my arms moved and the circular ink painting his chest shifted too. Or perhaps I was losing my mind, because his exquisite rhythm was undoing me as he seated himself deeper and deeper, touching more than my body, lifting me up, making me bright and so very alive. The bond thrummed between us, power galloping alongside the rapid thumping of our hearts. It was madness and magic and Faerie and everything I'd wanted but could never have dreamed I'd have.

Pleasure broke over me, emptying out my mind, singing through my skin and beyond, reaching inside him as he pumped higher and faster, his desire as wild as he was. When his pleasure crested and slammed over him, freeing his cry, his magic and ecstasy poured through me, lighting me on fire with green licks of wispy life magic.

Talen's eyes blazed silver, and reflected in them, my dark eyes swirled with power too.

He was mine and I was his, and screw Faerie, and Oberon, and the wrongs they championed. Nobody could take this from us.

CHAPTER 24

A light finger traced my warfae markings, wandering over my shoulder, across my collarbone, and down between my breasts. Talen had tucked my back against his chest and encircled me in his arms. He'd been silently exploring my marks since I'd blinked awake. The touch of a single fingertip became several. They circled the lower plain of my belly, and then dallied across my hip before sneaking across my thigh. I knew where I wanted it to go next, but infuriatingly, the touch skipped back to my belly and followed the trail of warfae markings roaming my opposite side. By the time the fingers found my neck and skipped up to my bottom lip, my nipples were hard and the rest of me as primed and wanting.

I nipped at the finger and heard Talen chuckle—an actual chuckle. I hadn't known he could chuckle. Turning in his arms presented the delectable sight of a mussed-up fae. He lay stretched along my left side, head propped on a hand, his hair somehow everywhere *and* artfully poured across his chest and waist, like someone had spilled silver paint over him.

When I'd first seen his tribal markings, I'd wanted to lick him all over. I'd lived that fantasy multiple times in the past few hours, but my desire hadn't waned. With a gentle shove, I rolled him onto his back and trapped his hips beneath me. His long look beneath pale lashes demanded I continue. Who was I to argue with a fae lord?

I nipped at his shoulder and ran my tongue along the inked outline of the first small circle. He kept his gaze on the ceiling, so I saw up close how his throat moved when he swallowed. Another lazy lick and his cheek twitched. Oh yes, I'd found my fae's weakness.

"Are you never satisfied?" he asked, his voice wrecked. *I did that.*

The saru in me purred. "Never."

I mixed the licks with a few achingly light kisses and roamed the defined landscape of his chest. *All mine.* And then I flicked my tongue lower, into the dip at his waist, delighting in the sound of his short intake of breath when I found the little trail of permanent ink at the start of the v that guided me downward.

I trawled my gaze up his length. Violet eyes burned back at me, daring me, pleading with me. So raw. So open. So Talen.

I took his arousal in my hand from the solid base to the sensitive tip. He locked up, fingers digging into the bed. I worked my hand and mouth together, tasting the saltiness as he unwittingly rocked his hips. His face, peering down, told me all I needed to know. The more I pleasured him, the more the gentle shimmer of silver in his eyes brightened. I'd never known power like it. It wasn't physical strength, and it wasn't magic. It was me, as a woman, controlling him and his pleasure while he was at his most vulnerable.

When he threw his head back, growling in all the right ways, I shifted upright and lowered myself over him, easing him inside.

His hands clamped onto my thighs and dug in as I rocked my hips, bringing him to the edge of ecstasy where his skin glowed with magic and his dark markings absorbed the light.

A blaze of power surged again, shattering me with a sudden orgasm. Talen bucked, back arching, and groaned as he came. I kissed him messily, swallowing the sound, trapping all of him beneath me as we rode the dregs of pleasure together.

I could have lost myself in lovemaking forever if reality hadn't wormed its way back into my thoughts.

Later, I lay in his arms, my leg hooked around one of his, his hair wrapping us in silk while his fingers traced lazy circles down my back. How long had we lain together? I wasn't sure. The shower had been the beginning. I knew every inch of him now like I knew my own body, maybe more so. I'd had my mouth on most parts of him. And just thinking about it made me want to start over. But the worlds outside waited to be saved.

"You believe I'm a star?" I ran my fingers over the ripple of his abs. Back and forth, back and forth, circling his ink.

"Part of one." His voice rumbled with contentment.

"Oberon gave me my markings." He didn't reply, but his fingers still swirled on my back. "I was going to return to him." Talen's fingers stopped. I looked up, but he was gazing at the ceiling. "I can get close to him. I can stop him, or at least try to sway his thoughts, make him see the damage he's doing to Halow. Make him see he doesn't need to kill any more."

Sadness fell softly over his face. "Others have tried over millennia."

"Before I knew who you really are, I thought... perhaps I could make a difference and nobody else needed to get hurt."

Talen shook his head, rippling his waterfall of hair. I couldn't resist it and scooped its length into my hands to toss it over his shoulder, twisting in my left hand. I kissed him on his exposed shoulder. He turned his head, concern digging lines into this brow. I eased my hand around his waist, leaning into him, skin to skin, and saw the moment his thoughts wandered. The worry faded and his mouth quirked in that secret smile.

He twisted at the waist and plunged his hand into my hair to cup the back of my head. The kiss instantly plunging to my core, making me want him all over again. It was over too soon, leaving my mouth and body tingling.

"You can't go back to Faerie alone, Mylana." He bumped his forehead against mine. "The secrets you keep from Oberon are too big to keep alone. You are but one piece of a larger puzzle. Alone, he will destroy you. We must go together, all of us. Oberon responds only to force."

Oberon's wrath had razed cities, silenced planets. He would not hesitate to hurt those around me, those I cared for. "He'll hurt you. He'll hurt Kellee."

"I've been hurt before and so has the marshal." He let me go and withdrew, taking his warmth with him. I admired the sight of him as he stood and collected his scattered clothes. There was a symphony in the way the moved. I could watch him for hours and never grow bored.

"You had a life?" I asked. He methodically dressed, picking up the pieces of the Talen everyone knew and slotting them back together. He would be the distant, reserved Talen again in minutes. To keep himself hidden, he had to be. I missed my wild, raw, and hungry Talen already.

"I lived as a lord, seelie and unseelie, both and neither at a time when the courts were a mix of dark and light. But Prince Oberon sought to use a weapon against all the unseelie, denying they were as much a part of Faerie as Oberon is."

"What happened?" I asked, almost wishing I hadn't when pain hardened his face.

Talen tossed his jacket on. His fingers made quick work of the buckles, tying himself up tight. "I had a household, saru and fae alike," he said, his voice already adopting the level, direct tone that kept his emotions buried, but I felt the distant pang of regret as if it were my own. "There was one saru who I was... She was a brightness in my life." His fingers stalled on the buckles. "Oberon threatened to kill her if I didn't help *deal with* the unseelie. I agreed in exchange for Shanna's life, and I sent her away." His shoulders stiffened. "Oberon didn't kill her. He didn't lie."

"But something else did?"

"The Hunt took Shanna."

"He does not control the Hunt. Nobody controls them. They are Faerie's will."

Talen worried his lip between his teeth. "I do not know how he did it, but Shanna did not deserve to die. She did not deserve the Hunt's attention."

He had to be wrong. Oberon was powerful, but only as far as Faerie allowed him to be. The Hunt was Faerie. If Shanna, his saru, had been taken by the Hunt, it was for a reason, for Faerie.

"I was left bound by my word to help the prince

vanquish the unseelie, but I did everything in my power to sabotage his efforts. That's when the Nightshade legend was born. In public, I was one of Oberon's greatest allies, but out of sight, I undid his plans at every turn. The unseelie and seelie fought for centuries, and I fought for the unseelie until Mab plucked a star from the night and crafted a weapon that would finally bring us down. With the light of the polestar, the prince and queen discovered the Shadow in their court. They shattered my power and then went on to drive the unseelie out of Faerie."

Stardust and shadow.

He waited for me to comment, looking every inch the aloof fae, like a different being to the one who had relished our lovemaking. A contradiction. Both dark and light, seelie and unseelie. Gentle and fierce.

"I am not looking for revenge. My anger waned long ago. I want justice. I want the unseelie back where they belong and Faerie whole."

He painted a pretty picture of a Faerie at peace but Faerie's peace was often reliant on the suffering of others. "What of the saru?"

"They will be free."

It was my turn to smile, because freedom could never happen for the saru while the fae treated us like lesser creatures. Saying something didn't make it so. Saru were a part of Faerie's fabric. They kept the households running. The sidhe would not give them up merely because Talen wanted them to. He was not a king, not of royal blood. If anything, he was a rogue, an outcast, and unseelie. The sidhe and ruling elite would never listen to him.

I gathered my clothing, aware of his heated gaze on me, and said, "The saru cannot be given freedom. They must take it, or nothing will change."

"Much is wrong on Faerie while Oberon rules. We can make change happen. The Nightshade is no more, but the Messenger is real."

I finished dressing, feeling each layer of the Messenger myth slot back into place until I too was the cold, detached thing that Halow and the saru needed to fight the fae. I scanned the floor for my whip. I didn't recall taking it off, but clearly, I had. It was nowhere in sight.

"You cannot go back alone," Talen said. It almost sounded like a threat, or was it a plea? With us both standing behind our wrappings, it was difficult to know the truth. But inside, I felt his fear, his uncertainty, and something else.

He approached and dropped to a knee, bowing his head. "You told me your name and you gave me your heart, Mylana. And now you have mine. I ask only that you don't break it."

Perhaps he was right. If I returned alone, Oberon or Eledan would try to manipulate me, and as strong as I was becoming, I was still vulnerable to both. But with Talen, Kellee and Arran at my side, as the Messenger, I was so much more than I could ever be alone.

I rested my hand gently on his head. "I swear on my saru name, we will get through this together." But as for breaking hearts, I could not promise to keep his safe when I could hardly guard my own.

The ship shuddered and he looked up. "Hapters."

CHAPTER 25

*H*apters had once been a golden marble sitting in Halow's velvety blackness. Now, as Kellee, Talen, Arran, and I looked through the observation window, it was an angry, bruised purple orb.

"How will we put countless wild unseelie back in their hole?" Kellee asked, gold star winking. When I didn't answer, Kellee's questioning gaze slid from me, past Arran, to Talen, who stood still and silent, peering down at Hapters.

"With light," the fae replied.

Kellee's eyebrow ticked. *"With light?"* The marshal bought a few seconds to rearrange his thoughts into words and said, "No."

Talen looked at him. We all did. And Kellee glared back.

"I warred for centuries on vague fae karushit. I followed orders and slaughtered thousands on the poetry of sweet fae words, so don't *vague* me, fae. You owe me more than that."

He had a point.

Talen lifted his chin and blinked at Kellee. "All unseelie are drawn to light. They cannot help themselves." Kellee's hard gaze flinched, some of its edges breaking off at the truth of Talen's words. "And so it is light we'll use. Shinj will corral the wandering unseelie using low-orbit ordinance. It'll alter the weather on Hapters, but the planet will recover and be habitable again in a few days."

"Just fireworks, no damage?" I asked.

Talen nodded. "You," he said to Kellee, "Kesh, Arran, Sota, and Sirius must close ranks and funnel the horde toward me."

Like on Valand. Talen had done something to the vakaru wraiths there, but those were more like ghosts. On Hapters, we were dealing with solid, angry monsters that could snap Talen in two.

"And how are you planning on trapping them?" Kellee asked, too astute to let Talen skip the details.

Kellee didn't know Talen had been the Nightshade, or did he? He'd always denied Talen was the Nightshade, but so had Talen. I studied the marshal and Talen looking back at him. Both powerful, both stubborn. Kellee had known Talen for centuries. He had watched the fae just as Talen must have watched him—and learned. There was no way Kellee didn't suspect Talen's identity. Perhaps he began to suspect the first time Talen had escaped his prison and turned the guards against themselves. Kellee was too observant, too careful, too curious not to figure it out.

"I don't plan on trapping them," Talen replied like it was the most obvious thing in the world. "They will kneel to me."

I gritted my teeth. Here it came, the moment Kellee realized the line Talen had drawn didn't align with his. The myth we had made together might fall apart right here. Kellee's glare darkened. They had always been enemies at their roots, and yet somehow, they hadn't killed each other. Yet. But Kellee knew what was at stake. This was the beginning of so much more if we were together.

Kellee checked me, the flicker so quick I almost missed it, and then he nodded slowly. "Just so long as you give the people their home back, I don't care how you do it."

Talen bowed his head obligingly, and I breathed again.

A fae pilot, the Wraithmaker, a saru gladiator, watching all this with quiet regard, and a vakaru war chief—we would never agree. The best we could do was work with our strengths and weaknesses for a greater cause.

The ship shuddered, and through the window, I watched a crackling stream of light arch toward Hapters's surface. Talen didn't stick around to see its impact and left, I assumed to get ready to disembark.

Arran handed me my whip, and before I could ask where he'd found it, he leaned in and planted a small kiss on my cheek. "Whatever happens here, know I'll always protect you."

I wanted to tell him I didn't need protecting, that I never had, but that he did. The boy in the cell next to mine, defiant and foolish, now a man on the cusp of warring for the greater good. We had survived, in our own ways. I nodded and watched him leave, thinking his promise back at him, *I'll always protect you too, Aeon.*

The ship banked, and through the observation window, stars slid sideways. Another shoot bloomed after the first and barreled through the atmosphere. *Fireworks.* The unseelie knew we were coming.

"We're on the edge of something important." Kellee

323

approached the window. Another blast sailed toward the growing planet, splashing color across his dark features. "There are few moments in time like these. Do you feel it?"

"I do." It felt as though fate were watching us, as though our choices would send ripples into a future we had yet to make. If I stopped to think on it too long I might start to come undone.

"You've come a long way, Messenger." He smiled as he said it and then turned that smile on me, melting some of my concern.

"So have you," I told him. My warm smile fought its way onto my lips despite my best efforts to hide it.

He closed the distance between us and stood almost as close as the moment he'd asked me to dance. That night seemed like a lifetime ago. I'd seen his past since then and knew Kellee more now than ever before. I'd seen his people reach for him and seen him weep for their deaths, deaths he had carried with him for centuries. By-cyn, I loved this vakaru war chief. His complexities, his stubbornness, his challenge.

"There are many things I want to tell you," he began, eyes sparkling, like he was laughing. I'd heard his laugh. I wanted to hear it again and wondered what it would take to hear it now.

"I imagine all the right ways to say them, but when you're with me, I—" He pursed his lips. Yeah, this was hard for him. I watched him squirm on the spot.

Well, look at this, an awkward marshal. More of my armor crumbled away. "Put a weapon in your hand and you know how to dance with me?"

The kiss was sudden. A step, a touch, his mouth on mine. I didn't have time to think, just react. I kissed him back, harder than I would have had I been thinking, and Kellee responded like a live wire pushed home. His touch slid into my hair and gripped, claiming territory. A heated rush of need had me clamping my hand on the back of *his* head and pulling him in, pulling him down. If I took that kiss and gave mine back any harder, there would be blood.

It was a dance, I realized, and a dangerous one. One wrong move and Kellee could lose control. But oh, how that thrill of knowing he walked the edge lit me on fire. I teased and tamed my unseelie monster, riding that kiss out until we had to break apart. The red-tinged gold in his eyes was a warning. He brushed a thumb across his parted lips, eyes heavy with lust, and dropped his other hand to my hip.

"I'm sorry," he said, "For everything."

"You are?" If I kissed him again, it wouldn't stop there. We would be on Hapters soon. There wasn't enough time to own Kellee in all the ways I'd dreamed of. I gripped his coat lapels in my fists and tugged. "How sorry exactly?"

His smile revealed white, blunt teeth. He bent forward and nuzzled my neck, below my ear. His tongue flicked, followed by a soft, sensual kiss that prompted a direct pulse of heat between my legs.

"You like that?" he purred.

"No." *By Faerie, yes.*

"Liar." His rumbling voice was undoing me. That refined accent had a link to all the feminine parts of my mind, allowing him to reach inside and stoke desire and lust.

"How about this?" His hand on my hip pushed lower, riding my pants seam, pushing inward. I was suddenly overdressed.

"No. Absolutely. Not."

"Hmm..."

I caught his hand and held him firmly in my grip. He looked down at me, eyes flicking over my expression. He was breathing hard, like me, I realized. He had said he didn't deserve me. There had been times when he'd thought he'd lost me, times he'd revealed how much losing me would hurt him. He had never been a monster to me. I bit my lip, careful not to draw blood. I loved him. I loved him so much it hurt in ways I didn't know I could hurt.

"Keep looking at me like that, Kesh, and I'll take you so damn hard the war will have to wait."

Another pulse. He teased his mouth over mine, not touching, just... torturing. I still had him in my fists. "You think I'm easy to *take*, Marshal?"

He smiled. His stance altered, tipping his weight to one side so that when he lunged, he would drive me back against the wall, but this close, and with his blood up, he was easy to read. When he pushed in, I twisted under his arm, sank my elbow into his shoulder, driving him down, and hooked my arm around his neck, jerking him back. It should have been an easy move, and for anyone who wasn't vakaru, it would have been. But Kellee would never be an easy catch. He bowed forward, using his strength to fling me over his head. My back hit the floor before I knew I'd been had. And then he was there, one thigh arched over my hip, one arm braced over my shoulder. So close, but not touching.

"Do you want your apology hard and fast?" he asked and leaned in to whisper in my ear, "or hard and slow?"

The ship shuddered, signaling we were entering low atmosphere, and Kellee pulled back, leaving me tingling and wet, all from barely more than a few touches and one kiss. A promise of what was to come. He was a wild thing barely caged, and I wanted him.

"Is there room in your heart for the last vakaru?" he whispered. How long had he waited to ask? How many times had he rolled the question over and over in his mind?

"You've always been in my heart, Kellee."

He looked away and clenched his jaw, letting those words sink in. It had been a long time since he had allowed anyone to love him.

He offered me his hand, golden eyes aglow, and hauled me to my feet.

We would finish this, and when we did, we would clash in all the right ways. But there was more behind the lust, all the parts he kept hidden, the parts too hurt and scarred by his past. The real Marshal Kellee was proud and wounded, fierce and complicated, and I loved all of him. Always had.

"C'mon, Messenger, let's go make history."

HAPTERS'S AIR smelled like rotten fruit, and its sky broiled, punctured here and there by crackling storm eyes and Shinj's atmospheric fireworks. Screeches and caws called out, some distant, some so close they tingled my spine. In the time it had taken us to travel to Valand and back, and with no resistance, the unseelie had claimed this planet.

Arran had brought the shuttle down on the landing strip we had departed from a few days ago. On the descent, we had left Talen in the center of the open prairie, exposed and alone with just the brooch as a weapon. But he had assured me and the others the unseelie would not harm him. As we had pulled away, the downdraft from the shuttle had whipped his long cloak and single braid around him, and he had stood like a rock, immovable and immune to everything. I knew otherwise and keenly remembered the unhurried grace of his touch, our fevered motions, and his sly, satisfied purr.

Pushing thoughts of Talen aside, Kellee, Sota and I circled around the prairie in one direction while Arran and Sirius veered off in the other, so we would create a closing pincer on Talen's location. The ship from low atmosphere would corral the unseelie toward us. We were the back flank, keeping them penned in, and Talen was the center of everything—the eye of the storm.

If we pulled this off, the Messenger would be worth her myth. Word would spread. The people would believe, and we all might have a chance at pushing back Faerie. As for the larger picture, saving the saru, stopping Faerie altogether, those thoughts had to wait.

"Sota, ready?" I primed the drone, hovering within sight but still some distance from me. The drone's sights turned tactical, sharpening my vision via our ocular link. In the distance, the drone scanned an incoming wave of dust and the pinpricks of heat signatures inside. The unseelie were coming.

"Ready," he responded.

All we had to do was hold them in place long enough for Talen to control them. The wild vakaru wraiths had bowed to him. Kellee had bowed. The unseelie here would bow too. Talen believed it, then so did I.

To my left, Kellee lurked in the long grass, claws out, eyes ablaze. Once he felled a few, the others would recognize him as a threat and fall in line, or so he had told me. As for me, I had my whip alive and lashing at my side, and the ever-present glowing warmth humming its own power. My coat shimmered, charged and ready. I might have looked like something Faerie had crafted, but my heat was saru, and that's where my strength came from.

This would be a victory. Losing Hapters was not an option.

The clouds boiled away, and the warcruiser's bulk loomed like the cleaving head of a scythe. It spat out powerful beams that crept ever closer, herding the unseelie right toward us.

The wind whisked, hot and abrasive. And my heart hammered like the hooves of the Wild Hunt coming for its prize. I lifted my chin. Lightning split the sky.

I was not afraid. We were together and nothing could stop us.

THEY CAME AS ONE. A galloping wave of darkness, an ocean of claws and teeth and wings and fangs. I felt the moment they hit Talen, felt the flare of power strike my soul and burst into flame. Light shot outward, slamming into the unseelie's ranks, knocking them back. The bond tugged, sharp and painful, until I let it go as I had once before, let it *flow* instead of fighting to hold on to it.

Power crackled down my whip and along my coat's silver lining, lighting it and me up. It didn't hurt, because it wasn't wrong. Saru could not steal magic, but it could be gifted, and Oberon had given me something powerful, believing it would stay hidden. That had been his mistake.

The eye of light flickered, its edges fading, and at its

center, a dark heart unfurled. Talen's wings. Enormous and hungry, they pulled the light into them, and pulled the unseelie too.

A few had broken free of Talen's thrall and scattered. One beast bounded toward Kellee. The marshal's claws flashed, the beast roared, and then I had my own fanged and winged thing screeching at me through the sky, talons thrust forward and open, ready to crush and kill.

The whip whirled and cracked, slicing through leathery skin and splashing blood onto Hapters's parched earth. The winged unseelie smacked into the ground, tumbled and thrashed, trying to lift itself into the air. Its movements were jagged, and its keen, wide eyes darted until it saw me. "Nightshade..." it hissed.

"Not me." I lifted the whip, circled it above me, and sent its tails in, coiling it around the beast's neck. "I'm just saru." The whip snagged tight, locked, and with one swift jerk, the unseelie's fragile neck snapped.

More broke free of Talen's hypnotic summons, but Kellee was there, wreaking havoc on the edge of my sightline, and I dealt with mine just as efficiently.

As more and more unseelie flowed in, more of Talen's hypnotic mix of dark and light flowed outward. I didn't need to be close to him to know he was a thing of dangerous awe and beauty. The bond shared it all, our combined strength and the sense that this was the right thing. Should we ever come to blows, sparks would fly, but that was not happening today.

Wraithmaker, no more.

Nightshade, no more.

Droch-fhoula, no more.

We were each something else, something changed and renewed, and we were winning. I'd only felt elation like it after the arenas, when the fae had cheered my name and the death I had wrought for them. A deep thrill surged through my veins, driving me on and lighting me up so the unseelie cowered back, trapped between Talen's consuming dark and my raw glow. They fell back from Kellee too, and Sota drove them closer toward Talen, his lens firing, blazing, washing Hapters in pulses of red light.

A crack sounded, and in the melee, I almost missed it. A heartbeat later, the bond stuttered, Talen's magic faltering. Talen's power, at the eye of all this, shrank in on itself, and the reaching dark edges of his wings curled inward, closing.

Something was wrong.

The unseelie moved as one, their mass breathing outward.

"Kellee!"

Kellee was looking up.

A mass of claws sprang from my right. I whirled and cut it down. More were coming from everywhere. No, Talen's hold on them was slipping. But why?

Another crack like thunder.

I looked up toward the sounds of cracking and saw the enormous warcruiser buckle at its center. It happened slowly, or perhaps it just appeared that way as cold, hard dread settled over me. There were hundreds of people on that ship, fae and human alike. Hulia too.

The crack sounded again, and a silver tek-leviathan speared through the clouds *above* the warcruiser. Bigger and bigger, the enormous metal ship swooped in, wings spread like a falcon's. It bristled with cannons, each one aglow with harsh red light as they charged for their next volley.

Earthens from Sol.

An icy dart hit my chest. Fear. Talen's.

"No. No!" I screamed uselessly at the intruders. We had this. We had it under control. We were subduing the unseelie. We were winning. And now the unseelie had scattered, masses of dark wings and rampaging hordes running chaotically.

I was running too, toward Talen.

The unseelie were on him.

I am not who I once was. He couldn't contain them, not torn between the ship and here. They would tear him to pieces.

Kellee was a blur, fast outpacing me, heading straight for Talen.

Another crack sounded, and I knew without looking up that the Earthen weapons had broken Shinj's back. Sorrow slammed into me, tripping my stride. The ship, our ship, was dying. And Talen felt it. I felt it. He wanted to help her, but the pain, the unseelie, they were everywhere, and he wasn't yet strong enough.

No. Damn them, no! Shinj had done nothing wrong.

"Sota, send a communication. Do it now! Tell them to stop firing!"

"They are not responding." My drone flew over my head and shot toward the heaving mass of unseelie blocking my way to Talen.

"We're not their enemy!"

Kellee plowed into the mob, Sota too. They fought and fired, claws and lasers tearing into flesh to get to Talen. I swung my whip, lifting it high, and was about to bring it down on the nearest heaving mass of unseelie, when a heavy, numbing weight captured my arm and lowered it softly to my side. Wait... why couldn't I raise my whip?

"Kesh?!"

Arran.

"Kesh…"

I turned, hands at my side, and walked toward the sound of my name on Arran's lips. I shouldn't have been able to hear him, but I did. I should have been heading the other way, fighting to free Talen, but I wasn't. What was wrong with me?

"Kesh…" Arran's hand settled on my arm. Yes, Arran was here and that was good. "Kesh, come with me." He pulled me forward, and that seemed like the best thing to do. I should go with Arran. He had kind hopeful eyes and they beckoned now, pleaded…

The light was all wrong. Bodies lay scattered around me. Unseelie bodies. None moved. We had killed some and we walked by them now as though they were nothing.

"Where…" I reached for my head, trying to brush the fogginess away, sure I must have gotten wounded to be thinking so slowly. I was in a fight, wasn't I? I was… doing something… important. Something I'd forgotten. It was right there, the thing I must do. Right there.

Arran pulled me on until we stumbled and staggered in a trot. Our shuttle gleamed ahead.

"Where's Kellee?" I asked. Kellee would know what I'd forgotten.

"Inside," Arran assured.

Inside? "But—"

I tried to see behind me, to understand what had happened, but a flicker of light and dark scorched my vision. If Kellee was inside the shuttle, then he was okay. That was good. That was important too.

"Talen?" I asked.

"Close."

"So much light and yet so little hope." The Dreamweaver's syrupy tones poured into my ear. I flinched and almost stumbled. Arran's arm tightened around my waist, and he urged me on, but didn't he know there was a ghost whispering in my ear?

"Arran, something is wrong with me. I shouldn't be here. There's something I need to do."

"Look around you, nothing girl. There is more happening here than your weak saru mind can comprehend."

I stumbled up the ramp into the shuttle and reached for the wall to stop the world from tilting beneath my feet. Blood was cooling on my neck, the wounds throbbing hot. Skin feverish. *Wrong.* I shouldn't have been hearing the Dreamweaver, not anymore. I'd beaten him back. Something terrible had happened, but I couldn't think around the fog to find its source. Why couldn't I think?

"Kellee...?" I called. He was here. Arran had said so.

He would know what to do. He always knew what to do.

The shuttle door slammed closed with a final *thwunk*, and everything rumbled as engines fired to life. But that couldn't be right. Where was Talen? Where was Kellee? And Sota... Sota had been fighting them with Kellee.

I turned too quickly.

"Queen of the hearts she steals..."

I squeezed my head in my hands. *No, no, no, get out of my head. You can't be here. YOU CAN'T.*

"Is she all right?" Sirius asked. Sirius was here too? A cold, hard tek-hand took mine. Wait. I looked at that hand in mine, the gleam of silver metal on my dark saru skin. Sirius was here. Arran was here. But not the others...

"It will wear off," Arran said with a harsh cold finality that didn't sound like my Arran.

What would wear off?

None of this was making any sense. My vision blurred around Sirius's autumnal reds. "Where's Kellee...?"

The floor moved, and I would have fallen had Sirius's metal arm not swooped around me.

Sirius.

Harsh and unyielding. Oberon's guardian.

Arran. Arran who had forgotten but remembered how to love.

Wait...

"Now she sees... but it's too late to save those she loves."

I shoved Sirius aside and stumbled against the copilot's chair. Arran was maneuvering the shuttle *away*. Outside, turning the entire plain into a play of light and dark, a battle still raged. Sota's red beams flashed. Kellee was a dark storm of his own, cutting a path through the horde. And there, at the eye, stood Talen, desperately holding the unseelie back even as they slashed and bit.

They were still fighting.

They didn't know I was in the shuttle.

Arran and Sirius were taking me away.

"No..." I lunged for the controls. Strong arms locked around my waist and hauled me back. "They're still there!" I whirled and swung for the guardian, but his tek-fingers caught my punch and squeezed, threatening to break my arm. I cried out, curling under the pain, and buckled to my knees.

The guardian's cool green eyes revealed nothing but harsh reality, like they always had.

"Don't hurt her!" Arran barked.

"Arran!" I shoved at Sirius with my free hand, but he

held firm. "Don't do this! We have to help them. The unseelie will swamp them. And there's a ship, an Earthen ship from Sol! It attacked Shinj—"

A warning growl rumbled through Sirius. "They won't let you go. This is the only way."

Fury raced through my veins. I bared my teeth at the guardian.

"In thousands of years," he sneered back, "I have never failed Oberon. I will return you to him at any cost. Their lives will pay for our quick exit before the Earthens overpower us."

My thoughts swam, sickness rising. "What did you do...? You drugged me..." But when? How? I hadn't eaten or drunk anything from Arran or Sirius. Argh, my damn mind wouldn't clear. "How did you do this?"

"Benrin's Spite." Arran glanced back. "When you had me guard Sirius's ship, I retrieved the syrup from the town, and earlier, when you were with Talen, I coated your whip handle with it. Just enough to make you susceptible to suggestion. You never would have left them otherwise." He said all this matter-of-factly. He wasn't sorry. Sirius and Arran believed this was right. Arran—my honest, carefree, trustworthy Arran—had drugged me.

Shock and disbelief left me grasping for the right words to stop this. I had to make him turn around. I had to make him go back.

Kellee would think I'd left him. He knew I'd struck a deal with Sirius. He would think I'd lied. After everything we had tried to accomplish, after everything he had shown me on Valand. It would all be for nothing. He didn't trust me enough. He would think I'd betrayed him. The realization hit me like a blow to the gut, and a pained whine peeled from my lips. And Talen.... I'd run from him once. Would he think I was running again?

"Take me back." My voice was cold.

"No."

"*Please, Arran. Please...* We had something. We were something. All of us. We were together. Don't do this. Please."

The shuttle rumbled harder as the vessel passed through Hapters's atmosphere. He wasn't turning around.

"You told me I was saru," he said, his voice as cold as mine. "That must mean I owe my life to Faerie and her king. I might not remember who I am, but I know what I feel. I love *them*. Love cannot be wrong."

I heard myself laugh a sad, twisted chuckle. "Oh, Arran..." Kellee had been right. He had wanted me to stop Aeon from taking the starfruit. He had said we were our memories. Love meant nothing without the memories to go with it. Arran's love was a lie, the same as the love of every single saru ever grown and harvested for Faerie. All of them were so in love with the fae, in love with a lie.

"Arran, you were my hero." I shoved against Sirius when he tried to pull me back again, and this time, he eased off. I gripped Arran's arm, turning toward me. There, in his eyes, something sparked, something I could hold on to. "You were brave and strong and proud. You were saru, and yes, you loved the fae. You loved them like all saru. But you knew that love was a lie. You tried to show me. You tried to tell me. I couldn't see, not like you. It took me years outside of Faerie to see it. Please, Arran, you might not remember, but I do. And inside, you must feel that too? Please. *Aeon* would never do this. Please, for the time we spent together. This is not who you are."

"It is now." He pulled his arm from my grip and returned to the controls. "Aeon is not me."

"No!" I reached for him again, but Sirius's hand came down between us. "Don't make a liar out of me! Please, Arran. I can't leave them like this." The ship, the people, my friends. This wasn't fair. It wasn't right. I should be there. I'd earned the right to be there. They needed me. I needed them. "Don't take them from me!"

Sirius's metal hand jerked me away from Arran. "Perhaps leaving them like this is for the best," he remarked.

I lunged at him with no real thought behind it and knocked the fae guardian off his feet. I tore myself free and dashed to the seat beside Arran's in time to see Hapters's storm clouds dissipate and a million stars blink in welcome. The shuttle lurched toward them, and around my heart, the bright, tight bond between Talen and me stuttered. I touched a hand to my chest, sinking my fingers in as if I could hang on to that thread. He would know I was leaving him. It hurt. The distance was hollowing me out, emptying me of Talen's connection. It hurt like grief.

Weaker and weaker, stretched too thin, it was breaking. And I couldn't stop it.

Arran hit a button, and the stars turned into long needles of light.

The bond snapped, taking my breath and the last of my strength with it.

"Why, Arran?" My body blazed, radiating heat and sickness. I clutched at the copilot's seat, feeling my heart hollow out with every labored beat.

Arran turned to me and dared to touch my arm. "Because I love you."

I jerked back, his words a slap in the face, and stumbled to my knees. The darkness was coming, and I wasn't sure if it was the same nothingness that always stalked me or if it was alive and hungry and watching, if the Dreamweaver had come to hide me in his arms and carry me away to the nowhere places where nothing hurt anymore.

"I love you, and even without my memories, I know I've always loved you." Arran left his seat and crouched in front of me. He peered into my eyes, seeing the horror and betrayal on my face and ignoring it, or wishing it away inside his own delusions. "That's why I must do this. We're going home."

How could he love me and hurt me like this? How could he leave Talen and Kellee behind when they needed us the most?

"I am saru." He smiled a sad knowing smile. "So are you, Kesh. Our king needs you."

Tears swirled in my vision. Aeon had never stopped loving me, but I wasn't the only one he had loved. And now he had betrayed me for the love of a king, like I had once betrayed Kellee and Talen. He was... Oberon's, just as I had been. "You think you love Oberon too?"

The resolve in his eyes told me he believed he was doing the right thing.

Had Aeon known this would happen, he would never have taken the starfruit.

And Sirius watched, having fulfilled his order to retrieve the Wraithmaker.

I couldn't hate either of them for following orders, and that made the pain worse.

They were taking me back to Faerie. I didn't want to go. Not alone. Not without the others. Not wrenched from them like this. We were supposed to go back together, all of us as one. As the Messenger.

I slumped against Sirius and let the numbness take the hurt away.

Sirius touched my cheek, collecting tears like he used to all those years ago. "Rest now, calla. You'll be home soon."

No, I thought. *You stole me from the only home I've ever truly known.*

CHAPTER 26

*L*egend said Faerie's crystal palace had been grown in the golden age of Faerie. The land, the essence of Faerie, had built it in appreciation of the sidhe who were birthed by Faerie to care for her marvelous creations.

Great glass archways and enormous halls had been built for the proportions of Faerie's wildest things, much bigger than the sidhe who inhabited the palace and city now. But Oberon had driven off those wild aspects of Faerie long ago, and now the expanse of glass and mirrors only made the palace seem cold and empty. Or it did to me as I walked alongside Sirius, keeping my chin high and eyes ahead. I'd been back on Faerie soil less than two hours, time enough to clean up and dress in something part gown, part uniform, and more courtly than Talen's torn coat and my Wraithmaker leathers. Oberon's most trusted saru had taken my old clothes away, keeping their eyes averted and words off their lips. I'd asked them to braid my hair in Faerie's current style, and they had silently obliged. Appearances were everything in the palace made of mirrors.

Outside of the silent saru, Sirius had been my constant guardian. Nobody else saw me. My return was a secret. It would make my execution easier.

The king would surely kill me. He had to after my failure to kill Eledan and the death toll at the Game of Lies. The question was whether it would be fast or slow, private or public.

"I know why you did this, but it doesn't make it right," I told Sirius. If I was about to die, I would speak my words. There was no point in taking them to the grave. "And just because he's king, doesn't make him right either."

"I do not need to seek your approval, and if you utter one more word against the king, I'll have charges of treason added to your roster."

I pressed my lips together and wondered where Kellee was, if he was alive, if Talen was okay, and what had become of the warcruiser and the people we'd tried to keep safe. The Sol humans, previously absent from this war, must have been watching us since we'd first arrived on Hapters. Talen had noticed them and lost them again. They had timed their move perfectly—while our backs were turned. When I closed my eyes, I saw the storm I'd left behind, the enormous Sol spacefaring vessel that had broken Shinj's back, Kellee and Sota fighting a path to Talen, whose dark and light had been collapsing under the weight of the unseelie horde.

Had they survived? Maybe I didn't need to know. I was on Faerie and the game had changed. The Messenger and her myth didn't belong here. But the Wraithmaker did.

"Wait here." Sirius left me in a small receiving chamber, one of many in the maze-like palace. Chambers led to chambers led to secret doors behind mirrors and around and around the secrets went. Like on the warcruiser, rooms sometimes changed, depending on which season was in favor. Summerlands allowed for bright, breezy spaces. If Winterlands was popular, then the rooms and windows shrank, hoarding warmth and light. I tasted spices in the air, rich and earthy, and suspected Autumn-lands was on the rise after summer had been in power. I hadn't seen the outside and hadn't cared to look as Arran had landed the human shuttle in a secluded spot hidden deep within the palace. It didn't matter though. Faerie was already under my skin and whispering its sweet nothings in my ear. It would take some getting used to after five— almost six years away. Six years playing human. Five of those spent hunting the Dreamweaver for Oberon, and afterward, I hadn't returned. Oberon would know it all. But he didn't know *I* knew the biggest secret of all. I still had a card to play.

The door opened, and Sirius beckoned me through.

With the twists and turns of the hallways, I hadn't real-ized where I was in the palace, but there was no mistaking the awe-inspiring size and grandeur of the shining throne room.

Oberon stood at a huge window, drenched in sunlight. His dark hair lay uncharacteristically loose down his back, its color made all the darker by the rich royal blue of his gold-lined cloak.

The mirrored pillars reflected me a hundred times as I approached. The mirrors amplified light and chased away the dark.

"Sire," Sirius announced, "I present to you the Wraith-maker." He kneeled and bowed his head.

I would have been a fool not to do the same and

remembered a friend who'd once told me how defiance was foolish and how there were other ways to subvert the fae. She was right. I could not openly defy the king.

I lowered myself to a knee and bowed my head. Even now, my battered heart leapt at the idea. It wasn't real, this love I felt for him, but that didn't make it any less powerful. I understood why Arran had helped Sirius bring me here. I understood how Kellee had fought for Oberon all those centuries ago. I understood so much more now. I'd left Faerie as Oberon's tool and now I returned... as a weapon.

Oberon sighed as though a great weight had lifted from his shoulders. He turned, and from my position, I saw the cloak sweep around his boots. Not courtly shoes, but thick, outdoor ranger boots, reminding me and others how Oberon was a warrior king beneath all this delicate finery.

His hand settled on the back of my head, and a rush of saru pride swelled within me. His hand came around, touching my cheek, and then his soft fingers touched my chin and lifted my head, inviting me to look up.

I barely noticed my tears falling. He was beautiful. And now that I had met Eledan, I saw the resemblance, but where Eledan's features were sharp, Oberon's were much softer. More like his mother's. Piercing blue eyes reached into my soul and peeled back all my defenses. I had thought I could hide from him. How wrong I'd been.

Love. Oberon had made us to love them, to love him. What was love? Just some strange ingredient poured into our making, something to make us loyal and obedient? But whatever he had made me, I was saru, and that love warmed me, wrapped me in its embrace and told me everything was well.

"Do not weep, my Wraithmaker." He brushed his knuckles down my cheek, smearing the tears. I fought to keep the pain off my face and be brave for him, but it had been so long, and I'd lost so much, and the compassion in his eyes could not be meant for me? "I do not blame you for any of it."

I do not blame you, the Dreamweaver had once told me. *She killed a queen, made a king, but they say she thinks it's all a dream...*

The tears fell freely, and I gave up fighting them.

The king's gentle smile made me fall in love with him all over again. "How can I, when you only did as I asked of you?"

I cupped his hand in mine and kissed the backs of his fingers. If there were words I was supposed to say, I couldn't remember them. He wasn't angry with me. He still loved me. He had not forsaken me.

Oberon stepped back, smiling. "Bring in the gladiator."

Fae guards escorted Arran in through the hidden door. By the way he held his shoulders back, I assumed his wrists were bound behind him.

"But someone must be held accountable for the many... mistakes," Oberon added.

I glanced at Sirius, but the guardian watched it all unfold, still on one knee, his eyes shallow as always.

The guards shoved Arran to his knees and held him down. He didn't struggle. He saw me and smiled. "My king, I thought only to bring her back to you, as I knew you wanted."

Oberon silently regarded the saru kneeling before him. The quiet stretched on, as did Oberon's long assessment.

Arran's smile withered. He looked up at Oberon, but he couldn't stand the weight of the king's gaze for long and bowed his head. "Was that... was that wrong?" he asked, facing the floor.

"No." Oberon touched Arran's bowed head too. The king lifted his gaze, spearing it through the room of mirrored columns. A dozen of his reflections looked back at him. "You brought me something I feared I'd lost. The Wraithmaker's return is welcome." His hand slid down Arran's cheek, as it had mine. He lifted Arran's chin. "Your actions at the Game of Lies cannot go unpunished."

"My... I..." Confusion stole the rest of his words.

Oberon let him go and stepped back. "Thousands of innocent fae perished."

"I..." Arran flicked his gaze to me.

"The Wraithmaker cannot help you."

Arran bowed his head again. "I don't remember. I... Sire, please, allow me to explain. I ate starfruit. I lost—"

Oberon lifted a hand, silencing Arran. "It is well known how you have an affinity with tek, gladiator. Do you deny it?"

"No. I mean, yes, I use tek, but I—"

"Do you deny you have murdered innocent fae?"

Arran's face paled. His lips trembled. "I don't remember."

Oberon's gaze found me. He knew. He knew it was me, but Arran was nothing to him, just someone to take the fall for my crimes and solve the problem of how to placate the court and the fae.

Oberon turned with a flick of his hand. "Sirius, have it known that this saru is to be charged with the massacre at New Calicto. He will be publically executed for his crimes."

"Yes, sire." Sirius rose to his feet.

"No..." Arran stammered. His fearful eyes flicked from the approaching Sirius to Oberon. "N-No!"

I couldn't allow this.

"Let it be done at Nightfall." Oberon's thin fingers flicked again, delivering Arran's sentence as though he were tossing away something worthless. "Let us give the lords time to return to court."

"No... I... This isn't right." Arran tried to lunge, but the fae guards held him down for Sirius. "I love the fae. I feel it. I know it's real. My king, I could never hurt you."

"Your past says otherwise."

Aeon had tried to kill Oberon ten years ago. I'd stopped him. But today, Arran was the perfect scapegoat, and if I was going to work my way around Oberon, I needed the king to love and trust me. But Oberon already knew I had killed those fae. *Everyone* knew it.

"Kesh?" Arran's plea struck like a knife to my heart.

Sirius pulled Arran to his feet.

Kellee told me Aeon hadn't survived me before, and now I was killing him again. Arran would die and I would live, and I'd get my chance to bring Oberon down. I should let him go. I should let events play out and use Arran's death to my advantage. It was what the Wraithmaker would do.

I got to my feet, tears rapidly drying. "My king, please... let him live."

Oberon had long ago perfected the emotionless gaze. I had no chance of reading him. But I held his gaze as long as I dared.

"You've left me no choice," Oberon said.

"Kesh! I only tried to save you! Don't let him do this!"

I closed my eyes. None of this was Arran's fault. All his life he had served and survived the fae. I couldn't let them execute him for my crimes, even if part of me wanted revenge for his actions bringing me here. I'd intended to come back and turn Oberon away from his crusade, and now I was falling at the first hurdle. But making things right couldn't stem from more deaths. Talen had told me I was made of light. I had to start there.

I opened my eyes and saw the king had moved back to the window, and for a second, with his face in profile, I saw the expression on his face was one of longing. But what could Faerie's king long for? If I knew, I could use it. But it wouldn't save Arran here, now.

"My king..." I lifted my voice, letting it fill the throne room. "I know what I am."

He didn't appear to react, and with his back to me, I couldn't read his face, but I let the words settle. "I have served you with love, loyalty, and admiration for years. I have never asked anything of you." I swallowed. "Spare him, please."

Arran was sobbing, his words muddled as Sirius led him away. I had seconds to stop this, seconds in which to change the king's mind.

"Stop," Oberon called out.

Sirius obeyed. Arran sagged in his arms, hope keeping him on his feet.

The invisible weight of Oberon's magic encircled me, urging me down to my knees. I knelt and watched the king turn to me.

"Your *companion* should hear this." The king's blue eyes turned as cold as the steel that made up his guardians' blades. "What you are... is mine." Faerie's king smiled, but it was not a kind smile. "Who you are remains to be seen." He breezed past me and tossed his parting words behind him. "Your actions, not mine, condemned this man. He will die when night next descends."

I heard Arran's cries long after Sirius had dragged him from the room and wondered if they would join the cries of all the saru I'd killed. Kellee had been right. Aeon would die for me again unless I changed the king's mind.

She killed a queen, made a king, but they say she thinks it's all a dream...

Arran would not die for me. Not again. Change wasn't coming. It was already here. It was me.

I had made a king. I could unmake him.

I smiled into the now-empty throne room. Countless reflections smiled back.

Arran would live. Oberon would fall. I was home, and the Wraithmaker was exactly where she needed to be.

To be continued...

THE MESSENGER CHRONICLES continues in *Prince of Dreams*, coming December 2018. Sign up to Pippa's mailing list for all the news. Turn the page for an excerpt and an exclusive *Prince of Dreams* chapter from Marshal Kellee.

PRINCE OF DREAMS ~ EXTRA EXCERPT

Kesh

My presence, by now, was well known. Gossip traveled fast on Faerie's winds. But knowing the Wraithmaker had returned and seeing her beside the king were two very different things. I was to keep to the miles of servant corridors, far away from the ever-watching fae.

I rattled around a royal receiving chamber, alternating between watching the darkening skies through the window and pacing the elaborately decorated suite.

For what I was about to do, Kellee would call me a fool. I could hear him and his high-and-mighty marshal tone. *Don't be a martyr.* But he wasn't here. And Talen would look at me with all the answers in his eyes, but none he could speak.

An empty ache hollowed out my heart.

I couldn't think of them, left behind, battling monsters.

I'd been back on Faerie for only a couple of days, but with the travelling, I'd been away from them longer.

Sirius entered the room, his face grimmer than usual. "This is unwise."

I assumed that meant the king was coming.

"They are preparing the gladiator for his execution."

I paced faster, boots beating against the carpeted floors.

A wall of rusty reds blocked my marching. "You'll get yourself killed," he said.

I stepped around him and kept on pacing.

"After all this time, after everything that has happened, you would die for the gladiator?" he asked, each word clipped with restrained frustration.

"You don't understand. He tried to save me once, and I killed him for it. And even after he forgot our past, he tried to save me again. He thought he was doing the right thing. The saru..." How could I explain what being a saru was like to a fae like him? "They can't help the way they are."

"You're right, I don't understand. Your life is worth more than his."

I stopped pacing and faced the guardian. So proud, so fae, so sure of his place in the world. "No. One life is not worth more than another. All lives are equal. All saru are equal. All fae are equal to saru—"

"That's absurd," he snorted.

He would think so. "I'm doing this."

He glared back. "You're not saru."

"I am."

"No, you're not." He approached, and his cloak flared out, making him seem bigger. He wasn't small to begin with, and as he approached, that old saru part of me urged me to drop to my knees. I lifted my head and looked him dead in the eye. His steps faltered, halting him outside of my reach. "While I was not part of your harem and not privy to its secrets, I saw enough. Saru are not Faerie touched."

I stood my ground, once again looking up at a fae looking down on me. "Whatever you think you saw changes nothing. I was born saru."

He turned his head away, grinding his teeth, and then lowered his voice to a hissing whisper. "I saw you summon light, a Faerie power few possess. It was minor and ill-directed, but it was there. I witnessed it. You cannot lie about this." He spoke as though angry, like this was all my fault, but the whispers weren't for my benefit. He didn't want Oberon knowing what he'd seen.

I glanced at the closed door. Sirius hadn't told Oberon any of this. Not Talen's words on how to save Faerie, nothing of the Nightshade or freeing the unseelie. He was a Royal Guardian, the crown's stalwart servant, and he was keeping secrets from Oberon. His silence, should it be revealed, would get him executed alongside Arran.

Sirius lifted his hand. The cloak fell back, revealing the smooth beauty of his tek-arm. My finest work. He despised it. Cold metal fingers touched my bare shoulder.

There was more in his eyes than stubborn denials, more emotion than I'd seen from him in all the years I'd known him. More than these last few weeks in my company could account for. Why did any of this matter to him?

"And that is why I must do this." I closed my hand around his and lowered it back to his side. "I am nothing in Oberon's shadow, but in death, I can show all of Faerie the truth. I will die for one worthless saru, but my death will change everything." It was a lie, but here, in Faerie, the fae thought themselves immune to lies. They forgot my greatest strength. I had no wish to die, but I would save Arran, and in a palace made of mirrors, I had to tread carefully.

The chamber door swung open, and Oberon strode in, a storm of royal blues and golden threads, his hair night-black and tightly braided. His rowan crown snared my attention. It suited him. He wore it well. Eledan had fashioned himself one of oak that had looked just as good, albeit a lie.

Sirius shut down, hiding the emotion away.

"My king." I dropped to a knee.

The guardian failed to kneel. Realizing his mistake a second too late, he dropped, bowing his head low, but in his haste, he had failed to cover his arm. His tek-hand gleamed, fingers spread. In this, the seat of power, human tek on display was an affront to all things Faerie. Too late, Sirius curled his hand closed and hid it behind his back.

"Sirius, at ease," the king ordered, his voice ringing with a dangerous note.

The guardian straightened and stepped back to the edge of the room, blending in with the shadows.

"Do not think to petition for the life of the gladiator," Oberon told me. "My decision is final. Preparations are underway. I will not be persuaded otherwise in this."

I stood, carefully reworking my words in my head, and regarded my king in the same cool, studious manner in which he regarded me.

He checked the door, now closed, and narrowed his eyes at me once more. He made his assessment and looked around him, reading the small, informal room with its fine furniture and flowing drapes as though it were the first time he'd seen it. Perhaps it was. There were dozens of rooms like this one and all looked the same. Satisfied, he unbuckled his cloak and tossed it over a daybed, then loosened his gold-inlaid waistcoat. "My Wraithmaker," he murmured, thoughts wandering.

With the waistcoat hanging open and loose, he rolled his sleeves up past his elbows, revealing warfae markings that snaked up his forearms. He discarded his lithe, courtly softness along with the pretty attire. Beneath, was the general, a fae of power and prowess, a king-in-waiting. This was how I'd always known him. I'd been alarmed when I'd first seen Eledan, his brother, outside of Faerie and how he had been built for combat. Oberon was the same, but he deliberately hid his warrior physique beneath kingly robes at court.

His wooden demeanor melted away, revealing the fluid, relaxed sidhe beneath. I wondered if any at court saw this side of him, the truth of him. At least one truth. He likely had many.

"I often thought of you," he said.

He had?

"I hadn't realized..." He trailed off as he came to the window, entranced by the inky darkness pushing out daylight. "It is a dangerous thing to wish for the dark. It answers."

Sirius was behind me, watching this exchange. The guardian had always been good at making himself almost invisible during these moments between Oberon and me.

"I killed those fae on Calicto," I said. "I programmed the drones to attack. It was a slaughter. They didn't stand a chance."

"Oh, I know." Oberon turned his back to the window and smiled a devastating smile. I'd seen Eledan wear the same seductive smile a thousand times before. They were more alike than I'd realized. "Sjora was looking for a fight and a way to undermine me," he said. "You gave her exactly what she wanted and eliminated her treasonous followers."

So, the massacre was... acceptable? I hadn't expected that smile or this reaction. I might be the Wraithmaker, but I'd always followed Oberon's orders to kill. The Game of Lies had been different. I'd chosen to kill his people. "I should be the one to pay."

"Yes. I am fully aware it is you who should be executed." He melted into a high-backed chair and drummed his fingers on the arm, his face pensive. "The gladiator's death is a small price to pay to keep you alive."

"Killing Arran is a mistake."

Oberon breathed in and tilted his head, studying me once more. "I have missed your obstinacy. No other dares to defy me openly. Behind my back, they twitter. I'd rather they openly challenge me. The whispers always reach me..." Again, his attention wandered toward the window.

"And that's a problem, my king."

"Whatever you are trying to do, do not waste your breath. I will not allow you to die in his place. Your life is worth too much."

I didn't need to look to know Sirius was smiling at the king echoing his sentiments. "All of Faerie knows I killed the queen."

Oberon's sharp gaze cut to Sirius. I couldn't see what passed between them, but I guessed Sirius hadn't known the truth, not for certain. That had just changed. If Sirius made himself too much of a liability, he would need those secrets he was holding on to so tightly.

"They want justice," I added.

"Justice?" the king drawled. "Faerie is dying. There is no time for justice."

"And what are you doing about it, as their king?"

"More than you can comprehend."

I'd come here to push back. Now was as good a time as any to start. "Sjora wanted to see Eledan on the throne. I doubt she was alone in that desire. Your rule, my king, is precarious."

At the mention of his brother, Oberon's expression locked. His fingers stopped drumming, and the king fell still. "My *brother* is as good as dead." He pushed from the chair and crossed the distance between us in a few short, sharp strides. "You performed perfectly." His penetrating blue-eyed gaze roamed over me from head to toe, softening as it did, becoming keener. "Strip," he ordered.

I blinked and unbuttoned the gown his saru had dressed me in. It was a plain thing, functional with minimal decoration. And now it was coming off. This wasn't unusual, neither would be what came next, but it had been years, and where I'd once been delighted to have my king's attention on me, the anxious flutter in my chest suggested I no longer felt the same.

I eased the sleeves off my shoulders, pulling my arms out, and pushed the gown down until it pooled at my feet. I toed it aside, crossed my arms over my body, grabbed the vest, and lifted it over my head. The undergarments were next. I reached behind my back and worked at the fastenings, like all of this was perfectly acceptable. Only it wasn't. Sometime since fleeing Faerie to hunt down Eledan, while living a normal life on Calicto and in all the time I'd spent with Kellee and Talen, I'd changed. Calicto had changed me. Halow had changed me. I didn't want this, not anymore. But now was not the time to take a stand. *We survive today to fight tomorrow.* Hadn't Kellee said that?

Oberon folded an arm across his front and propped his elbow on his loose fist, tapping a finger against the side of his head in thought. There was no heat in his lingering gaze, just raw concentration.

I discarded the chest wrap and pushed my panties down. When I straightened, Faerie's light air touched my deeply marked skin.

Oberon took a few steps one way, then the other, studying the markings wrapped around my thighs, torso, and arms, and then he circled me, examining every inch. My saru heart rattled in its tiny cage.

Oberon's hands clutched my waist, the king at my back. I slammed my teeth together and stared at the pattern of vine-like art painting the walls. His hands were smooth, like the hands of all immortals who healed their scars. His touch was soft and warm. They'd been soft and warm when he'd marked me too. I tried to block out the sensation, tried to block out everything. This hadn't bothered me before. Why was this time different?

His fingers kneaded and swirled over the marks he had made in my flesh, pushing in, up my spine and over my shoulders. Part of me hated this intrusion, but an old part of me *wanted* it too. Faerie's king was touching my flesh. Hands that had built armies, killed millions, commanded Faerie's legions—roamed my body. I tried and failed to steady my breathing. If he saw my shivering, if he heard my shortening breaths, he'd punish me. This was nothing to him, just a clinical examination, but his hands reminded me of the last time a fae had touched me, the last time fingers had swept along my marks, his body beneath mine, hands stroking, mouth bringing me to life.

Oberon came around to face me, and brief confusion gathered lines on his brow.

My skin had risen in goosebumps, and there was no hiding my hard nipples. Oberon saw it all.

Heat warmed my face and chest. The heat of shame. I wanted to snatch up my clothes and cover myself or maybe fall to my knees and beg his forgiveness. No saru was to look upon a sidhe without permission. And to desire one? To desire the king? It didn't matter that it wasn't him I wanted, it was Talen. I ached to have Talen back, to have him here with me so I wasn't alone.

Oberon turned away, saying, "You have earned more markings."

More markings. Once, I would have wept with joy. Not anymore.

"You spent time with Lord Devere?" the king asked, heading to the window.

I swallowed to moisten my parched throat. "I did."

"What happened to him?"

I considered lying, but Oberon already knew part of the truth, if not all of it. "We fucked. I killed him."

The king's stride faltered. He turned, arched an eyebrow, and said, "He was not the only fae to touch you?"

How much had Sirius told him? How much did he already know about Kellee and Talen? A lie would undermine the king's faith in me. "No."

"Your pilot." Oberon stopped at the window and gazed out at Faerie. "Tell me about him."

"I needed him to navigate the ship." Technically true. I filled my head with thoughts of the unnamed pilot I'd shot between the eyes and felt the lust ease as sadness crept in.

"And the vakaru?" Oberon asked, keeping his back to me. "Tell me of him."

I had known this day would come since Talen and Kellee had captured me. Fate would always bring me back to Oberon, and the king would ask his questions. I'd spent nights awake going over my answers, making the truths work for me so I didn't have to lie.

"The vakaru was a Halow lawman. A marshal. He detained me after I secured Eledan." I reached down for my clothes. I could do this. I'd lied to Mab for years. "Eventually, he released me, with conditions. I've spent the last few months trying to escape him."

"I have not instructed you to dress." He hadn't turned, hadn't looked. "Does he know you're mine?"

I dropped my vest. "Yes. He tried to kill me on numerous occasions."

"That's unsurprising. His kind was only good for killing."

"Do you... know him?"

"A lone vakaru is of little concern," he replied, ignoring my question. *Listen to what he doesn't say.* Considering everything I had seen on Valand, Oberon knew exactly who Kellee was.

The king turned and faced the room and me once more. "We have more pressing matters." He crooked his finger, and Sirius stepped forward. I'd forgotten the guardian was here and felt him keenly as he stood beside me. He'd seen me naked hundreds of times, but this time —everything about this time felt different. Because I was different. Before, I'd been glad to be in the same room as Oberon, to have him look at me, notice me, touch me. Now, all I wanted was to find a weapon and run it through him. Through them both.

"Sire?" the guardian asked.

"From this day until I say otherwise, you are *my lana's* guardian."

My lana.

My star.

My slave name.

He had never called me that before, but clearly, he had known it. Somehow, impossibly. All saru names were sacred. The only thing we truly owned. We never told the fae. So how did the king know mine?

There was only one possibility. He'd named me as a babe. But if he'd named me, that meant he had always been watching me. He'd let me grow and seen me kill fellow saru and climb through the ranks until the day I stopped Aeon from killing him. I'd survived everything Faerie had thrown at me. I'd thought my survival was my doing. But we had always been connected, this new king and I. I had always been his, just like Kellee had said. Worse, Eledan had said it before the fae came and ruined Halow. Eledan had told me the truth.

"We gave you that name. We built you up. We made you what you are today. From the moment the saru breeding bitch squeezed you out, bawling into this world, you belonged to Faerie. Every-thing you know, everything you are, we gave you." I heard it so clearly, as though the Mad Prince were standing beside me, hissing the words into my ear. I'd thought he had meant the Wraithmaker name. But what if he'd known the truth, even then? *We made you what you are today.*

I was falling. If my past was a story, if everything was a lie, then what part of me was true? Was *anything* of me real? I *was* saru. That was real. They could not take that from me.

"You want me to guard *her*?" Sirius asked, barely suppressing a snarl.

Neither saw my trembling. I closed my hands into fists and pushed the bad thoughts away. It didn't matter. The past couldn't hurt me. Not anymore. I was my own person now.

"No, I want you to be her *guardian*," the king said. "You will not leave her side. You will be with her every moment of every day. You will watch everything she does, and every word that passes her lips you will report back to me."

The king knew everything I'd told him was karushit. Kellee, Talen—Oberon knew they meant more to me than tools with which I'd tried to get back to Faerie. How could he not? And so Sirius was my punishment, my cage.

Sirius stiffened. "Sire, have your saru observe her. I am a Royal Guardian. I have served you and Faerie in battle for thousands of years. My place is by *your* side—"

"Should any harm come to her," Oberon cut in, "that same harm will be inflicted upon you. You are to protect her with your life. If she dies, so will you. Do you understand?"

Oberon couldn't mean it? Sirius was immortal. To kill him for my short life? It would be an insult.

Sirius fell to a knee. "Sire, please... do not cast me out like this."

Oberon's gaze grew heavy. "Do not beg, Sirius. It's beneath you."

"Guarding her is beneath me—"

"Do not presume—"

"The arm!" Sirius lifted his arm and rocked back on his heels. "This monstrosity was not my doing! *She* did this to me. She mutilated me. *She is a curse!*"

"Silence!" the king boomed in a voice designed to command armies. "Or by Faerie I will see you executed alongside the saru gladiator."

Sirius closed his eyes and wearily rose to his feet. When he opened his eyes, he was the immovable wall of guardian he'd always been. "You are punishing me."

Oberon smiled. "No, I am promoting you. Mylana is everything and must be guarded at all costs." He turned his attention to me. "The gladiator will die in your place. If I hear a single word of protest fall from your lips, I will confine you to the catacombs." He nodded toward the door. "You are both dismissed."

I gathered my clothes and followed Sirius out of the room. The guardian marched ahead like an angry wall of fire, leaving me trying to dress and jog to catch up. "Sirius..." On and on he walked, cloak flaring. Any faster and he'd be running. "Sirius, wait!"

He stopped rigid in the corridor, radiating the kind of fury that had my saru instincts gearing up to fight or flee. I stepped in front of him, blocking his path. His cheek twitched as he glared far over my head, probably wishing I didn't exist.

"I'm sorry. I didn't know he would do this."

His throat moved as he swallowed. "For all the gifts he has bestowed upon you, you are mortal. You'll eventually wither and die, and I will live. All of this will be another moment in the tapestry of my past. I *will* survive you, Wraithmaker." He shoved me aside and stopped at a turn in the corridor. "Come, *saru*. You will need to secure shared sleeping quarters."

Sirius would not let me out of his sight. He would follow Oberon's words to the letter because he had everything to prove. My plans to save Arran and the fate of all saru had just become a whole lot more difficult with Sirius as my shadow.

Marshal Kellee

I had always protected others. Since Oberon had taken my people from me, I had always righted wrongs, fought the injustice for those who couldn't fight for themselves. I had thousands upon thousands of deaths on my soul, and I had always planned on balancing those scales. The star cradled in my hand stood for that justice. It represented the laws that governed Halow, represented everything right. But those laws had died when the fae returned, and I wondered if "right" had been a dream. I continued to wear it, this small golden star, as a token, a shield. Now tarnished and scratched up, it still stood for something. It had to.

I stood for something.

"You've been staring at that star for hours. Unless it is also a key, what do you hope to get from it?" Talen inquired. The fae was sitting cross-legged in the center of the small cell the Earthens had locked us inside. The heat of the iron bars beat against him, but he showed no signs of pain. Not yet. He looked like something from the Earthen fairytales, effortlessly striking in his leather getup. I was still surprised they hadn't executed him on Hapters. When they had come blazing in through the chaos in their enormous ship, we had lost against the unseelie. They'd saved us, but we wouldn't have needed saving had they not attacked.

I pinned the star to my coat and leaned forward on the bench. "The law is gone. We live by morals now."

"Do Earthens have morals?"

Earthens were Oberon's original experiment, the origin of humans. Their kind had spread beyond Earth and Sol, prompting the first war with Faerie. After Mab's peace treaty, they settled Halow, grew, and developed, birthing tek cities like Calicto and Point Juno, cities in the stars. Humans of Halow were subtly different from the humans of Sol—the original Earthen families. I'd only met a few Originals in all my years, and all of them were better-than-you assholes.

I rubbed my hands together, pushing out the itch to free my claws. "They struck while we were already engaged in a fight. What do you think?"

Talen's eyes narrowed. "I could free us with a touch. I need only get close to one of them to incite their rage and have them—"

"No." He could do a whole lot more than that, but the last thing we needed was more enemies. I still hoped Hapters had been a misunderstanding. "Don't." *Not yet.* I would speak with their general and try to come to some agreement. They were keeping us alive for a reason. That meant there would be an opportunity to talk. Once I was out of the cell, I'd get a better idea of where we were and what our options might be. *Find a ship, get back to Hapters, assess the damage...*

"Is the ship alive?" The last I'd seen of the warcruiser, it had been bent and broken, lying limp in the sky over Halow.

Talen's fingers gripped his knees. "Yes, but she's in considerable pain."

I would never have believed the day would come when I'd pity one of the fae's world-eating ships. But ours—Shinj —had done nothing wrong. *We* had done nothing wrong. The Earthens had attacked from behind like cowards. All this time, all of Halow's people dead, and worlds destroyed, and they had been absent.

My fingers itched again. I got to my feet, needing to move, to think, to clear my thoughts of the increasing restlessness. The cell wasn't much larger than a few meters squared but pacing helped settle my thoughts, until they landed on Kesh.

I'd seen her run into the fray.

Watched her slow.

Turn back...

"And Kesh? Do you feel her?" I asked, careful to keep my voice level.

Talen bowed his head. "I don't know." He touched his chest and then dropped his hand. "The distance between us is too great."

She'd hurt him. By-cyn, she'd hurt all of us. But Talen hadn't seen the fierceness of her charge. He hadn't seen her rush into a wall of monsters to save him. I'd seen it. All of it. She would have toppled a dark army singled-handedly to save him.

"Do you think she left us?" the fae asked. He lifted his head, and that same indifference sat easily on his face, but his eyes held the truth. Always had. He loved her—the fool. She had made fools of us all, but damn her, I loved her for it too. Hated her most of the time as well, but we'd been working on that before she was taken.

"No." I gripped the bars and clenched my hands so hard the muscles ached. The way she had slowed, her shoulders dropping, her pace slowing. I'd seen that blank look on the faces of Hapters's folks when Sirius had drugged them. But Sirius hadn't drugged Kesh. The guardian, for all his many, many faults, had more integrity than that. I'd fought Arran. The gladiator liked to deflect, distract, and then make his move. "The kid took her."

"Arran? I don't see how. Arran is a skilled fighter, but Kesh is... ruthless. Had she not wanted to go, she would not have gone."

I smiled at all the times Kesh had gotten me on my back, at the precision with which she'd strike, at the raw, unyielding way she fought. She thought herself cumbersome and slow, but I'd stopped holding back in our sparring long ago. And every time I'd seen her in that Faerie coat, her whip at her side, her drone a constant death sentence in her wake—fuck, she took my heart and ripped it from my chest. Every damn time.

"There was a time, once, when she would have left." I'd had to lock her up, something I wasn't proud of, but it had been necessary. I'd known, given enough time, she'd come around if I showed her another way outside of Faerie. We all needed perspective before we could change. And she had. She'd more than come around. She'd taken up the challenge of becoming the Messenger and embraced it. To come back from the puppet she'd been and remake herself anew? That took strength and courage. "She chose to fight alongside us." *She made the right choice.*

"So he's taking her back to Oberon, back to Faerie."

I turned my back to the bars, leaned against them, and flexed my fingers. "By my count, she's already there." For all her crimes against Faerie, the king would kill her. But he'd make it slow, draw it out, let all of Faerie watch her demise. Everything was a pantomime with the fae. And I couldn't get to her. She was a million light years away, facing execution, and I was stuck in this cell.

Talen watched my hands move, knowing me well enough to understand why I had started rattling around this damn cage. I couldn't afford to free my claws here. I looked human. The Earthens would talk to me, trust me, but if they discovered who I was, they'd kill us both. Earthens had written legends in my name. They had turned me into a monster that rampaged through their ranks, drinking their blood, slaughtering thousands, driving spikes through their severed heads, and I couldn't blame them. They were right. I had been that monster.

I winced and pressed my teeth together, forcing back their ache.

Talen's gaze darkened with knowing. "They shouldn't have caged us together."

"They don't know—" *What we are.*

It would be fine. Someone would come soon. The restlessness would pass. Unleashing the beast in me wasn't an idea I relished, and not with Talen trapped here too. He might not be the Nightshade anymore, but he was nightmare enough for the Earthen to lose their collective shit if we showed them our true selves.

Maybe it would come to that. If it did, this cell wouldn't hold us. We'd have to fight our way out of this mess, Nightshade and Droch-fhoula together. That was Plan B, and I hoped I didn't have to put it into action, even if a deep-seated raw part of me wanted it all to go sideways just so I could tear through them again. It had been a long, long time since I'd been Droch-fhoula, but the hunger never left.

Talen picked a speck of dust or fluff off his leathers. "Attack me and I'll put you down. Again."

I grinned. For a fae, his right hook was lethal, and he was fast too. When I'd lost control with Kesh, I hadn't known he'd moved until I'd hit the floor. "Try it, fae."

"And have you lose another bet with Sota?" The corner

of his mouth twitched. "I'll let you keep your pride, Marshal."

I huffed a laugh and the tension in my muscles eased.

The distant clanging of doors sounded and human voices traveled through the walls. I straightened and faced the bars, putting myself between the closed entrance and Talen. The fae could look after himself, but Kesh would kill me if anything happened to him.

"How do you want to do this?" he asked.

"With diplomacy." I looked behind me at the silver-haired fae sitting upright and proper on the floor. He looked harmless, unless you knew the fae, then you'd know he was as lethal as any predator. If I were Earthen and on the other side of the bars, I'd kill him. We just had to hope that whoever was about to greet us had better morals then me. "If talks fail, we'll try Plan B."

"Plan B?"

"Stardust and shadow."

Edge of Forever (#6)

The 1000 Revolution

#1: Betrayal

#2: Escape

#3: Trapped

#4: Trust

#5: Deliverance (coming in 2019)

New Adult Urban Fantasy

City Of Fae, London Fae #1

City of Shadows, London Fae #2